Nowhere to Hyde

By

Michael Porter

Copyright © 2021 Michael Porter

All rights reserved.

ISBN: 9798763435436

DEDICATION

Special thanks to my wife Jackie, who's namesakes are nothing like her. Thanks to Whistle Test and 5th Element for their musical contributions. To Peter Cave, for those wonderful hells angels books from the 1970's, my style more than a little different, but his books had a real impact on my life.

No matter how evil may assail you,
remember there is still love in this world.

This is a work of fiction, well mainly. There are real people in here, and so many fictional people, some of us are in here more than once, some not at all. Any correlation with real people is entirely accidental. If you believe yourself to be here, I hope that you like who you see yourself to be, if not, then it's not you.

1: Wednesday. A gloomy night on the A49.

Jackie left the Railway Inn after her shift, she stepped out into the dark, the drizzle of earlier had blown away, her walk into work had been extremely nice, the sun shining, the breeze cooling, now, after midnight, the temperature had crashed, the wind whipped her short skirt around her legs, she pulled her jacket tight, her thin shirt was barely enough to keep her warm, but it was good for the tips. In her four years as barmaid, she knew how to dress to increase tips. 'It's not raining so I'll not call Dad, he's got work early, I'm walking.' She thought walking down the hill towards the bridge that took the road under the railway. Just before the bend was that sunlit path, not so lit now. Dark hedged and narrow, up to the bridge across the motorway. Less than half a mile to home that way, by the road more than two miles. "Bugger it." she whispered crossing the road and taking the path, the streetlights reached as far as the first bend, where the track turned along the line of the garden of the big house on the corner. She took her phone from her pocket, checked its battery, then switched it into torch mode. A small pool of bright LED light showed her the path, if only a very short distance, at the next turn the lights from the motor way cast a little yellow glow, but not enough to see by. Suddenly they were gone. "Damn. Penny pinching," she muttered to no one in particular.

"You really shouldn't be here alone." A voice so low it sounded like it came from the grave. She swept the tiny light around until it picked out a large man, dressed in black, resting against the hedge, smoking a cigarette. "Stop using your phone as a torch, use it as a camera, get all of my face and the three badges on my jacket." Stunned and for some reason unable to run, she followed his instructions. "Now send that to someone who knows you." He waited until this second task was completed and spoke slowly. "Feel safer now?"

"I suppose, what do you want?"

"There's been some trouble in this area recently and the cops are useless."

"You're here to walk me home?"

"I'm afraid so, it's not safe here for you alone, so you have escort."

He stood straight to his full height of over six feet. "Lead on my lady."

She turned up the path. "The badges," she said, "A name, master at arms, that's a soldier thing, but what does dilligaf mean?"

He laughed. "Do I Look Like I Give A ... you can fill in the rest yourself." Her smile un-noticed in the gloom.

"So, you're a road dog?

"No, The Roaddog, or just Dog, or sometimes Mr Dog."

"Don't you have a real name?"

"I used to, and a family, now a new name, a new family."

"So, you're some sort of guardian angel?"

"Angel, perhaps." She reached out and took his hand in hers, realising just how large his hands were.

"Wrong hand little girl, switch sides, leave the right hand clear."

She switched quickly before asking. "Why?"

"A gentleman keeps his sword hand clear when escorting a lady."

"I'm a lady," she laughed.

"You are tonight." She leaned against him, smelled that characteristic fragrance, patchouli, engine oil, and stale beer. As she pulled slowly away from him, she felt his hand tense in hers, three figures moved to block the path. Three young men, probably not in their twenties, bald heads and striped tracksuits.

"Looks like one of them hairy bikers, I'm gonna cut you wide an' deep old man." A craft knife appeared in his hand, the one to the left held a baseball bat, the one to the right a heavy dog chain. Roaddog dropped Jackie's hand and said, "Run little girl and don't look back."

She turned and ran, behind her she heard the sounds of a fight, the rush of air around the bat, the clatter of the chain and the dreadful scream, she stumbled to a halt. 'I can't leave him alone.' She thought. As she ran back towards the sounds of the fight, her little torch throwing shadows more than light, the fight was all over, Roaddog was panting, and bent over a little his long wavy hair hanging about his face, the torch picked out the hard blue of his eyes, the long knife in his hand appeared to collapse in on itself and then vanish into a pocket of his jeans.

"Are you hurt?" she whispered.

"Some."

"Are they dead?"

"Not so much. Can you go through their pockets? I want their phones." His right hand gripped his left upper arm, attempting to stop the blood dripping from his hand. While she was searching, he shrugged out of his jacket. He slipped the bandanna from around his neck and retied it at his left bicep, taking the broken handle of the craft knife from the ground he tightened the improvised tourniquet. Jackie stood from her search of the last of the young men, she handed Roaddog a bundle of phones.

"How can scumbags like these afford two of the latest stupid phones each?" That said he dropped them onto the ground and stamped them into tiny pieces. Whether it was the sound or the stink of smashed batteries one of the youngsters groaned and woke up, he raised himself on his elbows in time to feel Roaddog's knife at his throat.

"If I see you or yours in my town again, I won't cut you wide or deep, but you will beg to die. Am I clear?" A simple nod was all it took, the heavy fist slammed into the youngster's face and knocked him out again. The knife collapsed and vanished. Roaddog stood upright, unzipped his jeans, and proceeded to mark his new won territory. Jackie didn't know which way to look, so she turned away. Once she heard the zip again, she looked back. She picked up the discarded jacket and helped the older man into it.

"Let's get you back to mine, I'll bandage that properly."

"Far?"

"Over the bridge, turn right, first left, we're almost there now." She picked up his injured arm and carefully draped it across her shoulder then stepped under it, her right arm round his waist. "Keep it elevated, it helps stop the bleeding." He frowned at her. "Hey, I'm a first aider." He smiled as they walked up onto the bridge, traffic was light on the M6, but the passing of headlights illuminated them intermittently.

At the top of the bridge, he paused. The path to the road was overhung with trees.

"Do you think there could be more?" she asked, her voice shaking a little.

"I can't believe that those guys have more than two friends each. But it's not me I'm worrying about." He reached into his jacket and pulled out a phone, he spoke into it and it dialled, and was answered.

"Yes."

"Roaddog."

"I thought you called it a night, what you need?"

"How many still there?"

"Just me."

"Roll. I need you and your trike, M6 foot bridge, Leyland side, two minutes."

"Rolling."

"I didn't get half of that." said Jackie as they started walking slowly off the bridge.

"I called the club, Slowball is on his way to meet us at the road, we're almost into the trees and I can hear thunder."

"There's no rain forecast tonight."

"Damn girl. Please be quiet, I need to hear what's happening in these trees."

Jackie lapsed into silence, not sure what he meant, but equally not wanting to anger him.

"The trees feel fine, they are empty," he said. The roar of an approaching engine became so loud that it drowned his voice, the howl of tortured rubber filled their ears.

"Slowball's here," he said smiling. A voice called. "Dog."

"Coming," he yelled. "let's move," he said, pulling her quickly through the tree shrouded section. Across the grass she saw a huge red trike, with the biggest man she had ever seen standing up on it.

"Hey Dog."

"Hey Slowball, how's they hanging?"

"Slowly," he laughed, then pointed, "Trees." They turned and saw the three figures at the exit of the trees.

"What were you told?" shouted Roaddog. All three disappeared into the trees at a dead run.

"You want us to chase them?" asked Slowball.

"Nah, I don't think they'll stop running 'til they get to Yorkshire, anyway you'd never catch them."

"Mount up, we'll go to the club and get me stitched," said Roaddog.

"I can't," said Jackie, a little disappointed. "If mother sees that pic, she'll have kittens."

"I can't believe you sent my pic to ya ma," he laughed. "Fine. Slowball, you're taxi, tell the man where we're going." Jackie looked up at Slowball, daunted by his sheer size.

"You need to turn round, then first left number twenty-six."

"Damn," muttered Slowball.

"You still not got that gear selector fixed?" asked Roaddog. Slowball shook his head dejectedly.

"Jackie, please take a seat," said Roaddog, guiding her up into one of the high seats on the trike, then he took the other one. "This is a nice trike, it's really great, but because of its size it does make turning round a little difficult. A three point turn really makes Slowball sweat, perhaps one day he'll fix the gearbox." By now the trike was broadside on in the road, Slowball got out, slung the front wheel over to the left then started pushing the trike backwards.

"You could help him, or I could," Jackie said.

"No. He needs to fix the damned gearbox. Tell me my dear is your road one of those nice dead enders that seem to be so popular with everyone except Slowball."

"No, it's not."

"That will be nice for Slowball, won't it mate?"

"Yes, Dog." Slowball remounted the driving seat and set off along the road, first left came up in moments, and number twenty-six in no time.

"Pull into the drive," said Roaddog, a huge grin on his face.

"Bastard," muttered Slowball. As the trike rolled to a stop in the driveway, which to Slowball's joy was slightly uphill, the curtains of the house twitched and a face appeared for a moment, then vanished.

"Stay where you are until I get you," said Roaddog to Jackie, only just above the rumble of the air-cooled VW. Slowly he stood, and stepped down to the driveway, he walked around the tail, to where Jackie was sitting, held out his good hand to help her down, she smiled, knowing full well that by now her mother was at the open front door. She stepped daintily down and held onto his hand as they walked to the door.

"What the hell is going on?" demanded the short plump woman standing with the light from the hallway behind her.

"Roaddog, this is mother, you can call her Julie, or Mrs Bamber."

"Pleased to meet you Mrs Bamber."

"Why have you brought my daughter home on that ridiculous contraption and why is she covered in blood."

"I am happy to say that the blood is all mine, not hers."

"And shed defending me," snapped Jackie.

"You are home, and you are safe, my work is done," said Roaddog, "and I really need to get back to the club to get this arm stitched."

"Will I see you again?" asked Jackie softly.

"After tonight, do you want to?"

"Yes," she whispered.

"When you working again?"

"Tomorrow night."

"I'll be there when you finish, no walking home for you, and a proper bike." He smiled, nodded to Julie, turned and walked over to where Slowball was waiting. The trike rolled slowly back down the drive and into the road, then was gone with a roar of the motor, and a scream from the tyres. The short pipes of the VW made conversation difficult, but it was still possible.

"Where's your bike?" asked Slowball.

"At the club, I got a lift out with Bug."

"You rode bitch behind Bug? That must have been friendly."

"His bike is a little small, but fuck does it go."

"True." Slowball turned into the yard at the unit, rolled past his normal parking space and then let the trike roll slowly back down the slight incline until it was parked up against the wall. Slowball opened the locks and turned the heavy handle that released the door. He pushed it open and reached inside to disarm the alarms. Off to the right was the seating area, more like a lounge of a mansion, admittedly one run somewhat to seed. Slowball snatched the first aid kit from behind the corner bar, while Roaddog peeled off his jacket, a sharp intake of breath the only sign that there was any pain. Under the bright fluorescent lights Roaddog saw the cut in his jacket for the first time. There was no mistaking the double cut of two blades side by side.

"Bastard," he muttered.

"What's up?" asked Slowball. Roaddog showed him the jacket. "Fuck, I ain't stitching no double cut. That shit is for the professionals, quick look, then your choice, Chorley or Preston."

"My choice, is to stick that damned baseball bat up his ass, cut off his cock and choke him with it."

"You sure it's big enough to choke him?"

"Probably not, I'll give him a smile and choke him with the bat."

"Let's have a look first, eh?" Slowball untied the knot in the bandana, pulled it down and wiped the wound with it. Much of the bleeding had already stopped though it was going to start again once he started working on it. "You're lucky," smiled Slowball. "One of the blades must have broken off on your jacket and it didn't get through to the skin. One cut and shallow at that. Easy."

"I don't care, cunts that use a double blade like that need killing."

"I'll agree with that. Nova?"

"Yes, your stitching is bad enough, but if my muscles keep jumping around it's going to be dreadful. I'll have some jacks as well." Slowball went to the bar and took a bottle of American whisky out from under it, he spun the top off before passing it to his friend. Roaddog upended the bottle and took a good glug before releasing it.

"You going to have to talk to the vet," said Slowball slowly, "we're almost out of novocaine and sutures are low as well."

"I'll go see her tomorrow. Just fix me up I got a date tomorrow."

"Same little girl?"

"Yes, she may be little but them damned tits. I want to see them wrapped around my dick."

"You think she'll be up for it?"

"Can't tell, but god I hope so."

"She ain't no kid, ya know?"

"I had noticed. I'll bring her here tomorrow night, let her meet some of the guys. I'm sure she'll be cool. She's most likely to be working Easter weekend though, I'm certain we can work something out. Ouch, watch what you're doing with that needle."

"It's only the novocaine, stop being a pussy and have some more jacks."

"How come we've not got a run on this year?"

"Funds are low, shop work has been slow, and the other dealing has fallen to almost nothing. We've got so much stock here that sniffer dogs passing on the six are getting high."

"There must be some new suppliers in town. I'll find them and let them know that somewhere else would be better for their health."

"Fine. Now sit still and shut up. You'll only bitch if I don't get this thing straight."

It was almost two in the morning by the time Slowball was wrapping a heavy dressing over his handywork.

"You better hit the vet for some dressings as well, this thing is going to take some looking after. You riding home?" He looked at the half empty bottle of jack that Roaddog was holding.

"No, I'll crash here. Got a couple of jobs in first thing tomorrow."

"Fine take it easy, I'm gonna piss off." Slowball packed the first aid kit away and left closing but not locking the door. Roaddog listened to the heavy rumble of the VW as it receded into the night.

2: Thursday. With Civic and Billy.

Roaddog woke early, before his alarm went off, he rolled gingerly out of the cot, in the back room of the unit. There were ten more cots, ex-military bunk beds. There was some pain from the arm, but it wasn't enough to affect motion. He grinned and said a quiet thank you to Slowball and his needlework. The jacks he had drunk gave him a serious thirst, so he drank three glasses of water before starting the coffee machine. There would be more people coming in fairly soon, and that first or second coffee is important to most of them. He walked slowly outside into the clear day, blue sky and little wind, almost too good to be working. Around the corner he went to the caravan that was already set up for the morning rush.

"Hi Andy," he said. "Bacon egg and sausage on the biggest bun ya got."

"No worries Dog. How's things going, you're early?" Andy's thin face and skinny arms were all that Roaddog could see through the serving hatch of the caravan.

"Some shit last night, ended up too drunk to make it home, ya know how it is?"

"Yes, I can dream of such an exciting lifestyle, but if I did that my wife would be here serving my dick as a chipolata," he laughed loudly.

"How the fuck are you so happy this early?"

"It's not early for me, I've been on the road since six. Doing my bit to keep the workers from dying of hunger."

"Ya mean the ones too lazy to make their own damned breakfast?"

"Them'll be 'em, god bless you all," another raucous cackle filled the air. As the laugh died the rumble of the M61 came to the fore again.

"That'll be three quid mate," said Andy, holding a hand out through the window.

"Three quid? How much does it cost you to make this shit?"

"You know exactly how much it costs, cos I buy the knock off bacon and sausages from you guys. I don't dare to ask where you get the gas bottles, I use to cook the shit. Three quid pay up before the price goes up," Andy laughed again.

"You're a robbing bastard," said Roaddog dropping three coins in the reaching hand.

"But ya love me anyway." The hand vanishes and returns in a moment with a large bap in a paper bag. Despite the discussion Roaddog knows he's getting a far better deal than most of the punters that will show up today.

"Cheers Andy," he said turning back towards the unit.

"Hey Dog," called Andy, Roaddog turned around again.

"Yep."

"No runs this Easter?"

"No, funds are tight, sales have fallen off, I think someone is moving into our patch."

"I have heard of some bunch from Manchester way selling their stuff cheap."

"Thanks for that Andy, I'll look into it." Roaddog walked back into the unit and sat down to eat his breakfast. Drinking his coffee slowly, he knew that he had time before anyone else arrived. He was almost finished when he heard the rumble of the VW, this got very loud as it rolled backward towards the wall. The German motor stopped, and silence returned. Soon Slowball walked in with one of Andy's breakfast specials and a large coffee.

"How you doing man?" he asked.

"Fine, hurts a bit, but full range of motion, nice stitching man."

"No worries. What we got in this morning?"

"Some petrol head and a civic for a remap, and an old Harley for a serve 'n' tune."

"Green," laughed Slowball.

"What you mean?"

"Green, all those dicks with civics, they're always green. Stupid, look at me, fluorescent green, like those kwakers from the eighties."

"They do tend to be fashion victims," smiled Roaddog.

"Any bet some tosser has told him he can get twenty five percent more power and save on fuel."

"And he'll have a big bore pipe with fuck all baffle."

"Ear plugs and defenders today then?" asked Slowball with a grin.

"Could be a bet."

"Which one you want?"

"I'll have the civic, if you don't mind, I don't really fancy all that rolling around on the floor with this arm."

"No sweat," said Slowball, "hang on what you mean rolling around on the floor. Just how old is this bike."

"Two thousand lowrider."

"Bastard thing's too low to get on the lifts. I think I've just been had over again."

"Drag one of the old hydraulic lifts out of the back, we should be able to get it up on one of those."

"Not high enough for my old knees."

"We'll sort you something out, don't fret. Andy told me that some guys from Manchester might be moving on to our patch, that's why our sales have been down."

"They could be coming from anywhere, but mancs and scousers are the best bets. We need to do something about them."

"We will, once we find them." Roaddog stared into his coffee for a few minutes, then he looked up, and turned to Slowball.

"I think I hear something green." The unmistakable bell like note of a large bore exhaust was barely discernible, but it was getting louder. Roaddog got up and walked over to the door and hit the button that opened the roller door for the dyno bay. Sure enough a low slung fluorescent green Honda rolled to a stop in front of the dyno ramp. Slowball laughed loudly as the young man climbed out of his car. He couldn't have been much above twenty years old. He walked forward as Roaddog approached him.

"What's he laughing at?" he asked.

"He said green, I said yellow, he won a fiver the bastard."

"This is no ordinary green, my mate mixed it specially for me, I think it's great."

"And that's what counts. You want a remap?"

"Yes, I've been told that you guys are the best."

"Maybe not the best, but certainly cheaper than Greenacre." He turned to his friend.

"Hey Slowball, have Blackburn Honda got a dyno?"

"No Roaddog, I think they sub that stuff out to somewhere in Accy."

"So even if you went to Honda you'd be paying a percentage for someone else to do the work. We got all the machinery and the software to remap your car. What do you want from this re-map?"

"I've been told you can get me more power and save me some fuel."

"The only way to get more power is to burn more fuel. There is a way to cut the fuel at low revs, and punch it at higher revs, that way below say 3K you drive a grandpa carriage, and by 4K you've got a rocket ship. This does mean that when you drive it below 3K you'll be saving maybe fifteen percent, but once you hit 4K you'll be spending a fortune. What do you say?"

"That's the best you can do for me?"

"I'll make this thing fly, but you'll be paying in fuel. The choice is yours."

"I need it to fly."

"That I can do for ya. First thing is to get this up on the ramp, you don't have much in the way of ground clearance."

"Yeah, the front spoiler is quite low."

"Tell you what, you drive it, I'll tell you how much to go, if it gets too tight, we'll have to think of something else. Go on fire it up and roll slowly, if I say stop, do it."

"Does it end up on those rollers?"

"Yes, but take it easy OK?" The young man nodded and climbed back into his car. He started the Honda, it didn't fire quickly it took a few seconds, it spun for a while before it caught. Crackles from the tail and a short plume of fire. Slowball looked at Roaddog and grinned. The young man lowered his suspiciously darkened window and leaned out of it.

"Right," said Roaddog, "roll it slowly and keep it centred on the ramp." Slowly the car rolled forwards, not smoothly but in tiny little steps. "Keep coming," said Roaddog, waving a hand to bring the car towards the ramp, just before the wheels hit the bottom of the ramp, he held his palm up and called "Stop." Once the car was stopped, he stepped in front of it and ran his hand under the spoiler, there was enough space for his fingers but not much more.

"OK, roll it slow, the wheels are on the edge and the spoiler still has space under it. Easy now." He stood out of the way and the car started to roll forwards, as he listened to the engine, he worked out what the problem was. Someone else had remapped the ECU and really made a mess. 'Damn this is going to take more time than I expected.' He thought. Once the car was almost to the top of the ramp, he called another halt.

"Right, once it starts to fall into the groove, get on the brakes, let it down real slow, if your suspension compresses too much you may just damage your spoiler. Perhaps we should have taken the damned thing off to start with."

"Got it," said the driver. Roaddog nodded him forwards again. Inch by inch the car crept up the ramp, until it reached the rollers. The driver was quite quick on the brakes, as gravity started to work on the car, pulling down between the rollers. It settled into the groove, only millimetres of clearance under the spoiler, the side skirts were quite close as well.

"Hand brake, leave it in gear, kill the motor, and get out carefully, there isn't a lot of space to stand on." The young driver followed the instructions to the letter and stepped down gingerly off the ramp.

"Keys?" asked Roaddog.

"Inside."

"Great, go and get yourself a coffee and seat in the comfy chairs. This may take a while. Someone has already fucked with the mapping on this thing."

"How can you tell?"

"It runs like a bitch at low revs. No need for that shit, I can fix it." He waved the young man over in the direction of Slowball, who was already getting the man a cup of coffee.

"Here ya go man," he said. "Dog's a magician, he'll get it sorted." Then Slowball went over to the ramp to start strapping down the car while Roaddog was making the electronic connections. Once the connections were all made, he checked over Slowball's work, after all they didn't want this thing getting loose while on the red line. Slowball connected the exhaust fan pipe to the tail of the civic, and Roaddog set up the fans on the front and underneath the car. There wasn't a lot of space underneath, but the heavy mesh allowed some cooling air up onto the turbo. Roaddog reached in through the open window and turned the ignition to on. He noticed that the window wasn't glass. It was a lot thinner and lighter, polycarbonate. Only the front and rear screens were glass, everything else was plastic, the rear seats were almost non-existent. The front seats were aluminium framed with minimal padding. 'Someone has done some work lightening this.' He looked at the driver again, something didn't ring true. The centre console had too many switches and lights, two of them flashing red right now. After an instant of thought Roaddog went to the back of the car and opened the boot. Not a great deal of space in there, but even less in this one. Two large cylinder clamps fitted to the floor, and pipework with bayonet gas connectors. Roaddog shut the boot slowly and went over to the driver, he sat in a chair facing the young man.

"What's up?" asked the driver, more than a little nervously.

"You've had that thing fitted with nitro."

"Yes, but I took the tanks out before I came here."

"Wise move."

"I heard what happened to the last guy who tried his nitro on your dyno," said the young driver.

"So, tell me."

"I want it to run smoother at low revs, and then hot to the red band. Once you've got that sorted, I'll take it back to the nitro guys and they can sort out the settings from six thou up."

"If you'd said that on the phone we'd already be started, and by the way the price just doubled."

"No worries, I figured it'd go up some."

"I bet you brought a usb stick as well."

The driver pulled a small black pendrive from his pocket and handed it over.

"Fine," growled Roaddog. "If your nitro monkeys fuck it up, tell them to re-install my settings and start again. I'll make it a grand-dad carriage up to four k, hot up to six, and rocket ship to the eight and a half red line, you punch it through that red line, and it will blow its ass off. Do you understand?"

"I understand."

"You really shouldn't try to bullshit me, that is not very bright."

"I didn't think you'd do it, if you knew what I was up to."

"That car is either pursuit, getaway, or high-speed delivery. I don't care which, and black would have been better."

Roaddog walked over to his computer station and fired up the three screens. With the click of the mouse the civic's starter spun, in a few seconds the motor started. Roaddog pushed a joystick forwards and the engine revved, pulled it back and it returned to idle. After about fifteen minutes of tinkering Roaddog finally had the car release the clutch and engage the gear, the first run up to the redline sounded more than a little rough. The second better, the third, was smooth and sweet. The turbo howled like a banshee, and the exhaust sang. Roaddog nodded and shut the thing down, the silence was deafening.

"Right kid," he said, "you need more oil cooler if you're going to keep that turbo running, I'd suggest something off a big four by, probably two, and fit them with fans. With the gearing changes you've made and some extra power from the nitro, you should be good for 220 mph for short and I do mean short periods. Now for the bad news, that'll be three hundred."

"That's more than twice."

"And you got more than twice the work. Or I could reset it back the way it was when it rolled in here?"

"Seems like a fair deal to me. I only brought two though."

"The rest can go on your card."

"No worries."

Slowball handed the card interface to the driver and took his two hundred. The transaction went through with no hitches so Roaddog started to release the civic from the electrics and the hold down straps. He finally indicated that the driver should get in.

"Back it off real slow, we've still got to get it off the ramp without ripping off that spoiler." The driver nodded through the open window and turned the key, the engine fired in a heartbeat, and settled down to a smooth burbling purr. In a single motion it climbed out of the groove.

"Fuck," said the young man loudly, "it's a completely different car."

"It is, now go slowly down the ramp." The car rolled backwards under gravity until it reached the bottom, then the driver rolled it slowly up the incline and out of the bay.

"One more thing," said Roaddog leaning into the window.

"What?"

"If I hear of this car causing problems for bikers, then I'll hunt you down and kill you, are we clear?"

"I understand mate, I just need to keep the fecking cops off my ass."

"This should be able to outrun their chopper, but not the radios, understand."

"Oh yes. I only need to be out of sight for a minute or so, then they'll never find me."

"Manchester have evo's and scoobies, they're good for one-seventy at least."

"They'll never catch this baby. Thanks mate. See ya around." As the green civic rolled backwards into the yard an old Harley came around the corner, the rumble of the open pipes was un-mistakable. The youngster waited until the bike was parked in the yard before he set off, with a wave of a hand and the crackle of a full-bore pipe.

"Tag?" said Slowball looking at Roaddog, his reply was simply a smile.

"What you two grinning at?" asked the old biker walking towards them.

"You Billy Gibbons?" asked Roaddog.

"Nah, his beards shorter than mine," laughed the old guy. "Sorry I'm a bit late, had some trouble with the damned law."

"They can be a pain around here. What's up?"

"They didn't like my number plate."

"Damned pussies, ain't they got anything better to do?" laughed Slowball.

"I got somewhere to be at about two, can we get this done in time?" asked the old man.

"No worries," said Roaddog, "The hardest part is going to be getting the damned thing up on the lift. But with three of us it should be easy enough. You take a seat, we'll drag one of the old lifts out of the back, and get things started."

The two went into the back of the shop and returned with a dusty old contraption that used to be red back in the day, now it was dirty and rusty in patches. It was considerably lower than the nice shiny modern ones in the motorcycle maintenance section of the place. They rolled the bike in and put the lift under it, there was just enough clearance. Roaddog held the bike with his left hand and tapped his left shoulder, grinning at Slowball. Slowball laid down on the floor, and manoeuvred the lift into place, then jacked it up manually until the clamps engaged with the engine casing, this one was designed for the old 883 engine, tighten up the clamp wheels and then lift it clear of the ground, it didn't go up high, but it was clear of the ground and upright, which would make things easier. Working together it was only moments before the hot oil was draining, and the oil filter was off. Plugs, swapped in a heartbeat, air filter the same. Hydraulic fluid for the brakes changed, brakes cleaned. Drive belt tension checked, but not adjusted. Oil filter replaced and oil in the tank. Roaddog turned to the man sitting in the comfy chair reading and old copy of "Ironhorse".

"How good's your battery."

"It's ok, I suppose." Roaddog nodded and turned to Slowball, "Plugs out." He said softly. Slowball removed the plugs from the engine but put them back in the ignition leads and left them dangling against the engine. Roaddog turned the key, and pressed the starter, the engine spun quickly, the open sparkplug holes making a quacking sound as it turned over, he held the button down until the oil filter had filled with oil and the oil pressure warning light had gone out.

"Sparks are good." said Slowball as soon as the engine stopped, and he replace them both. Roaddog spun the motor again and it rumbled into life and settled down into that characteristic Harley beat. Slowball opened the inspection cover and checked the primary drive chain. No problems there. Leaving the engine running they dropped the lift and pulled it out from under the bike.

"Give it a quick wash." said Roaddog. Slowball shrugged and rolled the bike out to the jet wash station. While Slowball was washing the oil residues off the engine the motor spluttered a couple of times.

"Kill it," yelled Roaddog. He came out of the shop with some paper towels and a couple of spray cans. He pulled the plug leads, and gave them a rough wipe, then he sprayed them with one of the cans, he did the same to the ignition coil. He wiped both plug leads, and coil dry with the paper towels. Then sprayed them lightly with the other can. Leaving them a few seconds to dry he replaced the plug leads and restarted the motor. He let it settle for a minute, then went back into the shop, waving Slowball to continue with the clean-up. Roaddog walked back inside, stashed the cans in a locker and sat across from the biker.

"That's not WD40," said the old man.

"No, it's way better."

"What the fuck is it?"

"First is a switch cleaner, cleans the terminals and drives the water out. Next is a varnish, 0008/009. Once that has dried, which it had before I walked away, you can run those electrics underwater. It's good stuff, doesn't last forever but should see ya over a winter. Or in this area a damned summer," he laughed.

"Is it expensive?"

"Not really, switch cleaner about five quid, varnish is twenty. I can treat about thirty bikes with them. So not really."

"If I bring it back in autumn will you do that again for me?"

"Yes, and I'll only charge ya a tenner."

"Ya robbing bastard," laughed Billy Gibbons.

"It's a skill I can market. Pay up ya tight wad. You remember those cold damp mornings when everything is covered in dew, and you just know that motor is going to be a bitch to start?"

"Yep."

"Not anymore. I started this about five years ago, I was at a rally, one of those hot and humid days, with a freezing cold night. Everything was wet. My bike started in a heartbeat and warmed up nicely. All over the site people were running their batteries flat trying to get them started. Guys with cars were driving around giving people jump starts, it was crazy."

"But you were fine?"

"Oh, yes. I was sitting there watching everyone else."

"Did it help any of the guys there?"

"No, Once the water is in the electrics it's fucked. Ya just need a really good battery to spin the motor and give big fat sparks to get it fired, once the harley motor is running it's not going to stop unless you drive it through a river. Hey Slowball, you finished yet."

"Nearly mate, just gotta blast some of the oil off the bottom of the engine and I'm done here."

"How much do I owe ya?" asked Billy.

"Call it fifty."

The biker pulled a wallet from his pocket and passed Roaddog a debit card.

"Code is one two three four."

"You're having a laugh."

"No, that account has got a hundred in it, and no overdraft. So, the most ya can get is a hundred. I'll get a tank of fuel, a couple of beers, then when I get home, I'll send the code to the bank that tops it back up to a hundred. I may be old, but the tech shit is easy."

"No sweat man, you interested in joining our motorcycle club?"

"Not really, I've been a lone wolf all my life and there ain't that much of it left."

"The offer is open; we're looking to expand."

"I'm with Noel Coward I'm afraid." Roaddog frowned and thought for a while before replying.

"You gay?"

"No, he once said, or I think it was him, 'I have no wish to be a member of a club that would have people like me as members.' See what I mean?"

"I get it," laughed Roaddog. "If ya want to tag on a run or a meet you'd be welcome."

"You got a run on this Easter?"

"No. We have a meet on Monday night, we meet here, since the Woodsman decided we were too rowdy for their nice new image."

"I might turn up for a beer or two."

"Would be great to see ya. Don't forget, you are now called Billy."

"I don't play the guitar much and I can't sing worth shit."

"These days that don't matter so long as you look the part." Roaddog laughed and wandered off to the till to charge the work to Billy's card. Slowball had finished the washing and had wiped the seat and tank, polishing the mirrors with a soft cloth. He walked back into the shop, leaving the motorcycle running.

"You're good to go, mate," he said.

"Thanks man," said Billy, as Roaddog came back with his card.

"If you want a few beers with us on Monday, we'll be here from about nine, until we're too drunk to get home."

"I may just do that." he pulled his helmet on and walked out to his bike.

"You invited him to the meeting?"

"Yes, he's old but with a look like that he's gotta have a story or two to tell."

"Bone's gonna get pissed, you inviting strangers to meetings."

"What's he gonna do, fire my ass, or challenge me? Either way the result is the same, we get a new chairman."

"Don't forget that Lurch will back him all the way."

"Fuck them both and at the same time."

"What wrong with you? This club's been peaceful for a few years now."

"I don't know perhaps I'm just bored. And no Easter run is not helping."

"Perhaps you should go and sort out the competition whatever it is," laughed Slowball.

"You know that could mean all sorts of trouble?"

"You're bored, and you're not on your own. How long is it since we had a decent rumble?"

"I quite enjoyed last night's little fight, three on one, exciting I suppose."

"Wasn't the girl any help?"

"No, I told her to run. She did."

"She came back though?"

"Yes. That's really why I'm interested in her."

"So, it's not just those tits?"

"No, she came back and real quick, I had only just dropped the last one when she returned. I'm glad she did."

"Why?"

"It could have gotten real messy without a witness."

"Hey, they're still alive, and most likely still running."

"I'm not entirely sure they have that much sense. I feel they may make another appearance."

"Do we have any more jobs today?"

"No, not that are booked in."

"The phones not rung once today."

"Tomorrow is good Friday, anybody sensible has their bikes sorted, by now, emergencies will be tomorrow morning, we'll be open and ready for them. Today, I need a beer."

"Let's shut up shop and go for a beer then. Where?"

Roaddog simply smiled.

"Damn," said Slowball. "You and those tits." He laughed and went over to the roller doors, started them down, once they were down and locked, they both departed by the personnel door, Slowball closed all the locks and fired up the alarms. As he walked to his trike, he shouted at Roaddog, who was putting his helmet on.

"You shunted the phones?" A nod was the only reply he got; any voices would have been drowned by the sound of Roaddog's bike firing up. Roaddog took the lead, Slowball followed, there are clubs where trikes lead, but this is not one of them. The short ride to the railway took less than five minutes, past the Woodsman, and through the dip, Roaddog smiled and thought 'Remind me of the speed limit here.' They passed the pet cemetery and Roaddog let the big dyna howl for the pets gone from this world. They got held by the traffic lights at the railway bridge, it's not unusual for Roaddog to blow the lights and make the oncoming traffic give way, but today with Slowball behind him he wasn't going to risk his friend's life. When the lights turned green, he set off held first until he was under the arch shaped bridge. Between first and second, he let the engine rip, and the Vance and Hinds sang as only they can. They turned into the pub car park and Slowball found a place where the gradient was enough for his trike to roll backwards without actually having to push the thing. They entered the lounge bar together, as far as the bar man was concerned their conversion started with. "You're a fucking noisy bastard."

"I'm sorry mate," said Roaddog. "I just love the tone of those pipes."

"Four pints Wainrights," said Slowball turning to the barman.

"Four?" asked the barman, looking behind them.

"Four, afternoon beer," said Slowball, dropping a tenner on the bar.

"What you mean, afternoon beer?"

"Lightweight," smiled Slowball, taking the first pint before it had settled properly, and chugging it down without a single breath.

"You're just showing off," said Roaddog, taking the second pint and drinking it, not in one breath but in two. They took their second pints to a table, but not before the barman had picked up Slowball's ten-pound note, and said "Er, excuse me."

Slowball glared at him and said, "Yes."

"Er, nothing," said the barman.

Slowball and Roaddog continued to a table in a bay window where they could see the bikes.

"I'm going to like the discount we get here," laughed Slowball.

"Me too," said Roaddog.

"Where's your waitress?"

"Where's the menus?"

"I don't understand."

"No menus on the tables, no staff in the kitchen."

"How you get to be so smart?"

"Lucky I guess, it certainly can't be the people I hang around with," laughed Roaddog.

"Bastard," muttered Slowball.

"No one is arguing with that statement."

"So, what we going to do?"

"Couple of beers then back to the shop see what's happening."

"What are we going to do about sales?"

"I'll hit some of the dealers tomorrow, really can't be arsed today."

"Fine. More beer?"

"Yes, go on, one more then we'll go back to the shop."

"OK." Slowball went back to the bar, while he was away Roaddog looked casually out of the window. As he looked a small green van drove through the carpark and back out without stopping. The driver and passenger hidden by their baseball caps, and the darkened side windows of the van.

3: Thursday evening and Roaddog meets Nigel

The sun was almost down, but the sky was clear, the temperatures were set to fall slowly over night, but the weathermen had promised no rain, the entire weekend was set to be clear and warm. The clubhouse was almost in darkness, the sun was completely hidden, and the streetlights had not come on, they were high enough to be bathed in sunlight. Bone was sitting in his usual chair, drinking slowly and watching everything going on, not that there was much to see. The presence was light tonight, most waiting for the weekend to start properly. One of the girls brought him a beer, which he accepted without a glance, not what the young girl was hoping for, she wanted so much more from the top man of the club. Bone knew that any dalliance with someone so young would only result in injury or death, not for him, but certainly for her. Behind the small corner bar, stood a large woman, older than the younger girls that hung around with the club, always looking for some excitement, or action, but not her. She was the chairman's old lady. Her cut had no rockers on the back but had her name clear for all to see, her cut declared her to be Bandit Queen. She looked across at Bone and smiled, he was her man, and she would fight to the death for him. Her eyes turned to the young girl hanging behind Bone's seat, waiting to serve him in any way she could. Bandit Queen looked hard at the skinny ass and the small but firm breasts. 'It's been a while, these girls change so quickly nowadays, it could be time for a lesson, a quick lesson and all the girls learn, there aren't enough here tonight. Next time the girls are better represented, then that little bitch is going to be an object lesson for all the others.' She thought and then smiled, Bone caught the cruel smile and knew that a decision had been made, he'd try and get a quiet word with the kid. Though if she vanished then Bandit Queen would be pissed, but he'd been there before, and would no doubt go there again. A sigh bled from his lips as he realised how much Bandit Queen meant to him. He looked around the clubhouse, and considered briefly torching the place, and vanishing into the burning sunset. Just the two of them, on his victory. That would be good. As dreams go it was small and stupid. He knew he'd never quit, nor would she.

"Hey, Dog," he shouted.

"Yes Bone," replied Roaddog as he walked over to where Bone was sitting.

"Get Dog a beer," he snarled over his shoulder to the girl he knew was waiting. She shrugged and went over to the bar where Bandit Queen was already breaking the crown cap off a bottle. Smiles were exchanged neither were in any way honest.

"I hear you had a rumble last night?" said Bone.

"I wouldn't call it that serious," laughed Roaddog.

"You got tagged, or so the story goes."

"A small slash from a bastard using a double-bladed knife."

"What was the outcome?"

"I smashed their phones, and emptied their wallets, and marked them, they'll not be back around here again."

"You know that leaves your DNA for the pigs to find."

"My blood was all over the place anyway, so what the fuck?"

"How was business today?"

"Crap, though the civic that came in for a re-map will be quite interesting in a few weeks."

"Why?"

"I tagged it. It's had some serious work done, and I think we could get twenty for it in Birmingham, more with the petrol heads in London."

"It's that hot?"

"Oh yes, it's good for two hundred at least."

"Shit."

"Yes, and it's fecking green."

"No."

"Guy says special green just for him, but it's exactly the same as Kwaker green from the eighties," Roaddog laughed.

"Kid's today have no history, at least nothing beyond last week."

"I'll keep an eye on the thing, and once he's forgotten he even came here, we'll just drive the thing away. Paint it fucking black and sell it on."

"Good we could do with the cash; this week would be better."

"I have had a hint that some guys from Manchester are worming their way into our area."

"What are you going to do about it?"

"I'll find them and explain to them about our territory."

"And if they don't like what you tell them?"

"I'm fairly sure the survivors will get the message," Roaddog laughed.

"One of the things I like about you is that you get things done. What you got for tonight?"

"I got a girl to see, other than that, not a lot."

"Don't go alone, you could be a target right now."

"I'll take Slowball."

"And another at least."

"I'll see who wants to come for a beer, I don't foresee any problems, the bastards are still running."

"Ya can't be sure about that. Take some muscle with ya."

"Me and Slowball, anything more would be over kill."

"To quote Burt Gummer, it's only over kill until you run out of ammo. Take someone else."

"Fine, I'll take a third man, maybe Bug will be interested."

"Don't get your crazy ass killed OK?"

"OK boss, I'll do what I can to avoid the grim reaper, if he turns up, I'll spit in his eye and run like a bastard," Roaddog laughed and turned away, he didn't see the look on Bone's face. A mixture of concern and worry, concern that Roaddog could die and worry that his position as leader was under threat. He isn't the sort that worries about being ousted as leader, more that leaders die, they tend not to survive the changeover. Bone looked around the room, pausing momentarily on every member, and deciding which way they would go in a possible upcoming coup. Once the on-site members were finished, he moved on to the ones not actually here, gradually the tally progressed. The call was close. Roaddog could be the next leader, the club might even survive. If Roaddog doesn't make next leader, then the club dies without enough members. He knows he has to step away from the confrontation, at least until Roaddog has enough allies. Bone stares at Roaddog's back as he's talking to Bug, 'Now there's someone crazy enough to be sergeant if Dog gets a promotion.' He thought having absolutely no idea which way Bug would go, the guy's always been a bit of a maverick, he could even go rogue. He watched as Roaddog gathered Slowball and with Bug left, a wave the only acknowledgement. The sound of departing motorcycles filled him with momentary sadness. One day a war would come, and this would all change forever.

Roaddog led out of the yard with the other two behind him, back along the same road he had taken in the afternoon, this time with much more hope of meeting Jackie. An un-eventful ride led them back to the Railway, there weren't many cars in the carpark, so plenty of space to park the bikes. They walked into the lounge bar together, Roaddog walked up to the bar, the same barman was there.

"Three pints please," said Roaddog.
"Wainrights?" asked the barman.
"Nah, Hobgoblin, evening beer," laughed Roaddog.
"Only three?"
"Yes, still got shit to do tonight, is Jackie on?"
"Yes, she's here, waiting on."
"What time she finish?"
"About nine, if there's not too many in the bar."
"Good we got time for a beer or two."
"I hear that Jackie was involved in some sort of trouble last night?"
"What did she tell you?"
"Nothing."
"Then that's all you'll hear from me."
"Look I don't want any trouble here."
"There's but three of us, we'll not start any trouble for you."
"But you'll sure as shit finish it," the barman laughed. The three walked over to an empty table, not too close to any of the patrons who were still eating. Jackie came out of the back to clear an empty table nearby, her arms full of dirty plates she stopped to say hello.

"Hi Jackie," said Roaddog, Slowball just nodded.
"How's the arm?" she asked.

"I'll be fine, Slowball fixed me up, this is Bug, he's a bit of a nutter," he nodded his head in the direction of the aforementioned.

"Hi Bug. You ok?"

"I'm fine darling, who the hell is he calling a nutter?"

"You apparently," she turned away and went back into the kitchen.

"I like her," said Bug. "she's got sass."

"And tits," laughed Slowball.

"She has?" smiled Bug. Roaddog tapped the table with two fingers then pointed them in the direction of the other bar, not really separate, it was accessed by a large archway, the bar contained the pool table and the large TV's showing some football match or other. The people in that bar were all of the distinctly young variety, late teens up to early twenties. Track suits and baseball caps abounded, for the guys, the girl's T-shirts and short skirts. There was much discussion going on, and the bikers seemed to be the focus of it all. The chatting stopped, one of the young men shrugged and turned toward the bikers. He walked forward slowly his hands at his sides, open and empty. Roaddog watched his cautious approach, the baggy three stripe tracksuit could hide almost any weapon, the Nike air trainers spoke of wealth or cunning. He stopped a good five feet from the table. He even checked the door before he spoke.

"I hear your gang beat the crap out of the craft knife kid."

"Number one, we are members of a motorcycle club, not a gang," said Roaddog slowly. "Number two it was me, and me alone that beat the crap out of that dick."

"I heard that you marked them as well."

"True, what of it?"

"I'd just like, sorry, we'd just like to say thank you. That guy's been making an ass of himself for far too long, it's time someone smacked him down. Thanks."

"No worries, I don't think he'll be around here anymore."

"I wouldn't bet on that; he's backed by some big group of dealers out of Hyde."

"Manchester," muttered Slowball.

"Manchester indeed," said Roaddog. "Bug, who we got in Hyde?"

"There's Angels in Hyde and Outlaws in Stockport."

"I feel a battle royal coming on," smiled Roaddog. "Cars and bikes to the Angels, stock to the Outlaws, cash fifty-fifty."

"I got a contact in Stockport," said Bug.

"I'll talk to the Angels," said Roaddog.

"Wow," said the young man.

"Thank you," said Roaddog. "I think they'll all be out of our hair in a very short time."

"No sweat, you guys are crazy, you do know that?"

"I have been told that before," laughed Roaddog, as the younger man returned to his friends. Once there a girl went to the bar, tottering on the most ridiculous heels, as far as Roaddog was concerned. The girl tried to pick up three pints at once, but her hands just aren't big enough, she gives up and takes two first, over to the table where Roaddog and the others are sitting, puts the two down and wobbles back over to the bar to pick up the last one.

"These are a thank you from the guys."

"No worries," smiled Bug.

"My dad's got a jacket a bit like yours, his says Geronimo on the front."

"That's good," said Roaddog. "Slowball card her. Tell your dad if he's interested in meeting some modern-day bikers to come to the club house, address is on the card. It'd be good to meet one of the old guard."

"I'll talk to him. Thanks," she turned away.

"Hey chick," said Roaddog, she turned back. "Do yourself a favour, for fucks sake eat something, there ain't enough meat on your bones for a dog to worry over." With a look of complete disgust, she lifted her t-shirt and grabbed a small fold of belly.

"I'm still too fat," she snapped then turned away, stamping off didn't work out too well in those heels. The bikers laughed quietly to themselves. Slowly the spokesman of the youngsters came back.

"Did someone just tell my girl to eat something?"

"That'd be me, she's a tad skinny for my liking," laughed Roaddog.

"I've been telling her that for months, but she won't listen."

"What do you know of her dad?"

"Big guy, not tall, but built, if you know what I mean. He has some funny tattoos on his fingers, you know how some guys have love and hate on theirs, his say 'reka' on the right hand and 'myah' on the left. Just weird."

"You're kidding?" said Slowball, almost spitting his beer out.

"Why?" demanded Roaddog.

"Put the fists together and read them the wrong way. He's gotta be dead, he vanished years ago. He's Geronimo, he's a legend."

"Kid," said Roaddog turning back to the track suited figure. "Talk to the guy and get him to come to the club house tomorrow night, we'd all like to meet him."

"I'll try, but he's a stubborn old guy."

"Do that, and one other thing."

"What?"

"Do not piss that old guy off. While you're trying to work out what it says on his fingers, that left will put your lights out forever."

"He is a lefty."

"Ask him politely to come see us."

"I'll do that," he turned and went back to his friends, there was some chatter and they started to drink up in preparation to leave. Jackie came up to the table.

"What you guys up to?"

"Not a lot, back to the clubhouse, drink a beer or two and meet a few people. You want to tag?"

"I've already met one new guy, why Bug?" she asked.

"Oh shit," muttered Bug, while Slowball giggled.

"Well," said Roaddog, "very early in his time with the club this young man was on a ride with us, we were coming back from somewhere, I'm not even sure where it was now, but he made the mistake of swallowing some large and crunchy flying beetle. His guts were more than a little unhappy about this. So, they decided to get shut of said insect life form. At the time, Bug here, had four pints of beer inside him. His stomach emptied the lot before he had time to stop or take his helmet off. It was not a pretty sight."

"It was not a pretty smell," added Slowball.

"So, we took him to the car wash at Sainsburys and gave him a jet wash whilst he was sitting on his bike. Ever since he has been Bug."

"That's a very moving story," laughed Jackie. "I am very pleased to meet you Bug."

"Hi Jackie," said Bug. The spokesman of the youngsters approached again.

"We're off to Chorley to catch some karaoke, maybe we'll see you around."

"That's possible," said Roaddog. "See ya." He turned to the others. "Roll in five." Bug nodded and went off towards the gents.

"Jackie, can you introduce me to the boss?"

"Sure, come with me." She walked over to the bar and waved the barman over.

"Nigel this is Roaddog. Roaddog, Nigel."

"Hi," said Nigel, "what can I help you with?"

"Maybe we can help each other."

"What do you mean?"

"I'm looking for a venue for our monthly meetings, I think this place will do just fine, I bet it's quiet in here on Mondays. Meeting will bring between thirty and forty thirsty people in here, and I do mean thirsty. We'll not turn up while the kitchen is open, wouldn't want to put off your evening trade."

"Kitchen's closed on Mondays," said Jackie.

"Even better, is it actually worth opening on Mondays?"

"Some Mondays it's not, the only beers I pull are my own, Easter Monday is different, the kitchen is open. So, we'll have some people in."

"Let's hope it's better than tonight, the youngsters have gone off to Chorley for karaoke, and once we leave there's the two old folks in the corner, and that's your lot for the night."

"They're saving themselves for the weekend."

"Could be, you OK with us having a meeting here Monday night, should be a relatively quiet affair?"

"If you're going to drink beer and not make any trouble, I have no problems."

"Fine we'll see ya on Monday, I'll probably be around for Jackie here anyway."

"You look after her, she's a good girl."

"He already did that, last night he saved my life," interrupted Jackie.

"I don't know about life, virginity perhaps. I don't think they'd have killed you."

"Don't make me laugh," said Jackie. "That boat is long sailed."

"I'll take your word for that," laughed Nigel. "You look after Jackie, OK?" he said to Roaddog. Slowball came to the bar with empty glasses.

"Cheers man. Good beer," he said.

"Thanks Nigel," said Roaddog. "Let's roll."

The four walked outside, helmets were retrieved from the box on Slowball's trike, including a spare one for Jackie.

"You can ride behind me," he said.

"I've never ridden a motorcycle before."

"Don't worry about it, the backrest will hold you on, keep your feet on the pegs and follow me when I lean the bike. If you lean the wrong way you will make things difficult for us both. Try not to smack me on the back with your helmet, it'll take a while for you to get used to it, but it'll come."

"I don't even know how to get on."

"Don't worry about it. I'll talk you through it." He threw his leg over the seat and sat down, lifted the bike upright and flicked the kickstand up. With a touch of the button the eighteen hundred CC motor cracked into life, the rumble of the pipes filled the air, rapidly followed by the flat four of the VW, and then the V4 of Bug's Honda.

"Right," said Roaddog, loudly. "Stand close, put your hands on my shoulders, that's right, now left foot on the peg, stand up, step over, and sit down, really easy." Jackie followed the instructions and was sitting on the motorcycle, something she had thought that she would never do.

"Hitch back a bit. Just until you can feel the backrest behind you, then grip my hips with your knees." He pulled her legs in until he could feel her knees pressed against him, the pressure was sufficient for him to be fairly sure she wouldn't fall off.

"One last thing for you. Acceleration and braking can be quite harsh, you will have to lean forward when I am accelerating and backwards when I am braking, you are now an active part of the vehicle. Do you understand?"

"I think so," she shouted over the noise.

"Fine," he smiled to himself. "Let's roll," he shouted and slid the clutch out, the back-wheel scrabbling on the dusty carpark, he headed towards the road, and barely slowed at the exit, the road was clear, so he gunned the big motor and turned right down the hill. He felt her struggling to hold on for a moment, then her hands found his belt and her fingers wriggled under it. The lights at the railway bridge were against them so he slowed. As the speed dropped her wriggling became more of an issue.

"Sit still. If you must see the road, then pick a side," he called as he slipped down the last gear. Before they had actually stopped the lights changed and he accelerated quite slowly for him, he pushed the bike down into the right-hand bend, slowly and smoothly, then into the left, smoothly accelerating all the time, she stopped moving at this point. He couldn't tell if she was relaxed or frozen in fear. The traffic lights were all in his favour as they headed for the club house, even the right turn was good. He knew that the test was going to be the roundabouts, so he slowed it down into the first one, as he flicked from the left turn on to the right turn, he felt her tense but only for a moment, then the switch to the left turn off the roundabout she was perfectly comfortable. The next roundabout was a left turn so no problem, other than the tarmac getting closer as the speed went up and the lean increased. Seconds later they were slowing down for the industrial estate roads, narrow and littered with dangers. They pulled into the yard and Roaddog allowed Bug and

Slowball to pass so they could park in their usual places. He stopped and looked over his shoulder at her.

"Dismount is the reverse. Hands on shoulders, stand up, weight on left foot, lift right foot and step over, right foot to ground and you're off." The heavy bike barely twitched as she followed his instructions to the letter. Once she was clear he parked up in his normal space, Jackie stood still not knowing really what to do. Looking around she saw so many strangers, suddenly she wasn't sure she wanted to be here. So many of them looked scary. She remembered that rush of fear when she saw Roaddog in the darkness, 'Oh my god, was that only last night.' She thought. Relative silence fell as Roaddog's dyna shut down. It was only seconds until he was at her side, but for her it seemed like hours, everyone was looking, everyone was staring.

'What the fuck have I got myself into?' She thought.

4: Thursday evening. Learning new things

Roaddog came up alongside her and took her hand.
"You ok?" he asked.
"I'm not sure, I'm sort of scared, there are a lot of people here. I don't know any of them."
"You know me, and for them that is enough. Do you believe me?"
"I don't know," her voice cracked.
"You'll be fine, tell you what, let me introduce you to one of the most important people here, many don't see it. But I understand how things work. Her name is Bandit Queen. She'll look after you and get you through the hard part. OK?"
"If you say so. I'm still scared."
"Don't worry, come on." He gently pulled her into the club house, the roller doors were open, and the big burners were throwing heat into the room. He took her into the bar area where Bandit Queen was keeping an eye on everything that was happening, not that there was a lot. As they approached Jackie looked Bandit Queen over, she was different from most of the other girls around, she was late thirties to late forties, a difficult face to put an age on. She wore no makeup. She was wide at the shoulder, her arms heavy and sort of solid looking. Her hips wide and her thighs thick, as she turned Jackie noticed the muscles in her legs moving, there was some power there. Jackie's eyes moved back up the older woman and met her bright grey ones. They locked together for a long moment then Jackie backed down. There was a serious fire going on in those cold grey eyes.
"Hi Bandit Queen," said Roaddog. "This is Jackie."
"I've heard about you, you got our Roaddog cut."
"He saved my life which I think is quite special," said Jackie calmly. Bandit Queen smiled and turned to Roaddog.
"I like her, she's got a fire in her." She looked at Roaddog for a few seconds, as if expecting something, but he was unsure what she wanted. Finally, she spoke. "Fuck off." Roaddog turned to Jackie and smiled, then went to talk to Bone about the information he had picked up.
"Now we are alone," said Bandit Queen, "are you really sure you want to be around all these crazy bikers?"
"I don't know. I like Roaddog, he's sort of wild."
"Oh, he's that, he may just be too wild for you to deal with."
"I've seen him knock three thugs out take their phones and money, then he peed on them. That qualifies as wild in my book."

"He can get a lot wilder than that. You want to be his girlfriend?"

"I think so, he's been so nice to me."

"This is a motorcycle club, things run a little different here, than in your suburban world out there."

"What do you mean?"

"All these girls that you see, there aren't many here tonight, but then it is Thursday, weekends are better. They are here because they want to hang out with the scary bikers, they want to ride with them, and party with them. They understand the price they have to pay to be here."

"What price?"

"The guys like girls that are prepared to party, they expect some sort of sexual favours in return. You up for that sort of thing?"

"I don't know, this is something a lot different than I was expecting. Do you do these things?"

"Hell no. I'm Bone's old lady, it's almost like married, you want to be like that with Roaddog?"

"I'm not sure. I barely know him, I suppose."

"So, which is it to be?"

"Do I really have to decide right now?"

"Oh yes. If you want to be exclusive to our Dog, then he needs to declare that today, you're a new and pretty face, you're going to be very popular and very soon."

"I really want to give Roaddog a chance to get to know me, but I don't want to put him under pressure. I certainly don't want to be, oh my, I can think of no polite way to say this."

"Just say it," laughed Bandit Queen.

"I don't want to be a tart for the rest of them while he makes his mind up."

"I started out as one of those girls," whispered Bandit Queen, menacingly.

"I didn't mean, oh fuck," said Jackie.

"Don't fret, I enjoyed my days spread eagled for anyone with a hard dick, or a hungry tongue. I took up with Bone real soon though, and together we carved the old leadership out of the hot seats and took them for ourselves."

"Sounds like fun. Are your seats currently that safe?"

"To be honest no, there is a feel in the air that something is coming, I think it's going to be Dog, but he has no old lady to back him. You up for that sort of task? The woman I took out was smaller than you and no freaking push over I can tell you, it got too damned close for my liking."

"So, what happens to the ousted leaders?"
"They either leave or die."
"What happened to the ones you ousted?"
"They left."
"Alive?"
"Yes. Damaged but living."
"Sounds like a brutal way to live."
"It can be, but it's also fun."
"This problem that Roaddog had last night, how often does that sort of thing happen?"
"Not often, we get the occasional tussle with local thugs, they always seem to think that we are old men, weak and slow."
"Do they learn?"
"The ones that live do, and those smart enough to learn by someone else's mistakes. Sadly, not many are that bright."
"What about those three from last night? I'd not like to bump into them in the street."
"They'll be long gone. Roaddog beat three of them in seconds, they'll not be around here anymore."
"I think I'll hang around for a while, I'll talk to Roaddog about things and see what he has to say."
"Be aware, once you get to be committed to this lifestyle, it can be very difficult to leave it," Bandit Queen smiled, because she remembered not that many years ago, when she decided, one summer of fun then back to reality. A wild summer stretched into a wet winter, then another summer. Now she wouldn't change a thing. She glanced over at Roaddog, he was just standing up, having finished his conversation with Bone. She reached under the bar and grabbed a beer bottle, snapped the top off, and said, "Give this to Roaddog. He's going to be thirsty, judging by the look on his face, and the storm behind my man's eyes." She levered herself up from the stool and walked slowly to where Bone was sitting, he had a bottle of jacks in his hand and was drinking a good-sized belt from the open neck. She sat on the arm of the chair and he leaned against her. He looked up into her eyes and passed her the bottle, Bandit Queen took a belt and passed it back, quiet words were exchanged but Jackie had no idea what they were. She held the bottle of beer out to Roaddog.

"We need to talk," she said, so softly that he could barely hear her over the rock music pumping from the speaker above her head.

"What's up?" he asked.

"I'm not at all sure this is the life for me?"

"It's fun, crazy, mad, and utterly wonderful."

"I'm not sure I can survive long enough to find out."

"Bandit's been telling you about the lifestyle, hasn't she?"

Jackie nodded.

"What don't you like about it?"

"I'm not sure I even want to have any form of sex with you yet, let alone any of the other guys round here."

"If you're willing to give it a try, I'm sure I can work something out. No! Stop looking like that, I mean that we can call you like a prospective old lady, not just some run around chick. What do you think?"

"I don't know, I don't want to lead you on, and I don't really want to walk away, I'm having a hard time here."

"I understand, give it a few days, you'll probably like it."

"Did Bandit really start like one of these young girls?"

"From what I hear, not exactly, she came in from outside, was attached to Bone at the hip in a heartbeat, and they've been together ever since. A love made in heaven," he laughed.

"Or hell," she smiled.

"Hell indeed, sometimes. But they're still together. They've lasted longer than many marriages, and through some tougher times."

"I'm not sure I'm prepared to live like that."

"Maybe you'll turn me into a proper upright citizen?"

"I don't see that happening until you are dead," she laughed and leaned against him. He pulled her in close and kissed her, hard and hot. She moulded her body against his, feeling the hard muscles of his chest and thighs even through the heavy leather and denim he was wearing. After what felt like an hour the kiss broke and she stared into his eyes. As she stepped away from him, she collided with something solid. She looked at Roaddog, who smiled, she turned slowly, and looked straight into the chest of the new biggest man she had ever seen. Slowball looked positively small alongside this person. She smiled up at him and said.

"I don't remember putting a wall here."

"Who you kidding? Jammer was a short ass." The voice echoed from the depths of his throat, like from the bottom of a quarry.

"What the fuck are you two talking about?" asked Roaddog.

"It's from a movie, asshole. When you look long into an abyss, the abyss also looks into you," said Lurch.

"Nietzsche," laughed Jackie. "You're Lurch," she said reading his name badge. "I'm Jackie."

"You're small and cute," laughed Lurch.

"Hey," said Roaddog, "everyone is short and cute when they stand next to you."

"You ain't ever cute," snarled Lurch.

"Ain't that the truth," laughed Roaddog.

"She gonna be yours?" asked Lurch.

"I hope so."

"Hey Jackie, if ya get bored of the little boys, come look me up," he laughed and turned away.

"Just how fucking tall is he?" asked Jackie.

"Nobody is entirely sure, some say there is a navigation light on his hat, but that could be a rumour," smiled Roaddog.

"Is he Bone's number two?" she asked.

"Right, he's just the sort of guy you need behind you in a fight."

"He's certainly solid, I wasn't really joking about the wall thing."

"What's the movie thing then?"

"It's called 'The Abyss', it was directed by James Cameron, from the late eighties, it's a real good movie, you'd like the fight scenes, though they may be a little tame for you."

"We'll have to watch it some time. I never knew that Lurch was a movie buff."

"It's a good movie, it's sort of a cult thing as well."

"Sounds like fun."

"What's going to happen now?" she asked looking around.

"It's Thursday, so not a lot. I've gotta be back here early in the morning, the phone is going to be ringing with bikers in need of help."

"Why?"

"Good Friday runs, it's early in the year, but a lot of clubs have runs at Easter, you know four-day weekend. Lots of them are going to have their bikes fail tomorrow morning, and we'll be here to help them out, with batteries, and fast tune ups, all the things a bike that's been laid up for the winter needs."

"No run for the Dragonriders?"

"Strapped for cash right now. But we'll get that sorted fairly soon, I think we know where the cash flow has gone."

"So where would you generally go for Easter?"

"Sometimes fairly close, there's a couple of places just north of Preston, sometimes we go to the lakes for Easter, tends to be a touch chilly up there though. If you really want an out of the way place to go, try Whitehaven, end of the earth or what?" he laughed. He took her hand and led her slowly out of the seating area, to where an old Harley was the centre of attention, there were three guys crouched around it.

"What's happening?" asked Roaddog.

"I'm struggling with fuelling, can't work it out, everything looks fine, but I just got a shit flat spot about two thousand," said one of the men, he turned to face Roaddog. As he looked up Jackie could see that he was in his late twenties, cold blue eyes caught hers for a moment then moved back to Roaddog.

"Jackie," said Roaddog, "this is Sharpshooter. He's a bit of an ass." Jackie took in his rugged features, his hair was different, those that had hair had it long, not Sharpshooter, the nearest thing that she could think of was a square military cut, flat on the top, and short on the sides.

"And Dog's a bastard," laughed Sharpshooter.

"Let me in," said Roaddog kneeling beside the bike, a quick glance at the air filter on the ground showed that it was so clean it had to be new. The inlet side of the carb looked a little too grey and not quite shiny enough. He reached one finger into the bore and lifted the piston, it rose smoothly, a little less easily than he would have liked, then when he released it, it fell quite quickly to about halfway shut and slowed down a bit. He turned to Sharpshooter.

"Bores dirty and the diaphragm may be failing, clean it out and replace the diaphragm."

"Shit man I ain't got that much cash."

"Don't fix it then, that diaphragm fails, and it stops," Roaddog smiled at Sharpshooters dejected look. "Bring it in tomorrow morning, I'll help ya fix it."

"I definitely can't afford your rates," muttered Sharpshooter.

"I didn't say I was going to fix it, I'll sit over there in a comfy chair drinking beer you're gonna pay for, and I'll tell you how to fix it," laughed Roaddog.

Sharpshooter turned to Jackie. "See I told you he was a bastard."

"I don't know, seems like a fair deal to me," smiled Jackie. They all turned to the open shutter doors, there was a fair bit of noise going on. A woman was yelling. She was lying on her back across the picnic table in front of the shop. Her shirt and bra lifted to show her breasts, her jeans and knickers pulled down her legs to her knees, her legs lifted upright by Bug. Her voice was shut off as Slowball stepped up to her head as it hung off the edge of the table, he shoved his hard prick into her open mouth and pushed it all the way home. Her arms reached up and grabbed his wide ass, pulling him harder against her. Bug unzipped his pants and slid his cock into her pussy. Moving slowly in until his belt buckle hit her raised thighs, slowly he fucked her. She moved her hand and pushed Slowball backwards.

"Fuck me harder you bastard," she yelled, before pulling Slowball back into place. Bug obeyed her request, his thrusting caused her whole body to move on the table, jamming Slowball even harder into her throat.

Jackie looked at Roaddog, "What is going on?" she asked quietly.

"Looks like Doris has got her freak on," laughed Sharpshooter.

"She's certainly having fun," said Roaddog.

"But where everyone can see," mumbled Jackie grabbing his arm.

"That's just the way it is round here, Doris is a little extreme, she can be a real party animal."

"You mean she actually wants this?"

"Oh yes. Not normally on a Thursday, she must have had a dry week, see the way her chest is going red?"

"She's chocking."

"No, she's coming any second." Doris started shaking, she pushed Slowball off for a moment to scream, them she pulled him back, the depressions in her cheeks showed she was sucking very hard, Slowballs twitching, and groaning showed her success.

"I'm having some of that," said Sharpshooter, he unzipped his jeans and walked over to stand beside Slowball, stroking himself until Doris pushed Slowball away and grabbed Sharpshooter by the cock.

"Fuck me," she yelled before Sharpshooter disappeared into her mouth.

"Does this happen often?" whispered Jackie.

"Not usually quite so loud, but she must have been without for a while."

"I've never seen anything like this."

"I'm not surprised. She likes it, the guys the same, sometimes the girls join in as well."

"How often?"

"Not every night, but almost every weekend, there will be some sort of sex going on around here. Normally a couple in the corner, or a trio in the back room. Sometimes when people get really stoned there'll be naked dancing."

"This is part of your life?"

"Yes, has been for a few years now. Look over at Bone and Bandit

Queen."

Jackie looked into the seating area, there the leader and his woman were sharing a chair that was far too small for the two of them, she had his penis in her hand, and his hand was inside her jeans.

"So, orgies every night?" asked Jackie.

"Not every night," laughed Roaddog. "Come on I'll take you home. Someone else can lock up tonight."

"You're not going to come back?"

"No. I need to get some rest; I'm getting very tired and I'm working early."

"This is a lot for me to think about you know."

"I understand, it can be a big step for such an uptight citizen. These girls were three quarters feral before they met us."

"And how does that occur?"

"What do you mean?"

"How do they meet you? Do you send the child catcher out with a cage and lollipops?"

"No," he laughed, "love the film connection though, they may look young, but they are all legal, at least I think they are. Though I'm not entirely sure about that one over there, the one staring at Bone's cock, with a hungry look in her eyes."

"Does she know that Bandit Queen will eat her up?"

"She has been warned and warned again. She might just learn."

"Bandit just caught her staring."

"Again?"

"Yes."

"On another topic entirely, are you working tomorrow?"

"Yes, evening kitchen and then bar."

"Fine, I'll pick you up after work, if that's OK?"

"And what do you plan for so late on a Friday night?"

"I don't know, back here for a few beers and see what happens."

"Just so long as you don't expect me to lay on that table, I'm not even sure I could sit at it now." They both turned back to watch the continuing show.

"Don't worry, I'll give it a good jet wash tomorrow."

Doris pushed Sharpshooter away and screamed her orgasm into the night sky. Her shuddering triggered Bug, he grunted and filled her pussy. Once she stopped twitching, she wriggled her ass to push Bug away.

"Lurch." she shouted. "Get the fuck over here and gimme that cock." Lurch walked slowly over to the picnic table.

"You sure baby girl?" his resonant voice filled the yard.

"Fuck me you bastard," she muttered looking up into his eyes, he smiled. She pulled Sharpshooter back into her mouth as Lurch walked round to the other side of the table. He unzipped his jeans and released his manhood.

"Holy fuck," whispered Jackie.

"Yes, don't ya just hate him, bastard is in perfect proportion."

"She's gonna take all of that?"

"Normally, Bug was just the warmup, and he knows it," Roaddog chuckled.

"Take me the fuck home," said Jackie, struggling to take her eyes off the length of Lurch slowly disappearing into Doris.

5: Good Friday. Old friends, New friends.

Alan had taken some time deciding what to wear, his old boots weren't up to it, rotted to almost nothing in the bottom of the old wardrobe. He was wearing his heavy and comfortable trainers, well protected but not with steel. He'd decided to leave the car here, and his last bike was a lost cause at the moment. Even though it was the driving force behind this visit. The taxi was on its way, or so the wonders of modern technology had told him. 'Bound to be a damned nigger driving it.' He thought. He laughed softly. 'That was alright back in the day, but now you can't even think it.' The irony of the thought caused him to smile even more. A shiny white Avensis pulled up at the door, taxi company logos emblazoned on the doors. Alan left the house and checked the door was secured before he walked away, he stashed his keys in the pocket of his jeans, checked phone, wallet and belt knife, this one used to fit nicely in a sheath in his old boots, the long black zip up jacket covered it adequately. He stepped across the pavement to the car, and sat in the front, some taxi drivers don't like that, but he really didn't care, a quick glance told him that he was correct about the driver, he wasn't too happy being so close to the customer and he was definitely a darker shade than his car.

"Where to mate?" the driver asked. "All I got was Walton Summit." The accent left no doubt that the driver was from sunny Blackburn, Alan smiled and passed him the card that the young pup had given him.

"You sure you want to go there?" asked the driver. Alan simply nodded.

"Your funeral, seat belt please, let's at least get you there in one piece." Alan fastened his seatbelt and the driver pulled away from the curb.

"You know where it is?"

"Yes, and I stay away whenever I can, those bastards can get a little rough."

"I've been invited."

"Again, your funeral."

There was no more talk until they pulled into the industrial estate, the taxi driver turned off the main drag and pulled up.

"It's along this road a ways. If you want me to take you back home, no charge. I'd advise against going there, those people are crazy." Alan smiled at the driver.

"Drive on please."

"Jesus," muttered the driver, he rolled slowly along the street and round the corner. He stopped a car length from the gateway to the yard. "You sure mate?" asked the driver.

"Yes, I'm sure, in fact I'm looking forward to it now. This shit really gets the old heart racing."

"That'll be a fiver then." Alan hitched forwards in the seat and reached under the jacket to get his wallet from the right hip pocket, the knife at his hip came into full view. Alan handed the driver a five pound note from the wallet.

"You know that knife is illegal, don't ya?"

"Didn't used to be. Why don't ya stay and watch?"

"Not sure I want to."

"If you do, whatever happens don't call the cops, OK?"

"If you say so, man, if you say so."

Alan climbed slowly out of the car, settled the jacket back into place, as he walked away from the car, he heard the doors lock and the driver's window open a little way. 'Damn these modern cars are too quiet.' He thought as he walked up to the gateway, he unzipped the jacket. He stood for a moment, then filled his lungs and shouted loudly.

"Did one of you bastards tell my daughter to fucking eat something?" He dropped the jacket and caught it with his left hand, the right on the hilt of his belt knife. He smiled to himself as he heard the scream of rubber as the taxi's tyres scrabbled for grip as it took off.

Roaddog was in the clubhouse drinking slowly, he was planning on picking up Jackie later, so he had to stay sort of sober. It was much busier than the night before, more members and more girls, Bandit Queen holding court by the bar, she seemed to be drinking slow as well, not necessarily a good sign, sometimes she made Roaddog nervous, so he was leaning against the bar, just chatting. He was always aware of what was going on around him, one of the reasons he had come so far in the club, nothing happened without him seeing it. He caught a sight of a man appear at the gate, he smiled to himself and almost laughed as the guy waited to attract some attention. Then the shout made silence fall like midnight in the club.

"This one is mine," shouted Roaddog as Bone was starting to get up, the leader glanced across and sat down. As master at arms it was his right to take this threat. Others started moving, either to give themselves some space, or a better view. Roaddog waved Slowball off, with a smile, they both knew who this was. Roaddog walked out of the clubhouse towards the entrance, his hands open and empty.

"That would be me," called Roaddog, when he was halfway to the old biker, loud enough so everyone could hear him.

"You're not wrong, she's more than a little scrawny," laughed

Geronimo.

"And she's seriously unsteady on those skinny legs," smiled Roaddog.

"That's more the shoes than anything else."

"You could be right there. You want to come meet the guys?"

"I'm not sure. Would I be welcome?"

"I think you'll be OK, I'll vouch anyway, and Slowball's just dying to meet you."

"I'm currently not thinking of coming back, you understand?"

"Yes, I get it. Don't sweat it."

"Fine, I'll meet, then we can see where it goes."

Roaddog reached a right hand to be shaken, wrists were clasped, and a serious hug ensued. Together they turned to the unit and walked towards the clubhouse. Slowball came out to greet Geronimo, shook his hand, then followed him inside. Roaddog took Geronimo to meet Bone. The leader stood to greet the older man.

"That's a damned old cut," said Bone.

"Yes, it's been around a while, most of its life in the damned cupboard. Call me Alan."

"Fine, Alan," said Bone. He looked round at everyone. "Rest of you lot fuck off. Man talk." He waited briefly as the others slowly drifted away.

"Alan," said Bone, "You've been away a long time."

"Yes, twenty years and some, I can't believe that anyone actually remembers me."

"I don't think anyone remembers you, but tales of Geronimo are still told occasionally," said Roaddog.

"You're kidding."

"No," said Bone, "you're somewhat of a legend."

"I don't believe it."

"Beside the point, why did you leave?"

"Got a short stretch for cutting some bastard that needed it, when I came out everything had changed. I drifted by and didn't recognise a single face, I thought I'd take a break. Got a real job, and a woman, then a child, so I've been away for about twenty years. Then the daughter's boyfriend drops your card in my hand. I thought I'd come by and see how much has changed."

"Would you be interested in coming back?" asked Bone.

"Maybe, you don't seem to be making the newspapers as much as we did in my day."

"That's true," laughed Bone. "There's much worse shit going on in the world than us. There's been a change in the last few years, the whole world is smaller, those old forces that keep groups together have faded, as have the old gangs that you remember."

"What do you mean?"

"The skinheads, they've just about gone, no real presence anymore, the paki gangs, they've gone, most of these are generally just followers of a specific brand of music. The football gangs, they're just about dead as well. The only real competition we have is the drug dealers, the citizens don't mind if we carve up a few of them. So, we don't get that much in the way of violence. It can be boring sometimes."

"I heard that your lot kicked the crap out of three thugs this week."

"That would be Roaddog here."

"Three on one?"

"Yes," said Roaddog, "they tagged me as well, but they lost."

"They live?"

"Yes," said Bone. "Though if the girl hadn't been there, Dog here would probably have dropped them off the motorway bridge."

"I never even considered that," said Roaddog.

"You're losing your touch."

"Thanks boss."

"You came by taxi, why?" asked Bone.

"I thought I might have a beer or two, so I left the car at home."

"You got a bike?"

"Sort of, it's old, and I do mean old."

"How old?"

"Nineteen sixties, no way it'd keep up with your Japanese crotch rockets," laughed Alan.

"Hey," said Roaddog, "some of us ride American and British bikes. Sixties, Enfield, Triumph or BSA?"

"Not even close," laughed Alan. "Douglas Dragonfly."

"No shit," said Bone. Alan just smiled.

"Is it running?" asked Roaddog.

"No, I can't get points, and I think the coil is fubar."

"Bug," yelled Roaddog. "Get your hairy ass over here."

"What do ya want?" demanded Bug.

"Alan here has a Dragonfly, needs points and coil. What ya got?"

"You're shitting me?" asked Bug looking at Alan, who shook his head. "Fine. Give me a few minutes." Bug wandered off, to the computer in the office.

"Will he be able to find the parts I need?" asked Alan.

"If anyone can it's him," laughed Bone, he looked around and caught the eye of one of the girls, and signalled that he'd like a drink, and held up three fingers. Cherie got three bottles of beer and brought them over. Then drifted away again.

"So, what was the club into twenty years ago?" asked Bone.

"Well, we didn't have such a swanky shop or clubhouse; we were working out of a sort of garage under the railway in Preston."

"What were you dealing in?"

"Usually stolen cars and bikes, we had a team that could tear a car into its component parts in about thirty minutes, and have the parts shipped out to various scrap yards for sale. We dealt a little dope, usually stolen from the black guys."

"Major bad boys then," laughed Bone, looking left as the young girl Amanda came up with a bottle of jack, she passed it to Bone, then knelt by his feet, pressing her chest against his leg, the bottle passed around the three, then returned to Amanda, she stood it on the floor, and ran her small hand up Bone's thigh.

"Hey Bone," said Alan. "We were respected back in the day, most of the other groups only messed with us the once. Then they vanished or paid heavy."

"What you mean paid?"

"Two of the local drug dealers used to pay us money and dope to leave them alone. It was a great arrangement, they paid up and we didn't even need to bruise our fists."

"Love it," laughed Roaddog. Bug came back. "What you got?" asked Roaddog.

"I got points that will fit given a tiny mod, and about four different coils, two will be here tomorrow, and the other two on Tuesday, battery is off the shelf, minor mods to connections but it will fit, and be ten times as good as the original." He looked down briefly at Amanda's hand which was now slowly stroking Bone's crotch. He shook his head and picked up the bottle of jacks, took a swig. "You want I pick the Dragonfly up with the van tomorrow, we could have it running in an hour or two?"

"I'm not sure I want to commit to that sort of thing," said Alan.

"No commitment, just let Bug and Roaddog work on it, they're suckers for old British basket cases," laughed Bone.

"She's not in a basket yet," Alan grinned. "She just needs more time than I've been able to give her for a while."

"When these guys get her running and I have every confidence that they will, you can ride with us if you want, but if you're not going to commit to the club then you can't wear the cut."

"I understand, I thought long and hard about that as I was getting dressed to come here, it was either an introduction or a possible offence. I can take it off if you want."

"Don't sweat it," said Bone, "we can talk about that another time." There was a scream from behind them.

"Bitch," howled Bandit Queen. She came storming towards them, Bug clutched the bottle of jacks and stepped backwards out of her way, she reached down and grabbed a fistful of Amanda's long hair. With one hand she dragged Amanda away from Bone and swung her over a sofa, out into the front yard. The girl scrambled to her feet as Bandit Queen came around the sofa.

"Bone help me," called Amanda, just before Bandit Queen's heavy left fist smashed into her belly and knocked her to the ground.

"You were warned, and better warned," said Bone, watching his old lady move as only she can. "Time to pay." Bandit Queen grabbed the girl by the jaw with her left hand and hauled her to her feet. The right arm cocked.

"Not her face," snapped Bone. Bandit Queen looked over her left shoulder at him.

"You want her pretty?" she growled.

"Not especially, but you can't show her off if you smash up her face." Bandit Queen looked back at Amanda and grinned wickedly, the right arm cocked again, as it came forwards the girl threw both arms up to protect her head, Bandit's target was a little lower, the fist slammed into the young girls left breast, flattening it against the ribs, she was lucky she was so light, the ribs flexed but didn't break. The white flash of pain took away the girl's consciousness, as she was thrown through the air to land in a heap. Bandit Queen stamped over and picked up an arm, the limpness was obvious to all.

6: Good Friday. Late night train party

"She dead?" asked Bone. Bandit Queen reached down and felt Amanda's throat.

"No, just out. Fuck."

"You really ought to pick on people more your size, say Lurch."

"Somehow I don't see Lurch stroking your cock."

"So, what you going to do now?" asked Bone. Bandit picked up an arm and let it drop again, still out of it. She looked back at Bone and grinned.

"Shit," whispered Roaddog.

"Cherie, Doris, help me here." she called. "Roaddog get me some gaffer tape."

"Shit, shit, shit," muttered Roaddog going into the office to retrieve the required tape. By the time he came back with the roll in his hand Amanda was already without her shirt, shoes and socks, Bandit Queen was working on her jeans, Amanda was awake now and struggling only a little, the jeans peeled off like a second skin. There was no underwear to be seen, nor any body hair at all, this made her look even more like she was underage. Bandit Queen dragged her over to the picnic table and dropped her face down on the end of it, she kicked Amanda's feet apart.

"Roaddog, tape her ankles to the frame." Roaddog knew better than to disobey at this point, in short order Amanda was spread-eagled face down on the table.

"Bone," called Bandit. "Over here." He walked over slowly. "Look at that pretty ass, and shiny bald pussy. She wants you to fuck her, will you fuck her for me?"

"If that's what you really want?" he was a little confused.

"Should I say, will you fuck her first?"

"Of course, I'll fuck her first."

Bandit Queen turned to the girl.

"You wanted to fuck my man, now you get to, I'm going to stick his cock in you personally, and when he's finished, every other guy here is gonna do the same. If you get too full Doris will suck all that cum out of you, because she likes it so much. When they've all fucked you once, they can all go again and fuck you in the ass."

Amanda tried to wriggle free, but strong hands held her and the tape on the legs would have to be cut.

"Please," she whispered, "I've never done anal."

"You haven't?" laughed Bandit Queen. "We have an anal cherry here. I claim that cherry by right of conquest, I will give that cherry to whoever I decide, and if you are really lucky girl it won't be Lurch." She waved Bone up to the table, he already had his prick out and he was more than ready. She took hold of him and guided him up to the girl. The table was a little low, so he had to spread his legs quite wide to get the right angle. Slowly he entered Amanda. She moaned at the harsh intrusion. Bandit Queen leaned down and whispered to her.

"This is the only time you will get my man; you're going to be a busy girl tonight, I have something else in mind for you as well, you may even like it. Do you like the feel of his cock moving inside you? You'll get plenty of that tonight." She stood upright again and watched Bone slowly fucking the girl, she leaned in close and whispered to him. "Fuck her hard." He continued at his slow and even pace, turn his head to Bandit Queen.

"I want her to enjoy this one time, then the rest can fuck her." he whispered. "Why don't you help her along?" Bandit Queen smiled at the cruelty of his words. She reached down with one hand and stroked the girl's backside, before sliding her hand around a hip and underneath, she moved her hand until she could feel Bone's cock moving in and out. Then she moved her fingers to the young girls exposed clitoris, and swirled them around it, she felt the excitement build slowly in the young body. Despite Amanda's anger and embarrassment, her own body started to betray her; she shook her head from side to side as waves rolled slowly down her abdomen. Suddenly she stopped moving and shouted out her orgasm as her whole body tensed and arched. Her pussy clamped down hard on Bone and triggered him, with harsh grunts he emptied into her. Even as he pulled out and stepped to the side Sharpshooter was driving in. Bone tucked his cock back into his jeans and returned to the seats. Bandit Queen followed him a moment later after whispering to Doris.

"Get the guys hot before they fuck her, we don't want to be at this all night."

Doris nodded as she was already sucking on the next man in the line.

Roaddog, Alan, and Lurch were talking in the corner.

"Is it often like this?" asked Alan.

"Nah," replied Roaddog. "Sometimes it's quite boring, tonight is different, we've got new people visiting, and a possible coup dismantled by the Queen herself."

"These are the good things I remember," said Alan.

"There are bad times as well, battles lost, and friends as well. It must have been hard for you when you got out of jail and everything was different."

"It was a dark time for me, but I got sorted out. Lurch, you not joining in the train?"

"No, Doris is right there, she'd be pissed if I tagged on that, and that Amanda chick is too small, she'd die."

"Why is Doris so important to you?"

"It's something special for a guy like me to find a woman who can take it all. I'm not gonna fuck that up."

"I don't understand?"

"He's six foot forty inches tall, and carries a dick to match, not many can take it, and Doris over there, is one of them," laughed Roaddog.

"The only one," rumbled Lurch. Alan raised his eyebrows in disbelief as Bug came back from his turn.

"Alan. How's the carbs on your Dragonfly?"

"Carb, it's one of the early ones. The later models had twin carbs. It seems to be OK, could probably do with a strip though."

"No sweat, we can do that as well. You be in some time tomorrow, I'll come pick it up in the van?"

"I'll be in all day, nothing planned."

They heard the rumble of a harley as it turned off the main road, it could only be coming to the clubhouse at this time of night. The single headlight turned into the yard and pulled up alongside the other bikes there. The motor fell into silence and the rider dismounted.

"Hey, it's Billy," laughed Roaddog. He walked out snatching a bottle of beer.

"Hi Billy," he called as he neared the bearded biker.

"Hi Roaddog, what the fuck is going on here?"

"She tried to replace the boss man's old lady and lost. Bandit

Queen decided she needed a lesson, she's still breathing, and I think she's learning something about endurance."

"I've heard about this shit, but thought it was just one of those urban legends."

"Doesn't happen often, but it does still happen."

"That's one cute looking ass, would it be OK if I joined in?"

"Hey Bone," yelled Roaddog. "Would it be OK if my mate Billy here tags on the train?"

"Of course, it would Dog," shouted Bandit Queen. "The more the merrier." Roaddog led Billy over to the table.

"Doris girl," he said, "get him hot, he's an old man, he'll need all the help he can get."

"Fuck you asshole," laughed Billy.

"Hey Amanda, look who's come to fuck you, it's Billy Gibbons." Amanda's tear-stained face turned and her eyes went wide as saucers. Then she rested her head on her hands, Cherie had long since left her alone. While he was there, Roaddog cut the tape holding her legs. She made no attempt to get away as Billy entered her. Once Billy had finished, he picked up his beer and wandered over to Roaddog. Doris helped Amanda stand up and took her over to where Bandit Queen was sitting. Bandit looked her up and down. There was a large bruise on Amanda's left breast, and a long straight one where the edge of the table had been hitting her upper thighs.

"Now girl," she said. "Have you learned who this man belongs to?" Amanda nodded, but said nothing.

"Good. For the rest of this weekend, you will be wearing your shirt, and a short skirt, seeing as you failed to bring any underwear today you can do without, your pussy will be on display at all times, for anyone to stroke or touch, or lick, is that clear?"

"Yes, Bandit Queen," was the tremulous reply.

"Doris, take her in the back, get her cleaned up and properly dressed, and fill her full of vodka, that'll help her." Doris nodded and dragged Amanda into the back of the shop.

"Fuck. I don't believe this place," said Billy to Roaddog.

"Yes, it can be fun."

"Hey Geronimo, your cut looks far too old, what's happening there?" asked Billy.

"Call me Alan, it is old, like years, I've been away for a while, and some guy sent me a card, said come down Friday night."

"I was here yesterday, these two guys fixed my bike up real good and real fast. Can't believe how good they are."

"You'd recommend them?"

"Hell yes, and so much cheaper than the main dealers."

"They've said they can fix my dragonfly, should I let them?"

"You got a dragonfly, fuck my dad used to ride one of those, awesome in their day. Yes, I'd trust them with anything."

"Hey Billy," asked Roaddog, "just how old are you under all that beard?"

"I'm nearly fifty man, November this year."

"That face fur makes you look about sixty-five," laughed Bug.

"Alan. You got an old lady?" asked Roaddog.

"No man, cancer took the wife about two years ago, got a teenage daughter to bring up."

"She ain't so teen, if you ask me."

"She'll be nineteen next time, but she's still my baby girl."

"If you ride with us, you'll have to make do with the chicks, or bring yourself a woman more your age, not many can cut this life."

"Yes, I know what you mean. The wife wanted to burn my cut; she was frightened I might just come back. She'd heard the stories and read some of the books from the seventies, she thought I'd die in some knife fight, or get wiped out by a van full of skinheads."

"We've lost more guys to BMW X5's in the last five years than we have to fights," said Roaddog. "In fact, I think my fight this week was the first one this year, before that was late last year. Two guys fighting over a chick."

"What happened there?" asked Billy.

"Bandit Queen stepped in and beat the crap out of them both. Now they share her, she always has a ride, always has a place to sleep, and always has at least one dick in her," laughed Roaddog. He checked his watch and realised how late it was.

"I gotta cut," he said. "I got a girl to pick up."

"You need escort?" asked Bug.

"Nah, I'll be fine, if anything was going to happen it would have been yesterday. I'll be back in an hour or so." Roaddog walked slowly over to his bike and fired it up, the short run to the Railway was now almost auto pilot for him. As he made the left into the carpark a small green van was turning left out. It flashed in his brain, but he had no idea why. He parked up and walked in, the bar was almost ready to close, and there were still a few people drinking. He walked up to the bar, and Nigel stopped talking to a customer and came over.

"Wainwrights please Nigel," said Roaddog.

"But that's for daytime, isn't it?"

"Yes, but I've had a couple already and I've a distance to ride, so something light, ya know?"

"I do indeed." The full pint appeared above the bar. Money changed hands.

"How's it going?" asked Roaddog.

"It's been quite busy in here tonight, a few big parties, and some couples. TV room's been pretty full of kids all night, they only left about an hour ago. So, a good night for me."

"That's great, we like it when our local businesses do well."

"Hang on." Nigel went to the middle of the bar and rang the brass bell that hung there. "Last orders," he called. There were no obvious takers, so he returned to Roaddog.

"Why do you like businesses doing well?"

"It means that the local economy is thriving, and there is even more money to be made in the niche services that we provide."

"What do you mean?"

"We have a motor repair shop, and we provide temporary security for people, we provide night watchmen sometimes. Since we moved into our unit on Walton Summit crime rates have fallen, insurance premiums have dropped. We have been a benefit to the community."

"That's only because most of the crime was perpetrated by small fish, and they don't dare to swim in your pond."

"And we do nothing to let them think otherwise. Stay away is the safest policy," Roaddog smiled.

"Actually, I really hate this weekend."

"I know you do; come Monday night you have four days takings in your safe. And a nervous ride to the bank on Tuesday. We'll be here Monday night anyway; we could leave a couple of guys to look after the place for you. And give you an escort to the bank Tuesday."

"How much would that cost me?"

"Call it fifty quid and a few beers."

"You guys can really drink, define for me a few beers?"

"No more than another fifty quid's worth."

"You my friend have a deal. I'll sleep so much better knowing that there'll be a couple of guys looking after the place."

"Great, so why don't you night safe it?"

"The money the banks charge is crazy for only a couple of weekends a year, and I'm not walking out of here at one thirty in the morning with a few hundred quid in my pocket."

"You can night safe during the day you know?"

"I'm not completely stupid, even so, I'd rather take the risk once. Normally I have a couple of friends turn up, and we all leave in different cars at the same time, so no one can be sure which is actually carrying the cash."

"Well this year, you're going to be riding in style on Slowballs trike, and surrounded by the meanest looking motherfuckers you've ever seen." He laughed, then continued. "I wouldn't be surprised if we have a police escort by the time we get there, and perhaps on the way back."

"Here comes Jackie. You sorted Jackie?"

"Pretty much, just the tables in here to clear and not too many of them."

"Don't worry about them, I'll sort that lot out, you two get off now." Nigel smiled at Jackie and Roaddog. Roaddog drank his beer, and they left the pub together.

"You OK?" asked Roaddog.

"I'm fine, just a little tired, it's been a heavy day."

"You want to go home, or to the clubhouse? It's been a busy day there too."

"Clubhouse, I could do with a beer or two to chill before I go home."

"No worries." He climbed onto his motorcycle and started up the big twin motor. "Mount up," he called over the noise.

"I've been looking forward to this all day," she shouted, as she settled into the pillion seat. Her hands gripped his belt and off they went, a short pause at the exit, waiting for a car to pass, then out into the main road. A quick squirt on the throttle and Roaddog blew past the car they had waited for, down the hill and under the bridge, he'd cleared sixty miles an hour before he was out of the left-hand bend, he could feel that Jackie was getting to be more comfortable with the actual riding. She was actively leaning into the bends on the last roundabout. Off the main road and into the street where the clubhouse is, she's actually smiling and almost letting go of Roaddog's belt. He rolled into the yard and parked in his normal space. They walked towards the clubhouse and Jackie saw Amanda sitting on the picnic table. Her legs spread wide.

"Why is that girl showing herself off like that?" she whispered leaning close to Roaddog. He smiled at Jackie and walked them straight towards Amanda, when he was almost up against her knees he reached in between her legs and stroked her pussy gently. Amanda flinched at his touch.

"Still sore?" he asked softly. "It will get better." Then he turned to Jackie. "She's been a bad girl, she's currently under punishment for trying to steal Bandit Queens man. She was warned, she'll heal, but she'll not forget."

"Damned right she'll not forget," called Bandit Queen. "Show them your tits."

Amanda lifted her shirt and showed Jackie the bruise that covered almost the whole of her left breast. Then she lifted the skirt and showed the bruise across her hips.

"Bandit Queens lessons are short and effective," whispered Roaddog. "There may be other girls who were thinking of the same sort of thing, not anymore."

"That's brutal," whispered Jackie.

"Yes. Better than a knife in the back though. Amanda here will learn from this, she'll learn to fight, and she'll learn to live. She'll be stronger and better in a few weeks."

"I have a new name," whispered Amanda, "I am now Man-Dare."

"That's a good name, a name of great meaning. Did I miss the christening?"

"Of course not," called Bandit Queen. "I'm just building up a little pressure." She laughed loudly holding up a bottle of beer. Roaddog patted Man-Dare on the leg and walked into the clubhouse to get himself and Jackie a beer. She followed closely not exactly sure if she should. Doris met them with a bottle for each, Roaddog nodded his thanks, and walked them over to where Alan and Billy were standing.

"Jackie," he said, "this is Alan, who's maybe considering coming back into the fold, and Billy who's just some old fart that tagged along," he laughed.

"Alan. Your cutoff is denim where all the others here are leather. Why?" asked Jackie.

"It's old, from a time before the leather ones became fashionable."

"Billy." said Jackie. "You remind me of someone, but I'm not sure who."

"I brought my bike in for a service, yesterday. As soon as he saw me, this mother, called me Billy, and it's sort of stuck."

"Billy, er, who?" she asked.

"Billy Gibbons," he replied, Jackie still looked confused.

"Try the TV series Bones, Angela's dad," laughed Alan.

"Yes, you do look like him, he plays a crazy texan rock musician."

"No," laughed Roaddog. "He is a crazy Texan rock musician playing at being Angela's dad, though there are some conspiracy theories going around that he may be just that, and he's doing nothing to deny them."

"Roaddog," whispered Billy, "is there really going to be a christening? And should I leave?"

"Yes, and not necessarily, christening's not like an initiation, so I don't see why you should leave. However, if Bone or Lurch suggest that you leave, then do so, with speed."

"No sweat, I'd love to see it, but not willing to die to do so."

"Judging by the look on Bandits face it's not going to be long. Jackie, do me a favour, this is going to be way outside your experience, please don't make a scene, or any rash judgements." He looked into her eyes. She could tell he was preparing her for something as best he could, so she finished her beer and nodded slowly. He held her in his arms briefly and whispered. "Be strong." Sure enough Bandit Queen stood up and walked out into the open air, she turned to face the bright lights of the clubhouse.

"Listen up all you scumbags and slags," she spoke clearly and loudly. "We are having a very special day here, we have a naming day, it doesn't happen very often, we are a small club, it happens even less often for a female, so few are worthy of a name at all, but this one has earned hers." She waved Amanda forwards, the girl walked slowly and stood beside Bandit Queen. "I have three questions for you girl. You will answer them, and you will answer them truly. Do you accept your new name and all it stands for?"

"I do," said Amanda.

"Do you promise to uphold all the values of womanhood within our club?"

"I do."

"Do you hate me?"

"I do."

"Good, nurture that hate, grow strong on it, and one day you will be here christening your own replacement. Lie down upon the ground and accept your baptism." Amanda lay down, on her back with her hands at her sides. Bandit queen stood by her head, slowly released her belt buckle, and unzipped her jeans, she pushed them down below her knees and crouched over the girl. Bandit Queen released a torrent of hot yellow liquid all over the girl's head, Amanda didn't make any move to protect her face, Bandit Queen shuffled her feet and moved the spray down the girl's chest and belly. Once the stream had stopped, she stood and raised her pants.

"Come on you mother fuckers, baptise the bitch." Most of the men came forwards to add their own pee to the baptism, Alan and Billy were personally invited by Bandit Queen. Once all the bladders were emptied Bandit Queen spoke again.

"Stand up woman, stand up Man-Dare." Man-dare rose slowly, and a little wobbly to her feet.

"Revel in your new name, enjoy the power of it, and grow strong sister." Bandit Queen reached forwards and kissed Man-Dare firmly on the lips. Then she stepped back. "Someone turn the hoses on the bitch, she stinks." Bandit Queen laughed heartily as two jet washers fired up and a fountain of water filled the night, throwing rainbows in the streetlights. Roaddog walked over to Jackie and took her hand.

"Talk to me," he whispered.

"That was absolutely disgusting."

"Did she object?"

"That's probably the worst part about it, she accepted it, as if it was normal."

"Nothing here is the normal that you are used to."

"That's for fucking sure. I've never witnessed anything so barbaric. And yet she just lay there and took it, why?"

"Bandit Queen was right about that girl from the first day she walked into the yard, she knew that Amanda was going to be trouble. She didn't just feed her to the dogs, she's testing her, look at it more like forging a blade. Bandit Queen is making a knife who's only purpose is to stab her in the back."

"Why would she do that?"

"The club needs strong leaders if it is going to survive, Bandit Queen was forged in the fire, now she's making Man-Dare strong in the same fire. Though I see ice in her as well. She is going to be strong, but she could be fragile as well. Only time will tell."

"You want to be leader with her at your side."

"Fuck that, too much hassle. I go where they say, fight who they say and fuck who I want."

"And who do you want, her?"

"No, you ya fool." he grabbed her and kissed her long and hard. She didn't struggle at all, she melted into his body and kissed him back.

7: Friday into Saturday, Moonlighting.

When the kiss finally broke Bandit Queen was standing next to them, with a bottle of beer for each. Jackie nodded her thanks and took a swig, under the gaze of Bandit Queen.

"Well Jackie, what did you think of the christening?" Jackie stared at her for a moment before speaking slowly and clearly.

"That has to be the most disgusting display I have ever witnessed, and the craziest part of it is that she accepted it. I couldn't believe my eyes." Bandit returned her gaze for a moment or two, then turned to Roaddog.

"I've already told you I like this one, don't let her get away. Tell her about the train. That'll make her mind up." She patted them both on the backside and turned away, as she walked through the crowd it appeared to fade away in front of her and reform after she had passed.

"What did she mean train?"

"Well, remember you asked."

"Tell me for fucks sake."

"Bandit caught Amanda with her hand on Bone's cock, she was only stroking him, she didn't have it out of his pants or anything. But she was stroking him, and Bandit flipped. He went on to tell her the whole story he missed nothing out. Jackie was having problems believing all this, so she turned to Billy.

"You fucked her as well?"

"Yes, a chance like that doesn't come around every day for an old guy like me, so yes I was a bad man and fucked her. You should have seen the look on her face when she thought that Billy Gibbons was about to fuck her." Jackie glared for a moment then turned her gaze on Alan.

"Not me. I didn't." he said.

"Why not?" she snapped.

"I'd rather not say."

"There's a young girl tied to a table and raped by all and sundry and you didn't join in, why?"

"Fuck," he muttered and looked at the ground for a while, then he looked her in the eye and continued. "I couldn't, she reminded me of my daughter."

"Face down on a table she reminded you of your daughter," growled Jackie, "you are going to have to explain that."

"Fine. It was a couple of weeks ago, there was a really warm evening. I'd had a few beers in the back garden and went to bed quite early. Just after midnight I woke up, old man's bladder, I heard a noise in the garden, so I went downstairs quietly, I snatched the back door open and stepped out onto the patio, a boy with his pants around his knees was backing up as quickly as he could until he hit the wall. Bent over the table, where I'd been drinking beer, was the daughter, skirt up round her waist, knickers hanging off one ankle. Brilliantly lit by the almost full moon.

'Dad.' she said.

'What the fuck is going on here?' I asked.

'I'm trying to get a quiet fuck in the garden, and now I'm going to have to try to wake that fucker up again.' She just glared at me until I went inside."

"Alan," said Jackie. "you need to get that girl under control, she's likely to end up in a bad way if you don't"

"She's been real crazy since her mother died."

"You need to get her back on the rails before she gets hurt."

"The boy," said Roaddog, "he the one that gave you our card?"

"Yes, that's him."

"He showed proper respect and had the balls to talk to us in the pub, not many will do that."

"He does seem like a nice guy."

"Getting back to tonight's entertainment," said Jackie. "What's to stop that sort of thing happening to me?"

"You're not as stupid as she was, for a start. And I wouldn't let it happen."

"How'd you stop them all?"

"I most likely would fail, but I'd die doing it."

"He's right," said Alan. "Once you're in a club like this one, it's like family."

"So how did you get left out?"

"The ones who remembered me died, everything changed while I was inside, I decided to try a different life for a while."

"Now you're coming back?"

"Maybe. The biggest problem is my daughter, she gets a hint of this lifestyle and she'll want in."

"You can't let that happen, she's too young," said Jackie.

"She's only a year or two younger than you and you are considering it."

"I suppose, before you introduce her, tell her everything, especially about tonight, if anything that will put her off."

"Is it putting you off?" asked Roaddog.

"Let's say it's not helping," She drank the rest of her beer, then looked at Roaddog. "Take me home, I have a lot to think about."

"No worries." He looked around and called over to Slowball. "Can you take Alan home?"

"Course I can," was the distant answer.

"Slowball will get you home, how does ten in the morning sound? We'll come in the van to pick up your old bike, we may not be able to get it running tomorrow, but we can give it a real old-fashioned try."

"Ten sounds fine to me," said Alan.

"See ya tomorrow," said Roaddog, he took Jackie by the hand and walked slowly out to his bike. "You ok?" he asked.

"I don't know. This is all so new and different."

"Well, I know the best place to think," he smiled, put on his helmet, zipped up his jacket, fired the big V-twin, and rolled the bike backwards. He turned and smiled at her.

"Trust me?" he asked.

"I suppose," she said.

"Load up," he called. She climbed on and grabbed his belt, not too tight, he smiled because he knew that was going to change.

He rolled slowly out of the yard, on to the road, he didn't take the normal route to her house, he turned left at the first roundabout then straight on at the next, cruising at a steady fifty the V was barely beating. The next roundabout took them up onto the M65, gradually he wound the power on, and snicked up the last two gears, Jackie was shielded from much of the wind behind him, and completely out of sight of the speedometer, the needle hung short of the hundred mark but only for a minute then he started to slow down, off at the next junction and down to the normal roads. Traffic was light as it always is at this time of night, off the roundabout heeling hard over and accelerating he climbed the hill on the A675, long sweeping bends, just the sort of thing the heavy Harley was built for. It only seemed like a minute and he was slowing down for Abbey village, nothing moving but better safe than sorry. Exiting the village, he turned on the power again, downhill into the left, then climbing up onto the moors, open fields around them, flashing past faster than she could see. The road here had an experimental centre line, small but bright blue LEDs, Roaddog preferred the old-fashioned cats-eyes, at high enough speed you can see these LED's pulsing, and it makes the line move in your brain. Screaming passed Belmont reservoir he slowed down again for the village. Passed the speed camera he raised a single finger in salute, at the Black Dog he turned right, and up the narrow walled section of road, the stonework bouncing the sound of the heavy motor back and forth until it was deafening, then comparative silence as they came into the open once again, he slowed right down, and turned the bike around in the road, pulled over, and stopped the motor. The silence made their ears pop. Jackie looked around.

"Where are we?" she asked.

"Some call it Wards reservoir others Blue Lagoon. When it's been raining and there's a good moon, the water running down from the moors, can be quite spectacular, we've got the moon but no water. Unload." She stood up and swung her leg over the bike, he tipped it down onto the kickstand and stood up off it.

"Why did you bring me here?"

"I told you, it's a good place to think." He gently took her hand and walked her across the road and sat her on the edge of the tarmac. He sat alongside her and slid his hand over her thigh. "Look at the stillness of the water, the moon shining like it's on a mirror of the hardest glass, yet across the water is the spillway that empties a stream from the moor, there's a little water in it but not much, it's been too dry recently."

"It's certainly pretty and peaceful. What's it like in the daylight?"

"Personally, I prefer the moon light, sun makes it look somehow depressed, oh, it's open and green and natural, but like one of those depressing landscape pictures you see screwed to pub walls. It looks too real in the day, under the moon it's an entirely different place, I think it's sort of magical."

"You're crazy."

"What do you mean?"

"One minute you're fighting for my life in an urban jungle and the next your sitting by a lake talking about magic."

"That's not crazy, that's life. What were you thinking about while we were riding here?"

"Well, nothing really, I was feeling the road, and the beat of the motor, the wind and the forces in the turns."

"So, you weren't thinking of anything at all beyond the moment you were in."

"I suppose."

"Well now you can think about all those other things, the road has stopped, the motor has stilled, the wind has dropped, and the forces are gone. All that is left is the two of us and mister moon."

"If you're crazy," she whispered, "then so, I think, am I." She leaned towards him and kissed him, his tongue darted into her mouth swarming around, hot and hungry, his hand tightened on her thigh and slid further up. He pulled her in tight, his breath rushing loudly through his nose. Then something changed. He stopped, he leaned away from her.

"What's wrong?" she muttered. His head cocked to one side, he looked up to the road from the moor, and sure enough there were lights sweeping round one of the bends. Then they vanished behind the hill.

"Fuck," he said.

"What's up?"

"This road, this time of night, it's either pissed up yahoos, or cops." The lights came into view as the car came down the steep slope, before it disappeared again the blue and yellow squares showed brightly in the moon light and the large orange dot as well.

"Cops," he said. Seconds later the car came out of the dip, its headlights lighting up the sky briefly then sweeping down passed the church spire in the distance and striking them both in the face, Jackie turned her head so that her face was hidden in Roaddog's jacket, he closed his eyes, but it was already too late, the hot white halogens had wiped out his night vision, the wide tyres skittered for grip as the brakes hit hard, the tail of the car wriggled as the driver fought for traction. The car stopped, the motor humming softly, the exhaust ticking loudly as it cooled. A spotlight hit the two in the face. And Roaddog closed his eyes again.

"What are you two doing here?" demanded a voice from the car.

"We were watching the moon on the water, but with that light in my face I don't think I'll be watching much for a while." The motor was still running, and the cops hadn't got out of the car yet, so Roaddog heaved a quiet sigh, he got to his feet and lifted Jackie to hers. Together they walked to the car.

"Who are you?" asked the voice still hidden behind the light.

Roaddog gave them his name, well, the one he knew matched the registration plate they were looking at.

"You?" he asked Jackie, turning the light more her way. She told him, her voice shaking with nerves.

"You two got ID?"

"No," said Roaddog, opening his wallet and showing the policeman that all he had was cash. Jackie shook her head.

"These roads aren't safe at night you know."

"They're not much better during the day," said Roaddog.

"What do you mean?" snapped the voice behind the light.

"The dip you just came through, I've had a friend killed there, the bend further up with the tree, I had one taken off the road and killed there, the road down into Rivington village, I've had three killed there by some dick in a four by, these roads are much safer in the dark. But there is a lot less traffic, just you and me."

The policeman was silent for a long moment, then the radio in the car squawked.

"Silent alarms, BP and Spar Bolton road," said the second cop.

"You two drive careful and stay out of trouble," said the cop as he killed the light, selected a gear and set off along the road, tyres screaming. Before the car entered the village, the lights were scattering blue beacons across the countryside, but it was a little too early in the morning for sirens.

"That was scary," said Jackie pulling Roaddog against her and nestling her face against his shoulder.

"Two days ago, you were involved in knife fight with three thugs and talking to a cop is scary." He laughed and turned her face up, to look into her eyes.

"You were in the fight I just turned up as it ended. Is that your real name?"

"No, but it matches the bike. I'll get it changed when I remember."

"You can do that?"

"No, but I do know a man with access to the DVLA databases."

"I'm shaking," she said.

"I know, exciting isn't it?" he smiled.

"Yes, no, fuck, I don't know, shit, kiss me." The words tumbled over themselves, so he kissed her to stop the noise. After a while he broke the kiss and said.

"You do realise we are standing in the middle of the road?"

"Are we?" she asked still a little breathless. Roaddog, looked up the hill again as he heard a ting, ting, ting. Two separate lights came round the top corner.

"Fuck," he said. "Can I not get a break?"

"What's wrong now? Those are bikes, aren't they?"

"Not exactly." The sound of the two strokes got louder as they came down the hill. Then vanished briefly while they were in the dip, the two came over the brow and stopped beside Roaddog and Jackie.

"You guys ok?" asked one of the young men.

"We're fine."

"We just got hassled by the damned cops, documents, ID's the works, fuckers."

"The bastards got a call to a break in, so they fucked off and left us alone, they didn't even stop the car," laughed Roaddog.

"They checked tyres, exhausts, speedos, everything bar rip the feckers to pieces. Anyway, what you two doing out here this time of night?"

"Watching the moon on the water, it's pretty."

"You're kidding."

"No, moon, water," laughed Roaddog.

"You know that carpark just up the way is a favourite for doggers?"

"That's why I stopped here."

"You're crazy. Which way the pigs go?"

"Bolton, some spar and petrol station."

"Good were going to Preston, you wanna tag? Safety in numbers thing."

"Jackie you ready to go home?"

"Yes, be good to get some sleep, though I'm not working until tomorrow night."

"Lucky you, I'm working in the morning."

"Fuck man, it's Easter Saturday." said one of the young men.

"And I got a motorcycle shop to open, And Jackie here has a waitressing job to go to in the evening."

"We're lucky we got the whole weekend off. Hey, don't the Dragonriders have a clubhouse in Walton Summit. Perhaps we should drop in one day?"

"How do I put this? Some of the guys are old and old school."

"Right, you're not."

"You seemed like nice guys, so I have no issues. Had you been ten or fifteen years older, then most likely there'd have been a problem here."

"Our old guys no different from your old guys."

"That's for sure. I'll ride with you, I'm going to the 65, and then south on the 6. You two?"

"We'll take the 65 into south Preston."

"Fine, you two lead the way, when we get to the 65 I'll cut in the horses and leave you to your ride home OK?"

"Fine by us. Let's hit the road." They two turned key's and kicked their starters to bring the little strokers to life. Jackie and Roaddog got on the Harley and he thumbed the starter, and the rumble of the big V filled the air. He waved to the two scooter riders. They set off, blue smoke filling the air behind them as Roaddog, slipped the clutch out to follow, the return journey was more sedate than the outward one had been, and without incident, other than the single finger salute to every speed camera that they passed. They pulled up the sliproad to the M65 the little scooter engines struggling with the incline, once on the flat Roaddog pulled into the outside lane, and kept pace until the scooters were flat out, the riders hunched over the bars for that last half mile an hour, Roaddog waved to them then rolled on the power, the dyna leapt from eighty to ninety, to one hundred almost faster than it could be said, the bright lights of the scooters falling backwards quickly in his mirrors. He smiled to himself and focused on the empty road. The hypnotic effect of the dark motorway always focused his mind, with no other traffic on the road it seemed to Roaddog that the road was created when it came into the range of his single headlight and ceased to exist the moment it left it, the road was in front of him but gone before he actually reached it. South on the M6 wasn't much different, though there was a little more traffic. As they pulled up outside Jackie's house, he realised that he could barely feel her presence, she was becoming part of the bike, feeling the ride and going with the flow. The big motor stuttered into silence. Jackie dismounted. Roaddog did not.

"You had enough time to think?"

"I'm not sure."

"How about I pick you up in the morning and you spend the day with me at the shop? It could be fun."

"Yes, what time?"

"Nine-ish?"

"I'll see you in the morning."

She leaned down and kissed him hot and hard. When she finally stepped away, she was breathing hard. He wasn't much better. He waved as he pressed the starter and rolled the bike back into the street. In a moment he was gone.

8: Easter Saturday and News at ten.

It was about nine when Roaddog rolled up to Jackie's house. She was ready but her mother was at home, and her father was looking out of the window. It was obvious from the body language that there had been harsh words exchanged. He had heard some of them when he had talked to her earlier. He stopped on the driveway, but at the bottom nearly on the footpath. He smiled to himself as he blipped the throttle and hit the kill switch, the exhausts popped mightily as the motor died. 'Love those Vance and Hinds.' He thought to himself as the whole neighbourhood woke up. He walked towards the door, his shoulders and hips rolling with his stride, Jackie smirked to herself at the performance he was making of a simple walk. He smiled at Jackie and spoke softly.

"Hi Mr's Bamber."

"Don't you hi me."

"What's wrong?"

"Where were you two until nearly two in the morning, and don't give me any of your bull."

"We went to Blue Lagoon to watch the moon on the water, we met a nice policeman and a couple of scooter boys. It was fun," he smiled.

"I don't want her out until that time of night in all sorts of stupid places."

"You have nothing to worry about, she is perfectly safe when she is with me."

"But she's not safe from you."

"Surely that's for her to decide?"

"I don't like it; I don't like you."

"That is your prerogative, Jackie of course likes me, and likes to be with me, because there she is, dressed and ready to ride. Shall we go?" The last addressed to Jackie pointedly. Jackie walked around her mother and down the drive toward the waiting motorcycle.

"I'm sorry but I have to go, I have work to do today," he said to Mrs Bamber, then he turned and went to the bike, he threw a leg over the seat and hit the starter. The Harley started with a crack and he rolled it backwards into the road. Then nodded at Jackie to mount. Knowing her parents were watching she performed this motion with a grace that she wasn't actually sure of, as soon as her hands dropped to his belt, he threw the clutch out and set off with a roar. Once they were out of sight he backed down on the throttle and set off in an unexpected direction. Only minutes later they were pulling up outside an unremarkable semi, there was already a van parked up with the rear doors open. While Jackie was dismounting Slowball and Alan came from beside the house, pushing a small and obviously old motorcycle. It was a nondescript beige colour, though there was something about it that was strange even to Jackie's untrained eyes. She tapped Roaddog and said.

"It looks weird at the front."

"Oh, it's weird. Only the dragonfly had that sort of front end, they didn't put them on anything else after these." He jumped up into the van and pulled the ramp out, locked it into place as the others lined up the motorcycle. Three of them pushed it up the ramp and strapped it down. While Slowball was securing the ramp in place Roaddog spoke to Alan.

"You want to take your car, or ride in the van?"

"If I ride in the van then someone has to bring me home."

"That's not a problem."

"Here's another, I'll call the taxi driver who dropped me off."

"That'll blow his mind, he might not even come to the shop."

"His choice. Van it is." He walked up to the passenger door of the van while Roaddog and Jackie were getting on the bike. They set off in convoy, Roaddog stayed behind the van, it was after all carrying a very precious cargo. Alan had no idea just how few of these machines were still running today. There would have to be some talk about that once they got to the shop. They arrived in short order, and Slowball pulled the van up in front of the main doors, Roaddog parked in his usual place, Jackie walked into the shop where Bug and Sharpshooter were lounging and chatting, the music playing from the speakers the same sort of rock as the night before but at a much lower level. After a brief hello the two went back to their conversation about the vocal skills of Gillan and Coverdale. Neither of which meant anything to Jackie. The Dragonfly rolled out of the van and into the shop, Alan returned it to its centre stand. Conversation stopped.

"Fuck," said Sharpshooter. "I never thought that I would see one of those."

"Me either," replied Bug. "But there it is."

"Who could even think that was a good colour?" laughed Sharpshooter.

"How did you come by this rare classic?" Roaddog asked of Alan.

"I sort inherited it. It was my grandfather's, grandmother said take it away before he kills his stupid self. He loved it, I couldn't bring myself to sell it, even after I'd sold my commando, and my rocket I just couldn't."

"In good condition those will go for ten k at auction."

"You're kidding?"

"No, there can't be more than fifty still running."

"I'd like to get it running but I'm still not selling it."

"Good man." He turned to the men seated. "Bug, get your hairy ass over here and let's see what we can do for this venerable old lady." Bug and Sharpshooter came over and started to lend a hand, Bug liberated the battery in a few moments.

"This heap of shit is fucked. I've got something far better." He dropped the dead battery into the recycling bin and went into the back of the shop. Sharpshooter had the carb off and took it over to a work bench to strip it down. Roaddog was working on the points cover which was hiding under the generator, he worked for a while then decided the genny had to go first. Alan watched the men working for a while then decided to go and sit down, he was of no use to them at all. As he sat down next to Jackie an orange delivery truck turned up. Roaddog went out to talk to the driver, collected the parcel and signed the delivery documents, without the driver even getting out of his cab. He dropped the box on the bench where Sharpshooter already had the carb in lots of tiny pieces.

"Carb OK?" he asked. Sharpshooter looked up.

"Should be good, float's intact, the slide needs a clean and a polish, the needle and the jets look OK, just old and tired." Roaddog went back to working on the points.

"How did your evening go?" asked Alan of Jackie.

"He took me out to Blue Lagoon."

"Shit, it's been years since I've been there."

"He's right it is beautiful when the moon is on the water."

"Did you talk things out?"

"Not really we didn't get much of a chance."

"What do you mean?"

"We'd only been there a few minutes when the cops turned up."

"That must have been fun."

"Not really, I've never had any dealings with the police, I was frightened. Dog took it all in his stride. Eventually the cops got a call and went off to Bolton I think."

"So then did you get to talk?"

"Not really," she laughed, "There was the kissing and then the scooter guys turned up."

"That must have got a little rough."

"No, they seemed nice and we rode back to the motorway with them."

"You are shitting me?" he said loudly.

"No. We left them at the motorway, and he took me home."

Alan shook his head and stood up.

"Hey Roaddog. What the fuck is this I hear about you riding with fucking mods?"

"Relax Alan, they weren't Mods as you understand them, those days are gone, pretty much gone. Nowadays they ride scooters, wear parkas, and listen to northern soul music. They aren't the rabid gangs that they used to be, there are the exceptions of course. Hell, even the scooter clubs will go out of their way to keep the peace between us."

"That's gotta be bollocks."

"No it's not, there are still some dinosaurs that just like to fight for no reason, but there aren't so many of them left. What happened to your old crew?"

"They died or turned citizen."

"And so did you. Now you're thinking of coming back, but things have changed not so much around here, but in the world in general. When you were riding, the cops couldn't catch your Norton or your Triumph, could they?"

"No, their cars were dog slow."

"Now they got scoobies and evos, they're good for close to two hundred, and their drivers are quite good as well. Bike cops got Hyabusa they're as quick as the scoobies or would be without all the extra weight. They got radios ya can't outrun, and their choppers. We gotta play things smarter these days."

"Sounds boring," snarled Alan, he sat back down.

"What's the problem?" asked Jackie.

"All the years I was riding with this club, we'd go fifty miles out of our way for a rumble with the damned mods, now it seems we ride with them."

"They were nice young men, who'd been hassled by the cops just as we had, they ride nearly bikes, and wear funny coats. What's the problem? You've got more in common with them than someone like my dad, who's only ever driven a car, and is the most upright of citizens."

"But they're mods for god's sake."

"They did mention something I didn't understand."

"Go on."

"They said that the carpark up the hill from that little lake was a favourite for doggers, what are doggers?" Alan looked at her his eyes wide, he stood up again.

"Roaddog, you gotta get this girl educated."

"Why?"

"She just asked me about doggers."

"Sheltered life, what can I say, you educate her." Alan sat down again.

"Well," demanded Jackie, a little embarrassed that everyone else knew about something that she didn't. Alan looked at her calmly.

"Doggers. Doggers are people who go to out of the way carparks, woods, playgrounds. They go there to have sex in public and to have strangers join in with them, most of these strangers are men looking for a blow job or a shag, and not too bothered about sloppy seconds." Jackie stared at him for a while then glanced at the empty picnic table. Then looked back at Alan.

"Not unlike what happened here last night."

"Perhaps, but Man-Dare was only open to club members, perhaps available would be a better word."

"Club members and you and Billy."

"Yes, invitees as well, but I didn't."

"I see," she said slowly, she paused before continuing. "Looks like there's a whole world out there I know nothing about."

"You really don't want to go there. Look it up on some porn sites if you are that curious, but don't go there."

"I don't think I'll do that either."

"I am glad. I wonder how they are doing with my old bike?" He looked across at Roaddog and called out. "How's it going?"

"Points are being modded by Bug, Sharpshooter almost has the carb cleaned and back together, coil is changed, I'm gonna change the sludge in the bottom of the engine for something like oil, give it some new fuel and we'll be ready for a start."

"You're kidding?"

"Will you stop asking that," Roaddog took his phone out of the inside pocket and stared at it for a moment. "Slowball get the big display up. Punch in the tracker." The large TV on the wall came to life and a map showed, in the centre of this map was a marker.

"What's that?" asked Alan.

"That is a car we put a tracker on Thursday, it's a super shit hot civic, and it's in Hyde. We have heard that some competition has moved into our area, and they are based in Hyde. Where the fuck is that Slowball?" said Roaddog.

"The main street that you can see is Commercial Brow, Hyde. We've got a motorway junction, railway station, waste processing centre, car showroom, car body shop, and a garage. There's a pub called the Railway Inn, and just around the corner is the cop shop. It's perfect."

"We still don't know where the driver has been, all we know is that he's just started the car."

"He's headed for the motorway, if he's coming here, he's going to be carrying." said Roaddog.

"We can't hit him on the motorway. Too many cameras," said Slowball.

"Track him when he gets here, I'll ring Bone." Roaddog walked outside into the yard. He called a number on his phone. The conversation was short. He returned to the shop.

"Track him on the screen, when he gets here, get eyes on him. That's you Bug your bike looks like it's off the shelf. I'll ring Bandit and get her to send in one of the girls to be additional cover for you. Hide your colours. We need to find out where he goes and where he unloads whatever he is holding. Everyone clear?"

There were nods all around.

"Right," said Roaddog. "Let's see if we can get this old lady running."

9: Easter Saturday, Fire in the hole.

Once Bug had modified the points, just enough to make them a good fit on the timing plate, Roaddog started fitting them, and setting them up. Gap first then location, turning the timing plate was quite difficult, access to the holding screws was limited and visibility inside the housing a serious problem. He turned to Alan.

"Can you imagine how hard this job would be without a lift or a racketing screwdriver?"

"Must have been a bitch back in the sixties."

"This was built in 1957, last of its kind. Not as rare as the twin carb versions, but still rare enough, there were only fifteen hundred ever built. Douglas folded in 1957."

"How do you know so much about it then?"

"Looked it up this morning. If we can get this set up right it won't need anything like as much maintenance as they did back in the day, the points are far better, and this condenser won't fail."

"Even if it works, I won't be riding it much, the roads today are just too scary."

"There are certainly a lot of dicks about. But hey, there's only two things certain in this world."

"Aye, death and taxes."

"How old is the petrol in this tank?"

"Years."

"It's gone," Roaddog got a bucket and drained the remaining fuel from the tank. Poured in a little fresh, sloshed it around and drained it out too. "When this old girl runs, and I am sure she will, remember, modern fuel is like two star and lead free. So, don't forget your fuel additives," He waved a bottle for Alan to see. "We sell it, there are a few guys around here still running really old bikes, lead free plays havoc with the valve gear."

"How long until she's ready?"

"We are almost ready for a trial now, I think I'll change the plugs though, nice modern plugs will give better sparks." Sharpshooter finished installing the cleaned carb, then stepped back.

"Turn it over a few times while I'm setting these plugs," said Roaddog. Sharpshooter cranked the engine over using the kick starter. The engine turned quite well considering it hadn't actually moved in years.

"No clanks and no tight bits," said Sharpshooter.

"Stick it in gear and do it again," Sharpshooter follows the instructions and calls out.

"More resistance, but nothing too tight."

"Almost there then," said Roaddog, coming over and fitting both spark plugs into the leads. "Ignition on and spin it," he said. Sharpshooter kicked the engine over a few times and they both saw big sparks at the plugs.

"Plugs in then off we go," said Roaddog, as he fitted the plugs to the cylinders.

"There is a trick to starting it," said Alan.

"Yes, it'll be the same as all the other old bikes, get some fuel in the cylinders before you start it. No worries." They lowered the lift and rolled the bike onto the ground.

"Alan would you like the honour?" asked Roaddog.

"No man, you've put the work in you do it."

"What you really mean is that you can't be assed kicking the crap out of this thing trying to make it run."

"Got it in one," laughed Alan.

"Fine, here's your lesson in starting old bikes. Ignition off, petrol on." He turned the petrol tap. "Flick the pipe to be sure the petrol is moving, not really necessary here because we know it is full." He flicked the pipe. "Tickle the carb." He pressed the small button on the carb that pumps extra fuel into the barrel. "Kick the motor over a couple of times." Twice down on the kick start. "Tickle again, then feel for the compression." He tickled the carb and pushed the kick starter until he felt the compression. "Ignition on and kick it hard." He turned the ignition switch to on and looked Alan straight in the eyes. "Fire in the hole," he said as pushed down hard driving the motor round as hard as he could. It sort of fired, first one cylinder, then after a moment or two the other started to fire, then engine smoothed out and the rattles went away as the oil pressure came up and the lubricant started to fill all the oilways. The steady beat of the engine continued as blue smoke came from the tail pipes.

"Don't worry about the smoke, I've overdosed it, seeing as it's not been run for a few years, that'll go away. Motor sounds sweet, a bit tappety, but that might settle down as it warms up, if it doesn't, we'll have to adjust the tappets." He rolled the bike over to the rolling road and dropped the front wheel in between the rollers. Slowball came over and started the rollers turning. Roaddog slowly applied the front brake, watching the gauge that measures brake force.

"Get the airline in there, they'll be full of crap" said Roaddog. Slowball left the rollers running and blasted air into the brake drum. Roaddog tried the brake again.

"More air," he said. The third attempt seemed to meet his standards, so he heaved the brake on, as he would for a real test. The test dial showed that the brake was working well enough to pass the test. The same performance was repeated for the back brake. Roaddog rolled the bike back off the brake tester and turned to Alan.

"There you go, one old girl already for the road."

"I can't believe it, it's not even lunch time."

"I'd change the tyres as soon as you can, these are old and perished, cables could do with replacing, but no real urgency there, they'll most likely last the summer out, or die in the first two days. Take it round the block, see how it feels."

"I've no lid."

Slowball handed Alan an old-style pisspot helmet, and Roaddog stood up to hand over the bike. Alan took the handlebars and sat on the bike.

"Remember, drum brakes, almost anything out there can out brake you," said Roaddog with a smile. Alan grinned and gingerly rolled out into the yard, then off into the road. Roaddog looked up at the big screen on the wall. The marker was now on the M61 and still coming this way, he hoped it didn't come off at Bolton or Chorley, and where was the girl that Bandit Queen had promised. A soft voice behind him made him turn quickly.

"What do you need?" asked Cherie.

"Your body," smiled Roaddog.

"You dragged me all the way here for a jump, I thought you had a new girl, and there she is," she pointed at Jackie. Then looked back at the screen.

"We're tracking a green civic, I think it's involved with some dealers that have been moving into our patch. We need to know where it goes and who the driver meets. Simple observation that's all."

"And I get to ride with you."

"No, you get to ride with Bug, his bike is less noticeable than mine."

"Damn," she muttered.

"Bug, you leave that damned pipe closed, you're going to be tooling around the towns, he'll not be hitting the gas, and if he does, let him go. We can always pick him up another day. Don't go giving him the idea that he has a tracker on his car. You lose him he stays lost, got it."

"I understand. Come on Cherie, he'll be at the M65 interchange very soon."

The two walked out into the yard, Bug latched his phone into the dash on his bike, it was showing a smaller version of the tracker on the big screen. As they pulled out of the yard Alan returned. He rolled to a stop in front of the large open doorway. He dismounted and hauled the Douglas up onto it's rather clumsy centre stand. Alan walked slowly up to Roaddog and held his hand out, Roaddog took it and they shook solemnly.

"Thanks man," said Alan. "I'd never have been able to get it running. How much do I owe you?"

"Call it twenty to cover the parts."

"That's not right."

"Fine twenty for the parts and I get to take photo's and video of the bike."

"Why?"

"Advertising, she came in a basket case and rode out in half a day. Your recommendation included of course."

"Do for me. I'll bring it here if it needs anything, and one of the things it's going to need is an MOT."

"No it's not, it's more than forty years old and substantially unchanged, engine and frame numbers still match."

"I'll need tyres at the very least."

"No worries there, tell you what, you bring it in and leave it with us for a few days. I'll do the tyres and at the same time, seeing as wheels are off, I'll check out the brakes and the chain and sprockets. These are all going to wear out very soon, if we know which ones we need before we take it apart then we can replace them in one day not four, I don't expect the brakes to be easy to get nowadays."

"Great when should I bring it in?"

"Say Tuesday, you can have it back before weekend, and I'll start sourcing the other hardware that you're going to need."

"That sounds like a plan to me."

"I'll take some pictures, then shoot video as you ride it out. OK?"

"Certainly."

"New question, you got AA?"

"Actually yes, why?"

"Great, we'll be going to Rivi tomorrow be here about 10 am you can ride with us."

"Why is AA important?"

"If you get a tyre failure then they'll bring you back home."

"Again, sounds like a plan. Go get your camera."

"Always got it with me." Laughed Roaddog taking his phone out of his inner pocket. Together they rolled the Dragonfly out into the sunlight and Roaddog took several photos of it.

"Right just ride it out of the gate while I run the video."

"Helmet?"

"Nah, look better without it."

Alan started the Dragonfly and rode it out into the road and then back again.

"That will be great. I'll get our website guys to mix that up on a new page with some words from you. Be great."

"What words do you need?"

"Don't worry about it, we'll think of something," he laughed.

"Can I trouble you for a ride home?"

"No worries, Slowball," he called. "Get the van and take Alan home will ya?"

"Course I'll be a couple of minutes," said Slowball, going into the back.

"See you even get a ride home," laughed Roaddog.

"One more thing. Ya can stuff your twenty quid, here's fifty and you can like it."

"OK, I'll like it, and I'll see ya tomorrow."

"Definitely."

"You might even sell the Dragonfly while you're there."

"Not happening."

"It's going to be popular, and there will be some willing to buy it, but don't take less than seven for it."

"I've told you I'm not selling it."

"I heard you, come on let's get it loaded, I can't help you at the other end, I have to be here for a while yet."

Alan rode the Douglas into the back of the van and the pair had almost finished strapping it down when Slowball appeared.

"Sorry guys, must have been a dodgy kebab on the way home last night."

"You didn't have a kebab," laughed Alan.

"It's always the kebab, even if you don't have one," laughed Slowball as he walked up to the driver's door.

"See ya tomorrow," said Alan, shaking Roaddog's hand again. Roaddog walked into the clubhouse and sat next to Jackie. He checked the big screen, then took his phone and sent the pictures and video to the guy running their web site, the text message returned only seconds later said that the new page would be up before tomorrow morning. Roaddog checked the screen and asked Jackie.

"How long has that car been stationary?"

"It's not moved for a few minutes, maybe as many as ten."

"Isn't that B and Q?"

"It was, now it's a monster charity shop, furniture and electrics, carpets and curtains."

"He's come from Hyde to go charity shopping in a car that can't carry two carrier bags? That's weird."

"He's probably not shopping. It's a big carpark and generally quite empty."

"He's making a switch," He sent Bug a text message saying it was a switch. In moments the reply was 'Into a green van, following the van.'

"Green van, Bug's following the van."

"Does it feel good when you get an old bike running?"

"It's almost the best feeling in the world. I suppose I'm a really lucky guy, I get to do a job I love, and ride bikes, so lucky."

"Have you not found anyone to share it with yet?"

"Not yet, but bike club gives a guy plenty of opportunities to burn off the frustrations of life, so no rush really."

"Alan said that the club is like a family?"

"Not like, is."

"So last night, when Amanda was taking her punishment for being an unruly teenager, where all those men fucking their daughter or their sister?"

"Good question," laughed Roaddog, "and the answer is yes, and no. Man-Dare is now more of a sister than she was, and less of a daughter, but even with these labels, she is both less and more. What you suggest as incest is a rule decided on the outside, and as such has little sway inside the club. Think about Alan's response."

"He didn't join in because she reminded him of his daughter."

"Yes, but was that because when he saw her bent over that table, he wanted to fuck her?"

"He didn't because she looked too much like his daughter."

"Wrong girl."

"You mean when he chanced on his daughter in the back garden, he wanted to fuck her?"

"Maybe, and when he saw Man-Dare he was scared that he would think of his daughter while he was screwing Man-Dare. Now that would be a road he would not want to walk down."

"This is all very confusing."

"Agreed," laughed Roaddog, "on one hand there are few better ways to blow the minds of the citizens than the open rebellion against rules that are so ingrained they are viewed as natural laws, what is the worst thing that could have happened to Alan in that situation?"

"I've no idea."

"For Alan, his world would end if his daughter rejected him."

"You think he might actually try to have sex with his daughter?"

"He already loves her, he would kill and die for her, why not share their love physically. She's of an age where she can make that decision for herself. But this is of course so forbidden by our society that she's far more likely to reject him than accept."

"There are some good reasons why these rules are in place."

"Agreed, but most of those reasons are now gone, we no longer live in tiny villages where the gene pool is already too small, pregnancy can be easily prevented, idiot offspring are no longer an issue."

"Are you saying that you would have sex with your own daughter?"

"Much as I like to break the rules of society, I'd say no, children are to be protected above all else. However, I'm not sure that I would like to be put under pressure to decide."

"Have you any children?"

"Not anymore."

"Sad story in only two words?"

"Nothing to tell right now," mumbled Roaddog, his eyes darkening. Jackie smiled before continuing.

"How would you react if Man-Dare turned out to be your child?"

"You really know how to ask the difficult questions. For Man-Dare to be mine I'd have to have got her mother pregnant when I was twelve, or there abouts. So, putting that information to the side, I would hope that my child would not be here offering herself to crazy bikers, I may even chain her to a wall to stop that happening."

"So, to get things straight, it's acceptable, now what were Billy's words? I remember, it's OK to 'Pull a train' on someone else's baby girl, but not your own?"

Roaddog laughed aloud.

"Double standards I know, but hey, I ain't perfect."

"I have another question, next Friday, Man-Dare's father turns up. What happens?"

"You are really good with the difficult questions. Best case, she takes daddy aside and explains things, he accepts her explanation and goes away. Middle ground, they argue he storms off, she becomes ward of the club. Worst case, they fight, he hurts her, and we have a corpse to deal with, and a girl who's lost her daddy."

"More double standards, you can hurt her, but he can't."

"Parents are allowed to chastise their children."

"So, rape is a chastisement?"

"In this case yes, she was planning to use her body to tempt the leader into taking her as number one woman. The punishment sort of fit the crime."

"So, though you all rebel against the rules of the society the rest of us live in, you still have a set of rules to live by, and these are often contradictory and confusing?"

"Pretty much, but we do have an awful lot of fun. We ride, we party, we live."

"You live fast and die young."

"Often the case. When members actually manage to live as long as say Bone, they are promoted to less risky duties. If Alan does come back in, he'll get night watchman jobs, the occasional delivery run, but never will he be expected to go into a fight situation. Well almost never."

"What do you mean by almost?"

"Occasionally situations crop up where there isn't any time to move the elders out of the way."

"Or the women?"

"Do you see Bandit Queen ever backing down from a fight?"

"Actually no, she's one batshit crazy bitch."

"That she is," laughed Roaddog. "Tell her she'll love it. Another thought, next time you see Man-Dare stroke her pussy and kiss her to show that you care."

"I can't do that, I'm not a lesbian."

"There you go with the labels again. Man-Dare would love a display of support like that especially where everyone in the club can see. You'd definitely get the sisters behind you."

"I'm not sure I could do it."

"It would certainly be pushing your boundaries, but up to you." The van rolled into the yard. And Slowball got out of the driver's side.

"Hey Slowball, where've you been? It doesn't take this long to get to Alan's and back."

"Come here," replied Slowball going to the back of the van. Roaddog went to the van, a quizzical look on his face. Slowball opened the back doors and Roaddog looked inside.

"Fuck," he said.

"Exactly," said Slowball, "it takes a while to load so much beer."

"Sharpshooter, get your ass over here and help with the beer," called Roaddog.

"OK." was the reply.

"Fill up under the bar, then stick 'em in the storeroom," said Roaddog before turning to Slowball. "Did he say how he came by so much beer?"

"No, I didn't ask. And this is less than half what he had in his garage."

"Looks like we've got a potential new supplier for beer," laughed Roaddog carrying two cases out of the van. With three of them unloading the van it didn't take long at all. Once it was empty Slowball parked it around the back.

"Slowball, can you and Sharpshooter mind the store while I take Jackie for some lunch?"

"No sweat. Where's Bug at?"

"No idea, the civic is in Preston, but Bug I'll check." Roaddog sent a text to Bug and Cherie. Either way no one was going to answer if Bug was moving. Seconds later, there was a reply from Cherie. Industrial estate off Golden Hill in Leyland. Package went inside nothing moving for thirty minutes now. Roaddog thought about it for a moment, then sent back 'return to base.'

"Bug is coming back; we have a location for what might be their processing centre. No point in tipping our hand until we have to."

"Good," said Slowball.

"Jackie, want to go to lunch?"

"Yes, it'll be nice to get out in the sun."

"Ok, guys we won't be too long, just keep an eye open for customers, and no one get too carried away." Roaddog had no issue with Slowball running the shop, but Sharpshooter, Bug and Cherie in one place is likely to turn into a party. Well, they weren't going far. As he rolled his bike backwards out of his parking place Jackie asked.

"Where we going?"

"I know a little place that bikers are always welcome, you'll like it." She thought of the run out to Blue Lagoon, and decided to trust his choice, it would most likely turn out to be fun. He took them out onto the main road, and headed towards Preston, they blew past Sainsburys, and the end of the M65, a few more roundabouts and she recognised the road to the tip, where she'd been with her father a time or two. The roundabout there had changed since her last visit, now it had traffic lights on it, roll fifty yards and stop. Roll fifty yards and stop. Roaddog pulled hard left off the traffic island and parked up behind the tank that was set up on the edge of the roundabout, a centurion tank built in Leyland. There were a lot of bikes parked up, and a mobile snack bar.

"This is a lunch out?" asked Jackie.

"Yes, for the lady I'd recommend the quarter pounder with cheese, none of your plastic cheese here, real cheese, and proper burgers as well."

"That'll do for me."

"Great. Take a seat on the grass and I'll be back directly."

"There's a bit of a queue."

"Is there," he smiled and walked away, he walked towards the queue, before he reached it the guy running the place called out.

"Hey Roaddog. How's they hanging?"

"I'm doing OK, keep on rocking you know how it is." As he was saying this, he was passing by people waiting in the queue.

"What do ya want?"

"Two quarters, cheese and two beers."

"Hey there's a queue you know," said a small voice behind him. Roaddog stopped and turned slowly and looked down into the glaring eyes of a young boy, not too young as he had a helmet in his hand with the gloves stashed inside it.

"I'm sorry, please excuse my son," said the man next to the boy. "It seems I have been a little lax in his education, I shall rectify that oversight immediately. OK?"

Roaddog smiled, nodded and continued his slow walk to the front of the queue. As he arrived at the serving hatch two burgers and two beers were presented to him.

"Thanks Mac," he said.

"No problem Roaddog," replied Mac. Roaddog turned and walked towards Jackie, sitting in the sun with the tank behind her.

"He didn't even pay for them," said the boy quietly to his father.

"What part of shut the fuck up is not clear?" Was the hoarse whisper he got by way of reply. Roaddog smiled as he continued his walk to Jackie.

"I've never had a burger from one of these roadside places," she said.

"Another first for you," he laughed, "you've got to be careful though some of them are really bad. Mac is good though."

"He lets you jump the queue?"

"Yes, he owes us, and we don't take the piss of his hospitality."

"What do you mean?"

"If there's more than one or two we always pay, and we don't jump the queue. It's nice to have somewhere to get a lunch even when you're broke."

"Actually, I meant the owe part," Jackie laughed.

"We happened to come by one evening when he was having trouble with some scousers."

"Were they refusing to pay or something."

"Oh, they had no intention of paying for anything, and they were going to take the whole thing, van, car, stock and cash."

"So, what happened?"

"They paid in blood and broken bones. Me and Bone gave them a good kicking. Eventually they fucked off back to scouse land."

"This burger is really good and the beer's not bad either."

"I told you, the burgers are good, and the beer he gets from Lidl, it's cheap and comes in small bottles. Sadly no toilet facilities here."

"That doesn't normally stop you," she laughed.

"Yes, but somehow the citizens get offended when the girls leave a big puddle in the middle of the carpark," he smiled widely, then noticed the boy walking towards them. Roaddog scanned for the father but couldn't see him.

"Hi, I'm John." said the boy.

"Hello John."

"I'm sorry about earlier, I didn't realise who you are."

"No worries."

"How do I join your gang?"

"We are a motorcycle club, not a gang. How old are you?"

"I'm sixteen."

"You need to grow six inches, put on three stone of muscle, but there's no rush, you have three years at least before you would even be considered. Tell me did your dad go off for a pee?"

"Yes."

"Well, he's just come back, and now he's struggling with what he should do."

"I should go to him before he does something stupid."

"That is exactly the right thing to say, so I'll see you in three years, OK?"

"Certainly," the boy smiled and turned to face his father, who's relief was so obvious.

10: Easter Saturday. A quiet night in.

By the time they got back to the clubhouse Bug and Cherie were there, each with a beer, just sitting and shooting the breeze. Sharpshooter and Slowball were fitting a new battery to a bike that had come in, the owner of the bike was sitting where he could stare at Cherie's tits without being observed. Roaddog and Jackie sat opposite Bug and Cherie.

"Where'd you two end up?" he asked.

"We went charity shopping to start with, watched a deal go down, and decided it was too rich for us, then we ended up in Leyland, at an industrial estate, looked interesting, found a couple of spots that could be useful, but only time will tell."

"That's good, so no drama then?"

"Only this crazy bastard," snapped Cherie.

"What?" asked Bug, a big grin on his face.

"This twat popped a wheelie away from a set of lights and damn near dumped me on the road, fucker."

"I knew you was ready, you're a big girl, you can take care of yourself."

"You try that shit again and I'll cut you from cock to coccyx," she snapped.

"Careful Bug, she gonna add your ball sack to her collection," laughed Roaddog.

"Just give a girl a warning, dick," Cherie snarled, her hand dipped to her right boot, and returned holding something small and black, with a flick of the wrist the blade appears, a four-inch stiletto, sharp on both edges, black on the faces, but the edges glistened in the overhead strip lights.

"I am sorry, Cherie, I'll give ya the heads-up next time," Bug turned to Roaddog. "Sometimes these chicks are just too sensitive."

"Bug, my friend," said Roaddog slowly. "I have never heard anyone accuse Cherie of being sensitive, sorry that's not right, I've never heard of anyone survive, that's the word I was looking for." They both smiled broadly at Cherie.

"Bastards," she muttered and the knife folded and went back into the boot.

"Here ya go mate," said Slowball handing the keys to the visitor. "Cash or card."

"Cash," replied the man getting to his feet and pulling his wallet from his back pocket.

"Forty," said Slowball. The guy counted four tenners out of his wallet, while staring down Cherie's top. He handed them to Slowball.

"Do I get a receipt?" he asked.

"For a receipt you pay VAT," said Slowball.

"Fuck them," said the guy, after a moment's thought. 'These guys have a good reputation.' He shook hands with Slowball and jammed his helmet on before leaving.

"Cherie, can I ask you some things?" asked Jackie.

"Course you can, anything."

"Do you really like riding with this lot?"

"Yes, it can be great fun, cold wet winters not so much, but summer is coming."

"How long you been riding with them?"

"Since I was fourteen."

"Isn't that a little young?"

"Yes, but better than the other options that were around at the time."

"What do you mean?"

"Do you really want to know?"

"Yes, I want to understand how this life is better than, well, anything for a fourteen-year-old girl."

"You asked. My mother was a junkie, and I ended up in care. By the time they were thirteen many of the girls were sneaking out and taking up with older guys that would give them fags and booze, or drugs. Many of them came back with cash, and some came back pregnant. Some came back with tales of wild parties where they had sex with loads of men. One night a friend convinced me to sneak out with her, so I did, we were just around the corner when she walked up to a car, and a guy got out. 'Come on we're going to a party.' She said. I didn't want to go, the guy grabbed me by the arm and dragged me towards the car, I was screaming and kicking, but he was so much bigger than me and so much stronger. There was a noise, but I didn't identify it at the time, then the man was punched in the face, he released me and staggered backwards, the big woman kicked him in the nuts, and as he went down she stamped on his knee. He screamed. Another guy got out of the front seat of the car, she kicked him in the knee, slammed his head against the car then stamped on his other knee when he hit the ground. He screamed as well. She looked into the car, the driver was not moving, both hands in clear view on the steering wheel. 'If I see any of you around here again, I will gut you like fish. Now get the fuck out of my town.' She said. The three men left in a hurry, she put me and my friend on a funny motorcycle, it had three wheels. She asked where we lived, I told her. She took us there; it was only a couple of hundred yards away. She took us both to the door and kicked it until someone answered. She told the night assistant what had happened, how she had prevented us being abducted by three men. My friend started crying and saying how they had ruined everything. Ruined what? Asked the big woman. My friend told her that the men would have given her a hundred quid for bringing me to a party. Why? Asked the woman. Because she is a virgin. The woman took my friends phone, asked who is he? The girl told her; she found his number. She called out the number. 'Find me that phone.' She yelled. 'I'm going to turn those bastards into dogfood.' She screamed. She dropped my friends' phone on the floor. She turned to the assistant. 'You take better care of your charges, maybe you'll never see me again.' Someone in the darkness shouted something. She looked down at me and said softly. 'Remember.' Then she vanished into the night. I have never forgotten her, and I never will.

 "Who was she?"
 "Bandit Queen."
 "What happened to the three men?"
 "It seems there was some sort of racist incident at the hospital, or so the papers read. A car was found burned out in Chorley, but the three men were never seen again."
 "You think she killed them?"
 "I have no idea, the cops came by and asked lots of questions, or so I heard. They could find nothing to tie anyone here to the disappearance. So, they gave up. Three less scumbags in the world."
 "Are you happy with that?"
 "I was still a virgin when I left that place, no one ever bothered me, it seems that word got around. Bandit Queen came and picked me up on a regular basis, we talked, we rode, there was no pressure. Life was good

with the club. I was like a daughter to them all."

"How did you end up here?"

"The childcare system is just great, until you are no longer a child, then you're out, no family to support you, no idea how to look after yourself. 'Here's a scumbag flat in a shitty neighbourhood.' Sink or swim they no longer care, you're off their books. I lasted four months, then I came looking for people who actually cared about me. And I'm still here."

"No longer a virgin?"

"Hell no, but it was my choice and no one else's."

"You planning on settling down at all?"

"No, I want to live before I die."

"No special guy in your life?"

"There was for a while, but he died."

"I'm sorry, that must have been hard?"

"It was, for a while but I have my family here."

"They really are a family?"

"Oh yes, and so much more, we all look after each other."

"That's good."

"That's why I'm still here."

"Yes," said Roaddog. "she's still here but be careful where you take her to eat."

"You're mean," smiled Cherie.

"I don't understand," said Jackie.

"Our lovely Cherie has a party trick that really upsets the citizens, don't take her anywhere near a hotdog stand."

"Why?"

"You know those foot-long hot dogs, the big bockwurst, not the skinny frankfurters?"

"Yes."

"Well madam here has a tendency to take said sausage from its bun, tip her head back, then swallow the whole thing in one slow steady move. The citizens can really lose their cool, the guys can't believe it, the women hate her immediately, and the kids just want a replay."

"It's fun," laughed Cherie.

"Not good for the digestion," said Jackie, laughing. "You really should chew your food you know."

"Roaddog," said Cherie. "I like her, don't let her get away."

"I'm trying," he said. "What time you working?" he asked.

"In about an hour."

"No great rush then, you got everything you need?"

"Oh yes."

"I'll get you there in plenty of time, what time you finishing?"

"You don't have to worry about that, dad's picking me up."

"How did that happen?"

"I think mum bullied him."

"Should I arrange escort," laughed Roaddog.

"Nah, let him have his day, I'm not working tomorrow though."

"Ok, I'll pick you up about nine, we're planning a little run out, should be nice and calm."

"Why don't I believe you?"

"Well," said Cherie, "should be and gonna be are equally unlikely." She smiled broadly.

"Fine," laughed Jackie. "Take me to work, you crazy person." She stood up and started to put her helmet on. Roaddog shrugged and got up.

"You guys be OK for a bit?" he called.

"No worries," said Slowball. Roaddog and Jackie set off to her work, on their way out of the industrial estate they saw two Harleys going the other way. Roaddog glanced backwards and saw no cutoffs, so he thought nothing more of it. He carved easily through the Easter traffic, and arrived at the pub, the carpark was almost full. Jackie got off and said.

"I better get inside they look really busy, there were nowhere near this many booked in."

"It's a nice day, so people are out for a family meal."

"Probably. See you tomorrow." She said kissing her fingers and moving them inside his helmet so he could kiss them. He laughed as she turned away. First gear cracked into place and he shot off, gravel spitting from the fat rear tyre.

In a few short minutes he was back at the unit, as he parked up, he noticed that the two Harleys were still there, and two strangers were sitting in the seating area. Walking slowly towards them he saw that their jackets were open and cut off leathers were now visible. 'This can't be good.' He thought.

"Good afternoon gentlemen, who are you?"

"We're from the central Manchester chapter, we're asking a few questions of the clubs that we think are dealing in blow. Your man Slowball decided we should wait for your return," said the older of the two. His cut identified him as Wolf.

"What are the questions you are asking?"

"Have you noticed any fall off in sales recently, any competition moving in?"

"Actually, we have."

"Have you any idea who and where this is coming from?"

"We do."

"Come on man, share please."

"Our information is recent, and so far only gives a general location."

"You actually know something?"

"Yes. We think they're operating out of the Commercial Brow area of Hyde. We tracked a shipment from there to Preston and then on to Leyland. We're not certain what the shipment was, but we intend on finding out this week at some point."

"You're shitting us?"

"No. The goods were moved out of Hyde in some very specialised transport. Then switched to a small van in Preston and on to an industrial unit in Leyland."

"Fuck," said the younger one, Banjo. "We've been all over the northwest looking for these bastards and they're right on our doorstep."

"Nothing is certain until we search their shop in Leyland," said Roaddog.

"Maybe we can expedite that for you?" asked Wolf.

"I'm not making that sort of decision without clearing it with the chairman."

"Only right," smiled Wolf. "Can you contact him?"

"Easy," Roaddog pulled his phone from his pocket and called Bone. He was surprised when Bandit Queen answered. Her response was terse to say the least. "Three minutes out and loaded." The phone went dead.

"Fuck," muttered Roaddog. Then he spotted the small blinking red light beside the till. "Which dick pressed the alarm?"

"Sorry Dog that was me, I saw their colours and panicked," said Bug.

"Cherie, your knife nice and sharp? You might be getting Bug's ball bag after all." He turned to the visitors. "Gentlemen, please stay calm, nobody get hot. It's going to be tense for a little while. You have my word you are in no danger." He turned to the open doorway as the sound of motorcycles filled the air, in only seconds motors were stopping and the men were unloading.

"Everybody relax. False alarm. Damned Bug panicked. False alarm."

"For fuck's sake," snapped Bone. "It's been a while I was looking forwards to a fight."

"Not today, OK?"

"Fine," Bone looked round, then caught Slowball's eye. "Get some beers out for the guys, they deserve it. Good response time guys, maybe next time we'll get to break some heads."

"By the way the beers on Alan," said Roaddog.

"Fine by me," said Bone sitting in front of the visitors, who were now seriously outnumbered and nervous, though trying to look relaxed. Their chapter is bigger than the Dragonriders, but Manchester is a long way away.

"Bone," said Wolf. "your man Roaddog says you know where the guys from Hyde are processing their blow, we'd like to tear their place apart, but it is in your back yard."

"We know this do we?" Bone looked at Roaddog.

"It's possible, we won't know for sure until we get inside. I haven't had time to tell you, the information is less than an hour old."

"Where is it?" asked Bone.

"Braconash industrial estate."

"Can you hit them tomorrow?" Bone asked.

"I'm sure that can be arranged."

"You planning on selling their drugs round here?"

"God no, we'll take it home and flog it there."

"Even better, you take any drugs you find and split the cash with us, we'll be up at Rivington, until mid-afternoon, send a rep there with our cut."

"We take all the risk and you want half the cash, seventy-five/ twenty-five."

"Sixty/forty, we found them for ya."

"Deal," said Wolf. He reached forwards to shake Bone's hand. The contract made Banjo muttered.

"If there's no drugs Cyrus is going to be pissed with you."

11: Easter Sunday. Run to Rivi

Roaddog pulled up outside Jackie's house at dead on nine AM, he smiled as the curtains of so many houses around twitched. The big V died and fell onto its kick stand. He stood up and walked slowly to the front door, feeling the eyes on his back. He smiled broadly as he tapped politely on the door. The muffled sounds of motion inside and some voices sneaked through the heavy plastic of the door. He wondered who was going to open it. He was surprised when it was the least likely face of them all. Jackie's father stood before him.

"Hello," said Roaddog.

"Yeah, well," said the older man.

"How's Jackie?" Roaddog sounded more than a little worried.

"Personally, I think she's lost her mind."

"What do you mean?" quietly Roaddog felt the anger grow within himself.

"Her association with you is insane."

"And."

"Sadly, I can do little about it, she's a grown woman, even if she is still my little girl."

"So, what will you do?"

"I will be there to pick up the pieces, if you hurt her, I will tear your life apart and feed your entrails to the pigs, are we clear young man?"

"As crystal, old man." Roaddog held out his hand for Jackie's father to shake. As their hands clasped Roaddog went on. "Rest assured I will protect her with my life."

"Good, you can call me Chris."

"That's sort of a strange coincidence. My name used to be Chris, then I was given my new name."

"Weird, you look after my little girl."

"That I will sir." Chris nodded and stepped back into the house, he waved Jackie out, and kissed her gently as she passed him.

"See ya dad," she whispered.

"Ready?" asked Roaddog.

"Sure, where we off to?"

"Clubhouse first then Rivi. You'll love it." Together they walked down the driveway to the bike, and slowly mounted. Jackie was surprised that the motor was still quiet when she took her seat.

"I don't believe your old man just did that," said Roaddog.

"What?"

"He threatened to feed my entrails to the pigs."

"Uncle Henry is a pig farmer."

"Now that is interesting information, I'd like to meet this uncle of yours at some point."

"Fine, are we going to sit here all day?"

Roaddog chuckled softly and thumbed the starter button. He rolled the bike back into the road and set off for the unit.

The yard was full of bikes when they got there, far more than she had ever seen there. Roaddog still found his place to park in, together they walked towards the club house. As they neared the front of the shop Man-Dare came into view perched on the edge of the picnic table, her legs spread wide, her skirt lifted. Roaddog paused and smiled at her. She smiled back and twitched her legs to guide their eyes to her crotch. Roaddog leaned in close to Jackie and whispered in her ear.

"Go on, make her day." Jackie shook her head. "She'll love, it and so will all the other girls."

"I can't," she replied.

"Yes, you can." He licked her ear and made her shiver. She turned to him and mouthed one word, bastard. She stepped away from him and crossed the distance to the table. Jackie stared into Man-Dare's eyes, and placed her hand on her thigh, Man-Dares eyes widened as the hand slid slowly upwards, her muscles twitched as the hand moved. Jackie slid her hand across and cupped the soft pussy, she was surprised by how soft and warm it felt. Man-Dare swallowed and pressed herself forwards against the hand.

"Still sore?" whispered Jackie.

"A little," was the equally quiet reply. Jackie slowly raised her middle finger, up into the warmth of the woman's body. Man-dare moaned softly. Jackie leaned in and gently kissed her on the lips. Jackie withdrew and pulled her hand from the girl's body, then she presented the finger to be sucked, Man-Dare licked and sucked it until there was no more taste of her upon it. Jackie smiled and stepped back into Roaddog's arms.

"Wonderfully done," he whispered to her and took her hand, they walked into the bar area and Cherie passed them each a beer. Billy and Alan were there.

"Hello guys," said Roaddog.

"Hi Roaddog," said Billy. He smiled at Jackie.

"Hi Dog," said Alan. "Jackie that was some sexy display you just put on out there, where can't be a soft dick in the place. Me included." She smiled.

"Me too," said Billy. "God girl you're hot." Jackie giggled, and leaned against Roaddog. He smiled down at her, then kissed her softly.

"They are not wrong, you are hot." he whispered. He glanced around the place, it looked like everyone was here, there were a few missing, but not so many. Bone caught his eye, from his position in the yard. Bone raised his left arm and tapped his watch. Roaddog nodded, then spoke out.

"Bar's closed, drink up it's time to get this show on the road." His shout started people moving, beers were emptied, and bottles dropped into the large glass recycling bin. Roaddog took his bottle and Jackie's to the bin, a quick glance inside told him that he would have to arrange a pickup in the next week or so, the pickup guys complain if the bin is too full, their hydraulics seem to struggle to lift this one. He returned to Alan and Billy.

"As guests you get to ride at the back, Slowball and his trike are always tail end Charlie, you ride just in front of him. If anything goes wrong, he'll call us, and someone will come back to help. OK?"

"Fine by us," said Alan, Billy just nodded.

"Come on Jackie, let's roll." Roaddog said and walked over to his bike, motorcycles were starting all over the yard, the shutters on the shop were coming down, the lights were all out. Finally, Cherie came out of the unit and closed the door. The column of bikes started to roll slowly out of the yard, Bone and Lurch in the lead as befitted their rank, Roaddog should have been next but he chose a much more mobile position in the convoy, he'd be moving up and down the line all the time, checking on riders and generally keeping an eye on everything that was happening.

He waved Billy and Alan off then sent Slowball off as well. He checked over the doors and the gates, then he rolled out onto the street. He closed and locked the outer gate. Jackie took her seat behind him and they took off after the club, he was behind Slowball as they started the climb up onto the M65, he blew passed the trike, and waved to Man-Dare sitting behind Slowball, he caught up with Alan and Billy, dropped in alongside them for a moment or two, then set off along the line of motorcycles. Jackie was enjoying the feeling of the motorcycle underneath her, the beat of the motor and the thrum of the tyres. She waved to the other riders as they passed, getting waves and smiles back from all. In moments they were slowing to exit the motorway, as the line started to snake off the roundabout she recognised where they were, the road she had travelled in the dark only two nights before, she could see so much more of the countryside as it went ripping past. The column slowed down for Abbey village and packed up tight, the roar of engines shook the windows of the houses as they blew through the village. Right in the middle of this village was a police van parked on the side of the road, its laser and cameras pointing at the oncoming motorcyclists, various hand signals were made as they passed the van, the operator struggling to capture all the registration plates as they rode along the road, before ten had gone he gave up. The final straw for him was the damned trike at the back of the convoy, the girl sitting on this one lifted her skirt and flashed him as they went by. He picked up his radio and called the local station, reporting a gang of bikers heading for the barn. 'The traffic cops will fix their wagon.' He thought.

Roaddog moves slowly up the column until he was in the third row, then he settled in for a while, the long sweeping curves up to the reservoir at Belmont, made the line string out a ways, but the slowdown to the 30 at Belmont village caused them to pack up tight again. The right turn coming up was going to be a problem with such a large number of bikes in the convoy, but Roaddog was ready for that. Everyone stopped and waited for Bone to make the right and start the climb up to the open moors, when there was sufficient gap in the oncoming traffic Bone made the turn, Lurch went with him, Roaddog did not. He rolled his bike forwards so that it was broadside on to the traffic blocking the entire lane. He sat and stared at the drivers coming towards him, daring them to run him over, while the column of bikes made the right turn. Once Slowball was past Roaddog waved to the leading driver and surprisingly got a salute back, then he gunned the big motor and set off up the hill after Slowball. Jackie watched the small lake that was Blue Lagoon fly past on the left, she agreed with Roaddog's assessment, it was somehow depressing even in the bright sunlight, the grass looked drab, green and alive, but somehow depressed. At the top of the slope a few scraggy looking sheep peered over the fence, sparkling white in their newly shorn coats, but still they managed to look somewhat down in the dumps. The tight roads at this section made it impossible for Roaddog to get passed the wide tail of Slowballs trike, but he was in no real rush. The only difficult section left was the drop into Rivington village. Once the trike had cleared the tight S bends, and the road straightened out Roaddog turned on the power and blew past, Jackie waved to Alan and Billy as they tore through. They were almost halfway down the column when the next set of bends came up. Out of those and he turned it on again. Before the tree turn he had made it most of the way to the front, he dropped in alongside Bug. After the tree, on the narrow descent, Roaddog exchanged some hand signals with Bug, together they slowly jumped up the line one bike at a time. As the road turned left and became Sheep House Lane, Roaddog hit the power hard and passed Bone and Lurch in a flash, followed by Bug, together they disappeared from view around the slight bends, Bone glanced at Lurch, who shrugged. Bone looked in his mirrors at the line of motorcycles behind him, and quickly decided that he would have words with that damned dog once they caught up.

Roaddog accelerated hard, knowing that Bug and his V-four would not be far behind. At speeds that were more than a little faster than advisable, and far above the posted speed limit. Roaddog keeping the motor revving high and making a lot of noise, Bug joined in by opening the port on his exhaust pipe, taking all the silencer out of the line and venting the noise and some small flames out to the side. They reached the section of road near the café, where there were always parked cars, once passed these Roaddog again blocked the road with his bike, and Bug joined him. In less than a minute a volvo four by four came around the corner, hoping to go up the lane. The car stopped only feet from Roaddog's motorcycle, the driver leaned on his horn, and waved at the bikers to move. Bug smiled and yanked the throttle open; the V-four redlines at fourteen thousand, it went all the way there before he snapped it shut. The plume of flame spat from his exhaust and dark smoke billowed around the front of the shiny red volvo. The car driver snapped a reverse and dropped back a few feet. Bug smiled at him, though the driver could only see his eyes through the opening in the front of the helmet. The noise of oncoming motorcycles grew as the column came down the lane. Bone shook his head as he came around the bend and saw the two in the road ahead of him. Bug's bike rolled forwards enough so the convoy could get through, Roaddog's impromptu roadblock and filled up the next junction, but the left turn they needed was clear, after Slowball had passed the two set off in pursuit, but not before Roaddog had given the volvo driver a friendly, if sarcastic wave. As they drove away Roaddog thought to himself, 'Perhaps I should learn to read lips.' Then he laughed, they were only a few hundred yards from the turn into the road to the barn.

They were lucky when they arrived at the carpark, a car had just left, so there was somewhere for Slowball to park the trike, there were many hands to roll it back into the space. Then bikes parked up in front of it, one of those Alan's ancient Dragonfly, the rest of the bikes went up to the circle in front of the barn. The bikes were parked in small groups, the barn was busy, even though it was quite early. The sunny weather always brings out the crowd. The burger van was running and churning out food in quantity for hungry bikers, they come from all over the northwest to Rivington Barn, Sundays only of course. There were a few other clubs represented, but not in any real numbers, Dragonriders was the only club with a real presence. Bone caught up with Roaddog and Jackie as they were walking towards the barn, Bandit Queen was behind him.

"That was some stunt you pulled."

"I know that section of road is quite dangerous, especially for Slowball, so I thought I'd make it easier for the brothers and piss off some citizens at the same time."

"Oh, it did that. The look on the guy's face as we rolled through, now that was a picture."

"I think he said something unpleasant to me as well, as I pulled away."

"If you're going to do that sort of thing again, please let me know in advance, surprises I don't like."

"No worries. I'm going for a beer, you up for that?"

"Why not?" The four of them walked slowly into the bar, and as if from nowhere Man-Dare tagged along. They walked inside and went up to the bar. There were few bar patrons this early, but those that were at the bar made space for the Dragonriders and gave up their place in the barman's idea of the queue. While Roaddog was ordering the drinks, Bandit Queen touched Mad-Dare's elbow and whispered.

"There are children here, you stay covered."

"Of course. Wouldn't want to frighten the little boys," giggled Man-Dare.

"Now look what you've done," laughed Bone.

"Damn it we don't need any shit from the cops today," said Bandit Queen.

"I don't know," laughed Roaddog. "It can't have been us; we were at Rivi being interviewed by officers from Bolton. Anyone think of a better alibi?"

"The only better one is being in the cells." Bone smiled hugely. As he turned away from the bar, Lurch came in, his head clear above any others in the room. As always Lurch could see his friends and came straight towards them. Bone raised a glass and asked a question with his eyebrows. Lurch shook his head and continued the slow walk to the bar.

"Bike cops have showed up," he said.

"They looking for anyone in particular?" asked Bone.

"Apparently some girl flashed her pussy at the speed camera guy, and he was pissed." Man-Dare spit a mouthful of beer out and laughed loudly. Lurch wiped his hand down his cut and grinned back at her.

"Do they have a description?" asked Bandit Queen.

"They have a very accurate description," said Lurch slowly, "shaved, open, very pink, and wet." Everyone laughed at this point.

"That's going to give them some interesting questions to ask," laughed Bandit Queen.

"Do you think I should go and hide?" asked Man-Dare.

"No." said Bandit Queen. "You could go outside and see if they'll ask."

"That might be fun as well," grinned Man-Dare.

"Not until we've finished our beers," said Bone.

"When do you think the Manchester guys will be turning up?" asked Roaddog.

"Can't tell, they'll most likely have hit the place by now, it all depends on how much opposition there was, and how much stuff they have to sort through," said Bone.

"I suppose, but the suspense is killing me."

"Of course, they could renege on the deal all together and not turn up at all."

"That would be so rude," Roaddog grinned.

"And angels are never rude, are they?"

"They are gentlemen after all."

"I really don't care how much of a cut we get; anything will add to the funds. If we get enough, we can put a run together for May day."

"Short, but I'm sure we could do it. It's been too long since we had a good party." Roaddog looked down the length of the old building for a while before carrying on. "I may know a band or two we can get on short notice."

"And there's always some DJ's loose most weekends."

"I'll talk to Andy about putting his truck in for the weekend. That should give us some decent grub."

"Hey, you're spending money we don't have yet."

"A guy's gotta have a dream," Roaddog glanced around the room again, and two cops strolled in. "Pigs," he whispered. Jackie glanced at them then looked away, the others just stared. Slowly the policemen walked down the length of the room towards the bar. Somehow their fluorescent jackets looked more than a little out of place, even though the place was full of motorcyclists, there weren't many with that much dayglow. It was obvious from their demeanour that they knew who they wanted to talk to.

"Good morning ladies and gentlemen," said the first cop. The bikers nodded but said nothing.

"We have had a complaint," said the cop.

"Keep taking the pills," said Roaddog. This got him a scowl from the cops, and a smile from his friends.

"It seems," continued the cop, "there has been an incident of indecent exposure."

"That'll be him." said Bone, pointing at Lurch.

"Actually, it was a young lady."

"We don't know any ladies," said Bone.

"Listen dick," said the second cop. "One of these bitches flashed her pussy on the road here today, and I want to know which one it was." Bandit Queen squared her shoulders to the younger of the two policemen. The other cop placed a hand on the policeman's arm and said quietly.

"Come with me constable. We need to talk." The two walked slowly away.

"Look around constable, tell me what you see?"

"A room full of people."

"How many witnesses do you see?"

"There must be a hundred."

"Really, how many don't actually see motorcycle cops as the enemy?"

"Now I think I see what you mean."

"Good, we are in a tricky situation here, let's not make it any worse than it needs to be."

"Should we call for back up?"

"No, that would be worse. A quiet word is all it will take."

"How can you be sure?"

"I know these guys, they can be reasonable, so long as you don't piss them off."

"You're going to trust them?"

"Yes. Watch and learn." The two walked back to where the Dragonriders were waiting.

"Please forgive my colleague, he's having a bad time," said the sergeant. "There are a lot of children around here today, we wouldn't want to frighten them, would we?"

"No worries," said Bone. "The roads around here are scary enough; we don't want to frighten the little ones any more than the roads do."

"That'll be good enough for me," said the sergeant. "Enjoy the day." He tapped the second cop on the arm and the two turned away. Once they were far enough away so that they couldn't be overheard.

"What do we tell the camera guy?" asked the constable.

"We tell him that given his description we were unable to find anyone that matched it and got no leads from our questioning."

"Do you think he'll be happy with that?"

"I really don't care that much; he needs to grow a pair. I mean would you complain if a young girl flashed her pussy at ya?"

"Probably not, but it is illegal."

"Maybe, maybe not."

"What do you mean? He got such a good look that he could tell her beaver was bald."

"To get indecent exposure you have to prove some form of intent. In this case, 'sorry the wind caught my skirt' and your intent is gone."

"So, we've got no case?"

"Pretty much, but if she flashes someone here, there's no wind. If you see her then so much the better."

"But which one is it? They brought a few girls with skirts."

"Go ask them if they've got knickers on."

"Wouldn't that be wrong?"

"Very, you might even get slapped. See the one called Bandit Queen, if you ask her, you'll probably end up dead."

"She's wearing jeans, so it can't be her. Hang on, dead?"

"Yes, if there's one psycho in that bunch it's her. I knew her from school. She's as mad as a bucket of wasps."

"How come she's still loose then?"

"The only thing that I can think of is that she works by a simple principle, no witnesses."

"That's just not right."

"I know, anyway let's continue our investigations, there are a lot of nice bikes here for us to question," laughed the sergeant as they walked into the bright sunlight.

"Damn," muttered Bone.

"What's up?" asked Roaddog.

"I don't like the cops being here, we're expecting a visitor at some point today."

"Don't worry about it, I got their badge numbers, they'll not forget that they met us here today, especial that constable." Roaddog smile did little to make Bone feel any better about the situation. He put his empty glass on the bar and took Jackie's hand.

"We're going for a mooch around. Catch up with you guys later," he smiled at her and they left the bar area and headed for the entrance.

"Do you always have trouble with the cops?" she asked, softly.

"No, Man-Dare certainly got the camera guy pissed, but that's nothing, she's got Bandit on her ass now, she'll be a good girl, at least until we leave."

"Could it have got violent in there?"

"It was possible, but a couple of cops aren't going to start anything, it's just too dangerous for them."

"What do you mean?"

"Look around," he said as they walked out into the circular carpark, only a couple of vans parked in the whole area. "How many guys do you see wearing cutoff's? How many motorcycle clubs here today? None of those guys like cops, most of them would gladly drown a couple of cops in the pond, and then vanish into the sunny afternoon, most could be at devil's bridge in less than three quarters of an hour."

"Do they hate cops that much?"

"Yes, they do make our lives difficult in patches, sometimes I wish I lived in the era when Alan was a member, the cops just couldn't catch up with us most of the time."

"You could live like that?"

"Yes, I think so."

"I'm not sure I could, I like having a place and a job, and people around me."

"Oh, there's no shortage of people, look around you."

"Yes, there's a lot of people, but you don't know any of them."

"We'll see about that." Roaddog was watching a guy rolling a heavy bike backwards into a small space in the centre circle. Happy with the distances the man stopped the motor and got off, he hauled the bike up onto its centre stand. He stepped gingerly around the handlebar and dropped his helmet onto the right-hand mirror. As he turned away from the bike Roaddog was right in front of him.

"What is that thing? I've never seen one before."

"It's a Honda Magna, one of the last of the seven-fifties, they went down to seven hundred after this year." As he was talking the bike started to make a loud whirring noise. "Just the fans, they come on when the weather is this hot." The guy smiled, he reached out his right hand. "I'm Mick." Roaddog shook his hand slowly.

"Roaddog, this is Jackie." He tipped his head in the direction of Jackie. For the first time Mick broke eye contact with Roaddog and looked at Jackie. His eyes caught hers, the blue-grey of cold steel, she felt as if they were boring into her very soul, she smiled and looked down.

"Hi," said Mick. "What you guys up to today?"

"Just a little ride out, catch a beer or two, maybe see some good bikes."

"That's normally why I come here, sometimes there's a gorgeous pair of blue kettles, sometimes there's an amazing RD 400, occasionally the fizzie boys turn up, or if you're a monkey bike fan there's generally a couple of those here." Mick pulled the shoulder bag he was carrying to the fore, and unzipped it, he lifted the camera out and threw the strap over his head. "Have you seen anything good here today?"

"We've only just got here really, but there's a guy with one of them Magna's around somewhere, oh and there's a Dragonfly on the lower carpark." Mick smiled at the mention of the Magna.

"You're kidding me? A Dragonfly?"

"He came up with us, parked on the lower carpark with Slowball's trike."

"And a trike as well, this is going to be a good day."

"Maybe catch ya later," said Roaddog.

"That'd be great, gotta get the Dragonfly." Mick walked off towards the lower carpark.

"I had no idea what he was talking about, but he has some crazy eyes."

"There's some pain behind those eyes, maybe we'll find out later." They walk slowly around the open section of the circle, bikes coming and going the whole time.

"What didn't you understand?" asked Roaddog.

"Kettles, what are kettles?"

"Right, kettles, are Suzuki GT750's very rare now, water-cooled two strokes renowned for boiling. RD 400 a Yamaha from the same era, seventies. Fizzie, Yamaha FS1E mopeds, they have a sort of cult following these days. Monkey bikes are a tiny sort of Honda, it can fit in a large suitcase, you've got to fold the handlebars down, but it will fit in a suitcase. Everything clear now?"

"Not exactly, but what the hell. Is it always like this up here?"

"Only Sundays, and bank holidays, tomorrow will be good up here but the rest of the time, this is a wedding venue."

"So last night there was a wedding party here, and today it's full of hairy bikers?"

"Pretty much. You should see it when guys in suits turn up to collect the cars they left here in the circle, it can take them hours to get them out." Roaddog laughed loudly. He stopped suddenly and his jaw hung open.

"What's wrong?" asked Jackie.

"Look at those," he said pointing at a pair of bikes, parked side by side.

"They're a bit strange, but to me what isn't?" laughed Jackie. Roaddog looked around and spotted Sharpshooter only a little way off.

"Hey Sharpshooter, where's Alan?" he yelled over the crackle of motorcycle exhausts.

"I don't think he's got more than arm's length away from his bike yet," was the reply.

"Come on Jackie, he's gotta see these," laughed Roaddog, pulling Jackie towards the lower carpark. As they entered the carpark section there was Alan talking to Mick, who was on his knees beside the Dragonfly, trying to get the sunlight shining on the rocker cover. Beside them was Billy really rocking the Texan vibe, large, mirrored sunglasses, hat pulled down and a fist full of rings stroking his long beard.

"Hey Alan," called Roaddog as they approached. "There's something you got to see. Come on."

"I don't know," said Alan. "There's an awful lot of people here."

"Don't worry, the last time someone stole a bike from here they made it as far as the tree, sometimes call the hanging tree."

"You're joking, right?" asked Billy.

"Maybe," smiled Roaddog. "You OK Mick?"

"Thanks Roaddog, I'm fine." He was hunched over the camera trying to get the angle right.

"Are you sure?" asked Alan.

"Of course. No one steals bikes from here."

"OK, what is so urgent that I must see it?"

"You've love it, I promise." His grin gave Alan the impression that this was not entirely true. But he nodded and followed Roaddog and Jackie back up to the circle, and around, Billy came along as well. It didn't take long to get to the two bikes that Roaddog had seen only minutes earlier.

"What the fuck are they?" snapped Alan.

12: Rivington and Meetings

"The blue one is I believe a Lambretta, with what looks like a four-foot over-springer front end," laughed Roaddog. "The other is perhaps a Vespa with a crazy extended telescopic front end. Aren't they pretty"?

"They're scooters for fucks sake."

"They are indeed but look at the work that gone into them."

"Back in my day they'd put three extra lights and a couple of mirrors on and call them customs," said Alan.

"These are some serious scooters."

"Damn the paint's brilliant," snarled Alan.

"I do have a question though."

"Go on, Why?"

"No, why is easy, because they can. The question is how do they keep the chrome on those expansion chambers, no yellow, no blue, they've got to be real hot, but no signs of it."

"That's both simple and not so simple at the same time," said a voice from behind them. All four turned at the same time, there were two young men, in long green parka's each carrying a partially empty pint of beer. Roaddog smiled and said.

"Go on, tell us."

"Simple it's not the expansion chamber you are looking at, not so simple it's a stainless-steel heat shield made to look like an expansion chamber, now that took some doing."

"That doesn't explain how you keep the heat out of the steel work."

"The exhaust manifold has copper wire bound around it for the first four inches, then exhaust thermal insulation blanket bound around that, then the heatshield fastened to that."

"But it looks like it fastens straight to the engine."

"It doesn't actually touch, it's close but it doesn't touch, so there is no direct heat transfer."

"Who made these heatshields?"

"I did."

"The paint?"

"Not me, I have a mate who's a bit of a nutter when it comes to paint jobs, he's not cheap, nor quick."

"He does an awesome job."

"Thanks man. I'm Bob."

"Roaddog, Alan, Billy, and Jackie." He indicated each as he named them.

"What you riding?" asked the other young man.

"Two Harleys and a Dragonfly," smiled Roaddog.

"Oh my god. I'm Josh, my grandad used to ride a Dragonfly."

"What the fuck is it with Dragonflys? How come everyone's grandad rode one?" asked Alan.

"That's easy," said Josh.

"Go on," snarled Alan, "explain it for the stupid old man."

"Early sixties," smiled Josh, "national service, many young men pulled away from their homes, lots of them moved to the south. Dragonfly was state of the art, and cheap, they'd just gone broke. Many service men bought them and then brought them home to the northwest when their service was over. My Grandad bought his in Kings Lynn, he was stationed somewhere around there with the RAF. When he died, Gran sold the contents of his shed for scrap metal. Dragonfly went with it, I was only a youngster, I couldn't have bought it, but I would have, given a chance. Come on man, show me the Dragonfly." Josh smiled at Alan, looking so much like a kid after a birthday present. Alan turned to Roaddog.

"You are a bastard," he said gently.

"I know," laughed Roaddog.

"What's going on?" asked Josh.

"Alan here was a hells angel from way back. Now he realises that guys in green coats are just guys."

"Oh make no mistake, there are still some crazy mods out there, but not as many as there used to be, I mean look at this jacket of mine," He opened the jacket and revealed a brilliant red lining, and a small black label that declared Abercrombie and Fitch. "It's so much nicer than those old military jackets."

"Fucking fashion statement," Alan laughed.

"Definitely," said Josh. "Where's that Dragonfly? Lead on MacDuff."

"And now he's quoting fucking Shakespeare," said Alan.

"Classical education, I can't help it," smiled Josh.

"Fine. This way Mac Beth. Thane of Cordor."

"You know the bard as well," laughed Josh.

"Only some, but yes. Mainly from the movies." Alan, Billy and the two mods walked back towards the lower carpark.

"You OK?" asked Roaddog, looking over at Jackie.

"I'm fine, there's always a lot going on, isn't there?"

"Sometimes, other times it can be quite boring."

"Is this really a wedding venue?"

"Yes, and a damned expensive one. They made a lot of money last night, but today they'll make heaps more."

"How come?"

"Thirsty bikers, they drink an awful lot of beer, and they don't stay long, there'll be thousands of bikes through here today, and the burger van will have that queue all day." He waved in the direction of the van parked outside the barn entrance. There were about twenty people in the queue, all waiting in an orderly fashion.

"Somehow it's a lot more civilised than I expected."

"Well, as you look around, you can generally see the guys who are members of bike clubs, they wear their colours all the time. There are a few who don't, there are the rogues, ex-members kicked out for whatever reasons, usually failed coups. There are a lot of ordinary citizens here as well, far more of them than the club members. Some hell's angels, and some of the rogues are complete nutters, but you can't tell just by looking. So, when you are standing in that queue, and you accidentally step backwards onto someone's foot, there is a small, and I do mean small change that that guy is one of those nutters, and he will pull the sawn off from his belt and empty both barrels into your guts. Leather is all well and good but that sort of shit it can't deal with, so apologies all around, and civility reigns supreme. Did you notice something else?"

"No."

"When we were looking at the scooters, hands in pockets."

"I didn't notice that," Jackie said, but a rapid look around showed her that many people standing close to motorcycles had their hands in their pockets. "Why?" She asked.

"Look but don't touch is the order of the day, there are safety reasons for it as well. Most motorcycles have exposed parts that can be very hot, grab a downpipe and it will burn the skin off your hand before you know it."

"I didn't realise they got that hot, all that chrome looks far too pretty to be dangerous."

"I know. Shall we get some food? It is sort of dinner time."

"Why not?"

"Burger or hotdog?"

"Choices, choices," laughed Jackie. "You take me to the classiest places. Burger." She smiled and leaned in to kiss him. He put his arm around her waist, and they joined the back of the queue. The queue moved surprisingly quickly, two guys said hi to Roaddog as they walked away with burgers in their hands.

"Who are they?" asked Jackie.

"Millennium."

"You are going to have to explain these things because that means nothing to me."

"Members of Millennium Motorcycle Club."

"There are a few of them here today."

"Yes. They're local, Leyland Eagles are here as well, and I've seen the odd Satan's Sons patch as well. So, there are a few clubs here." They arrived at the front of the queue, Roaddog ordered two burgers, and parted with the necessary cash before they turned away. As they walked down the line, they passed Sharpshooter and then Cherie and Doris, the two girls had a box, a list and a pile of cash.

"Where is everyone?" asked Roaddog.

"They're all still in the bar," said Cherie. "Bandit Queen is keeping Man-Dare on a short leash."

"That's for the best, but I wouldn't say that to her, she'd most likely do it." They continued walking and turn in through the door. In the corner near the bar were most of the rest, three tables pulled together, Roaddog pulled up a couple of extra chairs, and seated Jackie in one, then he went to the bar. When he returned he sat next to Jackie.

"Anything exciting happening out there?" asked Bone.

"The bike cops are still there, and Alan's Dragonfly is getting a lot of interest, but other than that, not a lot. A couple of clubs out there, but not in any numbers, so quiet really."

"Let's hope it stays that way."

"There's a lot of citizens, lots of families out there, we definitely want the peace."

"No signs of our visitors then?"

"Nothing, you think they've crossed us?"

"No, they'll show, I just hope they don't bring too many, we don't need an invasion, someone will notice, especially those damned cops."

"They'd have to bring about twenty to be noticed, there's bikes coming and going every minute." Roaddog looked round the group and held Jackie's hand. All of them were feeling more than a little nervous. Cherie and Doris turned up with the box full of burgers, each one wrapped and marked with a name. Soon everyone was eating, the people running the café at the other end of the room were unhappy, burgers outside are half the price that they are inside, but no one was going to actually complain. Doris and Cherie were sent to the bar to buy more beers, and with their usual efficiency they returned with trays. Conversation a limited and quiet, Roaddog kept a steady watch on the door. Finally, he saw a face he recognised, a scraggy grey goatee, and a name tag that said Wolf. Next to Wolf was a shorter man, wider, and his face showed some oriental features, next to this new man was Banjo. As they walked towards the Dragonriders Bone stood to great the arrivals. Space was made so they could sit next to Bone.

"Beer, or lager?" asked Bone.

"Beer," said the new man. Bone snapped his fingers in the direction of Cherie, she jumped to her feet and almost ran to the bar. Lurch following her closely. The barman saw them approaching and stopped what he was doing to serve them. Lurch nodded a quick thank you to the customer who was made to wait.

"Bone," said Bone, holding out his hand.

"Cyrus," said the man carrying the chairman badge.

"How did it go?" asked Bone while the beers were being pulled.

"It was interesting."

"How so?"

"I think they were relying on the anonymity of the place, there was only one guard, and the fool opened the door without checking."

"He dead?"

"No but he saw nothing. He'll wake up, maybe Tuesday."

"So, what did you find?"

"It was a processing house, but sadly there seems to have been a fire, all those chemicals probably."

"How much did you recover?"

"The delivery that arrived yesterday was untouched, four kilos, almost pure, we won't know for sure until we get the results in but shit it's good stuff."

"Anything else?"

"Yes, about another five kilos of the street product. So, all in all a good haul, probably fifty kilos of street product that we can sell at home, and that you can now sell here."

"That should certainly help with our cash flow, speaking of cash?"

"Oh, we found a little, it took a while to get into their safe. But we did recover some cash."

"How much?"

"You will not believe it."

"Come on the suspense is killing me, no let me guess, ten quid in old one-pound notes."

"Not exactly, your share is twenty K."

"You're having me on?"

Cyrus shook his head.

"That means there was fifty in that safe?" asked Bone.

Cyrus nodded.

"Fuck," said Bone.

"Yes," replied Cyrus, "this is bigger than we thought."

"Could this be a network across the whole northwest?"

"Maybe."

"Are we going to get any fallout from this?"

"More than likely, but we left no clues, no witnesses, no evidence. By the time the fire bobbies get that thing under control there will be nothing to see."

"Let's hope so," growled Bone. Cyrus reached into his jacket and pulled out a small package, a tightly wrapped carrier bag from a local supermarket, he passed it over to Bone, who put it into an inside pocket without opening it. He slowly looked around the members of his club.

"Looks like we'll be having a run for spring bank," he smiled.

"Don't get too flash too soon," said Cyrus.

"No sweat, I think we'll tag on someone else's arrangements, I'm sure Centurions won't mind us joining them for the bank holiday celebrations."

"That'd be good," said Roaddog, "I think they've got a great band for the Sunday night, Fifth Element. Damn their singer is one hot chick."

"Hey," said Jackie sticking an elbow in his ribs.

"But not as hot as you, not as hot as you," he smiled and stroked her leg gently.

"Nice save," muttered Bandit Queen. Cyrus picked up his beer and looked pointedly at his lieutenants, they followed suit and all three emptied their glasses in a single swallow.

"We'll leave you to it," he reached a hand to Bone, who shook it firmly. "Your sales should go up, if you need any supplies just give us a call, suddenly we are quite flush."

"No worries," said Bone. "But I think I'm going to be a little slow getting our stock out there, you know, drive the price up a bit," he laughed.

"We've got so much stock now; we'll have to push the price down to shift it." Cyrus smiled and stood up. His lieutenants followed him.

"Maybe we'll meet at a rally somewhere," said Cyrus, as they turned and walked slowly out of the barn, Wolf and Banjo flanking their leader as they normally would.

"Well," said Bone. "Looks like we are going to have a party next month, did someone say that had seen some of the Centurions here?"

"Yes," said Roaddog. "It was me; I saw a couple."

"Was their chairman amongst the ones you saw?"

"I don't think so, and they have a president, not a chairman."

"What's the difference?"

"Name only."

"Let's go and see if we can find them, we need to check up on Alan and Billy as well." Bone finished his drink and all the others followed suit. Cherie gathered all the leftovers from the burgers and dumped them back into the box, Doris tidied up all the empty glasses, just to help out the people who work there on the weekends.

Outside in the brilliant sunshine the circle was crowded with motorcycles, and people, many of them not motorcyclists, this venue was also popular with people who like walking in the forests and on the moors all around. Sitting just outside were Billy and Alan, each smoking.

"I wondered where you two had got to." said Roaddog.

"We're just having a fag, then going inside for a beer," said Billy.

"What took so long?"

"It's that damned Dragonfly," laughed Alan. "Seems everyone has heard of them, but no one has ever seen one. So many questions. I can't believe it."

"Have you seen any of the Chorley Centurions around?"

"Yes, they were across the far side of the circle. Only a couple of them though."

"Ranking members?"

"I don't remember. I didn't see any patches," said Alan.

"We might have a party to go two in a few weeks, they're having a rally, usually at Chorley rugby club. We going to see if we can get an invite."

"We'll get a beer and catch up with you guys in a bit," said Alan dropping his cigarette to the ground and stamping it out. He and Billy went into the dark interior. The rest set off around the circle, checking out the bikes, looking for people they knew and enjoying the sunshine. There were a lot of modern sports bikes around, with all their fancy colours, and pretty plastics. Many Harleys and the occasional Buel, and Victory. There were a few Triumphs, the modern sports bikes, and they did see two of the Rocket threes. Roaddog stopped by one of these and pointed it out to Jackie.

"Look at the size of this thing," he said.

"It's certainly big."

"The motor on this thing is most likely bigger than your dad's car."

"You're kidding," she grinned.

"No, that's a two point three engine, it's only three cylinders but they're huge."

"So how is it different from all the other bikes here?"

"It's got so much power, and so much torque, it's just a serious piece of kit."

Jackie looked around for a moment and pointed at one of the nearby sports bikes.

"Is it faster than that one?"

"Well, no, that's a state of the art sports bike, so the Triumph isn't quicker than that one." She looked around again and picked a different bike.

"Does it do corners better than that one?"

"Well no, that's a lightweight, it's got to be good for at least ten miles an hour faster through the bends." She smiled and looked around some more.

"Is it prettier than that one?" She picked a Harley heritage soft tail with a stunning paint job full of skulls and bones and stars.

"Well no, someone has spent a fortune on painting that Harley, and it looks great."

"So," Jackie spoke slowly, looking at the Rocket. "It's not as fast as that one, it's not as good in the corners as that one, and it's not as pretty as that one." She paused for a moment. "I'm reminded of something Alan said earlier." She turned and looked up into Roaddog's eyes. She took each of his hands in hers and smiled. "It's a fucking fashion statement," she said smiling still.

"Bitch," he whispered. "How to destroy a dream. Well I don't care; I still want one." She threw her hands around his neck and pulled him down to kiss him firmly, his hands moved to grasp her waist and then slid down to cup her ass. Gradually he increased the lifting force on her ass, until her feet were barely touching the ground. She pulled back and whispered.

"Does that huge motor vibrate more than your Harley?"

"No, smooth as silk and limitless torque at the twist of the throttle, it's just so powerful and easy."

"Then I don't want it, I like the vibration of the Harley. Why does the Harley shake so much?"

"That's the V-twin engine, it's an old design, but still very popular with the ladies, it seems."

"Damn right it's popular. Makes me all tingly."

"It's not so good for us guys though, just makes the hands, feet and balls go numb."

"Show me some more," She smiled and pulled her hands down taking one of his and waiting for him to guide the way. He shook his head slowly and smiled.

"I'm not sure I want any more of my dreams turning into green anoraks."

"It's no worse than when Dad bought his last car, that one is faster, that one carries more stuff, that one is prettier, but the Astra estate I can afford. The Astra does all of these things to a reasonable standard. These things are always a compromise, unless money is no object and you can afford a bike to do the things you are going to do today, and a different one for tomorrow. Isn't your Harley fast enough? It does roundabouts well enough for me. Isn't it pretty enough for today? Doesn't it make me wonder about a sybian?"

"You girl are crazy," he smiled down at her and walked slowly around the circle. He pointed out a few classics that were there, and a couple of the modified ones that people had changed to improve looks, beauty as always in the eye of the beholder, or performance, a Bandit with nitrous kit on it. Jackie spent more time watching the people than the bikes. As far as she could tell the people fell into three basic categories. There were the citizens, usually families, sometimes with dog, they came here for a walk in the country, and perhaps a beer and a meal in the barn. The citizens always give way to the bikers, the bikers are the most numerous group, leather clad, generally, very occasionally with children, none too small though, and the kids equally clad in leather. Then come the club members, identified by their colourful cutoff jackets, with badges and insignia, with names and responsibilities. Everyone gives way to them. Jackie had a sudden thought and scanned the circle, it looked like the two dayglow covered cops had left. That somehow made her feel a little better. She squeezed Roaddog's hand to get his attention then nodded in the direction of the rest of the group, there seemed to be some members of another club with Bone and Bandit Queen, the body language told her that things were tense in some way. Roaddog walked up behind the two bikers that were having a discussion with Bone and Bandit Queen. The "Sons" patches on their backs identified then as fairly local. He walked past and checked their names, Adolf and Globetrotter. He walked on passed, and just down the road he pulled his phone from his jeans pocket and called a number from way down his contact list. A brief conversation that seemed to make him happy, though Jackie didn't understand much of it. He smiled at her and walked back to the others.

"What's going on?" he asked.

"Why the fuck should I go through all this again? I made a perfectly reasonable offer for that old wreck and the guy told me to fuck off. I'm not happy."

"How much did you offer?"

"I offered the old fool a grand."

"I'm not surprised he turned that down, it belonged to his granddad, he's never going to sell it. He's pushing sixty so you won't have to wait long for his daughter to sell it."

"I want the thing now, not in a couple of years."

"He's not going to sell it."

"What the fuck is it to do with you anyway he's not even a member of your club?"

"He's a friend, and I fixed that bike up only a couple of days ago."

"I don't give a fuck. I'm having that bike. You won't want the trouble coming your way if I don't get it." Alan walked up and cursed softly.

"Hey Bone. I'm sorry I hoped these guys would have fucked off by now."

"Don't worry about it," said Roaddog. "these guys aren't going to be any trouble for us."

"What do you mean?" asked Alan.

"I've talked to the Sons, they've heard of Adolf and Globetrotter and are anxious to talk to them, they were down at the lower barn having a chill and a bit of a nosebag, but I don't think they're there anymore."

"No shit?" asked Alan. Roaddog shook his head slowly, Globetrotter looked round. Adolf looked straight at Alan, even so he didn't see the left-hand move. Alan's heavy fist slammed into the side of Adolf's face, his head spun around then the body followed it, as it slowly twirled to the ground, Lurch's huge hand dropped on Globetrotter's shoulder and grabbed a large piece of both jacket and skin. Harleys started to arrive and gather around the group. Motors stilled one by one.

"Roaddog," said the first to dismount.

"That'd be me."

"You got some imitation Sons here?"

"Lurch has one by the collar, and the other is taking a nap." Adolf started to come round.

"We've been trying to catch up with these guys for a while, they've been pulling the same stunt all over the place, using our name and intimidating people into selling their bikes for ridiculous prices." He shouldered his way through the crowd and up to Adolf, the fear in whose eyes was unmistakable. A heavy boot dropped straight onto Adolf's crotch.

"Call your man with the van, tell him to come up here, if he gets the slightest hint that anything is wrong, I'll cut your dick off right now."

Adolf made the call.

"I'd like to make a small observation at this point," said Roaddog.

"Observe away," said the lead Son.

"The local lakes are reservoirs, people have to drink that water, it wouldn't be nice if there were dead bodies in them."

"People shouldn't drink the water anyway."

"Why not?"

"Because fish fuck in it." The Son laughed at his own joke and so did all the others it was after all at least slightly funny.

13: Rivington and on to the Saddle.

Once the three guys had been loaded in the back of their own van and driven away. Roaddog asked a question.

"What about their bikes? They've got to be here somewhere."

"They're usually on test rides and the van is a rental, it's made them sort of difficult to track down. They have so many identities."

"You've been looking for them for a while then."

"Yes. They've been doing this shit for about six months."

"They must have made a bit of money at it."

"Well now they've lost all that. If you guys need a hand with something, just give us a call OK?"

"No worries, we're glad to have been of some assistance."

The Son got on his bike and slowly rode away, the others had driven off in ones and twos. Obviously, they were going to meet up with the van somewhere and explain politely to the guys why masquerading as members of a bike club is not cool. They might even be lucky enough to survive.

"You OK Alan?" asked Roaddog.

"Yes, I'm fine, I can't believe the bollocks of those guys."

"Nor can I," said Bone. "They needed to use a club with some clout, but to pick the Satans Sons was a big mistake."

"I'm surprised they got away with it for so long, there's a lot of Sons in this area, and many more affiliates. Risky business," said Roaddog.

"I think it's time we move on," said Bone.

"Where are you thinking?"

"I don't know, open to ideas."

"How about the Saddle? It's not too far, motorways for much of the trip, big carpark, great beer garden, good beer, and food as well. There may even be a group of bikers there already."

"Sounds like a plan. Spread the word, roll in ten," Bone set off towards the barn, Bandit Queen at his side.

"Listen up," called Roaddog loudly. "We're moving on, heading to the Saddle. Roll in ten. Be ready," he turned to Jackie. "I've got to unload some beer, you coming?" Jackie nodded and took his hand, they set off towards the barn, only a few yards behind Bone and Bandit Queen.

"I assume you know where you are going?" asked Jackie. Roaddog simply nodded and stopped walking. He turned and called out. "Man-Dare with me." The girl separated herself from the crowd and strutted slowly in their wake. He turned back to Jackie. "Looks like Bandit Queen dropped the leash." Man-Dare caught up. Roaddog took her hand and leaned against her, he whispered in her ear. "Be a good girl, we don't want to frighten the natives now do we?"

"Speak for yourself," she laughed softly. The trio continued the walk towards the barn entrance. The contrast between the bright sunlight and the darkness of the entranceway was such that they were momentarily blinded as they crossed the threshold. They entered the main room and continued straight across. It was only as they approached the double doors on the other side of the room that Jackie noticed the toilet sign above the door. Given the age of the building Jackie was surprised just how modern the toilets were, light oak panelling and nicely tiled floors. She walked into the ladies just as Bandit Queen was just opening the door of a cubicle. Man-Dare came in behind her.

"Hi Bandit," she said. "Roaddog suggests that you dropped the leash," she smiled.

"Thanks for the pickup, I'd forgotten about her for a moment," she turned to Man-Dare. "Are you being a good girl?"

"Yes, Bandit Queen. I haven't flashed anyone at all. Though I do think there were a couple of teenage boys sitting at a table that saw more of my ass than their mother would be happy with," she laughed. "Have you any idea how horny I feel with the breeze blowing around my pussy?"

"I do remember exactly that feeling."

"How many years ago?"

"Yesterday, bitch." Bandit Queen tilted her head back and laughed. "Go pee." Man-Dare went into a cubicle. "Leave the door," said Bandit Queen. Man-Dare shrugged and turned around sitting down. "No, stand up." said Bandit Queen a huge grin on her face. The cubicle at the end of the line opened, and a woman in her thirties walked out. she came along the line of cubicles and glanced into the open one where Man-Dare was peeing.

"You people are disgusting," she snarled.

"Lady," said Jackie, putting a hand on Bandit Queen's arm. "I suggest you leave before you say something you will regret." The woman snorted and flicked her head around, her blonde hair flaring out as she stamped off out of the ladies.

"Thank you," whispered Bandit Queen. "I'd have smacked the bitch."

"You may still get the chance; I don't think she's going to drop this."

"Go pee girl, we got miles to go." Bandit Queen smiled and turned to Man-Dare. "You stay here." It only took a minute for all three to finish up and leave. There were none of the guys around, so they walked back out into the main room. There in front of them was the blonde, only now she was accompanied by a tall man about the same age, maybe a little older.

"You people are animals, you don't deserve to be around people, you should be in cages," he growled as they approached. Jackie dropped back; Man-Dare grinned widely.

"Fuck you asshole," whispered Bandit Queen. The man's eyes filled with rage. He slapped her hard on the face. Even before her head had stopped moving her knee came up. She hit him hard in the crotch, then as her head came back forwards her left fist took him in the guts, and he started to fold. As he fell towards the ground her heavy right took him on the side of the jaw. The sound of heavy boots behind her told of the approach of her friends.

"Leave him," she yelled. She glanced up and the blonde, then felt the man at her feet start to stir. She looked down at him again and spat a mouthful of blood into his face, he flinched. "Look at you big man, beaten down by a girl," she sneered. Then she looked up at the blonde. "You need to leave this bastard before he starts this shit on you." The look in the woman's eyes told her more than she really wanted to know. "How long before he starts on her?" Bandit Queen nodded at the young girl clutching frantically at her mother's leg. She bent over and spat another mouthful of blood on him then turned and walked past the blonde. Man-dare hawked and spat on him as she passed. Jackie walked round him, then the men came and most spat on him, Bone waiting until everyone else had gone. He looked down on the fallen man.

"You're a very lucky guy, she'd generally have killed you for something like that. Learn from this." He walked over to the blonde who stepped backwards, fear in her eyes.

"If he doesn't learn from today, call us, I'm certain Bandit Queen would like a rematch." He smiled at her and the little girl. Then walked away. He caught up with Bandit queen just outside where she was waiting for him.

"You ok?" he asked.

"Fine, the slap split my cheek a little, it's stopped bleeding now. I'm worried about her though."

"I told her to call, we can't do much else, she has to help herself first."

"And that little girl."

"And her too. Come on, let's get the fuck out of here." He looked out across the circle and Dragonriders were mounting up all over. Engines were starting, as leader they couldn't leave without him. He walked over to his bike, mounted up, and rolled it out into the open pathway. The big Victory started on the button, and Bandit Queen mounted behind him. Lurch with Doris rolled into place behind him. They drove round the circle and slowly collected all the others. Down the hill passed the lower carpark where the last couple of bikes and Slowball tagged on to the end of the convoy. By the time they got to the end of the avenue Roaddog and Bug were in position on the second row. As Bone and Lurch made the right turn onto the main road Roaddog and Bug rolled across the road and blocked any traffic. One car came up as they had the road blocked, he slowed down and rolled to a stop, Roaddog waved a thank you then set off as soon as Slowball had made the turn, the pair dropped in behind the trike. This road wasn't suitable for a passing at least not for a while yet. They weren't even up to thirty miles an hour when two police motorcycles came out of the great house barn carpark, the two dropped in behind Bug and Roaddog. Once they got to the straight crossing the reservoir Roaddog looked around Slowball's trike. Seeing as there was enough space, he snapped the throttle open and blew through, Bug on his tail in a heartbeat. The cops stayed where they were until the thirty limit was gone then they too opened the throttles and tore down the outside of the convoy. They had to squeeze into the line for a moment as a small car went the other way, but as soon as it had passed, they set off for the front of the line. Bone had started to slow down for the right turn at the top of the hill as the two cops went past. As soon as there was a space in the traffic the cops rolled out into the road and blocked it. Then they waved Bone on. The whole convoy rolled through the right turn and every rider waved to the cops by way of a thank you. From there the ride through Chorley and onto the M61 was uneventful, except for the spectators who witness the passing. Bikes riding in close formation and making an awful lot of noise in some cases. The M6 came up in only a few minutes, passed the tickled Trout and up to the M55 interchange. Here they came off the motorway and followed the roads around the north of Preston. only a couple of minutes later they were pulling into the carpark of the Saddle. There were a few cars, and quite a few bikes. It wasn't as busy as they thought it would be. They took over a fair section of the carpark, but by no means all of it. Bone caught Slowball and handed him the package from inside his jacket.

"You're treasurer, you look after this, and you can buy the beers." Then he shouted loudly. "Clubs paying, Slowball's in the chair, form an orderly queue, and someone find out which beers they've got here." He grinned at Slowball and received a two fingered salute in return. The sound of laughing children in the beer garden behind the pub made Bone's mind up, they'd take the picnic tables on the edge of the carpark. There were a few people at some of them, and a few helmets in sight. But he knew they'd soon move once the Dragonriders started to take up the rest. Roaddog walked slowly inside, he checked out the bar and then went back outside.

"Hey Bone." he shouted. "Thwaites, Bomber, or Wainwrights." The reply was exactly as he had expected.

"Bomber," yelled Bone. Making a point to pronounce the second B, as Lemmy did when introducing the song when Motorhead played it live. Roaddog went back inside to pass the news on to Slowball who had taken up a position at the end of the bar.

"Hey Slowball, two bomber and two bottles of lager, no make that three bottles. Slowball nodded then passed the order on to the barman. The girl behind the bar dropped three bottles on the bar and smiled up at Roaddog. Roaddog picked up the bottles and they disappeared into the pockets of his cut. He picked up the two pints as they hit the bar and walked out to where Bone was sitting with Bandit Queen and Jackie. Man-Dare was perched on the edge of the table, facing across the empty carpark into the fields. He put the beers down, Bandit Queen gave him a glare. He pulled two of the bottles and passed them to Jackie and Bandit Queen. It was Man-Dares turn to glare, so he pulled the last bottle from the inside of his jacket. Holding the bottle in one hand he placed the other on Man-Dare's knee. He slid the hand down between her legs. She spread them just enough so his hand could slide upwards, up under her skirt. He pushed on until he felt her pussy, then he probed her opening. He stroked her clit until she was squirming, but before she could come he gave her the bottle and withdrew his hand, smiling at her.

"Bastard," she whispered, taking a mouthful of the beer. As Roaddog sat down beside Jackie, he smiled and leaned forward to kiss her. Her tongue jumped into his mouth then they heard Bandit Queen speak.

"Stop that."

"What have I done now?" asked Roaddog breaking the kiss and glaring at Bandit Queen.

"Not you fool, her." She twitched her head in the direction of Man-Dare. She turned back to the girl on the table. "You don't get to come until someone else does it for ya."

"None of these bastards here will do it," snarled Man-Dare.

"I know, shit ain't it," laughed Bandit Queen. Conversation continued for a while, light and slow. But it stopped completely when a large blue MPV came into the carpark. It pulled up alongside some of the bikes and then reversed almost up to the front door of the pub. The big diesel died, and a man got out. He could have been anywhere from mid-forties to sixty, not tall, not fat, but with a confidence about him that was undeniable. He had seen all the bikers before he parked so he came over to talk to them. He nodded and said "Hi." To most that he passed then he saw what he was looking for, the tag on Bone's chest that said chairman.

"Afternoon," said the stranger, "you guys staying for the show?"

"Could be," said Bone. The stranger moved to the end of the table, and pulled a card from his pocket, he handed it to Bone.

"I'm gonna be singing, probably not heavy enough for you guys, but I'll put some of the classics in for ya. I got a full rock band as well, if you're looking for someone for a rally some time." He glanced down as he put the stack of cards back in his pocket, then he looked up at Man-Dare, who's knee was almost touching his hip. "Hey girl, you know I can see your pussy, don't ya?"

"You can touch it as well," said Bandit Queen. "But ya can't make her come, she's under punishment at the moment." The singer slid his hand up her thigh and Man-Dare groaned as his fingers found their target. She pushed against his hand, then scowled as he withdrew it.

"Fuck she's hot," he smiled at Bandit Queen. "I reckon I could make her come without touching her pussy at all."

"That I'd like to see," laughed Bandit Queen.

"You're on," said the singer, stepping in between Man-Dare's widespread knees. He leaned forwards and kissed her softly on the lips, his right hand pulled her towards him, and his cheek slid along hers until his mouth was right by her ear. He felt her heart beating in her chest, and her chest moving as she breathed, he matched his breathing to hers, and his words to the beat of her heart. He whispered directly into her ear, the words reaching straight into her mind, pulsing as she pulsed. Beating as she beat. He talked of the feeling of her most recent orgasm, not the self-induced one, but the great one that involved someone else. She thought of the moment that Bone fucked her and of Bandit Queen stroking her clit. The singers left hand reached up under her shirt and stroked her ribs. Slowly as if counting them, one to a heartbeat, until he reached the curve of her breast. Then he followed that crease across her chest, and up between the two mounds. Her breathing became gasps as did his. She was panting hard, and he reached forwards sucked her earlobe into his mouth. He pinched her left nipple hard rolling it between finger and thumb. Man-Dare grunted, froze, seized and shook. Her knees gripped the singer's hips and she fell backwards onto the table. The only thing that stopped her crashing amongst the drinks was the singers grip on her shirt. He let her down slowly and smiled.

"What the fuck did you do to her?" demanded Bandit Queen, reaching out to feel the pulse in the girl's neck, just to satisfy herself that she wasn't dead.

"I gave her what she wanted."

"She certainly came hard," said Bandit Queen, she turned to Bone. "Move." Then back to the singer. "You can sit here with me."

"I got gear to set up and a show to do," he said, but still he sat down.

"Don't worry dear this won't take long," She smiled at him then tipped her head back. "Cherie," she yelled. "Get your ass over here this man deserves a blow." Her voice dropped again. "Just lean back against me and let Cherie work her magic, you'll love it. What's your name?" Cherie came and knelt in front of him and unzipped his pants.

"Paul," The singer mumbled as Cherie reached inside his zipper.

"Fuck he's nearly as big as Lurch," she muttered, wriggling the hard dick out of the pant leg was not as easy as she had expected it to be. But she got it done in only a few seconds. She looked the singer in the eye briefly then inhaled his cock, all the way to the root. She pulled back, smiled at him and plunged down again. In less than thirty seconds the constriction of her throat caused him to come. She held him deep inside until he had finished, then she pulled back again, more than a little short of breath.

"Better now?" asked Bandit Queen.

"Wow, is all I can say."

"Good, Dog will help you with your gear, won't you Dog?"

"No worries," said Roaddog, as the singer stood up and tucked his cock away.

"You guys are crazy," laughed the singer as he followed Roaddog to his car.

"How much gear you got?" asked Roaddog.

"Not a great deal, should only take a few trips."

"Sharpshooter, Bug," yelled Roaddog. "Hands please."

The two came over immediately and leant a hand with the load in. It was only two trips each.

"Thanks guys," said Roaddog to his two friends. Then he turned to the singer, "Where's it all go?"

"I can manage, thanks."

"Bass bins either side, poles, then tops. Desk on that table over there, power from the back under those tables," said Roaddog.

"Fine get on it. Stage right not too close to the bar, landlord complains if they can't hear." It didn't take Roaddog long to install all the heavy gear and run the mains power round the place. When he'd done, he said. "Tricky stuff is all yours, too many ways it can go wrong."

"Thanks for your help, I never thought I would meet another Roaddog."

"What do you mean another?"

"There is a guy who's been known as Roaddog for a lot of years, he's been crew for a long time, he lives for this sort of shit."

"I'm not sure I'm happy about that."

"Wait until you meet him, he's an OK guy."

"We'll see. I don't think I'll be here for the end, so you'll be on your own."

"Not a problem, I'd rather not have amateurs involved anyway."

"You don't mind us helping though?"

"Big guys, you're not going to drop my speakers are ya?"

"I suppose."

"Stay for the show, you'll love it. Thanks again." The singer held out his hand, Roaddog shook it and went back outside.

14: Saddle and home again

Roaddog walked out into the sun and over to the table where the others were sitting. Man-Dare seemed to have recovered and judging by the smile on her face was quite happy.

"Hey Man-Dare, you OK?"

"I'm better than fine, I think I'm going to take that singer home, he'll make a good pet."

"You'll probably find he has a wife, and children, perhaps grandchildren and a couple of side chicks already. He's a singer for fucks sake."

"A girl can have a dream."

"New dream Man-Dare?" asked Bandit Queen.

"Damned right," smiled Man-Dare.

"You missed it, he's got a big dick, ask Cherie. She almost struggled."

"That's it, I'm gonna get that man."

"Not until Tuesday you're not," said Bandit Queen, a huge grin on her face.

"Tuesday. I'm going to hunt him down and make him mine."

"Good luck with that," laughed Roaddog.

"You think he's going to be any good?" asked Bone.

"That's a serious piece of kit he's got in there, but that doesn't always mean anything."

"True, any idea when he's playing?"

"It's Sunday, so he should be finished by six. Most places do that on Sundays."

"So, he'll be starting in the next hour then," said Bone looking at his watch. "Should we stay, or should we go?" he laughed.

"Stay. He says he's got a full band as well, more heavy music than his solo, apparently."

"Fine stay it is, good beer, nice bit of road here, plenty of bikes coming and going. Not too far from home either."

"That's good for me," said Roaddog, he reached a hand down to Jackie, and said quietly.

"Fancy a bit of a walk?" she smiled up at him and got up from the table. Together they walked towards the front door of the pub. They had almost reached the door when a group of six teenagers on bikes came around the corner and into the carpark. Two of them rode straight up the blue people carrier sitting there with its tailgate up. They were looking inside.

"OY," yelled Roaddog. "Fuck off."

"We're only looking," said one of the youngsters.

"What part of fuck off needs explaining?" Roaddog dropped Jackie's hand and walked towards them. The two started to move away, taking the others with them and Paul the singer came out of the door.

"Thanks man," he said. "I'd forgotten about the boot and the guitars." He took two heavy guitar cases out of the boot and dropped the tailgate; he flipped the switch in his pocket and the doors all locked. Roaddog held the door so the singer could go in, then he ushered Jackie inside. The drop in temperature was quite surprising. Jackie almost shivered.

"It's a lot cooler in here," she said.

"Old building, thick walls and painted white," said Roaddog, by way of an explanation. He guided her to the right and waved at the singer as they went through into the rear beer garden. This was very large and had a few families and some children playing on the slides and such. The happy laughter of the children filled the air, but the looks of the parents were nervous to say the least. Perhaps they didn't know the Dragonriders patch, but they knew the type of people that wore these things. Together they walked through the patio area, and out onto the grass. The place was almost as big as a football field but not the same shape. They walked out to the fence over which they could see cows in the fields, off to the left even a horse or two. Roaddog pointed out the horses they were a field over, but still in plain sight because of the slope of the land. The stallion was certainly excited about something, but the mare was not standing for him, every time he tried to mount her, she moved forwards.

"That horse is almost hung like Lurch," laughed Roaddog.

"You are a very sick person," said Jackie as she leaned in to kiss him, her arms wrapped around his neck, and his around her waist. She rubbed her belly against his and felt his excitement.

"You're not doing so bad yourself," she whispered.

"Damn girl, you know how to get a guy going. I think I'm going to have to take you home later and sort this stuff out."

"I've no objections, but I don't know what daddy will say."

"My home fool."

"Bikers have homes? I thought they lived free on the roads."

"Yes, I have a home, it's nothing special, but it is all mine."

"That should be interesting," she whispered and went back to kissing him.

"Are you sure?" he asked after a while.

"No, but I think it's something that has to happen eventually."

"When are you working?"

"Not until lunch time tomorrow and that is an all dayer."

"We'll be in late tomorrow, we're going to have a meeting, don't forget."

"I know, Easter Monday can be quite quiet. Or it was last year if I remember."

"That should be good."

"What else are we doing today?" she asked.

"We're going to stay for a while and watch this singer, see how good he is, he might be OK for a rally later in the year. Then we can go home if you want."

"Sounds like a plan," she laughed then pulled her phone from her jacket. Roaddog listened to one side of a phone call.

"Hi daddy."

"I'm perfectly fine, and no I don't need a rescue," she laughed.

"He's a perfect gentleman is so many ways," she reached up and stroked Roaddog's cheek.

"Can I hit you for a ride to work tomorrow?"

"I'll be home about ten in the morning."

"Yes daddy, I'll tell him," she looked up into Roaddog's eyes and said, "he says that if you hurt me, he'll kill you."

"Understood," said Roaddog loud enough to be picked up by the phone.

"No dad I have no idea what you are going to tell her."

"Love you," she looked back up at Roaddog. "Well, that went better than I expected."

"That's because you rang your dad and not your mum."

"I ain't stupid, my battery is only at eighty percent, she'd have bitched until it was flat."

"I got chargers for everything at home. We can give it a fill up later."

"Let's go and get some more beer," she smiled. Roaddog laughed, and looked over the gate into the field, he looked at the horses. "Don't give up horsey, ya may get lucky," he said quietly. She took his hand and pulled him away for the fence and towards the pub. As they neared the patio area where all the parents were sitting, there were a few stares and the occasional quiet comment as the tent in his jeans was noticed. He smiled as they passed between the tables and back into the cool darkness of the pub. He walked up to the bar and ordered beer for himself and a bottle of lager for Jackie. While the beer was being pulled, he looked to his right. The singer was almost set up, background music was rolling softly from the speakers, the lights were set up, if not actually on. On the floor at the back of the stage area was a fog machine with a small wisp of smoke coming from it, this was obviously hot. The singer came forwards off the stage with a black shirt in his hand, obviously off to get changed. Roaddog smiled at him as he walked past, the singer nodded and wandered off to the gents. Jackie came from the ladies, Roaddog was impressed by the shape and obvious strength of her thighs in the tight jeans.

"Enjoying the view?" she asked as she took the bottle from his hand.

"Most certainly. Where would madam like to sit? Comfy seat under the speaker stack, near to the door for the ladies, or here at the bar."

"I think at the bar, the view will be better, and that singer looks quite good."

"For his age you mean?"

"He's not that old," she laughed at the tinge of jealousy in Roaddog's eyes. Her smile gave away her joke.

"He's old enough to be your father."

"You mean grandfather," she laughed and leaned in to kiss him again. While they were kissing the singer walked past, he tossed his t-shirt onto the side of the stage area and picked up his guitar. A quick stamp on the control boxes, then he checked the tuning. The last thing he did was reach out to the tablet on a stand just to the right of his microphone stand. The background music faded, and then a backing track came punching through the PA speakers, the singer played guitar and sang to the track. The first song of the set of something by Bon Jovi, the rest of the set was in much of a similar vein, middle of the road rock. Some he played guitar, some he didn't. Occasionally he would pick up a second wireless microphone and walk out into the crowd to sing with the audience. He was definitely quite good. After about fifty minutes he finished the first set with that classic from Bryan Adams, the summer of sixty-nine. Though Roaddog noticed that some of the lyrics had been changed, this was certainly not a radio edit. The singer declared that he would be back shortly for another set, so hang around, it's going to be even better. The background music came up, but it seemed to be very quiet, simple contrast to the volume of the singer's performance.

"Want a beer man?" asked Roaddog.

"That would be great, singing is thirsty work." He looked around the room which was now almost entirely filled with Dragonriders. He spotted Man-Dare, and she locked her eyes on him. She wasn't able to move, currently jammed into a corner where Bandit Queen could keep a very close eye on her. Roaddog handed the singer a pint of Wainwrights. The singer smiled and drank half of it in one go, he wiped his lips with the back of his hand. "Thanks for that. Damn its hot in here."

"Those lights won't be helping," said Roaddog.

"They're not as much of a problem as they used to be, they're all LED, the old-fashioned ones were serious. It's mainly down to the number of people in here. It's good to see."

"There's even some citizens in. Though they are mainly round the corner near the pool table. Perhaps their ears are too sensitive."

"Is it too loud?"

"No, you can stand right in front of the speaker stacks with an open mike, so no."

"So, you're enjoying it?"

"It's damned good," said Roaddog.

"You've got a great voice," said Jackie.

"Thanks for that," he smiled at her. "Gotta pee, and chill." He turned away and put what was left of his beer on the floor by the mike stand and wandered off towards the gents. Roaddog stepped across the open area in front of the stage and spoke to Bone, who was sitting with Bandit

Queen and Man-Dare. They had their back to the stage, and the speaker almost directly over their heads.

"What do you think?" he asked.

"I think he's quite good," said Bone. Bandit Queen nodded.

"I want his babies," said Man-Dare loudly, she got an elbow to the ribs.

"As a solo he'll certainly do as support, we'll have to catch his band sometime. I can't see them being dreadful with him as the front man," said Roaddog.

"Good enough for headline at a rally?" asked Bone.

"Can't tell, we'd have to go see them. Maybe next weekend, I'll find out if they're playing anywhere near, and we'll take a run out to see the show."

"Sounds good to me. How long you planning on staying?"

"I'll probably stay for the second set then cut out," Roaddog smiled and glanced over at Jackie.

"Fair enough," Bone turned back to Bandit Queen and they looked at each other for a moment, then She looked up at Roaddog.

"Hey Dog, you got a damned leash somewhere?"

"No, why?"

"I'm trying to keep this bitch under control, and it's not that easy, I was thinking a nice heavy chain and I could chain her up outside. Entertainment for the locals, you know?"

"Sorry I'll try and remember for tomorrow. Anyway, I thought they prefer sheep round here?" laughed Roaddog.

"You may be right," laughed Bandit Queen, digging Man-Dare in the ribs again.

Roaddog returned to where Jackie was sitting at the bar.

"I'm going for a fag," he said and kissed her gently on the cheek.

"You don't smoke," she said, then she remembered the first time they met. "Or you don't smoke much?"

"I gave up years ago, now I have the occasional one. I'll be back in a bit ok?"

"I'll be fine, what can happen out here in the sticks?"

"Oh, you'd be surprised. Sometimes these places can get really rowdy." He smiled and walked toward the door. Once outside he cadged a cigarette off Cherie, and a light.

"What do you reckon of this singer?" he asked.

"He's a big dick," she laughed, "No, he's got a big dick," she smiled.

"I'm talking about his talent, not his cock."

"He can use that talent on me any day of the week," she smiled.

"You know," he said slowly. "I thought it was guys that are supposed to think with their dicks. What about his singing?"

"Well, if he can sing while he's dicking me, so much the better," she leaned against Roaddog and rubbed her not inconsiderable breasts against his chest. He sighed. "He's good," she said finally. "That voice has a sort of gruffness that reaches the places even Heineken can't."

"I suppose that counts as a vote for having him perform for a rally," he paused for a moment, "You got some handcuffs on ya?" he asked. She nodded. He held out his hand, Cherie reached into her jacket and pulled out a pair of shiny steel handcuffs. She held them over his hand and asked.

"What do you want them for?"

"I've a feeling Man-Dare is going to need to be restrained before too long." The handcuffs vanished back inside the jacket, and another set came out.

"Stronger," said Cherie, as she dropped them into Roaddog's open hand.

"These look like police issue."

"They're not, they're military and outdated. The other set are party versions, they can be released by the person wearing them, Man-Dare may know the trick."

"Nice to know, I think," he tucked the cuffs in a back pocket and went back inside. He returned to the bar and got some more beers in, he sat down on his stool and pulled Jackie into his arms. They kissed for a time while the singer came back to the stage. Halfway through the second song of the set Bandit Queen tapped Roaddog on the shoulder. She leaned in close and spoke loudly.

"Can you watch this bitch? She's starting to really get on my nerves," she nodded her head in the direction of Man-Dare who was standing behind her. Roaddog smiled and nodded. He took Man-Dare by the arm and guided her to the stool at the end of the bar, he picked her up and sat her on the stool. Then he took her left hand and, in a flash, had the cuff around her wrist. A moment later the other cuff was fastened to the mounting point of the brass rail that ran along the front of the wooden bar. She scowled up at him. He smiled as he sat down again. Bandit Queen laughed and walked off towards the ladies. He turned to the landlord and using hand signals indicated that he wanted more beers, one for himself and one each for the two women. The landlord laughed and pulled the pint while the barmaid got two bottles from the fridge and popped the tops from them. Roaddog passed two bottles to Jackie and indicated that the other was for Man-Dare. The song finished and the crowd applauded, the singer smiled and picked up the second microphone. One tap on the tablet and the backing music started playing, Roaddog smiled, "Don't stop believing" by Journey. The singer wandered through the crowd singing with various girls and guys. Everyone seemed to be enjoying it, Man-Dare really wanted to join in with this one. But the singer just smiled as he walked past her, his cheeky grin told Roaddog that he had something other than his arm up his sleeve. The next song started and Roaddog immediately recognised the classic by Free, wishing well. As the intro played the singer moved over to stand directly in front of Man-Dare. With the microphone in his left hand he slid the right up her leg and under her skirt.

"Take of your pants. Kick off your shoes," not the lyrics that Roaddog remembered.

"You know you ain't going anywhere," the singer looked pointedly at Man-Dare's left hand.

"Run around the town singing your blues."

"I know you ain't going anywhere." Again, the look and the cheeky smile.

"You've always been a good friend of mine."

"But you're always saying farewell."

"And the only time that you're satisfied."

"Is with your hand in the wishing well." The hand appeared from her skirt and the fingers were presented to her mouth, she licked and sucked them.

"Take off your guns you might shoot yourself."

"Or is that what you're trying to do." The empty right hand slid up her thigh and under her skirt again.

"Put up a fight you believe to be right."

"And someday your sun will shine through."

"You've always got nothing to hide."

"Something you can always tell."

"And the only time that you're satisfied."

"Is with your hand in the wishing well." The singer leaned forwards and kissed her briefly.

"I know what you're wishing for."

"Love in a peaceful world." The singers hand moving slowly under the skirt.

"Love in a peaceful world."

"Love in a peaceful world."

"Love in a peaceful world." The singer spun away for the short guitar solo; his right hand shiny with Man-Dare's special lubricant.

"You've always been a good friend of mine." The singer stepped in and the right hand returned to its recent home.

"But you're always saying farewell."

"And the only time that you're satisfied."

"Is with your hand in the wishing well." The last well rang on and on, while the right hand was moving furiously under Man-Dare's skirt. On and on the note rang, bar after bar, Man-Dare twitched, and writhed, then froze for a moment and slumped forwards in her seat. The singer stepped away, wiping his hand on her thigh and ran the note out another few bars before finally running out of air. Man-Dare's orgasm attracted the attention of the landlord, he came from behind the bar and went to where Roaddog was sitting. Then he glanced at Man-Dares left wrist, and the amount of thigh and other parts that where showing.

"You people are crazy. You can't go cuffing young women to my bar and then abusing them," he yelled. Roaddog smiled for only a moment before Bandit Queen spoke up.

"What makes you think she is restrained, and what makes you think she is abused?"

"Stupid woman, this asshole has handcuffed her to the bar." Total silence fell in the room.

"You're call Bandit," whispered Roaddog, pushing Jackie behind himself.

"Stand down Dog," was the quiet reply. Bandit Queen stood and stepped up to the landlord, he glanced around and suddenly was aware of the sheer numbers against him.

"Damn it," he said. "It's just not right and you know it." Bandit Queen looked at him for a moment, then turned to Man-Dare.

"I think someone needs a blow," Man-Dare smiled and moved away from the bar, leaving the handcuffs behind, she stepped up to the landlord and dropped to her knees. Her hands went to his belt, but he stepped back.

"You people are crazy," he turned to the singer and said, "You're being paid to sing, so sing." Then he turned and went back behind the bar. Man-Dare returned to her seat at the end of the bar and the singer went back to his singing. Very soon the place was rocking again as if nothing had happened. Roaddog stood in front of Man-Dare and retrieved the handcuffs, he unlocked them and checked them, he could find nothing wrong with them at all. He nudged Man-Dare and his face asked the question. How? She grinned and held up both hands. Her thumbs flexed in a peculiar way and suddenly both hands were small enough to slip from the cuff and she had very small hands to start with. He laughed and stepped up to Jackie, he hugged her and kissed her while he was shaking with laughter. She put her mouth up to his ear and shouted over the noise.

"Let's go," she pulled back and he smiled at her, then nodded. He turned to Bone and threw him a salute, and a small bow for Bandit Queen. Taking Jackie by the hand he walked through the crowd towards the door, on the way he dropped the handcuffs in Cherie's hand and shook his head. Only moments later they were aboard his bike and pulling out of the carpark. The approaching dusk was a lot colder than the afternoon had been, and Jackie tucked in tight behind him to stay out of the wind as much as possible. Crossing the river at the new bridge they headed for Leyland where he lived. Wide open roads with little traffic, they made good time, turning left at the tank. Then on to Farrington, a right at a roundabout and into the town itself. Roaddog shut down to spot on the speed limit as they went through the thirty mile an hour marker, just the other side they passed a police car. Roaddog rolled to a stop at the Centurion way lights, and sure enough the police car rolled up behind them. He smiled to himself and set off slowly when the lights changed, only a few more streets and he turned off into the street where he lived. He went down the alley at the side of his house and rolled up in front of the garage. The transmitter in his pocket turned off the garage's alarm system. It showed him a green LED to indicate that he could now open the door without a horrendous racket from the sirens. His keys opened the physical locks then he turned the bike around and reversed it into the darkened garage. While Jackie was waiting for him to put the bike away the police car rolled to a stop at the end of the alley. The two cops watched patiently as the bike rolled backwards into the garage. The door was closed, the locks set and finally the alarm reactivated. They were still there when Roaddog walked out of the alley and into his front gate, he waved to them as he opened his front door. By the time he'd reached inside and disabled the house alarm the cops had moved on, obviously something better to do. The two walked to the back of the house and into the kitchen, through the back window and over the yard wall Jackie could see the apex of the garage roof. Roaddog filled the kettle and set it to boil.

"Tea, coffee, beer?" he asked.

"Coffee I think, it's been a long and exciting day. But before that where's your loo?"

"As you are going up the stairs it's straight in front of you." He smiled she walked back towards the front door, then turned up the stairs. As she climbed the stairs thoughts raced through her head. 'Hairy biker lives on his own, what is his bathroom going to be like? The house smells OK and doesn't have too much dust on the windowsill halfway up the stairs. So, the curtains could do with a wash, but they are mainly just dusty.' The stairs turned left ninety degrees, then two more steps up. To her right was a partially open door through which she could see a bath. She paused for a moment then pushed the door open. In front of her the bath stretched along the wall, an electric shower on the far wall, a shower curtain hung from a metal rail. The sink next to the bath, and the toilet next to that, with of course the lid up.

"Men," she muttered, then laughed. She was surprised by the cleanliness of the place. By the time she got down the stairs again Roaddog was standing in the kitchen with two cups in his hands. He smiled as she walked towards him, he held one cup towards her, and she took it. He led the way into the front room. As they passed the door to the back room she glanced inside, it was dark in there but there were a lot of tiny lights and a quantity of electronic equipment. the lack of light hid the identity of the hardware.

They walked into the front room, a large leather sofa and one heavy chair, a small stack of hifi and a large TV on the chimney breast. Other than that, the room was pretty clear of any of the clutter that she was expecting to see. He sat down on the sofa and put his cup on the floor in front of it. He reached forwards and pulled up his jeans, he pulled the zips on his boots down and toed both off, he stood the boots up beside the sofa. He sat back and sighed.

"There is something special about taking the boots off at the end of the day."

"There are days when I feel like that, but not generally footwear," she laughed.

"Please feel free to get as comfortable as you wish."

"I'm not sure that is quite appropriate."

"You're worrying about propriety when earlier when you had your fingers in Man-Dare?" he laughed.

"That was different."

"Yes it was, you were deliberately putting on a show for everyone there, here, there's just the two of us."

"That's why it was different, there were a lot of people."

"So why is it different with just the two of us?"

"I don't know, it just is."

"Well, I don't know about you, but it's been a long, hot and tiring day for me, I'm ready for a shower then bed. Would you care to join me?"

"And they say romance is dead," she laughed.

"Neither of us are children, if you want, I can take you home?"

"No, it's just it feels a little strange to be so blunt about this sort of thing."

"So that's a yes then."

"I suppose. You are rushing things a bit you know?"

"Yes. But let's not be beating about any bush anywhere, we both know what is going to happen here. We're going to drink our brews, listen to some music, chat for a while, then go and have a nice shower together, and then sleep in my nice big bed. What time would madam like her alarm call for?"

"Well," Jackie shook her head and laughed, "I need to be home by about ten, so nine o'clock would be good."

"Eight will give you enough time for a shower and some breakfast."

"Fine eight will do nicely," she laughed. Roaddog pulled his phone from his pocket and dropped it into the charging station near the TV. Then pressed a few buttons and music started to come from the TV. Some sort of classic rock radio station.

"Give me your phone, I'll put it on charge." Jackie took her phone from her jacket and passed it too him, he found a spare charging lead, near the dock and plugged it into her phone. As soon as the phone showed its charging indicator, he put it down and turned to Jackie, he slid his waistcoat off and dropped it on the chair. He held out his hand to her and pulled her slowly to her feet, he slid the jacket off and dropped it onto the sofa, then wrapped his arms around her. They shuffled slowly to the sound of the music, each pressing their body against the other. He felt the pressure of her breasts on his chest, she was more focused on the bulge in his jeans pressing against her belly. 'Damn he's tall.' She thought, as she looked up to kiss him.

"This is nice," She whispered breaking the kiss for a moment. His hand slid slowly up her back inside her shirt, and with a simple motion released the catch on her bra. She leaned back and muttered.

"Tickles," then she moved forwards and kissed him some more. Their tongues fencing in their mouths, backwards and forwards then pushed and wriggled. In the outside world, that they weren't paying too much attention to, the DJ said something about a classic song by Free from 1972. The first few chords filled the air around them. They broke apart laughing.

"I don't think I'm going to be able to listen to that song without getting hard." said Roaddog. Paul Rodgers' voice singing 'Take off your hat kick off your shoes.'

"That damned singer certainly knows how to work a crowd," laughed Jackie, "or a pussy."

"It's no good, I can't listen to that right now," smiled Roaddog, "I think it's shower time." He reached across and killed the music; he took Jackie in one hand and his coffee in the other. She held him back for a moment while she picked up her coffee from the floor, then followed him to the stairs. As they climbed the stairs, she was staring at his ass moving under the tight denim of his jeans. She smiled as they got to the bathroom. He put his coffee on the sink and took hers from her to put it in the same place. He pulled her to him, and started to lift her t-shirt, slowly he lifted it and exposed her slackened bra, she lifted her arms so that the shirt could come off. He dropped it to the floor, and she performed the same duty for him, smiling as his hairy chest came into view. She ran her fingers through the coarse hair as her hands fell to her sides. He smiled and kissed her briefly, pushing the straps off her shoulders, so the bra fell into his hand and was dropped on the floor on top of the pile. Her hands reached for his belt buckle. She released it with a snap, she opened his jeans and pushed them down slowly until gravity took over and they fell to his ankles. He lifted his feet in turn to release them from the trouser cuffs. Then he reached down and removed his own socks. Her belt wasn't under as much tension as his own had been though taking her pants down was a little more difficult for him as they were such a tight fit. He peeled them down her thighs, and over the knees, he knelt at her feet to pull the bunched-up denim over her delicate ankles. With a flick of the wrists her socks followed in a moment. He reached up for the waistband of her knickers, and gradually lowered them. Unveiling the treasure hiding there, a small tuft of dark brown fur at the crest of her slit. Once the panties were gone, he pulled her towards his face and nuzzled against her mound. Inhaling strongly the pungent fragrance of womanliness. His tongue flashed out and licked her for a second as she gasped, and her hands fell to his head pulling him in for an instant. She pushed him away, and reached down, to pull him to his feet. He smiled as he allowed her to lift him. Once he was upright, she kissed him. Then sank to her knees, never breaking eye contact, she pushed her face against the mound in his briefs. Rubbing her cheek against it, revelling in the hot musky odour. 'My it has been a hot day.' She thought. She bit gently on the hard shaft hidden in his pants, then she pulled them down, His manhood lifted firmly once freed from its confinement. She leaned against him and nuzzled at the base of it. Her tongue sneaked out and licked around the base. She felt the prickly stubble and tasted the salty muskiness of him, he reached down and pulled her back up to her feet. He pulled her naked body against his, he felt the pressure of her heavy breasts against the hair on his chest. Her forehead was just level with his mouth, so he kissed it gently. He reached over and flipped the shower curtain to be certain that it was hanging inside the bath, and then turned the shower on. The dial didn't need setting and it only took a few moments to get up to temperature. He held her hand as he helped her into the bath.

"I gotta pee," he said and stepped over to the toilet. He pushed his penis downwards and closed his eyes, it took a short time to get the flow started, but once going it took a fair while to stop. A quick shake and he stepped over to the bath, he stepped in and pulled the curtain to make sure the water stayed in the bath. She pulled him under the spray and held him close. Jackie was giggling.

"What you finding so funny?" he asked.

"That just seems so, I don't know, sort of incongruous."

"What do you mean?"

"It was Friday, oh my god, that's only two days ago. Things happen awful fast around you. Anyway it was Friday, and a whole load of your friends, I didn't actually count how many. Peed on a girl in clear view of everyone, and now you go and pee in a toilet, it just seemed unlikely. And you didn't flush it."

"She volunteered, as you saw quite clearly, you have not. What did you say at the time? The most disgusting thing I have ever seen. And if I'd flushed, the water pressure drops, and you boil like a pink lobster under this damned shower. It heats up far faster than the thermostat can cope."

"I think you must be corrupting me; in the last few days I've seen and done things I would never even have imagined before I met you."

"New experiences, something outside what used to be normal for you. Some would call that corruption; I just call it fun."

"So, what does it feel like to pee on someone?"

"Some like it, some don't. It's like everything, people are different."

He pulled her out from under the shower and filled his hand with gel before he started to wash her. He started with the shoulders and worked his way methodically down her body, pausing for a while at each of the interesting bits. Once he was finished, he spun her back under the water to rinse off. Then he passed her the gel. She washed him much the same as he had done for her, when she got as far down as his penis she spoke again.

"Why do you shave this bit?" she asked, stroking him slowly.

"Some girls prefer it shaved, others don't care, and some think it's somehow creepy to shave. What's your preference?"

"It's not fun when the hairs get stuck in your teeth."

"Shaved it is then, but not right now, I'm too tired."

"You'd shave just for me?"

"Of course, wouldn't you?"

"Well, I suppose, I just don't see guys doing that."

"Some of us do," he smiled and pulled her to her feet and into his arms, the warm water pouring over their bodies as they kissed. His hands moved to her breasts, lifting and moulding, massaging and twisting slowly. She moaned into his mouth and then groaned as his thumb and forefinger twisted her nipple, none too gently.

"Enough," she whispered breaking away. She reached behind herself and nudged the power button on the shower with an elbow, it slowed to a dribble and stopped. She cocked her head to one side and smiled. He flicked the shower curtain back and stepped out of the tub, he turned to her and offered both hands to help her out. She stepped out of the tub straight into his arms again. They were both cooling in the fresh air of the bathroom, the steam settling out even as they watched. He took two towels from the cupboard and offered one to her, she took it and started to dry herself.

"No," he said, "let me." He started to dry her with the towel he was holding, starting at the top and working slowly down her body. Once he had finished, he dropped the towel to the floor, and looked at her. She smiled and got the message almost immediately, though he did have to bend a bit, so that she could comfortably reach his shoulders. If very short order he was dry as well. She held the towel up by one corner and moved it, so the opposite corner was positioned exactly over the one he had already dropped. Then she released the towel, it fell and created an even higher pile of discarded cotton. He laughed and took her hand, he pulled her gently out of the bathroom and into the rear bedroom. In the darkness she could see almost nothing, until he turned on one of the bedside lamps, a soft glow filled the room. Bike and band posters adorned the walls, except for the one that was almost completely mirrors. He pulled her slowly over to the bed, then turned her so her back was to the bed. He eased her backwards until she was sitting on the edge of the bed, then he pushed her back until she was lying on the bed. She smiled at him, though she was struggling to see over the mounds of her breasts. He pushed her legs apart and knelt between them. He leaned forwards and pressed his lips to her mound, his tongue licked out and across the small patch of hair above the top of her slit. Then he slowly moved downwards, licking her lips as he went, all the way down to the perineum. There he paused for only a moment before going down even further. Tickling the sensitive skin of the perineum all the way to her puckered nether orifice. He circled this and then started his way back up, slowly licking from side to side as he went. By the time his tongue arrived at the top of her slit her lips were far more prominent and her clitoris had grown enough to show below its hood. He captured the small nub between his lips and sucked it gently. She groaned and wriggled as the pleasure started to fill her mind, she felt a sudden bereavement as he moved away from her clit. This journey downwards his tongue penetrated deeper, and moved more to the sides, licking and slipping as it went. When he got to her perineum again, he picked up her legs and hoisted them over his shoulders. He delved even deeper into her anus, causing more writhing and much louder groans. He moved upwards again, pushing deeper and harder as he went. His tongue swept through her opening and across the sensitive nub that was the opening of her urethra, and on to her clitoris again. This time he gently caught it with his teeth and the end flicked and rolled by his agile tongue was more than her body could handle, the rush of pleasure took away her mind and her breathing, this was replaced with a clenching of her whole musculature. She pitched her hips upwards and her hands snatched at his hair and pulled his face even harder into her crotch. Her thighs crushed his head from both sides and her voice filled the room with gurgled shouts of pleasure. Her own personal juices filled his mouth as she relaxed finally. Her legs slumped down on to his back, then slid sideways off his shoulders. Her hands did not release his hair, they pulled him upwards. Sliding him up her body, until his mouth aligned with hers, she kissed him, her tongue savouring her own flavour on his lips. After a minute she pushed him away.

"That was great," she whispered. "Now fuck me." Her eyes hot on his. His arms caught her under the armpits and lifted her up, turning her so that she was in the proper position on the bed. Then he climbed on top of her, her legs opened to welcome him in. She reached between them to grab his cock, she placed it directly at her opening, and then spoke again.

"Fuck me," she said, clearly, her eyes shining in the dim lighting. After only a moment's hesitation he plunged forwards, filling her completely, in a manner that she had never experienced before. Orgasm shook her body before he was fully home in her. Her eyes opened again, and she reached for him, both arms clasped around his shoulders pulling him tighter in. Her legs lifted and her heels locked on his buttocks as she drove him into herself with far more force than he was willing to use. She released for a moment then drove him in again, she was the one controlling both speed and force to be used for these actions. Faster and harder she drove him on, her hot pussy clasping hard around his invading member. Her hips rotating to bring the pressure exactly where she wanted it, her crescendo built quickly. Her tension rising fast, her body racing for the soul-destroying orgasm that it craved so intensely. When that flower finally opened her entire body froze and trembled in the spastic pleasure of orgasm. Her spasms drove him over the edge, he pumped stream after stream into her. The further stimulation of his spend hitting her cervix drove her even higher, her screams filled the room, if only for a few seconds. She collapsed motionless on the bed, and he slumped on top of her. A single moment of lucidity made him roll sideways off her. His softening penis wrenched from its warm home and into the cooling air of the bedroom, it left a trail across his thigh as it shrank. A small river of spunk flowed out of her as her breathing slowed and relaxed. It seemed like hours, though it was only minutes before she spoke.

"Fuck," she whispered.

"I think that qualifies," he muttered.

"It's been a while," she said.

"That was great," he smiled and turned to her again, he moved his head so that he could kiss her. Their kiss went on and on, slowly the lights in their heads started to fade, and fail.

15: Easter Monday. Off to work.

Jackie woke slowly, she felt something hot hard and warm pressed against her buttocks, her barely opened eyes showed her a room that made no sense, and the light coming through the curtains was all wrong. Then the memories came flooding back, she remembered where she was, and who was pressed up against her. She smiled to herself and wriggled her arse. She got no response other than the hardening of the penis pressed against her, the arm across her belly tightened slightly, so she wriggled some more. His slow breathing caught, and then he breathed in a huge lungful of air, the arm tightened firmly across her belly and pulled her back against him.

"Morning beautiful," he whispered, his mouth only an inch from her ear, his hot breath made her shiver.

"Morning Dog," she shivered against him. "What time is it?" she asked. He looked around.

"Phone's downstairs. I think it's early." His arm slid away from her belly then pushed against her hip as he rolled from the bed. She watched as he walked around the bed and out of the door, his half hard penis bouncing in front of him, she watched the muscles in his buttocks moving as he walked out of view. She heard him go down the stairs and moments later come back up. He returned to the bedroom, carrying both phones. He passed her hers and dropped his at the side of the bed.

"It's only seven o'clock," she whispered. "Too early to get up yet."

"Sleep or something else?" he asked sliding into the bed and pressing himself up against her. "Damn, you're warm," he whispered.

"I have a question for you?"

"Ask."

"It's a little strange."

"I'm used to strange, ask, anything."

"OK," she paused for a while before going on. "how come Man-Dare's pussy is so much softer than mine?"

"Where does this come from?"

"When I touched her yesterday, I couldn't help but notice that her pussy was soft and warm, mine just isn't."

"I can categorically state that I have some experience of your pussy, it is without doubt soft, and warm, and wet and tasty. Where do you get the impression that it isn't?"

"When I touch it, it's just skin and hair."

"It must be the way you touch it."

"How can that be different?"

"I don't know, god girl, it's not even eight o'clock in the morning and you're expecting some sort of sense out of me. Here, let me try." He reached forwards and slid his hand down her belly, across her mound, through the small patch of curls and into her slit, he softly caressed it and she wriggled against him. "See, nothing wrong with that at all."

"It feels so different when you do it."

"How did it feel when you touched Man-Dare, talk me through it?"

"I reached down to her thigh, it was soft and warm, I ran my hand slowly up her inner thigh, I remember there was a little stubbly feeling where she had missed the last time she shaved her legs. My hand came up to her crotch, the soft skin of the crease was warm and damp, I slid my hand across and cupped the whole of her pussy, it felt really soft and warm, wet and inviting, so I raised my middle finger and it went up inside her, she trembled and pushed against my hand. It was all so soft and sensuous. My pussy doesn't feel like that to me."

"Well it feels fine to me, perhaps it's the way you feel it."

"I don't understand."

"How do you feel you pussy when you masturbate?"

"I don't."

"What do you mean you don't"

"I don't masturbate, it's a bad thing to do. At least that's what we were taught in Sunday school."

"You are kidding?"

"No."

"Well, that's not terribly logical, here you are before eight o'clock in the morning, in the bed of a man you're not married to, and you're telling me masturbation is wrong?"

"I suppose."

"If masturbation is so wrong, how did you end up losing your virginity?"

"I was being pressured by a guy to have sex with him, and by all the gods I was so horny, I did it, then I loved it. So, I end up in bed with some hairy biker I met only a few days ago, shit it's less than a week."

"But you've never got yourself off?"

"No."

"That's the problem."

"What do you mean?"

"When you touched Man-Dare you were soft and gentle. You were being nice to her, and attempting to stimulate her, when you touch yourself, you are anything but gentle. To be soft and nice would be masturbating, and that is not allowed. Do you see what I mean?"

"I think so, but I'm still sceptical to say the very least."

"So how long has this prohibition against the dreaded masturbation been in place?"

"I don't know, forever I think."

"So, when where you first told about it?"

"Sunday school."

"How old were you?"

"I don't know perhaps nine or ten."

"So, you hadn't experienced orgasm by then?"

"Of course not."

"So, it had to be explained to you?"

"Sort of."

"Explain it to me."

"It was one of the nuns that explained it to us, there were three of us in school of the right age."

"Oh my god, the penguins. I have experience myself of penguins," he laughed. "sorry, please go on. I'll explain later."

"The sister explained to us about original sin, and how all women are tainted by the same sin, and the sin is masturbation. At that time I thought the sin was eating apples, I knew nothing of the other thing. I was too shy to ask, but one of the other girls wasn't. I think she was desperate to avoid this sin but had no idea what it was. The nun explained that it was the gentle touching of the private parts that let Satan into your heart, and once there you were his and set to burn in hell. The sister went on to explain that cleanliness was next to godliness, but with a heavy brush and not a light touch. I had the picture of the stiff brush nana used to use for cleaning the doorstep. There was no way that was going anywhere near my pussy, so I compromised. I scrubbed with a coarse flannel." She paused for a moment then went on. "There was something about Satan's doorbell, but that went over my head."

"Oh my, the penguins certainly laid it in thick for you girls. We had something a little less daunting, or we were just a little more rebellious. We were told to watch out for the demons in the shape of women, because they would steal our souls by touching our private places. One of the boys said no one would ever find his private place, he used it to smoke his dad's fags, and no one would ever find it. That got him a slap round the head. And a further explanation about the actual process, it even appeared that the women concerned could even be completely invisible. I did make the mistake of asking how we watch out for invisible women. Another one with a crack round the head. But I at least didn't take this lecture to heart quite so much, as you did. Perhaps it's a guy thing, as soon as the dick started getting hard, we had to play with it, it's sort of compulsory."

"I still don't understand what you are saying. Is it my fault or something?"

"Yes and no, you are just being too rough on yourself. Try it, touch yourself as gently as you did Man-Dare."

"I don't see how that can work."

"Just kiss me and feel yourself with the very tips of your fingers, almost like you were trying to feel something without your touch being felt." He leaned over her and kissed her, his hand followed hers down over her belly, and through the soft curly hair. Her breath caught in her throat as her fingers slowly crossed her clitoris, and then on down her rapidly moistening slit. She shook her head and broke the kiss.

"That feels strange," she whispered.

"Good strange?"

"Very good."

"Don't stop, keep going, slowly and gently, slide a finger inside, like I did last night," she did as he said and groaned softly.

"That feels almost like it was you doing it," she mumbled.

"That's the idea. Feel how hot and wet you are. Is that how Man-Dare felt?"

"Yes, and it makes me feel good."

"Keep going," he whispered, moving slowly down her body, he held her nipple in his mouth for a moment, sucking and then flicking it with his tongue. He moved on, down her body, over her belly, pausing for a moment at her belly button, just to swirl his tongue in it. His cheek came up against her arm as he moved further down, he kissed her hip and then her thigh as he watched her fingers work on her pussy, dipping inside then rubbing across her clitoris.

"That's it," he muttered as her belly started to twitch. Then, all of a sudden, her thighs clamped shut, imprisoning her hand as her pelvis jumped upwards. She grunted and then relaxed. Slumping back down to the bed, her legs separated, and her hand was free. She looked down at him seeing the huge smile on his face.

"That's it," she whispered, "I'm going to hell." He moved round in the bed and kissed her firmly on the lips.

"If that's all it takes, then the place is going to be full," He smiled. "I still can't believe you've never made yourself cum before."

"I have now."

"And?"

"It was nice, but it's better when you do it."

"Is it?" Roaddog rolled away from her onto his back, he took his hard cock in his hand and started to stroke it. "It certainly feels nice to me," He said, looking her in the eyes while his arm moved between them.

"No, fool. It's better when it's your hand in my pussy." She reached down and replaced his hand with her own. She smiled and turned to him, kissing him for a while, then she rolled up onto her knees and moved across him. She held his cock as she slowly settled down on it. She smiled as he slowly filled her.

"Damn," she muttered. "That feels good." Once she was all the way down, she started to slide backwards and forwards, rubbing her clit hard against the root of his penis, her heavy boobs jigging merrily with every motion. Faster and faster she rocked, until she came again. She slumped forwards panting on his chest. He pushed her off to the right and rolled her face down, then he lifted her hips and got behind her, with a rapid thrust he entered her from behind and she grunted to be so full of him. He adjusted the angle slightly and drove in hard, the wide head of his penis dragging across the roughness of her g-spot, she groaned loudly. He plunged into her again and again, faster and faster, until her next orgasm clenched her whole body, she became so rigid and so tight, that he had no chance of carrying on, he blew on the spot, gushing again inside her. She slumped to the bed, he followed her down. Gradually their breathing returned to something a little more normal, at least something that made speech possible.

"That was good," he whispered, his mouth only a breath away from her ear.

"Damned right," she replied, flicking her head to get the hair out of her eyes. Slowly he rolled off her, onto his back. She looked over at him in the gradually increasing light and smiled.

"Fuck that was good," she muttered.

"Not too shabby," he grinned. "Damn, I need a pee." He rolled from the bed, and walked around the bed, her eyes followed him and noticed the string of stickiness hanging from the end of his flaccid penis. She smiled. Then she rolled out of the bed the other side, knowing that her own bladder issues would make themselves felt in a matter of moments. She walked into the bathroom just as he was finishing, she watched him shake the drips off and then he wiped the residue off his hand on the flatness of his belly.

"Sticky," he laughed, looking accusingly at Jackie, who stuck her tongue out at him. He reached across and turned the shower on, while she sat down to pee. He stepped in and started to wash the sweat and other effluvia from his skin. She watched him as he washed himself, silhouetted against the light from the window behind him. She smiled as she thought about everything that had happened in the last few days, surprised at just how small a number of days that it was. She stood and pressed the lever on the cistern, she stepped over to the side of the bath. Roaddog shouted and jumped out from under the stream. He turned to her and glared.

"Sorry," she smiled. "Automatic I'm afraid." His glare turned to a grin, he'd done it himself so many times, the flushing action is so ingrained that the only way he can stop it is to repeat over and over 'Don't flush.' Even that doesn't always work, then he just has to wait for the cistern to fill before he turns the shower on, today not so lucky. He stands back out of the flow as the triton stutters then slowly comes back to full force, Jackie steps in to get under the falling water. He grabs her gently by the arm and pulls her towards himself, squashing her large breasts against his chest.

"It's fucking with you," he said gently, reaching down and grabbing her ass.

"What do you mean?"

"It's sort of achieved a balance, but as soon as the cistern stops filling, or more accurately when it slows right down, the shower is going to lose it again and go freezing cold."

"Thanks for the warning," she wriggled her soft body against his.

"Woman you have to go to work," he laughed.

"But you're just so squeezable," she showed him just how. The shower gave another surge, then settled down.

"Shower is ready now," his smile made her giggle, as she turned away from him and pressed her ass against him.

"If you wake him up again, then you'll be late for work," he said, as she pushed back against him.

"Yes, but you feel so good pushed up against my ass," she glanced over her shoulder then stepped under the falling water. Roaddog helped to wash her, if only to get the task finished as soon as he could. Soon she was washed, rinsed and helped out of the bath, she picked up a towel from the floor and started to dry herself, she found some toothpaste on the sink and scrubbed her teeth with a finger. This finished, she dropped the towel to the floor again.

"You go make the coffees; I'll be down in a little while to make breakfast." he called from behind the curtain.

"OK." she answered, looking down at the clothes she had worn yesterday, and thinking, 'Stuff it, not yet.' She went to the bedroom to get the cups they had used the night before and went down to the kitchen. She'd been in there briefly the night before, but only to grab a coffee and retire to the lounge, the only thing she actually remembered were his hot blue eyes. This time she had chance to get a look around. Plate and knife in the sink, crumbs on the cutting board, he had toast for breakfast yesterday, but no evidence of anything older. She filled the kettle and looked around for the makings. Jars on the counter near the kettle. She was quite surprised as to exactly how clean and tidy the place was. She walked over to the fridge, thinking about the contents. Was this going to be a guy's fridge? She opened the door and took the milk from the door, two pint, semi-skimmed, and half full. As the kettle kicked off Roaddog walked in through the door, as naked as she was. He smiled as she was pouring the water into the cups, he opened one of the cupboards and pulled out a large brown plastic box. He opened the lid and she saw that the box was full of first aid supplies. Roaddog slowly removed the waterproof dressing off his upper left arm, no rush, though he trusted Slowball's stitching, he didn't want to put it under too much stress. The wound gradually appeared, a little hardened blood around some of the stitches, and at the ends of the cut, but nothing to worry about. No redness, no swelling, no hot spots. He soaked a chunk of cotton wool in TCP and wiped carefully around the wound. He got a replacement dressing from the bottom of the box and laid it on the worktop.

"That looks good," he said, "breakfast?"

"What you offering?" she asked stepping up to kiss him softly, then examining the injury.

"I was thinking, hash browns, I've got some in the freezer, bacon, eggs, and I've got some great mushrooms."

"A monster fried breakfast?" she asked.

"Why not? You're working all day and I got some shit I need to do. Thinking of one of the things I have to do." He reached up into the cupboard that had contained the first-aid box, down came a tall container marked spaghetti. She frowned a question, this hadn't been on the breakfast menu at all. He grinned and twisted the lid off the container and passed it to her. She looked inside and laughed loudly.

"Take your pick," he said. "If you're planning on coming back leave it in the bathroom, if not, throw it in the bin and I'll cry all afternoon." She picked a pink handled toothbrush from the tin, and pulled it from its packaging, passed the tin back to Roaddog and went to brush her teeth properly. He watched as her ass jiggled from side to side down the hallway, then watched her breasts bounce as she started up the stairs, he shook his head and turned to the task of cooking. When she returned to the kitchen things were proceeding apace. Hash browns in one frying pan with four large mushrooms, bacon cooking off in another and a third pan heating up for the eggs. She stepped in close and fingered the pinafore he was wearing, it looked like a very short French maids' outfit with quite a prominent bulge in the front.

"I learned a while ago," he said. "Don't fry bacon or eggs naked, it can cause some painful burns. It's not going to cause any major damage, but it can sting like a bastard." She laughed but moved far enough away from the cooker, not wishing any of the damage for herself either. From the other end of the kitchen she stared more at his backside than the food cooking. It didn't take long before food was being portioned out onto plates, from a rack near the sink came two cushion trays, just perfect for eating food while sitting in a comfy chair.

Roaddog gave one tray to Jackie and picked up the other.

"Follow me," he said, leading the way into the front room, he waved Jackie into the big chair, and he took the sofa. A few seconds with the remote and music was playing softly again.

"You should have drawn the curtains," she said. "People can see in."

"You're beautiful, I'm beautiful, people need more beauty in their lives. If they don't then they can look away." He laughed as a woman walked past the window, she glanced in. Looked away then looked back again.

"I think she's hungry," laughed Roaddog. Jackie looked round as the woman passed from view, then she laughed.

"I'll take you home then I think I'll swing by Braconash, see what's happening there."

"Is that wise? Someone could be watching the place. The police if no one else."

"We have cops as witnesses that we were at Rivington, don't forget."

"But why take the chance? Something like this will be in the newspapers tomorrow."

"There should be information out there already." He picked up the remote and in a short while, local reports were flashing up the screen, "chemical fire", said one article. "Industrial unit fire," said another. "Meth processing plant torched in turf war," said a third. There were lots of video streams of the raging fire, some from fixed cameras, some from drones. Finally, he selected the third link and followed through to a video news report. The reporter was facing the camera with a smoking ruin behind him.

"Here we have a once quiet Lancashire town, famous for its buses and military vehicles, today its peace was shattered as the building behind me was set on fire. Sources within local law enforcement suggest that this was a crystal meth factory, which explains the way it burned, there are many volatile and dangerous chemicals used in this process. Luckily there was no one killed, at least not this time. It is believed that this could be the start of a major turf war between opposing groups of drug dealers. How many lives have to be ruined? How many need to die? Before the police do something about these dangerous people in our small town. This is the question I shall be asking, and I shall keep on asking it until I get the answers that we deserve."

"That guys a complete ass," said Roaddog.

"But is he wrong?"

"Definitely. Meth comes from Liverpool mainly, and judging by the stability of the street price, supply is not an issue. Had it been a Meth lab, there would have been nothing left but a crater in the ground. It's relatively cheap and easy to make, but the risks are immense."

"I was more thinking about the turf war aspect, if word gets out then we could be in the middle of it."

"The angels won't talk; they just made a major score. This reporter is just after something exciting to say about Easter in Lancashire, nothing ever happens here."

"Where did he get that moustache?" giggled Jackie.

"He's just borrowed it from Ron Jeremy."

"Who's he?"

"The paradigm of nineteen seventies porn. Him and John Holmes."

"Never really been a fan of porn, you know?"

"Well, I suppose not, but maybe in the future when you get a little bored and lonely, you could give it a look, you never know it might just turn you on."

"Why would I need some moustachioed fool when I've got you?"

"There is that," he laughed.

"So, you'll stay away from that burned out shell?"

"Of course. Wouldn't want to attract attention, given that reporters stupidity the place is going to be crawling with cops. Their little CSI vans will be there, digging through the ashes."

"I've seen those little vans all over the place. Nothing like on the TV," she laughed.

"Wouldn't be much of a TV show if it was true to life for the Lancashire Constabulary. Boring guy called George, gets out of his little white van, with his little toolbox, scrapes a few things, snaps a few pictures and fucks off. Not much to watch."

"You forgot the dusting for fingerprints."

"Yes I did, that's just so exciting," he laughed. "If you've finished your breakfast, I'll take you home then daddy can take you to work."

"That means I have to put on yesterday's clothes," she frowned.

"I'm prepared to take you home naked; it'll be a bit chilly, and I'm sure that mummy won't approve."

"You are crazy," she laughed and stood up, holding her tray in front of her. He did the same and then led the way into the kitchen.

Once there he took the plates and scrapped off the leftovers and dropped the plates into the sink, she stood back to watch him at work, it was only moments before the plates and the frying pans were all stacked on the drainer, he took the cups as well.

"Time for a brew?" he asked.

"A quick one," she replied.

"And a brew?"

"Behave," she laughed.

"Never," he smiled. He filled the kettle and set it to boil. He was only a few strides behind her, and he got to watch her climb the stairs ahead of him. Her ass swaying from side to side. It only took a few minutes for them both to get dressed and return to the kitchen, where he made more coffee, and they returned to their seats in the front room, where the music was still playing, and the news was scrolling on the TV. There was no more news of the fire, they talked for a short time about the evening ahead, the plan was that the whole club would be at the pub for a meeting before closing time and he would take her home, either to hers or his. It didn't seem like any time at all, before they were getting dressed to leave. He set the alarms on his way out, and the same for the garage once the bike was out in the alleyway. Once they were mounted, he set off. Straight across the town, Jackie was amazed at the lack of time it took him to get from one side of Leyland to the other, he pulled up outside her house and killed the motor, she dismounted. Took off her helmet and kissed her fingers, passing them inside his helmet so he could kiss them. With a smile she turned to the house and walked towards the door, swaying her hips far more than necessary. Roaddog laughed aloud as he fired up the big V-twin. With a roar he was gone. He carved through the light Monday morning traffic considerably faster than when he had been carrying Jackie. He overtook two cars on the main roundabout, and carved up the front one as he pulled off the roundabout, his left foot peg striking plumes of sparks from the tarmac as he accelerated hard, the light ahead was green, the tail of the Harley squirmed under heavy braking as he slowed down to make the right turn before the lights went against him. This time it was the right-hand peg striking sparks. He was really starting to enjoy himself. The adrenaline riding high and pushing his heartrate faster. Climbing the hill past the railway station accelerating hard, the Harley howling, he knew that he should be slowing down for the mini roundabout, but he didn't, the car coming into the roundabout saw him at the last moment and stopped hard three feet over the give way line. Roaddog snapped the throttle wide open and tore across the roundabout, the small white hump in the road forced the Harley up into the air, if only briefly, both tyres hit the ground at the same time and the suspension eased out the shocks and Roaddog laughed. He started to slow down, closing the throttle slowly, by the time he passed the Rose pub he was almost down to the legal limit. He pulled up on the pavement outside his house and rolled the bike backwards between the gateposts, he kicked the side stand down and shut off the motor. The weight of the bike fell onto the stand a car with blue and yellow squares pulled up in front of his house.

'They can't have seen me; they are far too late for that.' He smiled, and slowly removed his helmet. He stood up and stepped over the bike, dropping his helmet on the right-hand mirror. He walked to the gate and met the policemen as they were coming toward him.

"Morning officers, looking for someone?"

"If you live here, then you," said the blonde cop.

"Then you've found me, now that was hard," he laughed.

"Can we go inside, there has been a complaint?"

"No worries," Roaddog turned to the front door, and went in, after disarming the alarms he waved the policemen in. "First door on the left gentlemen." He followed them in. "Please take a seat." The two cops selected seats and left Roaddog with the one he had been sitting in earlier. "Now gentlemen. What is the nature of this complaint? Music too loud?"

"This is more serious than that, the complaint is of indecent exposure."

"That's interesting."

"Interesting? I tell that we have evidence," said the cop with brown curly hair.

"That's even more interesting. Please tell me what you have."

"We have pictures of you sitting naked in that very chair," said the blond.

"I was having breakfast; it was very good. And my girlfriend, equally naked was sitting exactly where you are."

"That's right," said curly. "she's not in the stills, but is in the video, and she's naked too."

"Even more interesting. Any chance of seeing this evidence?"

"Here," said blonde, opening a laptop and it powered up immediately, showing a picture of Roaddog sitting with his breakfast on his lap.

"That's a fairly bad picture, probably a cheap phone, and as you can see nothing visible there to cause any offence."

"What about this?" said blonde, starting a video clip. This showed quite clearly, Roaddog and Jackie, getting up from their seats and walking into the kitchen. Sure enough Roaddog's genitals were barely visible in the dark below his breakfast tray.

"Now that's a much better shot, and judging by that dark blur on the right hand edge, I'd say the camera was in that alley across the road, making it about a hundred feet away, so for a shot like that, you have to be looking at a two hundred and fifty or three hundred millimetre lens." He paused for a moment. "Sorry guys no case to answer here."

"You think you can get this thrown out of court?" asked curly.

"And I wouldn't need a brief to do it, I could defend this one all on my own. Though I am sure the BNA will help me with a lawyer should I need one."

"The who?" asked blonde.

"The British Naturists Association, but I don't need them."

"Why not?" asked blonde.

"It is up to you gentlemen to prove some sort of intent on my part. Intent to frighten, harass, or embarrass. You may find that exceptionally hard to do."

"She's got a clear shot of you with your todger hanging out," said curly.

"So, it was a woman, I remember seeing her going towards the main road. So, she went to the main road, then came back and took stills on her crappy phone, then she went home, and was so frightened, embarrassed, and harassed that she got the good camera and the long lens, then set up in that alleyway. That sounds really frightened to me. Add to that the fact that I was completely unaware of her presence, so there can be no intent." The two cops looked at each other for a moment, then Roaddog carried on. "There is something far more important for you to look into."

"What do you mean?" asked blonde.

"Well, I have come to believe that someone is taking photographs and video of me inside my house, where I have a right to privacy under the human rights legislation, this person or persons as yet unknown have been broadcasting these images without my consent. Not only that but you already have the evidence, which should make things easier for you. Given the facts that you already have, I think this case is definitely provable." The two cops just looked at each other in disbelief.

"Come on guys. Let's get the paperwork started, this one will be a real feather in your caps, human rights prosecution, how many of your buddies can boast that sort of thing?"

"None," said blonde. "But she's a really nice lady."

"So nice she peeks into people's windows?" The cops were silent for a long moment.

"Alternative," said Roaddog. "Tell nosey woman that if she points a camera at my house again, I will make the complaint and you will have to prosecute her. How does that sound?" The cops exchanged looks for a while.

"That sounds reasonable to me." said blonde.

"And me." said curly.

"Something else you could tell her, if she wants to take pictures of naked people, or people having sex I can probably put her in touch with some who are looking for a good cameraman. All she has to do is knock on my door."

"Somehow I don't think she'll go for that," laughed blonde.

"Whatever." said Roaddog. "If you tell her to drop it, then that's an easy day for you. If she doesn't drop it, then it's going to get complicated, and she could end up with jail time. The choice is hers, make sure she makes the right choice."

"We'll do that, and you'll hear from us in due course." said blonde getting to his feet, curly only half a second behind, the two started walking to the door as Roaddog rose to usher them out. As they got to the front door. Roaddog spoke again.

"Once more question guys, not exactly law related if I may?"

"Go ahead," said curly.

"The guy that decides which cops go out on the road together, is he pushing sixty years old."

"Yes," said blonde. "Why?"

"Well, there was a cop show from the seventies, and I am sorry to say that you are Hutch, and you," he pointed at curly, "are Starsky. That guy's got a wicked sense of humour."

"Actually," said Hutch. "The old bastard not only put us on the same team but christened us Starsky and Hutch. That show was one of my dad's favourites."

"Sometimes life can be real strange," smiled Roaddog.

"Thanks," said Starsky. "We'll go and see the woman now, and make the options clear for her, if she insists, then we'll be back to take your statement. OK?"

"Definitely officers. Thanks for being so understanding, privacy is important."

"You could try using the curtains," laughed Hutch.

"Where's the fun in that?"

The cops got in their car and drove away.

16: Easter Monday Morning and mining

Roaddog smiled as the cops drove away, he went into the kitchen and made himself another cup of coffee. Then he went into the back-room downstairs. The electronics was humming away nicely, the air conditioner was blowing cold air into the intakes of the hardware. He woke the PC and ran a quick system check; everything was in the green. The rack of sixteen ASIC's was blowing hot air into the AC, to be cooled and returned to the intake fans. One unit was showing a slightly elevated temperature, a quick check showed that its intake fan was slightly clogged. He took it offline for a minute to clean the fan of the accumulated dust, then back into operation it went. The battery racks for the solar power units were showing slightly lower than expected but it was still early in the day, they were still filling, if only slowly, so the miners weren't actually using power from the grid. Given the weather forecast they probably wouldn't until tomorrow morning. He checked the light meter positioned on the roof, the power return from the panels was a little low, most likely they were a little dusty, not enough to be worth getting the hose out and cleaning them. The pool had hit three blocks overnight, his reward 0.1 Bitcoins, at current price that's about eight hundred pounds. Not bad for a night having sex with a hot girl. He laughed aloud at the thought, but it could be days before he got another hit, the hardware had cost him nothing, the aircon unit the same, the solar panels installed by a government grant, and they were paying him for the amount of electricity his panels generated. The extra panels he'd tagged on to the system on his garage roof had cost him almost nothing, the extra controllers the same, the only real expense in the whole system was the two additional battery packs, that said profits are extremely variable, but currently he's doing OK. On an average month he turns fifty percent of his bitcoin into sterling and leaves the rest. He drops his phone into the docking station beside his mining PC, the security software picks it up and flashes up the usual warning. He types in the security password and hits the encryption key. Passwords for wallets and banks are changed in a heartbeat, and all devices are synced in a moment, he checks for the word from the hidden phone. Gets the response from the phone in the floor safe, encryption complete. Now even if he loses his phone and his computer, he still has access to his banks and his crypto wallet. His thumbprint opens the safe and he checks the charge state of the phone, he drops into the dock to give it a charge, within the hour it will be good for another ten days at least. Finally satisfied that everything is running fine he takes his cup into the kitchen, thinking about another coffee, and notices the first-aid box still on the worktop. The un-used dressing still on top of it, he pulls up his t-shirt sleeve and checks the wound, after a moment's thought he wipes it around with the TCP infused cotton and put the new dressing on it.

"Should have done that before I went out." He mumbled to himself, then thought about the cops, had they seen it? They'd not mentioned it, so probably not. He returned his first-aid box to its place in the cupboard, then thought about what he was going to do with the rest of the day. He didn't plan on going into the shop, he knew it would be closed today, the guys won't start arriving until about six o'clock, and then after a few beers on to the Railway for the meeting. It could be in interesting day. He thought for a while about doing some work on the bike, but that was something he usually left for quiet times at the shop. Finally, the decision was made, quiet day, sit watch some TV, drink coffee, and just relax. He went into the front room and fired up the TV, the biggest question on his mind was what to watch, he wanted something that easy and different, but required only the suspension of belief and some small attention. Flicking through the list of favourites he finally dropped on to an American TV show, True Blood, that would do. 'Damn that girl's got great tits.' He thought laughing, bouncing down the menus he found the last one he had seen. "Was I drunk? Do I remember?" He muttered, deciding that he may have been the first and probably didn't the second. So, he hit the play button and settled down on the sofa, as the opening scene started to play, he hit the pause, and picked up his phone, he punched in the tracker app, and cast it to the TV. The marker popped up in the centre of the TV, travelling west towards Blackpool.

"Either being a bank holiday tourist or making a delivery." He selected the menu, and hit the history tab. A map appeared on the screen, the blue line traced a complex path but went nowhere near Leyland, so it hadn't been to Braconash, which was good. He dropped the app and went back to the TV. Sookie was riding her dead lover, tit's bouncing merrily. Roaddog smiled to himself. Out of the corner of his eye he was a shape move across the front of the house and turn onto the path. He hit the mute on the audio and went to the door. Through the frosted glass he saw a shape, it stood there, as if uncertain whether to actually knock. He waited, until the shape made up its mind, the knock was still echoing in the entryway when he opened the door. To reveal a woman in a long brown coat, she gasped and stepped back. He tipped his head to the left and smiled.

"Yes?" he asked softly.

"Er."

"Go on, spit it out."

"First," her voice stumbled on that word; it didn't do much better with the following. "First, I'm sorry for taking pictures of you in your house. I didn't realise it was illegal." His eyebrows rose slowly.

"Second?" his smiled broadened to see her struggling so.

"I don't have a second, and actually have no idea where to go from here."

"How about inside for a polite chat and a coffee?"

"Do you have tea?"

"I'm sure I can find you something you'll like. Please follow me." He turned away and walked slowly towards kitchen, he paused briefly waiting to hear her shoes on the tiles, the click of heels, and the clunk of the door closing, he started walking again. He went straight into the kitchen and put the kettle on, then he turned to see her in the doorway.

"Any specials that you'd like? I got, Earl Grey, Lapsang, Darjeeling?"

"Just tea." her voice soft.

"It's a bit late, but English breakfast?"

"Fine. You're a strange man."

"You are not the first to suggest that. Did Starsky and Hutch explain things to you."

"Oh, don't, I nearly peed myself when they knocked on the door. I more than half expected to see that colt stuffed in the back of Starsky's pants."

"You remember?"

"Yes, Hutch had a Python in a shoulder holster."

"You know your guns?"

"Dad was a gun fan, until the damned cops took his handguns away."

"How old are you?"

"That's not the sort of question a gentleman should ask."

"Well, gentleman I ain't." laughed Roaddog as the kettle kicked off, he filled the cups, then poured the milk in. He passed her the one with tea in it.

"Let's go sit somewhere comfortable." He walked past her, and she followed him into the front room. He waved her to the chair and took a place on the sofa for himself. She glanced up at the TV just as Sookie slumped forwards onto vampire Bill.

"What are you watching?"

"It's a TV series called 'True Blood'; you avoided my question."

"Fine I'm forty, I was nineteen when they changed the gun laws. Dad was so pissed. All because of some asshole in Scotland."

"I forget his name, but the town was Dunblane."

"My turn. How old are you?"

"Thirty some. So, I do remember, but not clearly. Did your dad let you shoot his guns?"

"Yes, I actually loved that 1911 that Starsky had, it was so easy to shoot, but it had a hell of a kick."

"Especially when you're a teenage girl?" laughed Roaddog.

"Definitely, but I could strip it down and rebuild it in 45 seconds."

"Is that fast?"

"Yes."

"I bet daddies hobby made boyfriends difficult?"

"It certainly sorted the serious from shit heads."

"How many ran on the spot?"

"Only a couple."

"So, when did you take up photography?"

"That was recent. Just before my cheating bastard of a husband left. Thinking about it it's probably for the best that they changed the gun laws, because I'd have stuffed that 1911 in his mouth and blown his head off, after I'd shot off his cheating cock of course," she laughed.

"Kids?" he asked, her smile vanished.

"No, that was part of the problem, some of my bits don't work too well, and I found out that he wasn't working nights, but not until his brood mare was on his second."

"Shit, that sucks."

"Yes, I got the house and a reasonable settlement."

"No guy in your life then?"

"No."

"Girl?"

"No," she laughed, "I've never actually tried that sort of thing."

"Perhaps you should."

"I don't know, I've always been partial to a good-sized dick."

"I've never tried that," laughed Roaddog.

"Did you really threaten to report me?" she asked softly.

"Yes."

"Starsky was quite clear that you hadn't broken any laws, but I had."

"He is correct."

"I wasn't aware of the regulations."

"That is no surprise, so many people are surprised by the actual rules."

"He also said something else. Was that a joke?"

"No. You walked past my bike, I'm a member of a motorcycle club. Some of the members can only be described as exhibitionists. If you want, I could put you in touch."

"I don't think so, I was simply taking pictures of someone I thought was breaking the law, and I know how much the cops like their CCTV," she laughed.

"You're not wrong there. They love their CCTV. Gives them hours of entertainment with no risk."

"Starsky mentioned the BNA, are you a member?"

"No, but they didn't know that."

"Are you a naturist?"

"Not as such, but equally I don't see what the issue is, we're all human."

"Yes, but certain parts are regarded as private."

"Why? It comes in two basic styles, and they're all much of a muchness."

"So why are you dressed now?"

"It gets chilly on the bike at any sort of speed, I've had visits from cops and now a complete stranger."

"How can I be a stranger? I've seen you naked."

"You're a stranger because you still haven't told me your name."

"I'm Sylvia, pleased to meet you," she laughed.

"I'm known as Roaddog. Likewise."

"So now we are no longer strangers, are you going to get your kit off?"

"Are you going to join me?"

"That I'm not sure about."

"Well let me know when you are," he smiled.

"Just how crazy are your biker friends?"

"Some very, some not so much. People are all different, you could come and meet some if you want, we're busy tonight, and the shop will be closed tomorrow, but we'll be open on Wednesday, there's usually a few guys around, and some of the girls. Just don't point a camera at them our you'll have more tits than on your garden feeders," he laughed loudly.

"You're kidding?"

"No, the girls do like to get their breasts out, and other parts sometimes." he thought about Man-Dare and the camera van and smiled even more.

"Well, I have to admit that things have been a little quiet for me since I kicked that no good husband out. I may just take you up on that, I'm not working Wednesday."

"Can't guarantee it will be exciting, but there's usually something going on. There's always customers to talk to, if nothing else."

"It has been sort of difficult to make new friends, I think it's my age."

"Nothing wrong with your age, it's just that it can be hard to move on from a failed relationship. I've seen it too many times."

"Your own relationships?"

"No, I generally don't have any issues moving on."

"I'm not sure what your biker friends are going to think of an old woman like me hanging around."

"I wouldn't worry about it, some of them are real old. Anyway, you're not that old."

"I'm over forty."

"It's only a number. Some people are old by the time they are twenty. Old isn't a number it's a state of mind."

"You think your friends would be glad to meet me?"

"Always, it's good to meet new people, it's not easy sometimes."

"I've found that since I've been single."

"You never know you may want to take up with one of them, or maybe two." Roaddog laughed.

"I'm fairly sure I'm not up to sharing, if you know what I mean."

"I do. Don't knock it until you've tried it."

"Have you?"

"Yes. It was fun for a while."

"Did it end well?"

"These things almost never end well, but in this case actually yes, it ended fine."

"You really do live differently from the rest of us."

"Again, don't knock it."

"I'm still a little confused by the naturist thing, what's it all about?"

"When you see someone in the street do you judge them on their clothing?"

"I suppose."

"Naturists wear no clothes. So, you can only judge them on their words and their actions. In many settings they only have first names as well. The lifestyle is still frowned on in many professions."

"I can sort of understand that, I suppose cameras aren't allowed?"

"Only with everyone's permission."

"I never heard of a nudist place anywhere near here."

"You'd be surprised there's a club on the road to Liverpool, not well publicised, nor well known, but it is there."

"How do you know all this?"

"I've been there, it's nice, they've got a pool, and some open grassland, surrounded by forests. It's lovely."

"So, you're not bothered about being seen naked?"

"No, to be honest I don't understand why anyone is."

"I'm not sure I could do that."

"It can be a big step for some people, but it is very liberating, or at least I found it so."

"You talk a good talk, but I don't think I'm going to go down that road, I'm too frightened."

"Your choice, I would never pressure anyone, it's a very personal choice to make."

"Even though I knew you were naked this morning, I was so surprised when you just stood up and walked out of this room."

"What did you expect?"

"I don't know, I sort of expected you to pay some attention to the window, but you made no attempt to cover anything."

"I saw no reason to, even if you'd been standing in front of the window with your camera I wouldn't. If you want to watch then feel free, it means nothing to me."

"But so many people would be embarrassed."

"Not me, I'm not like everyone else."

"I've noticed that. I'm still not sure how to take you."

"Any way you want. You'll find that I'm a simple sort of guy, I don't really worry about what people think of me, there is nothing I can do to control that, so I don't let it bother me."

"I wish I could be like that."

"It's not that difficult, once you accept that people will think what they want."

"You make it sound so easy."

"It can be, but you have to secure within yourself. So many people these days value themselves on what others think. It's not the best way to live your own life, you end up living the way others want you to."

"You don't do that."

"Of course not. How many people are there in this world that you really care about?"

"I don't know, there's a few, family and friends, quite a few."

"No, narrow that down, how many would you take a bullet for, and how many would take a bullet for you?"

"Maybe two or three."

"Those are the ones that count, the rest aren't important."

"You mean that these are the ones whose opinion should count, not all the rest?"

"Something like that, and not. If any of these suddenly decided to be naturists and refused to wear clothes, would you stop visiting them?"

"Shit. You're good with the hard questions, aren't you? No, I'd not stop but I might try to change their minds."

"How hard would you push them to change?"

"Not hard, it's their life after all."

"And they will think the same of you. These are the people that matter, not the others, the ones that want to make you in their own image. All you can do is be yourself."

"I think I get it," she laughed loudly.

"Go on, share that one."

"I just got a picture of sitting in my brothers living room, while him and his wife are naked, it's going to be hard to maintain eye contact, with his dick hanging out."

"You'd be surprised how easy it gets and how quickly it does it. Less than half an hour and you won't even notice."

"Oh, my god."

"What now?"

"My nephew, he's a big guy, I've seen the bulge in his jeans, it's enormous."

"Here's something else for you to think about, maybe it's you that does that to him?"

"You can't think that. He's my nephew for god's sake."

"He's a teenage boy, I remember being that, and almost anything gets a guy hard."

"You think he sees me as 'hot auntie Sylvia'?"

"Could be, I can certainly see why."

"But I'm far too old for him."

"No you're not. Judging from what you have said, you're not too old to look either," he laughed at her discomfort.

"Come on, it's difficult not to notice. He either wears tight, and I do mean tight, jeans, or baggy tracksuits. Either way it's easy to tell that he's turned on by something."

"There is a way to be sure."

"I'm not sure what you are suggesting."

"Invite him round to help with something, changing the curtains, or clearing the attic, something like that. Then watch him, if he's hard all day then it's you that's doing it to him."

"That's cruel."

"Oh, it's that too, but he'll love to spend the day with you, no matter what you are doing."

"I'm not sure I want to know."

"I don't believe that is exactly true, you already know you just don't want the proof."

"If it is me that he wants, then it would just be too wicked to do that to him, to get him hard all day then kick him out."

"How about you offer him a shower before he goes home, then catch him while he's jacking off, because he'll not be able to resist the opportunity in the place where you are so often naked."

"That's an even more wicked idea. I thought you were a pervert when I took photos of you this morning, but now I'm certain. That's immoral and illegal."

"Agreed," Roaddog smiled. "I do like to use the laws when they are in my favour, by the current mores and laws of society definitely wrong, but this has not always been so. Back in history it was not unusual for elder relatives to teach youngsters about sex. Even nowadays much of the taboo is without real cause, pregnancies can easily be avoided, and the genetic errors caused by such need no longer occur."

"Are you trying to get me to have sex with my nephew?"

"No, I point out an option that you could both enjoy, if he can be trusted to keep his mouth shut, and of course he has to understand that a long term relationship is so fraught with dangers that it would be extremely ill advised."

"And what would my brother think about this?"

"Older, or younger?"

"Younger, three years. What difference does it make?"

"Not much really. You were almost certainly his first real crush, to find that his own son has had sex with you would most likely make him both proud and jealous as hell."

"You really are crazy."

"Does your brother have any other children?"

"No. Why?"

"Because you are most likely your nephews first crush, after his mother of course."

"You really are full of crazy ideas," Sylvia smiled.

"That is also true."

"There is no way I am going to risk my relationship with my brother."

"I have another idea, it's getting on for lunch time, you fancy a ride and a beer?"

"You expect me to get on a motorcycle with a madman like you?"

"Why not? It could be fun, and a new experience for you?"

"It'd be new, that's for sure. But would it be safe?"

"Nothing in this world is safe. Riding with me is no more dangerous than crossing the road, and you've already risked that twice today."

"How do you know I've crossed the road twice?"

"You went out for a Sunday paper, the paper shop is across the main road, I don't count these little roads, damned twenty mile an hour limits mean they aren't roads."

"I know what you mean, about the roads that is. I'm not at all sure about riding on a motorcycle."

"With me you are perfectly safe, you'll probably even enjoy it."

"It's Easter Monday the roads will be packed."

"Only for the cage drivers, not even busy for me," Roaddog laughed.

"Cage drivers?"

"Cars, cages that blunder along the roads, with people trapped inside them."

"I get it," she paused for a while staring into his eyes. "Ok, I'll ride with you. Just don't let my brother find out," she laughed.

"Why?"

"He has more issues with motorcycles than I do, most likely he just doesn't want his son to ride them."

"Well, I'll not tell him if you don't. I have a spare helmet, should be OK for you, you're not dressed too well for the road, but you'll be OK so long as it doesn't rain." He picked up the TV remote and punched up the weather forecast. "The weathermen say it should stay fine for the rest of the day." He stood up and collected the cups, taking them into the kitchen and dropping them in the sink. He reached up on top of one of the high cupboards and pulled down an old open face helmet. She was surprised when he gave it a sniff. Then he reached into one of the cupboards and removed an aerosol can, gave the helmet a quick squirt and waved it around.

"It's not been used for a while." He showed her the can. She read the label, helmet sanitiser and freshener.

"Is that actually a thing?"

"Oh yes. In a hot sweaty summer, this is actually essential," he laughed, then passed her the helmet. She just looked at it. So, he took it back, put it on her head, and tightened the strap, checked it for motion and tightened it some more. This time it didn't move when he pulled on it.

"It's got to be tight, or it's useless." He waved her out of the kitchen and put on his own gear. He went to the front door with his gloves in his hands, he set the alarm and closed the door. He thumbed the starter and the motor started on the first turn. It settled into that steady beat. He gave her the normal instructions and she seemed to understand. She mounted up with ease and he rolled forwards onto the road. The drop down the curb caused Sylvia to grip him at the waist, he smiled. He waited at the end of the road for a long gap to make his right turn into, then he was off. Smooth and easy, by the time he arrived at the first roundabout he could hardly tell that she was behind him, easing through on the green light he wound on the power gently, overtaking a string of cars before the railway bridge made the road too narrow. Over the crest the solid white centrelines did little to slow him down, but he dropped into the traffic before they got to the roundabout, this complex was just too crazy to be tearing through. He stayed in the traffic, past the right turn into the local tip, sure enough the car in front turned without indication, he just shook his head and carried on into the roundabout, held up by the traffic lights he waited patiently. Once the lights changed, he was off, running wide on the exit of the roundabout he blew passed the three cars like they were standing still, not a twitch from Sylvia, once on the straight section he reached down and squeezed her knee, more to be sure she was actually there than to reassure her. Traffic lights, and roundabouts came and went, the only thing that slowed him down was a police car going the other way, a quick flash of the blue lights and he backed off, but only until he could be sure that the car hadn't turned about at the roundabout to follow them. They went all the way around Leyland, and left onto the Crosston road, passed the blue painted Elephant, and on through a couple more turns, before Roaddog slowed down and entered a pub carpark, he rolled into an empty space between a jaguar and a range rover. He smiled to himself as he turned and told Sylvia to get off. He helped her to remove her helmet, then did his own.

"Are you aware of the saying pork chop and bar-mitzvah?" he asked, a big grin on his face.

"I understand what that means."

"Well, that is how popular we are going to be in this place, the food is excellent, and the beer is great, but the clientele tend to be more than a little snobbish. It's a real twinset and pearls establishment."

"You couldn't find somewhere nice for us to go?"

"This is nice, there used to be pubs that catered to bikers, but with the drink driving laws most of us don't drink enough to make our own boozers worthwhile. We can expect a certain level of resistance once we get inside. It will only be as extreme as looks, or glares, the trick is to take no shit from these people, their opinion of us is of no importance."

"I understand. A laugh in their faces is like a smack round the head."

"You've done this sort of thing before?"

"Yes, on occasion."

"There is one important thing you must remember."

"Go on."

"Damn, your ass looks good in those jeans." He laughed and took her hand as they walked towards the front entrance, laughing together. As they arrived at the door, she pressed her shoulder against him and looked up into his eyes.

"You're mad, you know that?" she whispered, he only smiled in response. In through the doors they went and turned right to the bar.

Roaddog walked along the bar and squeezed in between two men, with a flash of the eyes he attracted the attention of the barman.

"Do you have a reservation?" asked the barman.

"No we don't, but if you've got a table with a long enough lead on it, we'll have a quick meal," smiled Roaddog. The barman consulted the book on top of the bar for a moment before speaking.

"I have a table for two not needed until two o'clock."

"Call that a recover."

"Drinks?" asked the barman.

"I'll have sheep." said Roaddog glancing at the pump clips.
"And for the lady?"
"I'll have tortoise, pint," smiled Sylvia.
"Your table is that one in the corner. I'll bring your drinks over in a moment."
"We have to wait until one o'clock for our table," mumbled one of the men at the bar.
"Life's a bitch," said Roaddog.
"Then you marry one," said Sylvia, as they turned towards their newly acquired table. They had barely taken their seats when the barman walked up, he placed a pint of slowly settling golden beer in front of Roaddog and a large tulip shaped glass of sparkling lager in front of Sylvia. She smiled at him and lifted the glass and toasted the scowling faces at the bar.
"I'll be back in a couple of minutes to take your food orders, Sunday menus by the way." laughed the barman.
Roaddog passed a menu to Sylvia and opened one for himself. The choices were limited, but nothing unusual for a country pub on a Sunday. The choices were made quickly, before the barman even came back the decisions had been made.
"You really like to create a stir wherever you go, don't you?" asked Sylvia.
"It gives the boring old farts something to talk about. Those smelly bikers that turned up in our pub, I was going to give them a piece of my mind, but the wife wouldn't let me. You know the sort of thing?"
"I can imagine," laughed Sylvia as the barman came back.
"What would you like to eat?" he asked.
"I'll have the roast beef," said Roaddog.
"Fish and chips for me," said Sylvia.
"Anything else?"
"No," said Roaddog. "Quick bite then back on the road, we've got things to do today."
"Speak for yourself," laughed Sylvia. "I'm going to have to explain why I had cop cars parked outside my house this morning. Nosey neighbours."
"Tell 'em to fuck off," laughed Roaddog.
"Your food will be ready in a short while. Thank you," said the barman as he turned away smiling.

17: Easter Monday Lunch and conversations

Lunch went quickly with polite chatter, despite the increasingly angry stares from the guys by the bar. They finished the food in a rapid but leisurely manner. As he had told her, the food was excellent. His beef was perfect, her fish she did actually complain about a little, it was just so big, the plates were quite large, and the fish hung off both ends. Once they had finished, Roaddog, got up and took their empty glasses to the bar. The barman walked up.

"Same again?" he asked.

"No, I'll have the forty-one deep."

"It's a nice light IPA, I'll bring them over if you want." Roaddog looked at the clock.

"Thanks, but no, I'll settle up and we'll get out of your way."

"No problem, how was the food?"

"Excellent as always, I should recommend this place to a few friends." He smiled and glanced at the man still waiting at the bar. The barman printed out a receipt for Roaddog and passed it to him. After a moment he glanced at the barman and nodded, a quick tap of the card against the keypad and the transaction was complete. Roaddog picked up the beers and went back to the table.

"Sylvia, you bring the lids, we'll go sit outside, weathers nice," she smiled and stood up from the table, taking both helmets she followed him out. They took seats at one of the picnic tables facing the road. Traffic running past at some speed. A heavy roar filled the air, and a tractor flew passed pulling a heavy trailer, one of those potholes in the road that the council should have fixed a while ago caused the trailer to bump, and a big fat carrot bounced out and landed on the table between the drinks. Sylvia jumped and choked a scream before it was fully formed.

"Hungry?" asked Roaddog picking up the carrot.

"No," she laughed. He tossed in into the road for the next vehicle to pulverise.

"What are you doing with the rest of the day?" she asked.

"I've got a few things to do, then the club has a meeting this evening, it'll be late before I get home, I'm not sure if the girlfriend will be staying tonight or not."

"Should I set up the camera again?" Sylvia smiled.

"If you want, I make no guarantees as to what you will see."

"There's no fun if you're not going to show anything interesting."

"If I were you, I'd turn up for club night, with your cameras. You can almost guarantee there will be some form of action, especially when they see the cameras."

"I think I'll just turn up; it would be nice to make some new friends."

"You may be surprised to know that sometimes it does get boring."

"I don't believe that."

"Oh, it can get boring, when you see a dozen people having sex on a picnic table, it gets to be just the same as last time."

"You're kidding me?"

"No, it has happened, the last time was a punishment, the girl in question has completely changed her attitude now. She's given up chasing the leader, she's turned into a seriously horny bitch instead, I don't think she'll be shy for your cameras." He laughed, something moving around in the periphery of his vision alerted him. He rose from his seat and turned back towards the pub. Coming towards them were four men, one the angry man from the bar, the other three somewhat behind him. Sylvia turned in her seat.

"Who the fuck do you think you are?" shouted the angry man. "You come into our pub and get served before us, that's not fucking right." He gestured with an empty beer bottle, waving it threateningly.

"They call me Roaddog," he held his hands empty and wide.

"Road fucking dog, what sort of name is that?"

"John, chill it's not worth it." said one of the men from behind.

"John is it?" said Roaddog quietly. "My name was earned in battle, was yours?" He rolled his weight forwards onto the balls of his feet, worrying a little about traction on the gravel.

"Dirty, smelly biker trash, that's what you are," yelled John, moving closer, not close enough yet. Roaddog smiled, hoping this would be the trigger he needed, his peripheral vision told him that the other men were still too far away, they really wanted nothing to do with this. Then John snarled and moved, the bottle swung in on the end of a straight arm aimed to meet Roaddog's face. Roaddog turned inside, his left hand took the approaching wrist and held it, his right elbow jabbed into John's chin and then the right hand snared the forearm. Roaddog's left hand moved to the body of the bottle, and his right withdrew briefly before slamming into the crook of the elbow, John's right hand released the bottle and was flung wide by the force of the blow. Roaddog stepped in even closer and slammed his right hand into John's body just below the rib cage, the force of this blow pushed John backwards and on to his ass in front of his three friends, they made no move.

"That camera has video of four armed men attacking me," snarled Roaddog, flipping the bottle from his left hand into his right. "Go away before blood is shed." The last almost lost in the traffic noise. There was a pause that seemed to last forever, then two of John's friends reached down and took him by the shoulders, they lifted him to his feet, and turned towards the pub, one of them spoke softly.

"You were told not to be here before one o'clock, just fucking relax."

"Fuck," whispered Sylvia.

"You ok?" asked Roaddog.

"I'm not sure. You said they'd not be happy to see us, but I wasn't ready for that."

"Fools been here for an hour drinking beer while angry that he couldn't force the landlord to bring their table forwards. Some people have no control at all."

"And you do?"

"Hey, I didn't kill the dick, that makes him up," laughed Roaddog, again peripherals alerted him, he turned to the pub, one of John's friends was walking slowly towards them, his hands empty and palms forwards.

Roaddog smiled, recognising his own body language spoken back to him.

"Look," said the man. "I'm sorry about John, he's been having a bad time recently, this family get together was to sort of celebrate his father's death two weeks ago, he's taken it very badly. He's been hitting the booze real hard."

"He should consider himself very lucky to have his parents for such a long time, mine have been gone years."

"Actually it was his mother that sent me out, John has been placed on a short leash, he's sitting in the rear garden next to his mother, her words are, please thank the kind man for not killing my stupid son. We've had enough tragedy in this family recently, we don't need any more."

"Please tell the old lady that I am glad I was not forced to take her son from her. There is something else you should be aware of, the more of you who stand behind him the more likely he is to get himself killed. If you can't stop him, then don't stand with him, I could tell you wanted nothing to do with this, but others are not so perceptive." With a sudden movement of the right hand Roaddog pulled his knife from the pocket in the leg of his jeans, and it unfolded to show a twelve-inch bladed black stiletto that slammed into the table. It stayed for a few seconds then was snatched and collapsed, then vanished back into the pocket. Roaddog smiled at the look on the man's face.

"Fuck," whispered the man. "I will tell the old lady," he giggled. "What you have said, will certainly improve her mood." He turned and walked quickly back into the pub.

"You," said Sylvia, "are a man of many surprises. Is your life always so full of excitement?"

"No, sometimes nothing happens for a whole fifteen minutes," laughed Roaddog.

"I'm not sure I'm ready for that level of excitement."

"It's not always like this, sometimes it gets positively boring."

"Why don't I believe you?" she smiled and stepped close to him; her face tipped up. He leaned down and kissed her softly, after a few seconds he broke away.

"I have a new girlfriend, and I don't do the side chick thing without permission," he smiled.

"I'm going to have to meet this girl, you do know that?"

"I'm fairly sure you'll meet her very soon. Shall we go?"

"I suppose, back to the boring reality of my life," she laughed, backing away and picking up her helmet.

"That's the plan, let's not make things too exciting for you." Roaddog checked the tension on her helmet before he picked up his own. They were walking towards the motorcycle when they heard a voice from the right.

"Excuse me," Roaddog turned and saw the man they had just been talking to walking quickly towards them.

"Good, you've not left yet. The old lady asks that you come and meet her, she'd like a chat. Her actual words were, go fetch me that crazy biker. Please."

"How many there?" asked Roaddog.

"Everyone, us four, three wives and assorted brats."

Roaddog looked round for a few moments, then took off his helmet, he waved at Sylvia to do the same.

"In the beer garden at the back?"

"Yes."

"Into the lions den then, or is that lioness?"

"Oh, she's that all right, please follow me." He turned and set off towards the back of the pub.

"Is this likely to get violent?" ask Sylvia quietly.

"No, sounds like mama rules with an iron fist, she'll keep things under control, her grandchildren are there." He smiled as he switched his helmet to the left hand, leaving the right hand clear. They turned into the rear garden through the wide gate, the gate was big enough to admit a car, or perhaps a delivery truck, but only open a foot. They passed through the narrow opening and into the rear yard. One side was taken up with a large group of people all now staring at Roaddog and Sylvia. John was sitting next an elderly lady, silver hair, and thick glasses, her swollen knuckles told of arthritis and pain, though her eyes gave away none of this.

"Mum," said the man who had brought them. "I present Roaddog and er, er." He tapped Sylvia gently on the arm. She glanced at him for an instant, then spoke as firmly as she could, though she wasn't at all happy with the situation.

"Sylvia."

Roaddog tried to make eye contact with the old lady, but she was having none of that, she focused entirely on Sylvia, which was making the younger woman even more nervous.

"Thank you, Adam. Sylvia," she said. "You can call me Nora. Does this man of yours always defend you so well?"

"He's not really my man, I only met him today."

"Hell of a first day?"

"You have no idea."

"You are not what one would expect as a couple, how did you meet?"

"Well." Sylvia paused and turned to Roaddog. He smiled and nodded, she raised her eyebrows, he smiled and nodded again. "Fine." she turned back to Nora. "I was shooting video of him naked this morning, then." she paused again. Nora waited she knew this was going to be interesting. Sylvia turned to Roaddog. "I just realised, I shot the video, then went and turned myself in to the cops. I don't believe it." Nora laughed.

"That has to be a story for another time there are more pressing questions right now. Do you think he could have hurt my sons?" There was a moments silence, Roaddog looked at Adam, he mouthed the word 'brothers' and got a small nod in return.

"Nora," said Sylvia, "given that he took John down in less than three seconds, had the others been armed, it could have become very bloody and very quickly."

"Would you have helped him to hurt my sons?"

Sylvia looked to Roaddog again, but he wouldn't take her eye, he was worrying where the old woman was going with this, the tension was mounting towards detonation and he really didn't like it, his right hand dropped to pocket in his jeans.

"I'm not sure whether I would be help or hinderance, but I would have had is back if I could." Nora held her eyes for a long moment letting the tension in the group rise some more. Finally, she made eye contact with Roaddog. Her hard-blue eyes locked onto his own, he felt as if they were boring straight into his brain, or maybe his soul.

"Roaddog," she said quietly.

"That's me," he said, not breaking eye contact.

"Would you defend yourself and your woman with ultimate force?" Roaddog was surprised by her use of the particular phrase so he avoided the question, buying some time.

"She's not my woman." Nora gave it a second before replying.

"Bollocks," her voice snapped hard over the noise of the garden, the intake of breath around the tables was intense. "She rides with you, she rides under your protection, ultimate force?"

"Ultimate force, yes," was his gentle reply.

"Outcome?"

"Four armed with bottles, hospitals are too far away, they bleed out in the carpark, and we are gone."

"How would you achieve this?" Nora asked as Adam focused on John. In a blur, with an ominous click the stiletto appeared in Roaddog's right hand, everyone gasped, John's face fell, Adam smiled.

"Fuck," muttered John, to receive a hard elbow from Nora. She looked hard at the blade, then held her hand out.

"May I see that please?" Roaddog was clearly not happy at releasing his only real weapon.

"You are safe here," she went one. "Anyone moves against this man and I'll gut them myself, he is under my protection. Please Roaddog." Roaddog turned to Adam, he was the closest and the only one of the brothers standing. Adam spread his arms wide and stepped away. Roaddog nodded his thanks and flipped the knife up, catching it by the blade and passing the grip towards Nora. She took the handle and waited for Roaddog to remove his hand from the blade before she moved the knife. She hung the knife and tapped the blade listening to the ring of the steel, then she checked the balance, she checked the edge, all along the front and three inches from the tip on the back. First by eye then with the pad of a thumb, a tiny sliver of skin was carved from her old and leathery skin.

"This is good steel, and it has seen some use, the balance is too far into the handle for it to throwable, but you can't do too much about that with a folding knife. The back edge could do with a little work. You know that the pivot is where it will fail eventually?"

"I understand, it has three sisters at home, they don't often get to go out together."

"When they do go out, similar holster arrangements?"

"Right and left jean leg pockets, and two more crossed in the back of the belt."

"Serviceable," she found the frame lock and folded the knife down. Then tossed it back to Roaddog.

"How do you know so much about knives?" he asked almost a whisper.

"Their father was a good soldier, I didn't marry him for his brain, luckily three of my sons got their brains from me, the other got his from his father, but none of the other advantages, my husband was a much bigger man in every way."

"Mother," muttered John. She shushed him and turned to the other three.

"Next time this fool picks a fight with a stranger, let him take his lumps alone, I'm too tired to beat sense into him now." She stared at each until she got a nod of acknowledgement. Her sharp elbow slammed into John again. "If you pick a fight with a girl or a child, I'll feed your sorry ass to the damned pigs." The silence lasted for a short time until Roaddog spoke.

"John, we now have something in common, my girlfriends father threatened to feed me to his brother's pigs," he laughed.

"What's his name?" asked Nora.

"Hang on." Roaddog ran through an old conversation in his head. "Bamber, yes Bamber."

"They've got enough head to get shut of a corpse in about an hour. I've got three times as many hogs as they have."

"So, twenty minutes?"

"Depends how big the pieces are? More axe work, the quicker the hogs work." At this point one of the children from the other end of the row of tables leaned away from the table and proceeded to throw what was left of her breakfast onto the ground, splashing a few shoes in the process.

"Mother," snapped one of the women as she rushed round to take care of her daughter.

"Sorry Roaddog," grinned Nora. "Grand children are a little sensitive. Sometimes I worry about what's going to become of the farm." The mother turned and glared at Nora.

"Nora," said Roaddog, "sometimes I think you are a wicked old woman." A huge smile split his face.

"Definitely, they don't let me out much so I've got to get my jollies when I can," laughed Nora. "Anyway we've taken up enough of your time, thanks for handing my son his ass, and not killing him."

"No worries, I always try not to kill people, the mess can take a while to clear up. You have a nice meal, the food here is always good. Goodbye." He turned and walked away; Sylvia hard on his tail. Adam only a step behind. Roaddog walked quickly to the motorcycle before he gave Adam a chance to talk.

"That was great man," said Adam. "You should have seen the look on John's face when you dropped that pig sticker. Talk about a picture, awesome."

"I couldn't look away, I had to see your mother's look. She's one feisty old lady."

"Oh, she's that and more. You understand she was joking about body disposal?"

"Of course, that was deliberate, just to get to the squeamish," laughed Roaddog.

"The one with the breakfast on the floor will be having soup and veggie special, she's a delicate little flower. She can't come to the farm anymore."

"I'm assuming you're eldest and the farm comes to you?"

"Yes, my kids aren't here, they've been at uni, and have little time to visit friends before they have to go back, so I let them off this family meal, they'd have loved your performance though. They'll take over after me. No problem."

"Your mother suggested she married your father for his dick, is that right?"

"Probably, he was a big guy, John on the other hand is not, he took it too much to heart and it made him a sour person."

"You have an interesting family, hold on to them they are important."

"I just hope John gets over this shit of his sometime soon."

"How do you know he's so small?"

"His ex-wife told me; on a good day he doesn't make six inches."

"Shit, there are other ways."

"Not for him, and he could never compete with father. That was another look I'll never forget."

"Explain."

"Pig farm, lots of pens, lots of pigs and lots of shit. If you're working anywhere near the runoff trench you take special care. One day one of the heavy boars nudged dad and he fell into the trench. I ran and picked up the rescue line, then turned towards the trench, John ran to the pump. Mains water just doesn't cut it when you've got so many pens to clean. I slapped the boar on the ass with the rope, he skittered off to the other end of the pen, I saw the hump in the trench and threw the rope towards it, hoping he would take it, if he didn't, I was going in. The carabiner bounced off the hump and it reached out taking a grip then wrapping it around the arm a few times, then I started to pull, behind me I heard the big pump start, that was the most welcome sound I can tell you. Dad slid slowly up the side of the trench onto the flat, and climbed to his feet, he started walking away from the edge as the water started to fall all around us. Gently washing the thick brown mess away. Now when you're covered in pig poo, the last thing you are is shy, that shit burns. He started stripping off and I was helping, not an easy job, by the end of it he was standing naked in the freezing water. John was completely transfixed, his jaw hanging open until dad walked up and killed the pump. The thing that really upset dad that day, wasn't the damned boar that had dumped him in the trench, it wasn't the grazes on his leg that he knew would become infected, it wasn't the fact that he was going to be puking and shitting for at least three days, it was the fact that one and only one of his new boots was in the bottom of that damned trench." Adam laughed heartily.

"John's had the inferiority thing going on since then, let me guess, sixteen."

"Spot on. He was never as tall, never as strong, and only half the man."

"Poor fucker, speaking of which he's walking towards us now."

"Mum says can you please come in she wants to order food," shouted John, before turning away.

"Better go," smiled Adam. "See ya Roaddog." He said holding out his hand. Roaddog shook.

"Lady Sylvia." Adam grinned, and held his hand out again. Sylvia pushed the hand away and reached up, pulling his face down, kissing him softly on the lips.

"I'm glad I didn't have to brain you with a stella glass," she whispered.

"So am I," he replied, "goodbye." He turned and followed after John.

"Now that is one crazy family," said Roaddog.

"That's for sure, those damned eyes, they cut straight into your brain."

"One scary ass bitch."

"For sure. Come on take me home."

"Your place or mine?"

"Yours," said Sylvia. "The neighbours have enough to talk about today."

"Fine by me." He reached out and checked her helmet, it was tight enough, he knew he'd not have to do that again. The Harley fired first time, and he rolled it backwards, they mounted up, the gravel made getting off the carpark a little difficult but given enough space he made the right onto the road. Roaddog made good time back to his house powering smoothly through the roundabouts and along the white lines of the straights. Never more than thirty miles above the posted fifty, Sylvia tucked in behind him out of the wind. She wasn't even looking where they were going, she was simply feeling the bike, and Roaddog in front of her.

'Damn she feels good behind me.' He thought the steady pressure of her body pressed against him, the squeeze of her knees in the corners and under acceleration, her weight against his back under brakes. 'Damn she's a natural.' He thought. He pulled up outside his house. He shrugged his shoulder and she moved, almost as if she was waking up. Sylvia dismounted, and he reversed the heavy motorcycle onto his front path. The silence fell as the motor stilled. Sylvia held out the helmet for him, he took it.

"You want a coffee, sorry tea?" he asked.

"No, I think I should go home, the vibrations of that engine are not helping my situation a great deal."

"I understand. I'm not sure what's happening tomorrow night, but Wednesday there should be a few of us at the clubhouse. Drop by, you'll meet some interesting people."

"I'm making no promises, but a definite maybe. OK."

"Fine by me," he said, settling both helmets in one hand and his keys in the other, the key turned in the lock and the door fell forwards, then he felt her turn and walk away. He smiled to himself. 'Maybe another time.'

18: Easter Monday Meeting and Mayhem

Roaddog looked at his watch again, only three minutes had passed since the last time. He hated the waiting, he didn't want to get to the Railway too early, Nigel would be having a great day, and he didn't want to frighten off any of the customers. There was still an hour left. He couldn't really polish the bike anymore, it gleamed almost to concours standard. His computer systems were running fine, no more scores, but perhaps tomorrow. He'd drunk enough coffee to float a battleship, his bladder was letting him know this on a very regular schedule. His hands were shaking with the caffeine, his brain jittery with the same.

"Gotta relax," he muttered, he turned the TV to his favourite rock radio station, and lay on the sofa, his feet hanging over the end. He closed his eyes and tried to settle. His thoughts turned to the meeting ahead, he was planning to table a motion to get Alan and Billy if not associate membership then friend of the club status. Then they'd be more welcome and get some of the perks of membership without too many of the responsibilities. The biggest problem was going to be getting this past Bone, he was against too many outsiders knowing too much of the club business. He was right, but Roaddog thought that these two men could be trusted, and perhaps even useful. He smiled as the thought of a pensioner like Alan being stopped by the cops in his beat-up fiesta, with a sniffer dog standing by. That's just not going to happen, not unless they had specific information, by then it would be too late for any of them. Billy with the caché of his celebrity look alike would be equally unlikely to attract anything other than autograph hunters. They could both be useful members and they are good guys. It may take some fancy talking but he expected Bone to give way if for no other reason than the fact that it was Roaddog asking. Arrangements for the Mayday rally with the Centurions, Bone should have news on that one. There should be some discussion on the subject of drug sales, Bug should have news of current street prices and sources by now. Any fallout from yesterday's demolition of the competition would be making itself felt by now, that may take a little time. It might take as much as a few weeks for the supply on the streets to dry up, though dealers may be holding back to push the prices up. He briefly considered opening a bottle of beer, but there was bound to be enough beer during the meeting, and after. The radio station gradually soothed his nerves, and settled his roiling brain, slowly he relaxed enough to doze. Not truly asleep and not actually awake, that dream state where anything was possible. His mind turned to Jackie and her soft body pressed against his, her hard nipples moving in the coarse hair on his chest. Her soft thighs gripping his as she moved above him, her eyes glowing in the darkness. The dream progressed slowly, the tension mounting. In the manner of dreams things started to get jumbled, her magnificent breasts became smaller, her face older and more lined. With a rush consciousness returned and with it a surge he sat upright.

"Wow," he muttered to himself, as he reached for the remote to turn off the TV. It was time to be setting off to the meeting, he grabbed his gear, and as a last-minute thought, he opened the heavy wooden box in the corner. Three more of the black stilettos were secreted about his person, now he felt dressed. Perhaps it was the disturbance of the dream that had upset him, he just felt better with all his knives on him. The ride to the Railway was almost uneventful. As he blew through a set of lights, he heard the howl of a v-four, and looking over his shoulder he saw Bug dropping in behind him. They were only a minute away from the pub, so there was little chance for conversation. They just turned into the car park together and rolled their bikes backwards into the line that was already there. Together they walked into the pub. A quick glance round showed that though the place had been quite busy, there were almost no customers not wearing club colours. Other than a couple of young men playing pool there was an elderly couple in a quiet corner, but that was it. Roaddog wandered over to the old couple, he stared at the gentleman briefly.

"What do you want, you young pup?" growled the old man.

"I'm looking at your tie, and I'm not sure which regiment it is."

"Welsh guards."

"You saw action in world war two?"

"And damned Korea, what's it to you?"

"You'll be used to young men blowing off steam then, it could get a little rowdy, but not too much."

"You youngsters have no idea what rowdy is. Hand to hand in the villages of France, or the foxholes of Korea, that was rowdy."

"I bow to your superior experience," smiled Roaddog.

"We'll stay a while longer; this could get amusing," laughed the old man.

"You're incorrigible," smiled his wife, lifting her gin and tonic to Roaddog.

"Same again?" asked Roaddog.

"That would be most kind," grinned the woman. Roaddog nodded and went to the bar. He returned shortly with a pair of drinks. He placed them on the table and said. "Thank you." Before turning away. The meeting was assembling by the time he had his own beer in his hand, so he took his place at the table. The report from the treasurer was brief but interesting, Bone proposed that the club pay for camping fees at the upcoming Centurions rally. The Centurions having already approved the attendance of a large contingent of Dragonriders. This was met with cheers, and a short discussion as to how many more beers could be drunk. Bug reported on prices and availability of the various products that they had in stock, prices of some were climbing quickly, but that wouldn't last once they started to release their own stocks. With the competition out of the picture, in the short term at least, things were looking better for the summer. There was a discussion as to holding stock back and pushing the prices up. But the sudden glut in Manchester would push our prices down, so Bug was given the task of getting a much of our stock out on the streets as possible. Before the competition got its act back together. Roaddog suggested the return to active, or semi-active status for Alan, and friend of the club for Billy. As Roaddog expected Bone didn't seriously contend either point. Geronimo was added to the active list and Billy as friend. A majority vote on both counts was well in Roaddog's favour. Billy was told to get a cut, but no club patches for the back, Alan was given permission to wear his old cut, until it fell apart. It was ten-thirty when the meeting was adjourned, and Nigel had to cope with a rush at the bar. Soon the bikers had returned to their seats, they were drinking and chatting. Roaddog was leaning against a wooden partition, Jackie in his arms, talking softly. Bandit Queen was by one of the entrances, alternatively putting money into and taking money out of a fruit machine.

Three men wearing balaclavas to cover their faces rushed in, one pressed the business end of a shot gun against Bandit Queen's not inconsiderable belly.

"Right fuckers," yelled the gunman. "This is a robbery; I want wallets watches and phones." He glanced at the bar. "Nigel, empty your damned safe, and your tills." Everyone froze. Except the old soldier, he was out of line of sight, so he stood and started moving slowly towards the masked men. Roaddog caught his eye and waved him to a halt, one of the masked men, armed with a machete turned to the old soldier, and lifted the two-foot long blade. Only one person was left moving, and this was Man-Dare. She leaned slowly back on her stool, spread her legs wide, lifted her skirt, and gently inserted two fingers into her naked pussy.

"Fuck," said one of the knife wielding masked men, "damned whore's fingering herself." The man with the shotgun glanced over. Bandit Queen moved. Her right hand jammed into the trigger guard, her left grabbed the barrel, she yanked the barrel upwards and the released the trigger. The gun spat its deadly cargo straight up into the ceiling. Bandit Queens right hand slammed into the gunman's testicles and he fell to the ground. His two companions were swarmed under by sheer weight of numbers. Only one of them made a move at all, but Roaddog was already inside his attack and the man fell hard. Bandit Queen slammed the shotgun down into the gunman's ribs.

"What sort of dick brings a single shot shotgun to a robbery?" she screamed kicking him hard in the ribs. She glanced upwards. "A fucking 4-10 poachers' piece and still loaded with fucking bird shot." She turned to Roaddog. "Blade me, I'm gonna gut this fucker like a pheasant." One of Roaddog's blades was already in the air when Bone yelled.

"No. No blood. Too difficult to clean up."

"Gut the bastard," shouted the old soldier, his voice not much less than it had been on the parade ground so many years ago. "Those cunts are the ones tearing our country apart."

"Sorry old man," said Bone. "We'd all end up inside, and you as well most likely." He turned to the barman, as the robbers were being taped. "Your call. Call the cops, they'll be out in a day or two. Or they can disappear. You and the old man have to agree. If they vanish, then there have to be no witnesses to say they were ever here, do you understand?"

"I understand, I want them gone," said Nigel.

"The Welsh Guards say they were never here," snarled the old soldier.

"Done," said Bone, he turned to Sharpshooter. "Can you fix that in the morning?" Looking up at the damage to the ceiling.

"I'll have two guys here before nine, they'll be gone before ten and no one will ever know."

"Right," snapped Bone. "We have a plan. Bandit Queen will take their vehicle, they certainly didn't walk here. Man-Dare, you ride with, they breathe wrong kill them. Everyone else back to the clubhouse and remember if asked everyone went back there. Move out." Pints were emptied in a hurry. Roaddog pulled car keys from the gunman's pocket. He tossed them to Bandit Queen.

"I'm betting it's a green van." He looked down at the gunman. "You're no better with a shotgun than you are with a knife, fool." Jackie came up behind him and spoke softly.

"What are you going to do?" she asked.

"These dicks are going to vanish."

"Is this what you do?"

"Only when it becomes necessary. Of course, if they'd been a bit brighter, and run off to Yorkshire when I gave them the chance, then they'd not be this deep in the shit. I didn't kill them on the motorway bridge, they threw that chance away."

"It's murder."

"Perhaps, but certainly deserved. If we call the cops, then these cunts will be out on the street in days. Next time they turn up here they'll be better equipped, and we won't be here to defend you."

"I don't like this."

"I know, I'll meet you back at the club in a while, and we can talk about it, OK?"

"And how do I get there?" Roaddog smiled, he turned. "Geronimo, you got a spare seat for Jackie back to the club?"

"Sure, I came in the car, not taking the dragonfly out in the dark."

"See you later." said Roaddog, hoping that he would. The van was loaded, and Man-Dare took another of Roaddog's knives, so she now had two. A long convoy of bikes left the pub and went to the club house. At the clubhouse, the van and a small group of bikes carried on. At a manufacturing unit only a few hundred yards away the gate swung open as they arrived. A security guard closed the gate behind them, then followed them into the processing plant.

The robbers were unloaded from the van, none too gently, one of the knife men had already peed himself. Their lives were ended without ceremony, a simple knife stroke through the ribs and into the heart. Barely a gasp from either of them. Their clothing was cut away and the security guard waved a wand shaped metal detector over them, it found nothing. The two naked bodies were carried up a ladder and dropped into a large metal hopper. The gunman was struggling hard against his bonds when an extra rope was fastened around his wrists, a winch hauled him up until his feet were an inch or two off the floor. His struggles became completely ineffectual, only causing a slight swing on the end of his rope. Bandit Queen stepped up to him.

"You stuck a shotgun in my guts and threatened to kill me, you are a fool." She snarled and sliced his jacket and shirt from his upper body. Two small golden hoops penetrated his nipples.

"I'm sure that the grinder can cope with these tiny fragments of metal, but I wouldn't want it to poison the poor doggies." She said gently, as she reached for first one, then the other, slicing both nipples from the chest, screams choked by the tape over his mouth. His eyes screaming silently into hers, she looked down and started to cut his tracksuit pants and trainers from him, he tried desperately to kick her away from him, but failed. He had no leverage, only his own body weight, which gave him nowhere near enough to be affective. In no time he was hanging naked, blood running down his chest, his slow rotation brought him around to face Bandit Queen. She grabbed him by the penis and stilled his rotation, he kicked his legs at her, then stopped as the knife approached his lower body.

"I haven't seen a Prince Albert in years." she whispered, taking hold of the metalwork that passed through his penis. "I think this will make a great belly button ornament, or really heavy earring." She placed the point of the knife along the axis of the piercing, she slowly pushed it into his urethra and once it was deep enough, she slashed downwards, slicing the end of the cock to free the heavy steel hoop. The gunman's screams were clearly audible despite the tape over his mouth, blood poured freely from the slashed end of his penis. Bandit Queen had no worry that he was going to bleed to death. She waved at Bone, and walked up to the hopper, climbing the ladder slowly as the winch raised the hanging man, then Bone moved the winch to bring the man closer to the edge of the hopper. Bandit Queen lifted his legs so that they dropped inside the shiny metal. He looked down to see his two friends already in there. The security guard threw a switch and the heavy rotors started to turn. The two bodies were torn to pieces in moments and ground to a heavy bloody paste. The screams of the hanging man became more urgent, more desperate. Bone pressed a control and the winched started to lower him slowly into the grinder. He lifted his legs as high as he could, gradually descending towards the slow moving rotors, eventually a foot caught in the machinery and the rest followed in almost no time at all, the screaming went on for about twenty seconds until the gunman was dead. Bone pulled the winch so that Roaddog could cut the ropes and the rest of the man fell into the rotors. In only a short time all three men had been reduced to thick pulp that would be turned into animal feed in the next couple of days.

"Let's get back to the club and get those clothes in the fire." Said Bandit Queen. "I'll take their van and leave it in Calan, Bone you can pick me up. Damn thing will be on cameras all over the city before they burn the bastard out somewhere." She tossed the knife back to Roaddog, knowing that all traces of blood will be gone very quickly.

"I'll dump the gun in the river on my way home." Said the security guard. "I'll add those machetes to my collection." As they were all walking out Bandit Queen turned to Roaddog.

"Your girl is the only one I'm not sure of. Make her understand."

"I'll do it. There are things she may not be aware of." He mounted his bike and roared down the road to the club. He parked up and went into the club. He dropped the clothing into the incinerator that was currently providing heat for the people gathered there. Music from the radio system filled the air, conversations were subdued. Roaddog snatched a bottle of Jack's from the bar and went to where Jackie was standing talking to Cherie. She glared at him, her eyes angry.

"I know where you've been," she whispered.

"Where?"

"There's a pet food factory up the road. You've been there getting rid of three bodies."

"How do you guess that?"

"Something Cherie said to me."

"I don't understand." He knew that no one would volunteer that information, especially not Cherie.

"When Bandit Queen rescued her, from the child molesters, Cherie said that she yelled 'I'm gonna turn them into dog food.' Well?"

"I'm not going to lie to you, you are correct. But there is something you need to know."

"Explain," she whispered. Roaddog took a large slug from the bottle before speaking.

"You've met those three before, on a motorway bridge."

"They were those."

"Yes, they had the chance to walk, or better still run. But instead, they stuck a shotgun in Bandit's belly. That was never going to end well."

"So, you've killed them and made them into dog food?"

"Not yet, they're meaty sludge that'll be made into dog food tomorrow. Fuck." The final word snapped. He pulled his phone out and sent Bandit Queen a text message.

"Where are our glorious leaders?"

"They are taking care of a couple of loose ends."

"That doesn't make this right."

"And threatening our friends is right?"

"No, but murder for god's sake."

"I'm sorry that it ended this way, but they had plenty of chances to avoid this. Most of all, they didn't need to be here tonight. Any sensible thieves would have seen all those bikes parked outside and gone somewhere else, but no, they had to be heroes."

"You think they were heroes?"

"No, but they did, by taking on the Dragonriders, they'd have been heroes amongst their friends, sadly, they have simply vanished. By this time tomorrow the only evidence will be our memories. Everything else will be gone."

"What if their friends know where they were going?"

"No evidence they ever arrived at the pub. Anyway who's going to tell the cops that they were going to the railway to steal the Easter takings? No one with any sense."

"Is this how you deal with inconvenient people? Will I be next?"

"No, you will never be next. I will make very certain of that."

"Remember I've just seen Bandit Queen take out a guy with a shotgun in her guts."

"Take my word for it, she's a pussy compared to me."

"So how is she leader and not you?"

"She's not, Bone is."

"Bollocks." snapped Jackie.

"What do you mean?"

"His name may be on the V5, but she does the driving."

"I don't understand." Roaddog looked confused.

"I watched that meeting of yours. Every decision that was made, she approved, not him, and when he wasn't sure, he checked with her first. She's the real power, not him. I have some more news for you."

"I disagree, but please say on."

"I believe that if she thinks that Bone has become too weak, she'll replace him with you. You'll be the "boss" and she'll be your woman."

"That shit is not happening. I don't need that sort of shit. That just shows how much she doesn't understand."

"Please explain that to me."

"I have absolutely no intention of taking that much responsibility. Hell, I'd fuck off and join the damned Sons rather than be in charge. I'm in this thing for the fun."

"Was it fun killing those three guys?"

"Not exactly, but necessary."

"How so?"

"You know what our legal system is like, they'd be back on the streets in hours, and by the time the case comes to court there are no witnesses left to speak against them."

"That can't be true?" she asked expectantly.

"How many times have you heard of some high-profile case that collapses for one reason or another? Evidence disappears, witnesses retract their statements. I've seen cases where witnesses have gone to jail for contempt, rather than tell the truth in court, simply because the cops cannot protect their families from the bad guys. That will not happen for the craft knife kid and his cohorts."

"You think this is the only option?"

"Realistically, yes. It's really sad to say, but our legal system is definitely in the favour of the criminals, they are the ones with human rights after all."

"You can't really believe that?"

"Can you afford a barrister to defend your human rights in court? I know that I can't, however, convicted criminals always get legal aid. We don't, we have to prove that we can pay the legal fees back, if we lose, cons don't."

"So, it's better to be in jail?"

"Yes and no. The system stacks up in your favour once you're inside, but it's difficult to ride a Harley in a cell."

"Have you ever been in jail?"

"I've spent a few nights in the cells, but never made it to the big house yet." Roaddog laughed.

"Luck or judgement?"

"Bit of both really. I've never been taken in for anything major, generally just a bit of a fight thing. By the time everyone is sober, there is no case to answer, just boisterous high spirits."

"And the cops let that sort of thing slide?"

"Yes, if no one is willing to make a complaint then there isn't much they can do."

"So, did you actually kill those three?"

"Personally no, the lieutenants were killed with a single knife stroke to the heart, the craft knife kid, he got something worse."

"How worse?"

"You really want to know? I don't think you do."

"Just tell me."

"You insisted, remember that, he went into the grinder, the others were dead first, he was not."

"He was alive when you fed him to the mincer?"

"Yes, he didn't have long left, his injuries would have finished him in a few minutes anyway."

"What do you mean?"

"He had some body piercings. We can't have metal fragments in the pet food, that's not right."

"So, what happened to his body ornaments?"

"Bandit Queen cut them off."

"What the hell were they?"

"He had two nipple rings and a Prince Albert."

"I'm assuming she took the nipples with the rings, but what the fuck is a Prince Albert?"

"Well, it goes into the hole in the end of a penis, and then turns down, the actual piercing is from the urethra out of the lower surface, then it is formed back into a hoop."

"And Bandit Queen cut this off?"

"Yes. He was bleeding quite badly at that point."

"Screaming as well, I bet."

"There was a lot of noise. Even more so when the grinder started."

"You understand that you are not really helping here?"

"Yes. Those assholes weren't going to stop, and the law wouldn't be able to stop them either."

"But you managed to?"

"They are unlikely to reoffend."

"They were someone's children."

"Sadly, that is generally the case, perhaps if they'd been trained a little better, they wouldn't have ended the way they did."

"Some children are untrainable," whispered Jackie.

"That is also true, if they don't learn about consequences early in life, then they aren't going to learn later."

"Have you learned about consequences?"

"Oh yes. Life teaches some brutal lessons. Had the scumbag been carrying that shotgun on the motorway bridge. Then the consequence would have been that I would have spent my life protecting a complete stranger. Hoping that you had the sense to keep on running."

"Why would you do such a thing?"

"Because it is the right thing to do. The innocents should always be protected from scumbags like them."

"I'm not exactly innocent," she smiled.

"Innocence is a spectrum disorder, and you are way down at the innocent end," he laughed.

"And you not so much?"

"Definitely, life has taught me many lessons, I have suffered some loses and learned from each of them."

"Do you want to tell me about them?"

"Not really."

"It might help me understand more about you and the way you think."

"Fine, but not here. Come back to mine."

"OK. Let's go." She turned and started walking towards his bike. Bone and Bandit Queen came through the gate as they crossed the car park. Roaddog paused while the two dismounted.

"Bandit Queen," he said. She looked at him, her brows raised in question.

"DNA," he said. She nodded, and then twitched her head in the direction of Jackie. "I'm working on it, I'll let you know in the morning." He said quietly. Bandit Queen nodded and grinned. She already knew how persuasive he could be. "Come with me a few moments," she said. Roaddog waved at Jackie, she followed him towards the clubhouse, behind Bandit Queen and Bone.

"Where's that bitch Man-Dare?" yelled Bandit Queen, Man-Dare came forward.

"I have a gift for you," said Bandit Queen. "Your distraction tonight gave me the time I needed to end this thing without any of us dead, as a thank you I present you with two nipple rings, you might want to remove the nipples from them." She dropped the rings in Man-Dare's hand. "I'm going to keep the Prince Albert for myself. Your punishment is over, you may dress how you want, you have proved to be an excellent member of this club. Thank you." A round of applause for Man-Dare lasted a fair while. By the time it had died away Roaddog and Jackie were on the road.

The ride back to his house was a little uncomfortable for him, with the three-quarters full bottle of JD kept moving around inside his jacket. When they arrived at his house, he went straight into the kitchen to make coffee, he added a good belt of jacks to each and took the bottle and two shot glasses into the living room. They sat on the sofa, soft music playing from a blues radio station.

"You want to know the history of Roaddog?"

"Please," she smiled at him.

"Right, I was a bit of a wild child at school, just down the road aways in Chorley. Dad thought it would be good for me to learn a little discipline, so he sent me to a local karate school, I was fourteen at the time. I learned fast, and became quite proficient, I was less of a problem at school, but only because the children there were no longer any sort of challenge for me. Not the brightest student by a long way but I was good with my hands. After school with precious little in the way of qualifications it appeared the only path open to me was a trade apprenticeship. While I was waiting for that to start, I happened to be in Preston, and there in the middle of town was a huge, armoured truck and a Scorpion light tank, along with a mobile army recruitment office. I had a long chat with a guy in there and signed up for a six-year stint. Dad was so pissed, mother was in tears, eventually they accepted that it was actually a good choice for me. Two weeks later I was whisked off to the barren wastelands of north Yorkshire. Six weeks basic training. Finally, I'd found something I was actually good at. My early training, my speed and my strength all stood me in great stead. Hand to hand I was great at, my knife work was excellent, I was a passable shot, not marksman but good enough. I blew through basic, and then moved south, near Salisbury. For some reason I just don't understand the fairy godmother department waved their magic wand in my direction and I got transferred to a mechanic trainee role. Something else I had a real aptitude for. Things were going great, in the three years I was there I met a girl, had a daughter, we were planning to get married. Then mother got sick, cancer killed her in twelve weeks. I was given compassionate leave to attend the funeral and make arrangements, Dad dived into the bottle, he never crawled out again. He drank himself to death in seven months. More compassionate and another funeral. I went back to Salisbury, trying to arrange a wedding for my girl and me. Then the shit hit the fan in Kosovo, I got 24 hours' notice I was shipping out. A quick chat with the padre and we were added to the emergency wedding list, no party, no fanfare, just married and loaded onto a hercules. Six months later I was called into the commander's office, and he informed me that there had been an accident at home, a bus drove through a bus stop, killing three people waiting there, my wife and daughter were two of the three. I was given yet more compassionate leave. I went to the naafi, drank a bottle of jacks." He lifted the bottle and took a large belt. "Then I went out to the motor pool, stole a jeep, an LMG, and drove out of the base. Everyone knew where the local warlords base was, but we weren't allowed near it. I went there in full on Rambo mode. I pumped a thousand rounds through that light machine gun and killed the boss and a couple of truckloads of his henchmen. Got myself shot up a bit, I was still alive when they finally came to get me. That got me a medical discharge, psychologically unfit for duty, and shipped back to England, fuck all here for me though. So, five years ago I turned up at the clubhouse looking for a mechanic job. Bone took me on, and I've been sort of stable ever since. Even the army shrink thinks I'm well enough to be lose on the streets. And that my dear is the tale of Roaddog."

"You still think of her?" she whispered, taking the bottle from him and holding the now empty hand in hers.

"Some days I can think of nothing else, those are dark days indeed."

"It will get easier with time," her voice still a whisper.

"People say that, and they lie," he snapped. "It doesn't get easier; we just deal with it better."

"And the dark days get further apart?"

"They do, but I'm not a person to be talking to on those days."

"Your life sounds so exciting and complicated, it's mine look boringly normal," she smiled.

"You've had your moments," he laughed.

"I suppose, but only in the," she paused, counting. "Fuck, six days since I met you. Less than a week and so much has happened."

"Maybe it'll quiet down a bit now."

"You think so?"

"One can hope," he laughed and pulled her to himself, she kissed him slowly and gently. Gradually the heat increased between them, suddenly she pushed him away, and stood up. She picked up the bottle of jacks, glanced down at the two as yet unused shot glasses, she spun the top off the bottle and took a slug, coughed a little, she held out her free hand to him.

"Come on, bedtime," she whispered.

19: Tuesday Early

Jackie looked at her watch as she woke, the time was two in the morning. She was unsure as to what had woken her, the house was quiet, the streets outside were quiet, the only sound was the slow breathing of Roaddog lying next to her, she rolled slowly out of his bed, she walked to the doorway, and looked back. The dim light from the streets that made it through the curtains gave her enough to see him in shadowed relief. The bed covers were so far down that she could see all of his back, the harsh whiteness of the dressing on his left arm picked out in the dim light. Down his back there were three scars, one about four inches long, and two that looked like puckered puncture wounds, perhaps the bullet injuries he had talked of. Further down into the deep curve of his buttocks, with the dark cleft between, down into the meat of his thigh, at least the one that she could see.

"Damn, that's why he looks so good in a pair of jeans." Her words barely a breath on the air. 'Perhaps it's the fullness in the bladder that woke me.' She thought as she moved slowly from the room. Having relieved her bladder, she grabbed a handful of warm water to wash away the crusted residue of their lovemaking, she returned slowly to the bedroom. As she stood again in the doorway her hand on the light switch for bare bulb on the landing, the white light picked out Roaddog's left arm as it lay against the pale blue of the sheets, palm upwards. A fine tracery of white scars ran across the wrist and one heavy one from mid forearm down to the wrist. 'Self-harm, and at least one serious attempt at suicide.' She thought. Her hand flipped the switch and the world became black. She waited for her vision to return before she moved back into the bedroom. She smiled to herself as she stepped over the discarded clothing on the floor. She turned and sat on the end of the bed, staring at him as he slept. His breathing stalled and caught in his throat. A twitch ran through the muscles of his shoulders and arms, before it returned to its normal slow rhythm.

'Life's certainly been hard on him.' She thought. 'He definitely fights back hard when it pushes him, he fights for his friends, and he seems to be loyal beyond what is normal in my world. How would dad have performed on that bridge faced by three armed thugs? He'd have died, without a doubt. Roaddog is a survivor, but do I really want a place in his life, or to give him a place in mine? This life of his is so dangerous, it could end up killing us both, do I want that? But as Cherie says, it's never boring. Has my life become so boring that I will entertain this madness? Is it madness? The real question is do I carry on with this madman, or walk away?' She stared at him while this question rolled around inside her head, she wasn't getting any sort of answer, at least not one that was definitive.

She turned and lay back on the bed, she reached down and pulled the covers up over her body. Perhaps that light movement brought Roaddog closer to consciousness, or it was the warmth of her body next to his. His breathing changed slightly, and his left hand moved slowly up over her belly and turned so the palm was resting on her softness. She felt his weight move as his body lifted and turned towards her. His hand moved down to her mound and suddenly his hot lips latched onto her left nipple. She moaned softly, as he suckled gently. The turmoil in her mind didn't lessen, she thought of the women she had met and talked to, from Bandit Queen, who seemed to be the most brutal of them all. To Cherie, whose life had been so hard that this club was a step up for her. To Man-Dare, whose mistake had led to her humiliation and on to newfound influence and a sort of power all of her own. To Doris and her exhibitionist nature, and her lust for Lurch. His fingers slid across her clit and entered her body, as his teeth softly gripped her nipple, her body clenched in both pain and pleasure. 'Could she become a part of this gang?' Her mind refused to accept the word club; it just didn't fit with her perceptions at all. 'Could she make the changes necessary to become one of the hard-faced women that ran with these bikers?' No, that question was wrong in itself, they are not hard faced. They care for the people in the group, it's the rest of the world that they, they don't hate it, they don't fear it'. Another finger entered her, and his left knee crossed hers. 'They just don't care what the rest of the world thinks, or feels, they live their lives exactly as they wish.' His weight crossed over her completely, and his fingers were replaced by his hard maleness.

"Fuck," she whispered as he filled her. 'That's what it is.' Her thought continued as he moved slowly above her. 'They just don't give a fuck for the rest of the world.' Slowly the pace of their lovemaking increased until she felt her world implode and pleasure swamped her mind. As her consciousness gradually returned, she came to the conclusion. 'Whatever the risks, I'm not giving this up.' She felt the roughness of his cheek as he held her close, then he rolled off her and sleep took her.

It was full daylight when they woke up. Roaddog turned to Jackie and kissed her firmly, her response was more than enough to elicit the normal reaction from a healthy male. The she pushed him away.

"You need a shave; those bristles are harsh on my baby soft skin." she whispered.

"That was definitely part of my plan for this morning. And you've got room to talk." He laughed.

"What do you mean?"

His hand slid slowly down her body, and to her mons-veneris, either side of her landing strip was enough stubble to cause some irritation.

"Fine." she laughed. "We both need a touch up."

"I'll touch you up anytime." he smiled, looking into her eyes for a brief time. "Breakfast or shower first?" he continued.

"Don't you have work today?" she asked.

"About ten o'clock I'll be part of Nigel's escort to the bank, but other than that I really can't be arsed."

"Isn't the shop open today?"

"Yes, but if Bone wants the place open, he can do it for a change. I need a rest after last night's hard work."

"About last night?" she whispered, he looked at her expectantly.

"Go on," he muttered.

"I'm not happy about what happened last night, but when I think about it, one of the scariest things that comes to mind is what if it was me he'd pointed that gun at? I'd not have done nearly as well as Bandit Queen."

"He'd have been forced to point it somewhere else, and shoot someone else, the rest of the guys would have turned them to burger meat in a heartbeat."

"But you'd have been dead."

"Chance you take. But a 410 loaded with birdshot? A good leather jacket can take a hell of a lot of punishment. I'd most likely have been bleeding, but he'd have had twelve inches of stiletto through his brain."

"Would that have been any better?"

"No, far too messy. The way it turned out, they'll be in cans today, their van will be a burned-out wreck, or ringed and for sale in Glasgow. In two weeks, all the evidence will have passed through dogs or be some petrol heads dream in the wilds of bonnie Scotland. This way is far tidier." He dropped onto his back beside her.

"Don't the pet food manufacturers keep samples for checking later if there are complaints?" She rolled half on top of him and looked into his eyes.

"I don't see Lassie complaining about an improvement in the quality of meat in the tins. They may be able to decide that there is human meat in those tins, but all three went through the mincer at the same time, it's going to impossible to separate them."

"They can do wonders with DNA nowadays."

"You've been watching too much CSI. In the mix they have DNA from three different sources, and they've been through an industrial blender, along with all sorts of other protein. Separating an individual is going to be impossible. I love watching that CSI stuff occasionally, have you noticed how they go to a crime scene that is a few years old and sift through everything there and find a pollen sample from the suspects garden that can only have got there on his shoe, isn't that magic?"

"I suppose, is this going somewhere?"

"In the very next episode the murder happened yesterday, in a hotel room, which has seen a five hundred people in the last year, and they find the victims DNA, and under a lamp a speck of blood from the suspect, but no mention of the five hundred that have left their DNA in that room in the last year."

"Well, the rooms are cleaned, aren't they?"

"Hotel cleaners get about fifteen minutes to clean a room, most of that is changing bed linens. Switch to Bones, suspected crime scene is a room that has been cleaned and repaired by professional crime scene cleaners, suspects are the crime scene cleaners themselves, Bones finds DNA on a nail used to repair a wall. I don't believe that hotel cleaners can empty a room of DNA evidence in fifteen minutes, do you?"

"I suppose not." Jackie grinned.

"Now CSI turn up with two scientists and usually a bunch of cops as back up, Bones arrives with her squint squad, Booth and a bus load of FBI. Lancashire Constabulary, one guy in a little white van. The reality is far different from the fantasy of TV."

"So, you believe there is nothing at all to worry about?"

"Let's just say that the risks are low. Anyone reports said scumbags missing, which is in itself doubtful, the cops are going to be real interested in a few well-known bad boys. They're going to come to the conclusion that the bad boys came up against some badder boys and most likely ran away."

"So, you're not worried?"

"There are more important things to worry about in this world. Like breakfast?" his smile made her laugh.

"Fine," she replied. "breakfast, but nothing like as heavy as yesterday, toast and coffee for me."

"No worries, but first, damn do I need a pee." He laughed rolling out of bed. Jackie rolled out of the other side and being nearer to the door made it to the bathroom first. She was already sitting down when he walked in.

"What can three men do with a bucket that three women can't?" he asked smiling.

"I don't know," replied Jackie, she blushed a little, due to his presence.

"Pee in it at the same time," he laughed as he waited for her to finish.

"Have you any idea how long it is since I heard that joke?" she asked.

"No."

"I was in school."

"You can't beat a good bit of schoolboy toilet humour," he smiled as he took her place, stroking her hip as she passed him.

"Breakfast or shower?" she asked.

"Shower, I think, we're both pretty sweaty," he finished up, and reached out to the handle on the cistern, then snatched his hand back. He turned to Jackie and smiled, then he crossed to the bath and turned the shower on. Once the water temperature stabilised, he climbed in, and held his hand out for Jackie to follow him. It didn't take them long to rinse off the sweat and various other things from the night together. Soon they were walking down the stairs. Roaddog led the way into the kitchen. He filled the kettle and set it to boiling, dropped four slices of bread in the toaster.

"I can't believe that I am here in your kitchen again, naked." said Jackie.

"No hurry to get dressed is there? I much prefer the view right now."

"You're not on your own, how do you keep so fit?"

"I don't work out or anything, but being a mechanic is quite a physical job, I don't eat too much but I do drink a lot." He smiled, as the kettle kicked off, followed in a moment by the toaster. "You make the brews and I'll do the toast." The tasks so divided it was only a minute before they walked together into the front room to have their breakfast. Sitting listening to the radio, eating toast and drinking coffee, the toast was finished in short order and complete silence. Roaddog stood up and spoke softly.

"I have something I need to do. It's not exciting but you are welcome to watch if you want."

"That sounds a little suspicious. I'll come and watch." He led the way into the back room. He took his seat at the computer and pulled out a second chair for Jackie. In seconds the room was illuminated by the monitor as it showed the login screen. Roaddog punched in his access code, knowing the even with the quickest of eyes Jackie wasn't going to able to see the keystrokes. A quick check through the monitoring systems showed him another small hit for the mining pool. He turned some more bitcoin into cash and stashed it in his bank, he left the rest as bitcoin. A systems check on the mining machines showed that they were all warm but not too hot. The air-con was working but not too hard. The solar panels were slowly filling the batteries. Records showed that the batteries had been empty during the night when the miners were at maximum output, so this most recent batch of bitcoin had been very expensive in electricity.

"Swings and roundabouts," he muttered.

"I don't understand any of this," said Jackie.

"Don't worry about it, I've got to keep an eye on all this every day, at least once. It's one of my money-making ventures."

"Is it working?"

"Yes, to some degree, the advantage that I have is that the electricity I am using is generally free, or very close to free. Last night the batteries were empty, so I was using juice from the grid, which is more expensive, but I've made a little money. If I get some sunny weather for next time, I'll make a lot more money, but every little helps."

"So, this computer just sits here creating money?"

"Sort of, It's mining for bitcoin."

"I don't understand."

"Bitcoin is a crypto-currency, it has no actual physical existence. It's traded all over the world, and often used illicit purposes, the transfer systems are encrypted and untraceable. It is outside the control of governments, but its value is exceptionally volatile, it goes up and down like a bride's nightie. That's why I trade enough of it into pounds so that I make a little profit. Then I'll trade more when the price is high, at the moment the price is in the toilet. I'll hold on to them for a little longer, when the price goes up again, I'll sell them."

"Are you sure the price will go up?"

"Yes, it keeps on changing, sometimes it appears to be linked to the price of oil, but then the next month it will be running contrary to oil. It's really weird. One day I'll spend some time and work out what the fuck controls it, if I can ever be arsed." he laughed.

"So how much are you making for being somewhere else and letting all this stuff run by itself?"

"I don't know, sometimes I make as much as a grand a week, sometimes it costs me in the electricity I have to buy from the grid."

"Sounds like you don't actually need a job?"

"That could be true, but then what would I do with my time?"

"I'm sure you have something else you could be doing, other than running around with a motorcycle club." She struggled with the last word, but still made the switch before the wrong one was actually spoken.

"Perhaps, but I like the way I live."

"In some ways so do I, but in others I worry about the risks."

"In this day and age, just living is a risk."

"That is true, but are you taking unnecessary risks?"

"I don't think so. It's all a matter of perspective."

"I suppose. Here's a question, how much would it cost to increase the effectiveness of your mining system?" Jackie waved an arm to include the whole room.

"For about ten thousand you could double the miners, then another five for the solar panels, and five for three more battery packs, and controllers. This would double the mining capacity, and that would most likely give about one hundred and thirty percent increase in success rate. So, between two thousand three hundred a week, and maybe as low as five hundred on a bad week."

"Is that not enough to live on?"

"I don't have twenty thousand lying around."

"How long would it take to pay back a loan of twenty?"

"Most likely about six to eight months. All this is a dream anyway, I have nowhere to put any more solar panels. Paying for the power is really the governing factor."

"Here's an idea, rent a warehouse type storage place, fill the roof with panels. Install enough hardware to make a fortune, rent out the storage space itself."

"Nice idea, now work out how much capital I'd need to do that?"

"It would definitely be a lot."

"The mining systems are so volatile right now, it's not worth the risk. All it takes is the Chinese to let loose one of their super computers and no one else gets a sniff, just not worthwhile."

"Do the Chinese do that often?"

"It's either them or the north Koreans."

"Well, it was only idea."

"A good one, but a few years ago it would have been a great idea. Now there are too many miners, and some of them are far too big, there's no room for the little people like me anymore."

"So how did you get set up in this if it is so expensive?"

"I was lucky and bought the gear real cheap from a friend who was going away for a long time."

"Why didn't he just lend it to you until he gets back?"

"I don't think he'll be coming back, neither does he."

"I see, one of those things?"

"Yes, it happens occasionally. He was in the wrong place at the wrong time, for some reason self-defence doesn't seem to count against coppers, especially not dead ones."

"That's not good."

"No, they seem to think that they are invulnerable, sadly wrong in this case." Roaddog glanced up at a shape moving past the window, he smiled before continuing. "How shy are you feeling today?"

"What do you mean?"

"I think I have a neighbour about to call. Do you want to run upstairs and get dressed? I'm not planning on doing so."

"You're going to receive visitors while naked?"

"Why not? My house, they don't have to come round."

"You really are mad. But I'll tag along." Jackie laughed. Sure, enough the shape turned into the path and waved to Roaddog.

"She's definitely calling, last chance to run off and get dressed," he laughed as he stood up from his place on the sofa.

"She, well I'm definitely staying naked then, let's meet the other woman in your life."

"She's not really in my life as such, be right back." As there was a knocking on the door. He walked into the hallway and opened the door wide.

"Hi Sylvia," he said.

"Are you nuts?" She replied looking around for other witnesses to his nakedness.

"No, I don't think so. You coming in?"
"Am I interrupting something?"
"No, we're just chilling before we start the duties of the day."
"Are you planning on getting dressed?"
"Not until I have to."
"We? Is your girlfriend here again?"
"Oh yes."
"Is she naked as well?"
"Gloriously so."
"And still you invite me in?"
"Why not? Not shy, are you?"
"Not as such, but this is more than a little weird."
"Make your mind up time."

"Damn it, fool get out of the way," Sylvia laughed as she pushed past him. She walked quickly into the front room, to find Jackie still seated. "Hi, I'm Sylvia," she said.

"Jackie," was the reply as Roaddog walked into the room. "How do you know Roaddog?"

"Now that is a story," Sylvia laughed, "how much has he told you?"

"Nothing," Sylvia turned to Roaddog and looked at him for a moment.

"You told her nothing of our day together?" she asked quietly.

"It was a busy night, I never had chance, I was planning to tell her this morning, but you interrupted," he laughed.

"So, what is going on with you two?" asked Jackie.

"Short story for ya," he smiled. "Sylvia called the cops on us. They came round to see me yesterday, I sent them away. Starsky and Hutch then went to talk to Sylvia, and convinced her to withdraw her complaint, as it wouldn't go well for her. Then she actually had the balls to come here herself, we chatted, went out for lunch, came home. Then I came out to the meeting last night and things got very busy. That's all."

"Why did you call the cops?" asked Jackie.

"I reported the pair of you for indecent exposure, I presented photos and video. The cops came back to see me later, they explained about invasion of privacy, so I withdrew my complaint."

"What did you have to complain about?"

"It seems that being naked in your own home isn't actually illegal but taking pictures from outside is." Sylvia smiled.

"Did you get some good pictures?" asked Jackie.

"All I got of you was your ass as you walked out of the room."

"No camera with you today then?"

"No, I just thought I'd drop in, on my way to the paper shop."

"I have a question for you Sylvia," said Jackie.

"Go on."

"Aren't you feeling a little over dressed?"

"What do you mean?"

"Everyone else here is naked, and you're not."

"You expect me to get undressed?"

"No, I'm just asking how you are feeling, if you wish to join us, then please feel free," Jackie smiled.

"I've never been naked in front of other people before," whispered Sylvia.

"Nor have I," smiled Jackie. "I've slept with him, so that's not so much of an issue, but I've never been naked in front of a stranger before you walked into this room."

"You people are crazy," muttered Sylvia.

"That has been said before," giggled Roaddog.

"No one wants to see an old woman like me naked, I'm forty for god's sake," said Sylvia

"And?" laughed Jackie. "You still look good."

"I ain't gonna argue with that," smiled Roaddog.

"Jackie's breasts are gorgeous and huge, mine are nothing like as good," said Sylvia.

"They're tits, aren't they?" asked Roaddog.

"After a fashion," whispered Sylvia.

"I'd like to see you naked," said Jackie. "And if you're fishing for complements then just look at the fishing rod that is getting all excited," she nodded in the direction of Roaddog, who's cock was indeed growing again.

"It's not my fault," smiled Roaddog, "that bastard has a mind of his own, and the thought of two beautiful naked women has got him all hot under the collar."

"You think I'm beautiful?" asked Sylvia.

"I think you're beautiful, but for the cock, naked will do."

"I think you're beautiful," said Jackie, quietly, a smile spreading on her face as Sylvia made eye contact. Slowly Sylvia looked from one to the other. Gradually she started to smile as well.

"I must be as crazy as you lot are," she whispered as she stood up. She grabbed the hem of her t-shirt and in a flash, it was over her head and dropped on the seat behind her. She reached behind and unsnapped the bra, a shrug of the shoulders and it fell forwards, to be flung behind her on top of the shirt. Her jeans were unbuttoned, and the zip dropped, then jeans and underwear pushed straight to the floor, shoes toed off, and socks joined the pile around her feet. She dropped back into the seat; in only seconds she was as naked as the other two.

"There you go," Sylvia said, she cupped her small breasts and lifted them, then dropped them for emphasis. "How do you like those forty-year-old saggy boobs?"

"In the interests of accuracy," said Roaddog. "They can't be older than twenty-eight," he grinned.

"And they are anything but saggy," said Jackie.

"You must have a different definition of saggy," said Sylvia.

"I'm sorry," laughed Jackie. "I get my description of saggy from an Australian comic singer, his says, 'They're like a footy sock with half a pound of wet sand in the end.' Sylvia, your tits are lovely."

"I've never heard that description before," laughed Sylvia. "My ex-husband told me they were saggy."

"That ass has no clue," said Roaddog.

"Do you mean that?" whispered Sylvia.

"Of course," replied Roaddog. "The guy was obviously a dick."

"Yes," said Jackie. "He just wanted you to feel bad about yourself, I hate it when guys do that."

"Sylvia," said Roaddog. "Do you want a brew? We've got enough time before we have to get dressed."

"That would be nice," said Sylvia.

"No worries," he stood and slowly walked past Sylvia, on his way to the kitchen. Sylvia couldn't take her eyes of his penis as he squeezed by, after all it was at head height for her, his excitement seemed to be fading a bit.

"So, what are you two up to today?" asked Sylvia.

"We've got to take the landlord of the pub that I work at to the bank this morning, he's got four days takings, and he's consequently a little nervous. The club are providing him with escort. After that I've no idea. I'm not working today, so I might just hang out with Roaddog."

"Can I ask a personal question?" Sylvia's voice dropped to almost a whisper.

"I might not answer but go ahead."

"Why do you shave a landing strip?" Sylvia, glanced at the door, nervous that Roaddog might be coming in. Jackie giggled.

"It was fashionable when I was at school, and I've sort of kept it up ever since. It really itches if you let it grow back. I have found that guys actually prefer it with less hair."

"I've not had a guy pay any attention for a few years now," muttered Sylvia.

"That's what happens when you're married to a cretin," said Roaddog from the hallway as he came in with a cup of tea for Sylvia. He passed her the cup then returned to his seat.

"I see that you shave as well," she said.

"Girl's don't like a mouthful of fur any more than guys do. Seems only fair."

"I really seem to be behind the times here," muttered Sylvia.

"I'm sure you'll catch up," laughed Jackie, she turned to Roaddog. "What are we doing today?"

"After our escort for Nigel, I've got nothing planned. You?"

"I'm not working so nothing planned for me."

"We could go to the clubhouse and hang with any of the guys that turn up." said Roaddog.

"Will there be many there?" asked Sylvia.

"Can't tell." replied Roaddog. "It was a busy night last night, so there could be a lot of resting going on."

"Should be a nice relaxing Tuesday," said Jackie, she smiled at Roaddog, suggesting that it couldn't be any more exciting that Monday was.

"Should I come down in the car?" asked Sylvia.

"No, get a cab, we'll be able to arrange a ride home for ya," laughed Roaddog.

"Just don't ride with a dick called Bug. He's nuts," smiled Jackie.

Roaddog passed Sylvia his phone saying. "Put your number in and I'll text you when it's safe to turn up. I'll Introduce you around, you can make some new friends and you'll most likely enjoy yourself. OK?"

"Seems fine to me, but I'll probably drive. That'll give me an excuse not to drink too much."

"There's too much?" asked Jackie, laughing.

"Yes there is," said Roaddog. "lying down and holding on is too much." He laughed loudly before going on. "We need to be going soon. It's time to get dressed."

"What? No sex?" asked Sylvia.

"Were you expecting some?" smiled Roaddog.

"Sort of. I was at least hoping for some moral high ground, and 'I'm not that sort of girl', but I'm not going to get even that?"

"Sorry darling," smiled Roaddog. "We have things to do and there just isn't enough time to treat you pair of gorgeous ladies as you deserve. Another time?"

"What if I don't want to share?" asked Jackie.

"Sharing can be fun."

"What if I don't want to share?" asked Sylvia.

"I'm sure an arrangement can be made," laughed Roaddog. He got to his feet and held a hand out to Jackie. Sylvia looked around, and jumped up, gathering her clothes in her arms.

"I'm not getting dressed down here on my own," she said. "Someone might walk past."

"Our clothes are upstairs," said Jackie, leading the way.

20: Tuesday Escort duty and Carousel

Roaddog turned into the Railway car park to find the place quite busy, there were half a dozen motorcycles there and Slowball's trike, a small van was just leaving as he rolled to a stop.

"Where the fuck have you been?" yelled Bone.

"Sorry I'm a little late." laughed Roaddog. "I had a couple of naked chicks to deal with and they can be a real bugger to get back in their clothes."

"Ask a jackass a question, get a jackass answer," said Bone. "You any plan for this thing?"

"Not really, simple escort, parking is a bitch though, there are a couple of shop fronts close by, they'll do. The place is too small to hold much of an issue for us, the only logical hit points are here and at the door to the bank. With the best will in the world Nigel's takings aren't going to be enough to bring out a heavy crew. We're only here to frighten off the chancers."

"Right," said Bone, "you lead out, Slowball, you're in the middle. Roaddog will check out the bank and decide how many we need in there. Start your engines." He turned to his own motorcycle and mounted up; Bandit Queen's absence felt a little strange to Roaddog. He rolled up to the exit, waiting for the convoy to form up behind him. He turned in the saddle and spoke over the noise of the heavy motors.

"I'll need you to unload quickly when we get where we are going, I have to check the bank before we allow Nigel to go in." Jackie just squeezed him with her knees and smiled, even though she knew he couldn't see her. Bone and Lurch formed up behind Roaddog, Slowball rolled into line next, Nigel perched in one of the high seats. The rest fell in behind Slowball, this is one of the occasions he was not going to be the last in the line. Once Roaddog was sure that everyone was ready he checked the road, the lights at the bottom of the hill had just turned green so there was no traffic coming up, and nothing coming from his left, he turned right onto the A59 going slowly down the hill giving everyone chance to get out of the car park. He went slow enough so that the lights had changed to red before he got there, no point if getting the convoy split up at the very first obstacle. When the green light came up, he set off at a leisurely pace, he revved the motor harshly whilst under the low arched bridge, as did every other vehicle in the cavalcade, much to the fear of the motorists waiting to go the other way. The traffic on the way into town was light and caused no problems for the column of bikes as they made their way at exactly the speed limit. It was only a few minutes later that they turned into Golden Hill lane, they arrived at Hastings road, Roaddog parked on the pavement on the street, Slowball stopped on the pavement the others parked around him, as Roaddog stilled his engine Jackie was standing up on the foot pegs, in a moment she was on the ground and Roaddog's bike fell over onto its side stand, he stood up and walked towards the bank. He looked in through the door and stepped inside. A quick glance around showed him a few customers, none who presented any threat to even one of the bikers. He stepped outside and waved two fingers up in the air. Nigel got off the trike and walked towards the bank, flanked by Bone on one side and Lurch on the other. When they got to the door Roaddog held it open and Bone stepped inside, he paused and moved in so that Nigel could enter, Lurch and Roaddog followed him in. The three stepped to one side and watched as Nigel joined the short queue of people, both of these customers suddenly decided that there was something better for them to do, somewhere else for them to be, so they left, at the same time as the customer at the window walked away. Nigel walked up to the window and the young lady behind it looked at him nervously, he dropped his documents into the drawer and waited for her to pull them towards her. Gingerly she opened the bag and found only bundles of cash and paying in slips already completed. She counted and checked the cash and punched all the figures into her terminal, in due course she stamped the receipts and returned them to Nigel with a smile. Nigel thanked her and turned away from the window, he was instantly flanked by Bone and Lurch, as Roaddog walked to the door and opened it, the quartet returned to their bikes as engines were started all around them. When Roaddog lifted his bike up from its stand as Jackie settled onto the pillion seat, he looked forwards to see a police car pull to a stop outside the Indian restaurant across the road.

"Damn," he muttered, there was no way Slowball was going to be able to make a U-turn with that cop car there. 'Change of plan.' he thought. He waited for a gap in the traffic, which just happened to coincide with the cops getting out of their car, he set off turning left, the others following. He smiled as the cops turned around and rushed back to their car. Up the hill and right at the roundabout, back through the housing estates and onto the main roads, back to the Railway. They were all parking up in the car park as the police car entered. The cops got out and walk towards the doors of the pub as Nigel was starting to unlock them.

"What have you lot been up to?" demanded the senior of the two.

"We've just been to the bank," said Nigel with a smile.

"Why all these people?"

"I have four days takings and feel a little unsafe in my hometown, can you do anything to make me feel better about walking down the street with the best part of fifteen hundred quid in my pockets?"

"Our town is one of the safest in the north west," said the policeman.

"We'll we're going in for a drink, care to join us?"

"It's too early for you to be opening the bar."

"Coffee only officer, coffee only," he opened the door and walked in, Bone and the others followed on his heels. The cops looked at each other for a moment then followed suit.

Nigel tried very hard not to look up at the ceiling, he failed, a short glance showed him that any difference in the paint had vanished. He sighed as he walked behind the bar. He pulled a jug of coffee from the machine and the heavy fragrance filled the air. Most of the bikers took seats at a few of the tables, but Bone and Roaddog sat at the bar, the policemen joined them. Nigel carried a tray of cups and a jug of coffee to the tables and turned to the men sitting at the bar.

"The next batch will only be a few minutes," he smiled going back to the coffee machine and loading another tray, he reached under the bar and turned the fans down on the air conditioning, the coffee would drown any residual smell of paint.

"How come the landlord picked you lot?" asked the cop looking straight at Roaddog.

"Nigel is our friend, we like his little pub, and he had a lot of money to take to the bank, it's only right to help a friend in need."

"Why is he so frightened?"

"You've not seen the news?"

"What do you mean?"

"Drug gangs having a turf war in our town, what are you doing about that?"

"That's just some journalist stirring the shit pot. Just a simple factory fire."

Nigel came up with a tray of cups and a jug of coffee.

"Help yourselves gentlemen," he said. Then reached into his back pocket, he took a small wad of cash out and handed it to Bone. "Thanks man, I felt so much better with you lot around me."

"No one is going to fuck with you when we are around," said Bone. Then he turned to the others. "Slowball," he called. "do the honours." He handed the cash to Slowball, who distributed it amongst the men. "Hey Nigel." said Bone, attracting the barman's attention. "Next time you have too much cash, just call Roaddog. He'll take it to the bank for ya, and it won't cost ya nearly as much as today."

"You honestly expect me to give this guy a grand and expect it to get to the bank?" asked Nigel smiling at Roaddog. Bone turned and looked Roaddog up and down.

"Yeah, you do have a point there, he don't look the most trustworthy of people, but there ain't no fucker going to try and mug him."

"There is that," laughed Nigel.

"Sitting right here you know," said Roaddog. He turned to the two cops who were quietly sipping their coffee.

"So that journalist is wrong, and it wasn't a meth lab that burned down?"

"Ongoing investigation, we can't say anything," said the cop.

"Given what I've seen of meth labs in the news, it'd have gone up much quicker, probably have left nothing more than a crater." Roaddog smiled.

"No comment."

"News said one man injured but not dead?"

"That's what the news said."

"I think your community outreach programme needs a little work," said Roaddog.

"You can think anything you want," said the cop, gruffly.

"For now, you mean?"

"I don't understand."

"Won't be long before thinking the wrong thing can get a guy jail time," whispered Roaddog in a conspiratorial fashion.

"What do you mean before long?" asked the other cop.

"Now I'm confused?" said Roaddog.

"It's not unheard of for us to investigate a person because someone was offended by something they said online."

"You're kidding?"

"No, been there done that, it's more common in the south, the Met have a whole department working on this shit, it's part of why I moved north."

"I'm glad I'm a motor mechanic, there are no politics in an engine. Spark plugs are never offended when you throw them in the bin."

"Any way, why are you so interested in that fire, your competition?"

"There are a few mechanic places on there, some motorsport places and an MOT station, but that scraggy little unit wasn't one of them, from the news report it wasn't high enough to get a lift in it," Roaddog smiled.

"It wasn't a garage," said the cop.

"No worries then," he turned to Jackie, "What you got planned for today?"

"Nothing, I'm not working today."

"I got nothing booked in the shop, what say we take off and just cruise somewhere?"

"The weather doesn't look too good," Jackie replied.

"I know, we could go to Southport and be tourists for the day."

"What about the unit?" demanded Bone.

"I think I'm having a day off," smiled Roaddog. "I'm sure the boss won't mind."

"Slowball," called Bone. "You got the shop phone on divert?"

"Yes," was the reply. "Good, looks like we're having a day off. If anyone calls tell 'em to come in tomorrow."

"Great boss, what we up to today then?" asked Slowball.

"Seems we're going to Southport for the day, should be relatively quiet."

"Fuck," snapped Roaddog. "There goes our romantic day out." He took Jackie in his arms and kissed her softly.

"Any one not got anything to do today, we're going to Southport. Who's in?" asked Bone loudly. There were a few dissenting voices, those that had jobs to go to, or other restrictions on their time, so it ended up that only Bone, Slowball, Sharpshooter and Bug would be going to Southport. The rest would be leaving as soon as they had finished their coffees.

"Should we warn Merseyside about the invading marauders coming their way?" asked the younger of the two cops.

"Stuff that," said his colleague. "They'll expect us to send reinforcements."

"There ain't gonna be but six of us," laughed Roaddog.

"For them that'd be an invasion," laughed the cop, finishing his coffee and nodding to his compatriot, "Time to go," he turned back to Nigel. "Thanks for the coffee, see you again soon."

"Any time officers, you're always welcome."

"We'll remember that." The two cops left as the Dragonriders were assembling to make their run to the seaside. As Slowball climbed aboard his trike and inserted the keys it started making a horrendous racket. He reached out and pressed a button on the dashboard.

"Hello," said Slowball.

"Hi mate, it's Billy here, where the fuck is everyone? The club is closed up."

"We're off to Southport. If ya want to tag along, we'll meet ya at the carousel."

"Fine. I'll see ya there," the line went dead.

"Ain't technology wonderful," laughed Bone. "They can find us even when we're not there."

"Some say that you're never there or is that all there?" said Roaddog.

"That too," laughed Bone. "Let's roll." Roaddog rolled out of the car park and turned left, then right at the lights at the top of the hill. A nice A road with some good bends and not too many speed cameras. The roar of motorcycles filled the countryside as they tore along the road, paying little attention to the posted speed limits. Roaddog kept the speeds down to a reasonable level, mindful that Slowball's trike wasn't too good in the corners, they raced through Croston in the blink of an eye, and on towards the A59, at the T-junction he turned right, he reached down with his left hand and tapped Jackie's knee. As they went round a right-hand bend, he pointed to a tiny side road to the left, it was signed as a dead end.

'That's where the naturist club is.' He thought. 'I'll have to tell her at some point.' A smile spread across his face at the thought of taking her to such a place.

Very soon the next T-junction came up, a left turn onto the Southport road. A wide road, with sweeping turns and that bane of all motorists, average speed cameras. Roaddog throttled back to spot on the speed limit, he wasn't sure if all the members of the group had secured registration plates, he thought that at least one or two had plates registered to their own addresses. He was safe, but worried about the others. In only a few minutes they were entering the outskirts of Southport, taking the beach road from the roundabout they passed along the salt marshes, the wind coming off the sea, though not strong, brought with it the salty flavour of the shore. While they were travelling over the dreadful bumps in this badly maintained road Billy caught up, his beard streaming over his shoulder with the wind of his passing. Roaddog led them up to the carousel and parked up on the pavement nearby.

Once everyone was unloaded, and the bikes were secured. Bone looked around.

"What's the plan?" he asked.

"Well," said Roaddog, "I had thought of a quiet romantic walk through the arcades, perhaps along the pier, and a ride on the carousel, followed by chips and a beer or two at the Fox."

"You're such a romantic," sneered Bone, setting off towards the amusement arcade, without waiting for the others to catch up. Jackie stepped up alongside Roaddog and whispered.

"Have I mentioned that you take me to all the really classy places?"

"He's planning on taking you to the Fox," laughed Bug. "Just you wait till you see that place," he laughed heartily and followed Bone. In no time at all the rest were following the leader, Roaddog was even more worried about the absence of Bandit Queen, in these sort of situations Bone can get really rowdy without her calming influence. At least they were all sober yet.

The arcade was quite busy despite the early hour, many teenagers were wandering around after all it is Easter, and the schools are closed. They walked into the arcade and spread out, Roaddog and Jackie walked along with Bone.

"Where's Bandit Queen?" asked Roaddog.

"She had something else to do."

"She'd love this place."

"She would, maybe next weekend."

"So, what was so important that she couldn't be here today?"

"You're not going to let this drop, are you?" sneered Bone.

"I'm worried about my friends," Roaddog smiled.

"Fine. You remember the blonde from Sunday?"

"Yes."

"She left a message on the club line last night. Bandit Queen and Man-Dare have gone to see her."

"You think that asshole husband has hurt them?"

"It's a possibility."

"You should have gone with her; I could have taken this escort run."

"She's old enough to clean up her own mess."

"You know she'll kill him."

"I know."

"You not worried?"

"Not specifically, she's a big girl."

"She's that all right."

"Don't tell her."

"Do I look like I have a death wish?"

"Not exactly, but sometimes I'm not too sure of you."

"What do you mean?"

"I get the feeling that you're going to be taking over sometime soon."

"Not happening, I like the fun, not the stress. You have nothing to fear from me."

"You know how many of the guys would side with you?"

"I've never thought about it."

"If you send out a call to arms, I reckon the numbers will be evenly matched. That would be the end of this club."

"As I said, not interested," Roaddog smiled. Bone turned to Jackie.

"Is he shitting me?"

"He has told me that he'd rather join the Sons than have the responsibility of being leader. I believe him."

"So, who's next in line?" asked Bone.

"Your seat is safe," said Roaddog.

"How can you be sure?"

"There's no one who could pull together enough of the members to oust you. With Lurch, me, and Slowball, there ain't no one going to stand up against that."

"What worries me is that Slowball and many of the others will always follow you."

"And they'll be following me, to stand beside you." There was a shout from across the room.

"Fuck off, you bastards." Slowball's voice filled the room despite the noise of the machinery. Bone and Roaddog started moving quickly towards the voice, Slowball was surrounded by five young men, they were harrying him like hyena around an isolated wildebeest. One of them, most likely the leader, was as tall as Lurch, but without the body mass. Slowball's heavy fist hit the tall one in the gut and he folded like a tower of cards. The others saw the Dragonriders closing in, they picked their leader up and hustled towards the door. Roaddog and Bone followed them to the door.

"This isn't over," yelled the tall guy, once he had his breathing back under control. The young men went out into the open air and ran off along the promenade. Roaddog watched them until they were out of sight. Then he turned to the others.

"The bikes are sort of exposed out there."

"Do you take his threat seriously?" asked Bone.

"You never can tell with scousers."

"They're from Liverpool?"

"No mistaking that guttural choking of the vowel sounds, central Liverpool, or somewhere close, perhaps Aigburth."

"And where the fuck is that?"

"Out towards the airport on the south side."

"They're a long way away from home."

"I still think we need to protect the bikes."

"Watchman, or everyone?"

"Let's have a wander out there, just for a little while." Roaddog waved his arm in the air, and the rest of the Dragonriders started to congregate.

"Right," said Bone once they had all gathered. "Roaddog thinks the scousers will be back. So, we need to look after the bikes." He led the way out onto to the concourse in front of the arcade, and out to where the bikes were parked next to the carousel. They had been chatting around the bikes for a couple of minutes when a police car came along the promenade, sirens screaming and lights flashing, it mounted the pavement, and slid to a stop just in front of the bikes. Bone and Roaddog walked towards the coppers, from their left, out of a transit van came the scousers and there were considerably more than the five. They ran towards the bikers, Roaddog noticed bottles in a few hands. He counted three.

"Molotov's," he yelled. Slowball ran to his trike, and flipped open the box on the back, his hand came out with a red cylinder clasped firmly. Three tracksuit clad arms snapped forwards and flaming bottles were launched, two dropped short and washed the pavement with flame. The third, hit Slowball's trike right in the middle. The wide and softly padded seat bounced the heavy jar full of golden liquid on. It fell just before the carousel, it shattered, and fire rolled across the ground and under the wooden bed of the antique fairground ride, Slowball ran towards the fire, his extinguisher spraying dry powder everywhere that he could see any flame. The ride operators stopped the carousel as quickly as they could and came running with their own extinguishers, water mist this time, more appropriate, but a little late. The fire from the petrol bomb was out, it was just accumulated litter that was burning under the platform. The water mist took care of those small fires in no time. The Dragonriders watched the young men running away, in moments they were all back in the transit and it pulled away from the kerb, turning across a taxi and a bus as it howled off down the promenade towards Formby its front wheels pouring smoke as they spun, failing to get enough traction on the sandy tarmac.

"Well officers," shouted Bone. "A van full of petrol bomb throwing terrorists, or some peaceful bikers who helped save a national monument from burning. The choice is yours." He laughed loudly as the cops ran back to their own transit van and set off with lights and sirens.

21: Tuesday Bandit Queen Social Worker?

Bandit Queen's car pulled up outside Man-Dare's house and the younger woman walked through the door even before the wheels stopped, her knee length skirt and biker boots a considerably different style from her recent apparel. Man-Dare opened the passenger door and dropped into the seat, automatically reaching for the seatbelt, snicking the latch into mechanism without even thinking about it.

"What the fuck is going on this early in the morning?" snapped Man-Dare. Bandit Queen pulled away from the kerb and set off towards the motorway junction that was only a few minutes away.

"We have a small job to do."

"How small?"

"Should be no problem, just some talking to do."

"Why so early?"

"We have a way to go, and we really don't want to be there too late."

"Where we off?"

"Leigh."

"Why are we going there?"

"Remember that blonde from Sunday?"

"Yes, what about her?"

"She left a message on the club machine last night."

"You think that bastards been hitting her again?"

"I'm not sure, but she needs help, and I did offer, so we go."

"Wouldn't it be better with one of the guys, I'm thinking Lurch, or maybe Roaddog?"

"I don't think so, any way if he's there and being a dick, then I can deal with him. She said he'd be at work this morning, so we probably won't even see him."

"What's the plan?"

"I'm not sure, just talk most likely simply to help her out, she's frightened, more for her daughter than herself."

"The curse of motherhood."

"Indeed."

"You ever thought of having kids?" Man-Dare's voice dropped so low that the local radio station almost hid it, she was a little frightened to be asking such a personal question.

"Maybe in the past, it might have happened, left it a little late now though, it just never seemed like the right time. Hey, I'm fat enough, without adding a baby to this belly," laughed Bandit Queen.

"Who's ever called you fat?"

"No one that wants to continue breathing, but there's no mistaking my silhouette, is there?"

"That's certainly true."

"These jeans are no size twelve."

"Mine are size ten," smiled Man-dare.

"I know, I've watched your scrawny ass wriggling its way around the clubhouse. Try a twelve, your feet won't go to sleep when you ride any real distance."

"How do you know my feet go to sleep?"

"I've been riding for a lot of years, tight jeans may look good, but too tight cuts off the blood to the feet when sitting on a bike for any length of time."

"My feet do get cold if we go any distance."

"Reduced blood flow will do that," laughed Bandit Queen.

"Many people think that size twelve is fat."

"Millions think that women wearing jeans should be stoned to death, that doesn't make them right." The steady thrum of the tyres on the motorway, and the quiet pop music from the radio filled the cabin for a few minutes.

"I have a question, but I don't want you to get upset, can I ask it?" Man-Dare spoke very quietly.

"Ask."

"How do you keep Bone as your man? I seen the way his eyes follow my scrawny ass."

"That's easy, your ass may be pretty to look at, and I'm fairly sure some guy is going to enjoy it sometime in the future, these legs of yours are gorgeous too." Bandit Queens left hand dropped onto Man-Dare's right thigh and slide a short distance up her skirt. The hand closed strongly on the soft flesh of the young girl's thigh. "That's the difference between us. I can feel your bone through your soft muscles. I have real muscles where you are pretty, I have real power where you look good. Some guys can see through the pretty surface and they feel what is underneath. When I kick a guy he goes down, when I stamp on a guy he dies. You can never do that. You have a different strength, you can use your looks to make guys do what you want, but it won't always work as you have found out. Just take things a little easier and have some fun."

"So how do I get a guy like you've got Bone?"

"Pick the right one, there aren't many young guys in our club, but as soon as a good one comes along, tie the bastard down until he'll do anything for you. Then you can be sure he's yours. But watch out for those young bitches, they can be a real problem."

"I think I understand, but what to do until a nice young guy comes along?"

"Tag on with one of the old guys, sometimes there is nothing better than being an old man's princess." Bandit Queen smiled briefly as she started the run down the exit ramp at junction 23.

"So, who would you suggest?"

"How about Billy?"

"Fuck he's old."

"He's not as old as he looks, he's less than fifty, doesn't seem to have a job, isn't short of money."

"He's old."

"And?"

"Well, he's just, I don't know, eeeww."

"He's old enough to understand the situation, especially if you explain it to him. He'll accept almost any conditions you insist on just to have you on his arm, on his pillion and on his dick."

"Could you be any cruder? You make me sound like a whore."

"You were willing to do anything for Bone to take over my position.

That didn't go exactly to plan."

"True." Man-Dare looked out of the window as the car turned off the A580 and headed into Leigh. She paused for a while as they passed through the centre of the town, and on to the residential areas. "So, I just tell him it's over when something better comes along?"

"Exactly. He'll most likely kiss your hand and simple step out of the way, but in the meantime, he'll keep you out of trouble, and maybe even teach you a thing or two about people. That long hair and the silly sunglasses may hide his eyes pretty well, but he's always watching, and he sees everything."

"How do you know?"

"There are two sorts of people in this world, predators and prey. He's a predator, and a topflight one at that, he has real alpha in him, it shows in the eyes."

"I haven't noticed."

"Most of the guys in the club fit into the predator class, we have no sheep. Some are alpha, most are not. Billy is definitely alpha material."

"Who else?"

"Think about it for a while." The residential streets changed to fields and the local recycling centre passed on the left. Bandit Queen checked the sat-nav on the dash, this showed that they were getting close to their destination. Passing many new houses, all of them small in the modern style. A right turn came up in a mile or so and they turned into Common Lane. After a couple of hundred yards Bandit Queen pulled over.

"Well?" she asked, making no move to turn off the motor.

"Bone, Roaddog, and Sharpshooter, they're alpha, the real surprise when I think about all this is that Lurch and Slowball for all their size aren't alpha."

"The two big guys aren't sheep, but they are followers and not leaders. What about Sharpshooter? He's only a few years older than you."

"There's something about him that gives me the creeps, I've no idea what it is, but his eyes give me the shivers."

"He's a cold one sometimes, but there is a fire in him. He could be good for you."

"No, I couldn't do that."

"So, Billy then?"

"Billy," laughed Man-Dare. Bandit Queen hit the start button and the engine stopped. She opened her door and the others unlocked in a heartbeat. The two got out and Bandit Queen led the way to the house that she had parked in front of. A heavy iron gate was closed across a driveway containing a small car. Man-Dare closed the gate as she walked through, she glanced across the road and took in the expanse of grass that ended in a line of trees.

"Nice place," she whispered as Bandit Queen knocked on the door. After a short time the door opened, but only as far as the chain on the inside would allow.

"Hi," said Bandit Queen.

"Oh my," said the surprised face. "I didn't actually expect you to turn up on my doorstep."

"You called us."

"I thought you'd call, I don't know what you can do."

"We can talk, and you can tell us what has been happening, through the crack in the door, or sitting inside, the choice is yours," Bandit Queen smiled.

"Sorry." The door close briefly to free the chain, then opened again. "Please come in." The two walked into the hallway and paused while the woman closed and locked the door, she was very careful to engage the heavy bolts, top and bottom.

"Now Janice," said Bandit Queen. "What's happened? I can see that someone has given you a slapping around, that black eye is new."

"That damned partner of mine."

"Here was I thinking you'd walked into a door." Bandit Queen smiled again as Janice led them into the front room, the TV was playing some children's cartoon, with the sound almost all the way off. The small blonde girl was sitting far too close and looked round as they walked in. She leaped to her feet and ran to her mother.

"Don't worry little one," said Bandit Queen gently.

"You hurt my daddy," said the little girl.

"Be nice Julie," said Janice.

"I only hurt him after her hurt me," said Bandit Queen, falling to her knees to bring her to the same height as Julie.

"He hurt mummy."

"I see that," smiled Bandit Queen. "We'll try to make sure that doesn't happen again. Is that OK with you?"

"He's gone away, will he be coming back?" Julie's blue eyes showed tears forming.

"That's for him and mummy to sort out."

"Julie," said Janice. "You watch your TV, and we'll go talk in the kitchen, is that all right?" Julie nodded and went back to sit in front of the

TV again. The two followed Janice into the kitchen, a final glance from Janice at her daughter as they passed through the door.

"So, what happened?" asked Bandit Queen.

"First off, what do I call you people?"

"I'm Bandit Queen, or simply Bandit." she pointed to the name tag on her cut. "And this is Man-Dare." Bandit Queen paused, then asked. "Where's your name?"

"It's Easter, I only managed to order it this morning. It'll be here this week."

"Bandit and Amanda." said Janice.

"No, Bandit and Man-Dare, she used to be Amanda, but she made a serious mistake, took her lumps and her punishment, then she got a new name."

"Was what I witnessed on Sunday part of her punishment?"

"That is correct."

"That's sort of brutal."

"Says the woman with a new black eye and a busted lip, if I'm not wrong."

"Yes, the swelling's almost gone, and it was only cut on the inside."

"So, what happened?"

"He didn't deal with the events of Sunday at all well, yesterday, the drunker he got the more it seemed to be my fault. Eventually Julie's screams caused the neighbours to call the police. They took him away; they want me to press charges. What should I do?"

"You want him back?" asked Bandit Queen.

"No, definitely not."

"The house shared?"

"No, all mine."

"You're not married?"

"No, we've been together just over two years, after my dead-beat husband ran off."

"Julie's not his?"

"No. He's been a good stepfather up until recently."

"So, what changed?"

"I don't know, he just got more and more angry about everything. Beaten up by you was just too much for him."

"So, what did the cops say?"

"I have to let him come back for his clothes and what not, but if he causes any problems, I have to ring them immediately."

"About par. When's he coming back?"

"I don't know."

"Right, we'll help you pack his stuff and wait until he's been to collect it. It is important that he doesn't have any excuse to come back here."

"That would be great. I really can't thank you enough, I just don't have any friends around here, that would even stand a chance of standing up to him."

"What about the neighbours?"

"They're old people, it was Julie's screams that made them call the cops."

"Have you thanked them for that?"

"Well, no."

"We'll go talk to them in a bit, something else, once he's collected all his stuff, you keep the doors bolted and change the locks as soon as you can. Alarm?"

"Yes."

"Change the code on that as well. Hopefully he'll just give up, but I'd not like to bet Julie's life on that."

"I'm no good at this stuff, is there anything else I should be doing?" asked Janice.

"Yes, there is. By now he's sober, and he's realised just how much he's fucked up. He's going to want to come back. Will you take him back?"

"I don't think so."

"He's going to promise the world, but is he going to change?"

"You're not making this easy."

"It's not going to be easy, and it's going to get a lot harder before it's over."

"I will miss him. He was very good with Julie, and she'll miss him."

"True, but can you take the risk? The choices are all yours, I'll help you in any way I can."

"Why?"

"What do you mean?"

"Why? For a complete stranger, who was actually quite rude when we first met."

"A scumbag like him made me who I am today. I have a real hatred for men that beat up women. I have a more special place for the ones that abuse children."

"He's never hurt Julie."

"But she was screaming, by hurting you, he is hurting her."

"I suppose."

"Choice is yours, even if you let him back in, I'll still help if I can."

"Let's get him moved out to start with." Janice was more than a little unsure about this statement, but she was determined to follow it through. She reached into a drawer and pulled out a roll of large black garbage bags. Bandit Queen smiled, both at the fact that everyone has such a drawer, and that his clothes were going into bin bags.

"Great." she said. "We'll get Man-Dare on the packing and then we'll go and visit your neighbours." She gently guided Janice towards the stairs and the pair followed her up. "Is his car going to be big enough? Asked Bandit Queen.

"It's not too big but it should be more than enough." They walked into the bedroom, it was quite spacious, wardrobes along one wall, and chest against another. Bandit Queen noticed a blood stain on the back of the door and growled.

"Chill," whispered Man-Dare. "Is that yours?" she turned to Janice; the only reply was a nod.

"Bastard," muttered Bandit Queen.

Janice opened one wardrobe, half of it contained men's clothing. Then she opened two drawers in one of the chests, one had socks underwear and colognes, the other a few t-shirts. She looked at Janice.

"It that it?" Janice nodded.

"Two years and that's it?" another nod.

"Cd's?" this time a shake.

"Books?" another shake.

"DVD's?"

"Nothing." said Janice.

"Computer?"

"Just his work laptop, and that goes with him everywhere. He's already got that."

In only a few minutes everything was packed into three bags.

They went downstairs and dropped them in the hallway, on their way to the kitchen. Janice put the kettle on.

"What do you know of his past?" asked Bandit Queen.

"Almost nothing, he doesn't talk about it, why?"

"Two years and all he's got is a few clothes, he's done this before. He's ready to fly. He's gone in a heartbeat."

"What does that mean?"

"He has a history, something he's hiding. I wonder how many women he has left in the lurch; I think he might be worth a look into. That temper of his has to leave some traces, even if he changes his name. Have you any idea where he came from?"

"He moved to Wigan for a new job, about three years ago, but before that I get the impression he was from Derbyshire or somewhere."

"Did he ever take you back there? You know visit his old haunts, meet some of his old mates?"

"Nothing like that ever."

"I wonder what he is hiding?"

"Don't you have things you'd prefer hidden?" asked Janice.

"Oh yes. That's what worries me. What is the bastard hiding?"

"I really don't care, so long he stays away."

"The truth of it will come out when he turns up, if he makes no attempt to stay then he's definitely been up to no good." Janice's phone made a buzzing sound and a tweeting noise at the same time. She picked it up and checked the incoming message.

"It's from him, he wants to collect his stuff, he can be here in five minutes. What should I do?"

"Tell him come ahead."

"I'm starting to feel frightened," muttered Janice as she sent the text message.

"He'll not be stupid enough to start anything while we are here, it's after we are gone that I worry about," said Bandit Queen taking her hands.

"Will you be able to keep Julie safe?"

"Everyone will be safe except him. Sadly, there are likely to be too many witnesses for my liking. I'd much prefer a dark alley and just the two of us."

"Are you not frightened of him at all?"

"Only enough to get the adrenaline running hot," smiled Bandit Queen.

"We'll have to keep Julie out of the way until he's gone," said Man-Dare.

"She'll be a good girl and stay indoors," said Janice. The three women walked into the front room and looked out of the window just as a silver car pulled up behind Bandit Queens.

"That's Simon's car," said Janice, "he looks like he's on his own."

"Does he have any friends?" Bandit Queen mumbled.

"No," was the quiet reply. They all went to the front door, and Janice opened it, her hands shaking as she withdrew the bolts.

She stepped out, then the other two followed one to each side.

"What the fuck are you bitches doing here?" he demanded.

"Janice didn't feel like getting slapped around anymore," smiled Bandit Queen.

"Well, the cops have said that I mustn't come inside the gate. So, I won't. Have you got my stuff ready?" Janice only nodded, and the others stepped inside to collect the bags. Bandit Queen didn't take her eyes off him, even though he was quite a distance away, and the gate was loud and heavy. Bandit Queen and Man-Dare went to the gate and handed him the bags.

"Clothes, shoes, toiletries. No books, no DVD, and no CD's," said Bandit Queen. "For a guy living here two years, you don't half travel light."

"What is that to do with you?" his voice very low.

"When I find out why you are so light, then the whole world will know," Bandit Queen's eyes bored into his. Simon paused for a long moment.

"Waiting for something?" asked Man-Dare. His head snapped over to her then he turned and walked away, back to his car, he got in and drove away without a single glance in their direction.

"Was it just me," said Man-Dare, "or did he twitch at DVD?"

"I don't know I was struggling not to kill the fucker."

"He definitely twitched," smiled Man-Dare.

"We better advise Janice, there may be a DVD lying around somewhere, that he doesn't want anyone to find."

The two of them walked back to the front door, watching the road is case the car came back. Janice was waiting not so patiently for them.

"What did he say?" she asked.

"Not much," replied Bandit Queen. "Man-Dare thinks there may be a DVD around somewhere, you'd better find it, or he may be back for it."

"I don't have much in the way of DVD's a few films, and a few TV series that's all. If anything, Julie's got more than me, cartoons and such," said Janice.

"Let's check those out then." They went to the DVD rack that was near the TV that Julie was watching, sorting through then didn't take a long time. One of the cases had a disc inside that didn't match the pictures on the case. Bandit Queen released the disc from the case and turned it over.

"This one is a home burn, it's purple." She went to put it in the DVD player under the TV.

"That one only works in daddy's computer," said Julie.

"Do you know what's on it?" asked Janice.

"It's movies of playtime," smiled Julie. "When will daddy be back, he always gives me lots of chocolate after playtime."

"I don't think daddy will ever be coming back, not after the way he treated me last night."

"No more playtime?" Julie asked, her lower lip sticking out.

"Not unless he gets himself sorted out."

"I'll miss playtime with daddy."

"Go and watch your TV." Janice said. As she went to her computer and hit the power button. "It's old and slow, but it works." She smiled at the other two women.

"What do you know of playtime?" asked Bandit Queen.

"Nothing, I'd almost swear that he never plays with her. Though she does like to sit on his knee and watch movies, or TV."

"Nothing too unusual about that," Man-Dare said.

"So why don't I know about this playtime?" asked Janice. Her computer finally finished it's boot up sequence, so she opened the DVD player and dropped the disc into it. She pushed the drawer and it closed slowly, they listened to the disc spin up. Then a window opened on the screen, it showed the contents of the disc, each folder on the disc had a simple date, the earliest being about eighteen months ago.

"Where do we start?" asked Janice.

"At the beginning."

"OK." Janice clicked on the oldest folder and it opened with a single video file. Janice hit the video and a player window opened. The picture looked like something out of a cheap porn movie, the quality was low and the only thing visible was an erect penis. Then a very young girl crawled into the shot and took hold of it with both of her small hands. Janice snapped the window closed before it could go any further. "Bastard." she whispered.

"I'm going to kill that cunt," muttered Bandit Queen.

"Both of you relax," whispered Man-Dare. The two glared at Man-Dare.

"Fucking relax," mumbled Bandit Queen. "Only when I stuff his dick down his throat."

"Janice," said Man-Dare. "Call the fucking cops, give them the disc, let them catch the bastard, once they have him inside, we'll arrange him a going away party."

"I want to kill the fucker," snapped Bandit Queen.

"Shush," snapped Man-Dare. "It's simply playtime for Julie, give her a couple of years and she'll forget about it, we need to keep this as quiet as we can for her sake."

"Man-Dare," whispered Bandit Queen. "I hate it when you are being rational. You're right, bitch."

"Janice," said Man-Dare. "Make the call. And tell them that you are frightened he might be coming back for the disc." Man-Dare went and sat beside Julie watching the cartoons on the TV.

"Does mummy enjoy playtime with daddy as well?" she whispered. Julie turned to her and replied quietly.

"No silly. Daddy makes mummy her special cocoa and she goes to sleep; playtime is just for me and daddy. Is he going to be coming back?"

"I don't think so."

"I want him to come back."

"Doesn't he hurt you sometimes?"

"Only a little bit, but he likes it, and there is always chocolate."

"I see." Man-Dare returned to Bandit Queens side and looked hard at the older woman's seething expression.

"You might get your chance if he comes back before the cops get here. There is good news."

"Explain," snarled Bandit Queen.

"Janice is not involved in any way, the bastard drugged her so she slept through it all."

"You're kidding."

"No, playtime is only for daddy."

"I want that bastard dead."

"I think his life expectancy is quite short about now anyway." Janice put her phone down and spoke softly.

"They're sending someone round right now they say, someone from a different unit."

"Let's hope they're not too quick," said Bandit Queen. She went to the knife block and took the two longest knives from it, she tossed the shorter to Man-Dare.

"Take the front, I'll have the back, he's most likely to try the back because the sliding door gives the quickest access, I'm betting he knows exactly where that disc was." Man-Dare went to the front window and declared.

"Clear here."

Bandit Queen stood by the sliding door to the back garden and watched the back fence carefully, if he was going to come from anywhere it was over that fence. Janice slumped in a chair watching her daughter, who was still watching her cartoons, she shook her head occasionally, not believing what was happening. After a tense ten minutes Man-Dare called out.

"Car."

"They cops?" asked Bandit Queen, not taking her eyes off the fence.

"I can almost smell the bacon from here," laughed Man-Dare.

"Fine, Janice go let them in, but make them show warrant cards through the front window." Janice did exactly as she was asked; the two policemen were not pleased but showed their ID as requested. Once they came into the house and the door was bolted again behind them, the greyer of the two introduced them.

"I'm DI Hopkins, and this is DC Lewis. You say you have some evidence that might help us." Julie looked round at the policemen if only for a moment. Lewis stared hard at Hopkins as the little girl looked back towards the TV. Hopkins raised his eyebrows but said nothing to his colleague.

"I believe there was a domestic disturbance here last night?" he asked looked Janice in the eyes.

"My ex got violent, and I threw his ass out," she snapped.

"And these two formidably armed ladies?"

"I suppose you could call them acquaintances."

"If that bastard turns up here," whispered Bandit Queen, "I'm going to gut him, don't get in the way."

"You found a disc after he came to collect his things?" He turned back to Janice.

"Yes," she passed him the DVD case.

"Do you mind if we have a quick look?"

"Use the computer, it won't play in the DVD player." Hopkins goes to the PC and loads the disc into the player, when the window opens, he picks a folder at random, and plays the file, only a few seconds, then he picks another one, again he skips through the video, until he finds something his is looking for. Another video, this one he jumps out of immediately.

"Damn," whispered Lewis. "This is important stuff. Is it the source?"

"Looking at the dates I'd say it is almost certainly just that. Webcam quality looks about right, and there's no mistaking that picture." Said Hopkins. He turns to Janice. "What do you know about these videos?"

"We found the disc after he left. That is all I know."

"According to Julie," said Man-Dare. "Daddy gives Mummy special cocoa, so she sleeps through playtime."

"Cocoa?" asked Hopkins.

"Cocoa." screamed Janice. "The bastard drugged me with cocoa. Sweet cocoa, with a dash of rum. I'm gonna kill him." Hopkins goes back to the computer.

"The most recent file on here is last week, Monday. Ring any bells?"

"I remember feeling damned tired all day Tuesday." said Janice.

"Well, we should be able to do a test to find out if you are telling the truth. We have to be certain; you do understand?"

"I suppose," Janice looked at her daughter and was very worried that she would lose her.

"Right," said Hopkins. "I think we have enough already to get things moving." He pulled his radio from inside his jacket. He spent a short time talking to the control centre.

"I am sorry," he said, "but we are going to have to take you and your daughter in for questioning on this matter, I'm sure you will be cleared of any wrongdoing, but we do need to be sure. Have you any idea where your ex may be heading?"

"None at all. I know almost nothing of his past, I think he came from the midlands somewhere, but he had no accent as such."

"We are almost certain that he is a person known as the unicorn, simply because of the unicorn picture that tends to appear in his videos."

"You mean the one he bought for Julie soon after he moved in with me."

"That's the one."

"So how long has he been at this?"

"It's been a few years now, he's been selling video on the dark web, for a while. We believe he's been selling live performances as well."

"How many victims?" asked Bandit Queen.

"We can't be certain, but I think Julie is his third sort of full-time victim. Video's of her have been turning up for about a year now."

"How are you going to catch him?"

"We have his car and his name we'll get him soon."

"Fuck that." she snapped. She turned to Janice, "give me his phone number." Janice showed her the number, Bandit Queen sent that number by text. Then called Bug.

"Bug, find that damned phone." Hopkins listened to a short silence as the other person was talking.

"I don't care if you are in Southport having a beer, find me that phone now."

"What is going on?" asked Hopkins.

"Bug is better than your shitty systems at finding people. He'll be back to us in a little while. So, what are you going to do for Janice and Julie?"

"They'll be taken into protective custody; a simple hair test will confirm that Janice has been drugged recently. Which I thoroughly expect to be the case. Then we'll try and find this ass, quick before he sets up a new identity." Bandit Queens phone rang. She answered it. She listened briefly then thanked Bug.

"The phone you are looking for is currently northbound on the M6 just north of Lancaster, it's making ninety miles an hour and is turned off."

"Do I want to know how you did that?"

"Call it the fuck in, and we can talk about it." Hopkins smiled and radioed to his control, his final words were, "Don't ask just go fucking look."

"I don't think I really want to know, but if you choose to tell me I am certain I can forget real quick."

"Phone systems leak like a colander," She turned her phone to show Hopkins a text she had just received from Bug. "That number is in the same vehicle, is operational, and is currently carrying a massive data load. Bug thinks he may be creating a new identity as he's driving."

"Is that possible?"

"If Bug thinks so, then yes. This is the twenty first century, and everything changes. You've got to be ready."

"I know that one," Hopkins pauses for a moment or two.

"That's torchwood," said Lewis.

"Torchwood indeed," laughed Hopkins. Bandit Queens phone rang again. She listened briefly, then hung up.

"He's using multiple VPN and fast switching encryption, Bug is sorry but his phone is too slow to break into the data stream."

"Have you any idea how many laws you are breaking?"

"If you catch him, do you care?"

"I should, but I don't." Hopkins radio squawked in his hand. He pressed the earpiece firmly into his ear. Then spoke into the microphone.

"If he runs, shoot the fucker, somehow I don't think he's going to survive long once he gets to jail." Bandit Queen smiled at the last statement. He turned to her and spoke slowly. "Traffic cars are on his ass, and a chopper is moving in, ARU (armed response unit) less than two minutes away. You know that I wish I could thank you for your help in this matter, but I can't."

"Just look after Janice and Julie."

"That I can do."

"Fine, I think our work here is done." Bandit Queen caught Man-Dare with her eyes and passed the knife she was carrying to Janice. "Janice," she said softly, "these nice gentlemen will look after you, you and Julie will be safe. We have to go now." She turned to Hopkins. "If you want to lose the fucker, just bring him to us, I'm sure we'll have a lot of information for you before he disappears from public life."

"You know I can't do that; you'll just have to catch him in a prison yard."

"That works too." She hugged Janice briefly and the pair walked towards the door.

"Are you just going to let them go?" asked Lewis.

"I believe so." Hopkins grinned. "I can't really stop them, if they aren't here. I think they left before we arrived."

"You can't do that boss," said Lewis.

"Actually I can, and so can you, I think this Bandit Queen might be quite helpful to us in the future."

"That is a possibility," said Bandit Queen, looking hard into his eyes. "Daughters?" she asked.

"Two, seventeen and eighteen."

"Children Lewis?" she asked.

"One on the way," Bandit Queen smiled, then glanced at Julie.

"She'll be fine, given a few years to forget, the real worry is the pervs that get addicted to his stuff, then go on to act out themselves. Either with their own children, or with someone else's. The innocent should be protected."

"I can't argue with that," said Lewis, stepping out of the way. Bandit Queen turned back to Hopkins.

"We will be watching."

"I understand," he smiled back.

Without another word the two Dragonriders left the house and drove away.

22: Tuesday Drag Racing

Slowball talked to the guys running the carousel, and they agreed to watch out for the Dragonriders bikes while they were away. So, the group set off away from the promenade, back towards the main street. Past an ice cream parlour, and a kebab shop, they arrived at a tiny little side street, the signs say Cable Street. With Jackie in his left hand Roaddog turned into Cable Street and walked the short distance to the pub on the right, the Fox and Goose. This particular place was well known as a music and biker venue, rock music and cheap beer, no food and no parking. Tuesday morning and it was only just open, the landlord was actually waiting a delivery of beer, and hadn't intended customers this early, but if people were willing to pay for beer, then he wasn't going to turn them away. It was close to midday, so Roaddog asked if it was all right for them to go and get some kebabs, people being hungry and all that. The landlord said that would be no problem, so Roaddog went to get food for the rest. They were all sitting around a pair of small tables drinking beers and eating when Bug's phone rang. After a brief conversation with Bandit Queen, he hung up and said.
"Who's got unlimited data and a fast, preferably 5G connection?"
"I'm on 5G." said Jackie.
"Lend me your phone." said Bug.
"Why?"
"We're looking for a paedophile." She unlocked her phone and passed it over to Bug, his linked hers to his and started his tracking software. In less than two minutes he had what he could get, and he sent Bandit Queen a text message and then called her, the conversation was brief.
"What the fuck is going on?" demanded Bone.
"Bandit is looking for some paedophile, and I've sent her his details,

other than that, I know nothing."

"Why is she looking for some asshole?"

"I don't know," said Bug, "and to be honest I don't care, I've done what she wanted, and she seems to be as happy as she can be. That's good enough for me."

"I'll have to talk to her," Bone seemed more than a little uncertain.

"I've a feeling she's sort of busy right now," smiled Bug.

A short time later all the kebabs were finished, and more beers were bought, a delivery driver came in through the front door and walked up to the bar.

"I got six kegs for you, where do you want them?"

"Just drop them by the front door, I'll get the staff to move them once they arrive." said the landlord. Roaddog glanced at Slowball and Bug. The three stood and walked over to the door.

"Where do you want them?" asked Roaddog.

"Just inside and over to the right will be great." said the landlord, checking the tags and dates on the kegs. He signed the delivery drivers dockets and waved him away. He turned to watch Roaddog and the other two manoeuvring the kegs, Roaddog tipped a keg up to about twenty-five degrees and then rolled it long on the bottom edge. It took him two attempts to get it up the step and onto the same level as the floor of the bar, wriggling it through the narrow doorway was a little difficult but he made it.

"You've done this before," the landlord said.

"I've done all sorts of shit before," laughed Roaddog. "Where's the cellar?"

"This close to the sea, there are no cellars. I'll get the door." He opened a wide door, and turned on the lights, the sound heavy fans and cold air flooded through the door. "Thanks guys, just drop them inside. I'll sort them later once they've had a chance to cool down a bit." The landlord killed the lights and locked the door again, returning behind his bar, he started pumping one of the beer lines through. The steady sound of liquid falling into a large steel bucket was quite soothing. Bone stood and said.

"I'm going outside to call Bandit Queen, see what the hell is going on with her today." The whole bar lit up for an instant as daylight from the street flooded in, to be gone a moment later. Bone returned to the bar in a column of light, and walked over to the others.

"Seems that dick she smacked down on Sunday is a well-known paedophile. Even better known now, dibble have his name and plate, and are pursuing his car up the six with orders to shoot on sight," he laughed.

"They can't do that, can they?" asked Jackie.

"I believe the copper concerned was actually joking, but they definitely want the fucker in a bad way."

"I bet Bandit Queen wants him as well," Roaddog grinned.

"Oh, does she. She's going through her diary to find out which psychos are in which jails; her only real issue is that his end is going to be too quick."

"Well," said Jackie, "at least she's done some good today."

"She thinks that some DI called Hopkins may think he's in line for some favours though," laughed Bone. "No good deed goes unpunished."

The door opened again, and four people walked in off the street, given the day the Dragonriders were having they all turned to watch, each of the men were towing a suitcase with wheels and three were carrying garment bags for suits. A little strange for a Tuesday lunchtime, but this is Southport. The four men blinked in the sudden darkness until the lights over the bar picked out the landlord, so they moved slowly towards him.

"Hi." said the first of them, "Have you any idea what time the bar across the road opens?"

"Not usually until about five this afternoon."

"Damn. We're performing there later and wanted to get in early, you know, drop the bags and go for a mooch around the shops."

"Give me a second and I'll call the guy that runs the place." The landlord picked up his phone from the back of the bar and made a quick call. "Chris says he'll be here in about half an hour, are you the team from Blackpool?"

"Yes, we are, why?"

"Because he says to get you a beer and he'll settle up later, he was dragged away by something that came up suddenly. So guys, what you having?"

"Desperado with lime."

"Four?"

"Yes. It's too early for real drinks." The landlord got four bottles from the cooler and popped the caps off, pushing lime wedges into the top of each. The four piled the garment bags on a nearby table and stood the suitcases with them. Sipping their lager from the bottles through the limes.

"Isn't that place a gay bar," asked Slowball walking towards the four.

"It is," said the tallest, "and we are drag queens performing tonight." His words almost a challenge.

"So, you're all gay?"

"Actually," said the spokesman, "The average is three in four are gay, I look good in a dress, and can sing and dance in eight-inch heels, and I make enough money to stop my wife and children from starving."

"Fuck me," said Slowball, "how tall are you in your heels?"

"With a good wig I get to seven foot four. You?"

"I don't do heels, some say I have enough trouble walking in my boots. I'm six three."

"Perhaps you should come catch the show, it'll probably be something different for you."

"You're not wrong there. But no, we've gotta get home to Leyland. How much do you earn for a night?"

"That's extremely variable, tonight if we win, the pot is five thousand."

"What are your chances?"

"Good actually, we've got three buses coming from Blackpool, so voting could be close. There are only three teams tonight, so we have a really good shot. Then on to the regional finals."

"Five K and it's not even a regional final. That's damned good money."

"It's damned hard work and the money isn't always good, but it's steady, and keeps the wolf from the door."

"Good luck for tonight." Slowball walks back to the table and sits with the Dragonriders again. "Can you imagine that guy in a dress?" he asked.

"I'd rather not," laughed Roaddog, "You fancy the idea Slowball?"

"Not much. They give me the creeps, but you've got to admit he's got balls."

"But why do it?" asked Bug.

"Money, he makes a living at it."

"You're kidding."

"No, if they win tonight they get five thousand quid." Slowball smiled.

"Shit," said Roaddog, "we're in the wrong business."

"You think you could make money dancing in a dress?" Bone laughed.

"I might need a little practice."

"Conservative estimate, about twenty years." Bone's grin had all the others laughing. The door to the bar filled the room with daylight again, and a lone shape walked in. He went straight to the bar.

"You guys the Blackpool crew?"

"That's be us." said the tallest.

"I'm Chris, if you'll come with me, I let you in, I've still got a lot of setting up to do." He dropped a tenner on the bar. "Cheers Jim."

"No worries Chris." said the landlord. The four followed Chris out of the door.

"Hey Jim." called Bone. "Any change of a second door? That daylight is really getting to my eyes."

"No chance, almost no one comes in here until it's dark outside."

"What's up? They all vampires?" Jim laughed aloud, and a scream came from the street outside. Jackie looked round to find herself sitting with Billy for company. The flare of light as the Dragonriders ran out into the street made her flinch. Roaddog was first through the door, and the view that met him was not what he expected. In front of the door to the pub across the road, the landlord Chris, and two of the drag queens were fighting off a group of eight young men, the other two queens were screaming.

"We don't want puffs in our town." One of young men screamed, hurling another punch at Chris. "Get the queers off our street." Howled another as he tried and failed to connect with the tall guy. The young men were not prepared for the tide of violence that over ran them. Roaddog was first to arrive, by only a second, he spun one of the men around and a fast right took the guy's breath way, as he folded over the fist in his guts a rising knee took him in the face and put his lights out. Bone took down one of the men with a single blow to the head, Slowball arrived grabbed two by the head and slammed them together, two more out of the fight. The tall guy slammed one in the face and he fell to the ground to be kicked into unconsciousness, Chris took one with a fast knee to the nuts.

"All you fucking bikers are gay." Shouted one of the last two standing, he was silenced by Bug, with a rapid left, right combination to the ribs, and a kick to the jaw as he fell to the ground. Only one left, he was rapidly surrounded by Dragonriders. Roaddog stepped up and grabbed him by the front of his expensive tracksuit. Roaddog hauled him over to the door of the bar and held him for the tall guy to despatch, the single blow splashed nose and blood all across the thug's face, he slumped to the ground as the others were starting to wake up. Slowball and Bug started collecting them together, there was little resistance after the first one got an additional slap from Sharpshooter. There were no broken bones, just some blood and pain.

"You're call Chris." shouted Bone. "Kill 'em, call the cops, or chase them off?"

"We need no more corpses on Cable Street, the damned cops aren't worth the fucking paperwork, let the fucks go." The corral of Dragonriders opened up to allow the men to leave. Staying close together they walked slowly towards the open end of Cable Street, watched all the way. Once they had turned the corner things started to relax. Chris got the door to his bar opened and started ushering the drag queens inside. The tall guy came over to thank the Dragonriders for the help. There was a loud noise from around the corner.

"What the fuck now?" muttered Roaddog.

Eight young men, some covered in their own blood came back into view, this time carrying the wreckage of chairs from the cafe up the road.

"We're going to rain on you Dragonriders," yelled the leader, as they came into Cable Street again. The Dragonriders spread out across Cable Street, Bone reached into his boot and produced a short length of steel bar. Roaddog stood in the centre of the road, a twelve-inch stiletto in each hand, next to him was Slowball, his right hand appeared from under his jacket, a length of triplex motorcycle chain dropped into view. Sharpshooter withdrew his hands from his pockets, each one with a shiny chrome knuckleduster. Bug stood at one end of the line, a military issue extending baton appeared in his hand and snapped out to its full extension. The tall guy and the other drag queen that had been fighting came to stand either side of Bone, even though they aren't armed. By the door to the Fox and Goose Billy pushed Jackie so that she was almost inside.

"Aren't you going to join in?" she asked him.

"This is a young man's game and I'm not actually a member, so I'll look after you if the crap comes this way. I don't think there's anything to worry about though." He could tell from the body language that some of the young men were only a moment away from running. He wasn't the only one that could see this. Roaddog called out.

"Your choices are run or die. Choose fast, because I am rapidly losing patience with you fools."

"We're going to rain on you," yelled the leader again, stepping forwards slowly, only three of his men came with him, he looked round, and three more threw down their weapons and ran, it seems they didn't like the odds now stacked against them. A fist fight with a few gays, is a world of difference from what now stood arrayed against them. In a moment the leader followed his gang, leaving only scattered fragments of furniture on the street.

"That's more like it," Bone said loudly, "really gets the heart beating."

"Thanks for that," said the tall guy. "We haven't had that sort of trouble round here for ages."

"No worries," Bone laughed, the sound of approaching sirens caused a flurry of activity, as the weapons all disappeared back into their concealments. The car went passed the end of the street as Chris was opening the door to his bar. The performers from Blackpool went inside and closed the door, and the Dragonriders returned to the Fox and Goose. They were sitting quietly drinking their beer a few minutes later when the policemen walked in.

"You lot seem to be in the thick of things today," said the first policeman.

"It's an exciting little town you have here," said Bone. "First, we prevent your carousel from burning to the ground, and then we protect some visiting artists from a completely unprovoked attack. I think we deserve a bonus for doing your job for you."

"I think that you instigated both events," snarled the cop.

"I'm sure you've talked to witnesses at both scenes," Bone smiled.

"We have, and you lot come out as heroes both times. Something I truly don't believe."

"We're just glad to help our fellow man."

"Personally," said the policeman slowly, "I'd prefer it if you lot left town immediately."

"Well officer, we're currently on our second pint, so we'll most likely be leaving fairly soon. Is that acceptable?"

"Try not to be involved in anymore, how do we put this? Incidents. We will be watching you."

"That's very kind of you officer, your local thugs have proved to be quite a nuisance for us today. We'd hate for any of them to get hurt."

"I wish I could say the same about you lot," snapped the cop as he turned to leave, his second followed him, with a big smile on his face.

"I think this town is just too scary for me," said Roaddog.

"Fine," replied Bone, "let's head for home."

"Agreed," said Slowball. "If we drink some more the bastards are sure to pull us as soon as we hit the road." He stood up and called to the landlord. "Sorry Jim, we gotta go, this town is just too rough for us."

"Yeah, right," laughed Jim, as the others drank up. Slowball collected the empty glasses and delivered them to the bar.

"Thanks Jim, we'll probably be back for some live music in the near future, unless of course the local mobsters kill us all on our way out of town."

"That's not going to happen, is it?" said Jim, "Dibble's going to all over your ass like a rash."

"We'll see about that," laughed Slowball, as they all walked out into the sunlit street. Parked directly outside was a police car, with the two coppers that they had just been talking to. Bone smiled as they walked towards the end of Cable Street. They turned left towards the carousel, and an Asian man approached them.

"You guys the ones that beat the shit out of those young thugs?" he demanded.

"We tried," said Roaddog. "But they ran off before we could do them any serious damage." The man turned to the police car as it rolled slowly out of Cable Street.

"Where were you bastards when the ass holes were attacking my business?" The man yelled. He turned back to Roaddog. "They were probably doing something more important." The next he called loudly. "Filling their faces at Crispy Creme." He went on much quieter. "If you get a chance, kill a couple for me."

"You must know that despite what the press tells the world, we don't actually kill people, we are simply a motorcycle club." Roaddog smiled and shook the man's hand. They walked on towards the carousel. The police car crawling along behind them. When they got to the promenade and looked across the road to where the bikes were parked, they all burst out laughing. There were two new motorcycles, each dressed up in blue and yellow, each with a rider covered completely in fluorescent green, the cops hadn't been joking about being watched, they were getting a motorcycle escort. As they crossed the wide promenade Roaddog nudged Bone and talked briefly to the leader.

"Let's fuck with the cops," suggested Roaddog.

"How?"

"Split, I'll take Sharpshooter and Bug through the middle of town, you take Slowball and Billy along the front. We can meet up at the roundabout on the way out of town."

"Sounds like fun, set it up." Bone laughed.

Roaddog nodded and tapped Bug and Sharpshooter.

"We're going to mess with the cops, you guys follow me, OK?" The two nodded. Roaddog moved on to Slowball and Billy. Once he had their attention.

"You two follow Bone. I'm gonna take the others a different route. Got it?"

The two nodded, by this time they were all at the bikes. The motorcycle cops had their motors started, even though no one could actually hear them. Once the Dragonriders were all mounted one of the motorcycle cops waved to Bone and told him to follow, he must have known something about the structure of motorcycle clubs, Bone looked at Roaddog, his smile hidden inside his helmet. Once all the cycles were set to roll, Bone set off along the front. Roaddog turned into Neville Street, he passed the end of Cable Street with Bug and Sharpshooter behind him, and the second motorcycle cop behind them, the car and the first motorcycle cop had followed Bone, Billy, and Slowball. Roaddog turned left onto Lord Street, the main street through the middle of town, this one had lots of traffic lights and roundabouts, definitely not the quickest route out of town. But the cop stayed behind him, and the other two. By the time they had driven through the centre of town and out to the roundabout at Churchtown, the group that had gone along the coast road had been waiting at the roundabout for a while, with traffic piling up behind them, the two groups re-joined and set off out of town, leaving the cops to their own devices.

23: Tuesday Home For Lunch

The six made their way rapidly back to the clubhouse, seeing as the time was just after two, they all went to Andy's burger van for lunch, he was quite glad to see them as the day had been quite slow, more than a few of the units around were closed for business, including the Dragonriders. The sound of approaching motorcycles brought a small smile to Andy's lips. When they turned up expecting food, he was even more happy.

"How's it been today?" Asked Roaddog, as he waited for his lunch.

"Fucking shit, I should have taken the week off, so many places are actually closed. It's crazy."

"Things have changed, used to be that businesses stayed open when the schools are closed, not today. People have to take their holidays so they can look after the kids, and businesses may as well shut."

"Yours being one of them?" asked Roaddog.

"Definitely," said Andy. "That'll be six quid."

"Prices suddenly gone up?"

"Hey, I got kids to feed as well."

Roaddog handed over a tenner and took his change with a shake of the head. Roaddog returned to the unit and handed Jackie her bacon sausage and egg sandwich and dropped into the seat next to her.

"Classy meals again, I see," she laughed.

"What can I say? I'm a classy guy," he leaned against her and they shared a greasy kiss. When they looked forwards again Bandit Queen's car was rolling to a stop in the yard. The two women got out and walked into the clubhouse.

"What you been up to?" called Bone.

"Helping the cops catch a damned paedophile," snarled Bandit Queen. She turned to Bug. "Thanks for your help, I believe the cops should have caught up with the bastard by now. With any luck they'll have shot him." Bug smiled and nodded.

"What had he been up to?" asked Bone, quietly.

"Taking video with that little girl and selling them on the internet." Bandit Queen walked over to the bar and grabbed a bottle of vodka, she took a large slug out of the bottle and passed it on to Man-Dare. She turned back to Bone. "He's been doing it for years apparently. The cops called him unicorn, there's a picture of a unicorn in his videos normally."

"How can he get away with it for so long?" demanded Slowball.

"He's good with the tech, and using the dark web, you can get away with almost anything," said Bug.

"Could we use it for selling our drugs?" asked Bone.

"It would take a little setting up, but yes it's possible. Though we'd be working in a world-wide market, so prices can be a little more variable than we like."

"Any other problems?" Bone enquired.

"The only real weak point is delivery. If just one package gets intercepted by a cop, then the whole network could be compromised."

"Think about it, come up with a way to avoid that." Bone smiled at the possibility of selling even more with no risk. "Surely the cops can track the money?"

"No, crypto-currencies are used, they can't track them," smiled Bug. Jackie looked hard at Roaddog, he shook his head, only enough so that Jackie would see. He'd rather not have the rest know about his bitcoin operation. Bug turned to Roaddog and grinned. He remembered helping Roaddog install the miners, he'd nodded to show that they'd talk later in private. By the time they had all finished their lunches Bandit Queen was a little more settled, still angry, but not cursing so much, the vodka seemed to be helping. The discussion turned to the upcoming rally in Chorley. All present were looking forward to it, and hoping for some good weather, but given enough booze that wasn't actually essential. While they were reliving rallies past a car rolled slowly into the yard. Two men got out.

"Pigs." muttered Bandit Queen, as she raced over to the car, only to find the back seat empty.

"Hello again," smiled Hopkins. Lewis nodded. "You didn't think I'd bring the bastard here did you?"

"I had hoped," said Bandit Queen. "So why are you here? Long way off your patch."

"I've come specifically to thank you and your people for their help today. Sadly, there can be no official recognition, your methods not being exactly de-rigour, location of the car goes to some sharp-eyed motorway bobby. But without you the bastard may have got away again. Our IT guys are confident they can break his laptop, we could get many more names and places from it. There's enough evidence in the car to put him away from a long time. I actually believe he may never see the outside again. Thank you."

"What about Janice?"

"Pending tests, but I expect her to be released today."

"With her daughter?"

"That's outside my control, social services govern that sort of thing."

"And they're a complete bunch of assholes. I knew I should have killed the fucker."

"Wouldn't have helped much," smiled Hopkins.

"Would have made me feel better, you better keep a tight hold on him."

"He's going nowhere right now. He's likely to be in solitary for the rest of his life."

"Here's hoping for a short life." She raised the bottle and took a slug.

"You do know that if he has an accident, we're going to come looking for you."

"I'm sure I'll have plenty of witnesses to say that I was somewhere else." She waved an arm at all the people sitting behind her.

"I'm certain of that fact," laughed Hopkins. He turned to the others. "Thank you all for your help today, we have caught a man who is a serious danger to children everywhere, and I can't say we'd have done that without you." Hopkins and Lewis turn back to their car and left.

"Now that was weird," said Bone.

"They were impressed with Bug's work," said Bandit Queen. "That Lewis though, he wanted to charge us with something."

"Phone tracking as we do it is illegal; I dread to think how many laws it actually breaks," laughed Bug. "Nice to get some recognition though."

"He's going to want a favour sometime in the future," muttered Bone.

"He can go fuck himself," snarled Bandit Queen.

The conversation turned to rallies old and the up-coming one for the mayday bank holiday. Bandit Queen smiled as Man-Dare moved in alongside Billy, their conversation gradually became more private and started to exclude the others.

Roaddog's phone pinged the sound of an incoming message, he glanced at it briefly, then showed it to Jackie, his brow asking the question. Jackie smiled and nodded. His fingers flew across the keypad and an answer was sent. In only moments a reply was received. Again, Jackie got to see the response and she smiled. The phone vanished inside Roaddog's jacket and the conversations continued.

"When are we planning to get to this rally?" asked Roaddog. "There's disco Friday, a band Saturday, and Fifth Element on Sunday."

"Preferences?" asked Bone.

"If we get there early Friday evening, take the gear and a stack of beer in with a van. I'm sure that the Centurions won't mind. We can be set up for the whole weekend."

"Who drives the van? There's bound to be ride outs, no one's gonna want to there without their bike?" Bone's question got lots of looks from the guys.

"I can drive the van," said Man-Dare.

"Sounds like a plan," smiled Roaddog. "You got a licence?"

"Yes I've got a licence. Cheeky bastard." Man-Dare laughed. "But I ain't driving it on no fucking grass, one of you bastards can get the thing bogged down."

"Deal," called Bone. "Tents and beer here Thursday evening, we'll move in as soon as they open the gates on Friday." He looked up as a car pulled into the yard and parked behind Bandit Queens. Thinking it was a customer Bone waved Roaddog to go and talk to the driver, along with a two fingered salute to tell them to come back tomorrow. Roaddog walked over to the car and opened the driver's door.

"You OK?" he asked.

"Not sure about this at all," was the reply.

"Time to meet new people, they're nice enough, if a little crazy."

"You're not joking there," she smiled and reached out with her right hand, Roaddog helped her out of the car, then she turned around to get a large bag from the passenger seat. Together they walked toward the bikers in the unit.

"Hey, Bone." said Roaddog. "You remember this morning when I said that I was late because of a couple of women. Well Jackie was one, and this is Sylvia, she was the other, she's a friend, she divorced, and looking to make some new friends, so I invited her to meet you lot. She's got a bit of thing for photography." At this point Jackie choked. "I'm sure you'd all like to meet her and have your photos taken."

"I'm OK with that," said Bone.

"That's good," Roaddog went on, "That's Bone, he's the boss. Slowball, he handles the money, Bug, Sharpshooter, Billy, Bandit Queen, Man-Dare, and of course Jackie you've already seen naked."

"Sylvia," Bone smiled broadly. "Roaddog told us that he was late this morning because he had to get two back into their clothes. Was he telling us the truth?"

"Yes," Sylvia grinned, "all three of us were naked this morning before he set off to do whatever it was he had to do."

"Well, I see no reason why you shouldn't fit right in with this bunch of loons," Bone's laugh filled the unit.

"So," Bandit Queen interrupted, "you spent the night with Roaddog and Jackie, was that fun?" She glanced briefly at Jackie to include her in the question.

"Actually no," grinned Sylvia. "I knocked on his door this morning, they were naked, so I joined in, it was different, and interesting, until it was time to get dressed again."

"You're a photographer?" asked Bone.

"It is a hobby for me," Sylvia replied, hefting the bag in her right hand.

"She takes some cracking video as well," laughed Roaddog.

"We've got a rally coming up." Bone went on, ignoring Roaddog. "would you be interested in shooting stills and video, to record the event for us?"

"That could be fun, what is a rally?"

"Oh, you are in for some fun," laughed Bone.

"A rally virgin," laughed Bandit Queen.

"I haven't been called virgin for a lot of years." Sylvia's eyes sparkled in the harsh lights. "Someone is going to have to explain."

"Well," said Bandit Queen. "you get somewhere between fifty and three hundred bikers, gather them together in a field, with beer and food and music, and then they party for the weekend, bank holidays are best because those are three day weekends, Easter is awesome, but we missed that one. Mayday is next, we're all going to Chorley. Chorley Centurions are hosting, it's a rugby club, so there's a proper bar, and proper toilets, even showers if you're brave enough to share. Camping on the rugby pitch is order of the day, there's disco and bands, burger vans and chippies. During the day, there's ride outs and bike shows. Just everything a crazy biker needs to have fun."

"Sounds different. What do I need?"

"Tent, is generally required, it can rain. Sleeping bag is preferable, but not always needed if you've got enough beer inside you. A change of underwear, if you feel so inclined. By the time Monday comes around we all smell like homeless guys anyway, so no one will notice."

"Suddenly I'm not so sure," Sylvia whispered.

"Don't worry," Bandit Queen smiled, "We'll look after you."

"That smile doesn't help," said Sylvia.

"You'll be fine," Roaddog's gruff voice cut through. "We'll have a lock box in the van or on Slowball's trike. Your gear will be safe, and we'll all look out for you. It's going to be fun."

"I've never been to a rally either," Jackie said.

"Two virgins," laughed Bandit Queen. "This is going to be so much fun."

"What sort of thing happens at these rallies?" asked Sylvia.

"Just the usual shenanigans." said Man-Dare. "Just be careful what's in the back of your shots. It could be surprising what people get up to in the dark."

"That shouldn't be a problem, if people behave themselves," said Bandit Queen.

"I'll be good," said Man-Dare. "Mostly." She laughed loudly and went to get herself a beer. The day was moving on and a case of beer made its way onto the floor as the chatter returned to rallies of the past and hopes for the future. Sylvia circulated through the group talking to everyone, she liked Roaddog and Jackie, she was nervous around Bandit Queen and Man-Dare, their confidence was just too much for her. She took a shine to Slowball, his size gave her a feeling of warmth and safety, he didn't appear to have the savagery of the others, or the coldness of Sharpshooter, something about his eyes frightened Sylvia. She took a small pocket camera from the bag, she was shooting pictures without flash and without framing, just after atmosphere for the small group. Slowball knew what she was doing and did nothing to let the others know. Evening came in and the temperature started to drop, Bug cornered Roaddog by the bar, while Sylvia was far enough away.

"You know about bitcoin?" he asked.

"Yes, what you need to know?"

"How do I get onto this dark web thing, and set stuff up to start selling our product?" He glanced round to make sure that Sylvia was far enough away.

"I'll send you a link when I get home, you need a good VPN, I'll send the link to the one I use. It's not free, but it's not too expensive."

"I'll cycle through mobile networks as well, should give me some extra protection. Any idea about the postal aspect?"

"I only deal in the intangibles, nothing physical. If we stick to small packages, we can use stamps, bought from various places with cash. Try for a sort of clean room for packing, minimise DNA traces. Drop in random post boxes. If we make sure the postage is over the top, then no one will question it."

"What about the damned sniffer dogs?"

"Not routine, dogs are too valuable to have them sniffing millions of envelopes a day. If we stick to fifty gram packs as a maximum, then we should have no issues. I do have a thought though. Vacuum pack and seal, then wash the outside with ammonia. Should reduce trace and kill off most of the scent. I don't care how good those dogs are, ammonia is going to fuck them up."

"Can we get the hardware we need?"

"I should think so, I caught something on a cooking program of all things. There's this new and wonderful method called Sous Vide. Food is sealed in a bag without any air in it and then boiled in the bag, all its natural juices are retained, and it's all entirely natural. Bags and sealing equipment available from Amazon for god's sake."

"New and wonderful, remember vesta boil in the bag curry from the seventies?"

"Hey, I've heard of it, but before my time. Anyway, they've got reinvent something every year," laughed Roaddog.

"Yes, the trick is going to be keeping trace evidence out of the seal on the bag."

"Agreed. An even older saying comes to mind. Cleanliness is next to godliness."

"Send me the links," said Bug, laughing. Roaddog turned to Jackie.

"Sylvia seems to be getting on all right with Slowball," he whispered.

"They're about the same age, and he's just a pussycat."

"Watch out, that kittens got claws," he smiled. He walked over to Sylvia.

"You OK?" he asked, "me and Jackie are going to split."

"I'll be fine," she smiled and leaned against Slowball. Roaddog and his large friend exchanged glances, then Roaddog left.

Thursday before the Mayday weekend.

Roaddog and Bone were in the unit chatting.

"It's been a bit quiet these last two weeks," observed Roaddog.

"Yes," replied Bone. "Sales are up, and Bug's getting the dark web thing rolling, it's taking a lot of his time though."

"It'll get up there and done right it's fairly secure. We should have the bitcoin rolling in once he's built up some trade."

"He's charging ridiculous prices though, and still selling it."

"The safety aspect. You want to risk approaching a drug dealer on a street corner, who may be a cop, or risk a few quid on a web trade? Once the ratings go up, we'll sell more."

"If it takes off big, we'll have to set it up for full time operation, keep your eyes open for an out of the way lockup with power and decent security," Bone said quietly.

"Will do, but if it gets too big, it's going to be easier for the cops to home in."

"Someone gets to make a delivery run out to Blackpool every day, then the cops will be looking in the wrong place," laughed Bone.

"If we're using letter post and post boxes, we could scatter them all over the north west and no one would be any the wiser."

"I've got a feeling for post boxes near courts and cop shops," grinned Bone.

"Pushing, but still possible."

"Do you think we've got enough beer in the van?" Bone's question was serious.

"Damn thing's half full, let's just hope we can get the rest of the gear in it."

"We should be able to, most of the guys have tents that wrap up small, and light, we should be OK."

"This weekend going to be good?"

"I hope so," Bone smiled, "Centurions always put on a good rally."

"Let's just hope it doesn't get too competitive."

"Talk to the guys, make it clear, we want no shit at this rally, we are guests."

"I'll tell 'em, not sure how much notice they'll take."

"You're master at arms, keep them in line."

"Yes boss," Roaddog laughed.

"What do you think about Sylvia and Slowball?"

"They're good together, maybe she'll tag along for a while, maybe not. More interesting is Man-Dare and Billy, what the fuck is going on there?"

"I think that is Bandit Queens doing, Man-Dare will stay out of trouble, and she'll look good on Billy's arm until someone better comes along."

"So, no wedding bells there either?"

"Unlikely, but who can tell. He's a nice guy, and she's a horny chick, there are worse matches to be had in this world."

"Are we going to invite him to become a full member?"

"That'll take a full committee decision, and there's no saying he'll want it."

"What about Alan?"

"Now that's a different question, I think he wants to be back in, but he's worried about that crazy daughter of his."

"He's coming this weekend, and let's not forget that most of the beer in the van is from him, and free."

"He's becoming quite an asset. Is he coming on the Dragonfly?"

"Yes, he said it wouldn't be right to come to a rally in his car."

"I want extra security on that damned bike. It could be a serious target as we already know."

"We got the heavy chains, and it's going to be chained to the van, once some of the beer is gone it can go inside the van."

"What about Sylvia's gear?"

"I've talked to Slowball about that, it's going in his lock box, and he's going to be looking out for her."

"Fuck, this is going to be some rally." Bone snarled. "At least four of us are going to be staying fairly sober, who's bringing some weed?"

"Slowball's got a nice big bag of some really good smoke, so don't worry about that, things could get quite mellow."

"That's good, as guests I'd rather not have anyone getting too hot, know what I mean?"

"I understand, I'll talk to Sharpshooter, make sure he brings only 'E'."

"That'd be good, let's have a nice mellow love in," laughed Bone.

"I'm sure Sylvia will get some great pics if that happens." The rumble of a VW motor filled the air, and Slowball rolled into the yard. He pulled to a stop and then reversed into his normal parking space. He took two small tents from the box on the back of his trike and tossed them into the back of the van.

"Two tents," laughed Bone. "You two not sharing yet."

"They're two-man tents and she says I'm the size of two men." Slowball grumbled.

"I call that a compliment," grinned Roaddog, "especially as she's seen Lurch."

"I suppose."

"I've noticed something else," said Bone.

"What?" said Slowball.

"Well, how long have we been bitching at you to get that damned reverse gear fixed? Must be eight months, and two weeks of Sylvia moaning and it's fixed."

"You can't underestimate the moaning power of women," laughed Roaddog.

"You two are a pair of bastards. Turns out it was a dodgy linkage, only took about an hour and I had it fixed."

"So, eight months of pushing that heavy bastard and it only took an hour to fix?"

"Yes, it took some grovelling around on the floor, but I got it in the end."

"And was Sylvia there, helping you out with good advice?"

"No, she was chatting with her damned neighbours."

"So, have they got used to her new friends?"

"Looks like it. A couple of the more adventurous ones may turn up Sunday night, it seems Fifth Element are one of their favourite bands."

"That could be interesting," laughed Bone, "Sunday nights can get really crazy."

"Do we know who's playing Saturday night?" Slowball asked.

"I've been told," Roaddog replied, "but I forget, some rock outfit from Blackpool way."

"Who cares?" grinned Bone. "So long as they're good, and preferably loud, cos most of you bastards are deaf."

"Who you calling deaf?" laughed Roaddog. All three looked around as a strange car rolled into the yard.

"Is the closed sign out?" asked Bone.

"Definitely," Roaddog replied. The car stopped and two men got out.

"Fuck," muttered Bone, "It's the cops."

"Good afternoon gentlemen," said D.I. Hopkins. "I was hoping to find that nice young lady Bandit Queen here?"

"Young you may just get away with but call her nice and you could just have a problem."

"Her phone seems to have gone dead and I was hoping that she could help us with a little something."

"Interesting," laughed Bone. "She did think that you may have captured her phone number while she was helping you previously, so she changed it."

"I'm sure she gave her number to us."

"Yeah right," sneered Bone. "What are you after anyway?"

"Well," Hopkins paused, "it's like this, that paedophile that she helped us catch, he's still locked up, and still breathing, we cracked his computer, but we can't break the encryption on his storage hard drive, all the useful information is on that. Our IT guys say it could take us years to break his coding. I was wondering if your guy could do better?"

"Our IT guy is busy, but I'll call him," said Bone, getting up and going into the office.

"Would you gentlemen like a beer?" asked Roaddog.

"We're on duty," said D.C. Lewis. Hopkins looked hard at his subordinate.

"A cold bottle of beer would go down nicely right now, thank you."

Roaddog got up and went to the bar in the corner, he pulled two bottles and popped the tops off, he passed one to each of the policeman, before he returned to his seat, he waved at a couple of empty seats, but the policemen remained standing.

"How's business?" asked Hopkins.

"We're doing OK, not rushed off our feet, but making a living at it you know."

"Closed on a Thursday afternoon?"

"And tomorrow, there's a rally in Chorley this weekend and most of the guys are going, so we thought we'd make a long weekend of it. Hey, we might not even open on Tuesday, at our ages hangovers can be a real bitch."

"I'm glad to say that I'm working all weekend, so I don't get to go to Filey with the wife and kids." Hopkins smiled. Bone returned from the back room.

"Bug is busy right now, he said something about chain of evidence."

"Yes, any information that you find for us cannot be used in court because we cannot prove that it hasn't been tampered with." Hopkins sighed.

"Bug says bitmap the drive, and send the data to a supercomputer, Oxford University has a good one, as does LSE, but the best one is the one that doesn't exist under GCHQ. He says to tell your decoders that they're looking for five letters in a row, 'gmail'. Shouldn't take much more than an hour to get the first stage done, then it's easy peasy. Does that make any sense?"

"Sort of." said Hopkins, looking at Lewis.

"I understand what he means," replied the younger cop, "but can we get that sort of time on a supercomputer?"

"I have enough people owe me favours," grinned Hopkins, "and some of them are going to be working this weekend." He turned to Bone. "Thanks for your help."

"We did nothing," said Bone. "You could have got this information from your own IT guys."

"I don't believe that they actually speak English, they speak some foreign lingo, it just comes out as gobbledegook to me."

"Bug says expect resistance, they don't like giving up time on their own personal supercomputers."

"He's not wrong there. I know just the boffin to talk to." Hopkins laughed. "I'll catch up with him tonight, when he's driving home from the golf club, with two-thirds of a bottle of good scotch in his belly, I feel he'll be most co-operative then. No Lewis, you are staying at home."

"But he'll be way over the limit," snapped Lewis.

"He always is, but he's almost impossible to prosecute, the stink will only affect his work for a short time, but if I can get a favour out of him, we'll have the data we need, and chain of evidence preserved."

"Bug said something else." Bone grinned.

"Go on." Hopkins raised his eyebrows.

"He said watch out for a keyboard map, whatever that is, and he suggested most likely is something called dvorak."

"Your guy is real sharp." said Lewis. "One of the reasons we struggled to break his computer was because he had a keyboard re-map built into the bios, god knows how he did that, but all the keys were wrong. Turns out it's a system used by some people to speed up their typing, it's far quicker than the standard 'qwerty' keyboard."

"Glad we could be of help," laughed Bone.

"Thank you gentlemen," said Hopkins finishing his bottle and looking for somewhere to put the empty, Roaddog stood and took it from him, and took the one from Lewis as well. The two cops returned to their car.

"Do you think they are up to something?" Lewis asked.

"If they are then they're awful cool about it. Is their idea good?" asked Hopkins as he started the motor.

"Oh yes, no doubt it's the only way to go, but time on a fast computer is difficult to get, and damned expensive as well."

"We'll see about that," laughed Hopkins as he pulled away.

Bandit Queen pulled into the yard in her car, with Man-Dare as shotgun, which seemed to be much the norm these days. She stamped across the yard into the seating area where the others already were.

"Was that the damned cops?" she demanded.

"It was, my dear." smiled Bone. "We helped them as we could, and they left."

"What were they after?"

"Decryption of a certain hard drive. I called Bug, and passed on the information he gave me, they seemed relatively happy when they left."

"I don't trust them," she snarled.

"Rightly so, it appears they snatched your phone number while you were at Janice's house."

"Figured he would, bastard. Was he after anything else?"

"He didn't give the impression that he was, but you never can tell with the slippery bastards."

"Well, Janice and Julie are together OK, and that rat bastard is so deep within the system that I can't find him."

"Maybe Hopkins can help you with that?" laughed Bone.

"Now that is a favour I can't afford," smiled Bandit Queen. "How's preparations for the rally going?" she asked.

"We're doing OK," Bone replied, "the van is loading with tents, and other gear, beer and drugs are set, all we need really is for Friday to come around a little quicker, and everything would be fine."

"Friday will be here when it is ready, and not before." She smiled as she sat in his lap. She looked across at Man-Dare, who seemed a little cast adrift as Billy wasn't there.

"Where's Billy?" she asked. There were many shaken heads, no one had talked to Billy that day, so no one knew what he was up to. Man-Dare pulled her phone from a pocket and punched in a speed dial number, she retreated off to one side, waiting for her call to be answered.

"Hi Billy." she said, eventually. "Where you at?"

"I'm a tad busy right now, can I call you back in a few?"

"Fine," she replied, "just don't keep me waiting too long."

"No problem." he said, as he broke the connection.

"Hey Man-Dare," called Bandit Queen, "you got used to having him around?"

"Yes, he's a nice guy and not too stupid."

"What do you mean?"

"He's real bright, some sort of computer consultant, and he plays a little guitar."

"What? A ukulele? That's a small guitar."

"No, he plays guitar, not professional, but he's good."

"How you know good?"

"I've listened to him, when he plays along to the songs that he likes, he keeps up very well."

"You getting hooked on the old geezer?" Bandit Queen laughed.

"Fuck you bitch," Man-Dare said, quietly. "And I think so." Man-Dare's phone rang, and she walked away to answer it. After a few minutes she hung up and returned to the group.

"He's got this work thing on, something fell over in Madrid, and he's got to fix it."

"How the fuck is he going to get back from Madrid for tomorrow?" asked Bone.

"Fool," laughed Bandit Queen, "He's working by remote over the internet."

"He can do that?"

"I'm sorry, my love," smiled Bandit Queen, "it's the year is two thousand and sixteen, not nineteen sixty."

"I've heard of that stuff, but I thought it was some guy pulling my pisser."

"No dear, it's for real."

"Could he be better than Bug?"

"Not likely, far too straight. I bet Roaddog knows more about the dark side of the web than Billy."

"Hey. Leave me out of this," Roaddog grumbled.

"We all know you have dealings on the dark side, we just choose not to ask too much," Bandit Queen patted his arm and smiled sweetly.

"Keep it that way," Roaddog growled.

"We all got secrets," she leaned in close and kissed him softly on the cheek.

"You can be a real bitch," he muttered as she pulled away.

"That ain't no secret," she laughed loudly.

24: Friday Rally Day One The Gathering.

The Dragonrider's unit was open, but not for business. The afternoon sun filled the yard and a fair way into the building through the open shutter doors. It was four o'clock when the bikers started to arrive, now with the time at almost five almost everyone was there. Bone took Roaddog to the side for a moment.

"Time to tell them the rules."

"Why me? You're the boss."

"Because you're the one going to be doing the enforcing."

"Whatever," Roaddog walked slowly until he was just outside the unit, looking back at all the people getting ready for a weekend party.

"OK people," he shouted. "Listen up. Slowball kill the music." The rock music pounding from the overhead speakers died.

"We have some rules for this weekend." Roaddog went on. "We are guests of the Centurions; we will behave as guests. Is that clear?" There were nods and groans and more than a few boos.

"Number one, there will be no competitions between us and the Centurions. Competitions can get out of hand easily. Number two, beer is acceptable in any quantity, weed and 'E' in moderation, no speed, no coke. We want a nice, chilled party for our first one of the year. Questions?" There were a few grumbles but no one willing to put their neck on the block.

"Number three, Sunday's ride out is to Rivington, this is not a race, it is a cavalcade, is that clear?" More grumbles.

"Number four, if there is any trouble, then we back up the Centurions, and we back them hard. Be aware we have already exceeded our quota for the month, so no corpses. Is that understood?"

"Hey, it's only the fourth of the month?" shouted Sharpshooter from the back.

"And we are still working off last month's carry overs. So be careful." He paused to let the laughter subside. "Right let's get this show on the road, anyone not here can catch themselves up. Move out ladies and gentlemen." He walked back into the unit and caught Man-Dare.

"Any word from Billy?" he asked.

"He's running late, should be clear by six tonight."

"That's good, you drive the van to the club and one of us will park it once we get there, OK?"

"No worries," she smiled, though her eyes told a different story, she was a little unsure about driving something so big.

"Don't sweat it," he replied quietly, "it's only a bit bigger than a car. It's real easy to drive, just don't cut the corners off." He turned around when he heard the rumble of Slowball's trike, almost directly behind that was Alan on the vintage Dragonfly. Seeing the activity in the yard the new arrivals simply turned their vehicles around and waited for the word to go. Roaddog turned back to Man-Dare.

"You follow Slowball, he'll stop just inside until we find out where we can all park."

He walked into the unit as the lights were going down, and the shutters started to close, in only a few seconds the place was locked down tight. He exited by the personnel door and set the alarms. He checked the chains on the rear yard, then walked towards his own bike, Jackie was standing beside it. He caught Bone's eye and raised his right fist in the air and pumped it twice. The signal to start engines passed quickly through the group. Bone and Lurch formed up the first row of the convoy, the rest falling in behind as the column advanced onto the road. At end of the line came Slowball and then the van. Roaddog rolled through the gate and then locked it. Heavy chains closed the gate and a temporary sign that said 'come back Tuesday' was hung on the inside. It only took him a couple of minutes to catch up with the van, Man-Dare didn't appear to be having any trouble with it. She even waved as he went past. Once he has passed Slowball, he dropped in alongside Alan for a few seconds to exchange greetings. Then he was off again, patrolling the convoy as usual. There where the occasional issues with roundabouts and traffic lights. Nothing the experienced bikers couldn't cope with. In less than twenty minutes they arrived at the rugby club. The gate was manned by two members of the Chorley Centurions. After a brief conversation one of the gate guys led Bone over to the area that had been set aside for the Dragonriders. Roaddog went back to drive the van across the grass, the ground was soft but not too wet. He knew the problem was going to be getting it going again on Tuesday, but by then it should be half a ton of beer lighter. The rules were no fires on the pitch. There was to be a huge bonfire on an open section for the pyromaniacs amongst the visitors, this was of course not lit as yet. There was more than enough fuel in the form of broken pallets to keep the fire burning all weekend. As soon as the van stopped Roaddog opened the driver's door and dropped the box of dinner plates on the ground. Dragonriders took plates from the box as they needed them, some only needed one, others two. The melamine plates serve an important purpose, a single underneath a kickstand and two under a centre stand. These stopped the motorcycles falling over in the soft ground that was all they had for support. In less than half an hour the van was empty of tents and they were all set up for the riders to take up residence once they had drunk enough. Tents all set up, Roaddog took Jackie by the hand and walked into the clubhouse. Up to the bar and they both got a drink, him a pint of Hobgoblin, and her one of lager. The DJ was already banging out heavy metal tunes to keep the audience entertained. Sylvia stood just inside the doorway, her two-hundred-millimetre lens snapping photos of Jackie and Roaddog's conversations. Sylvia wished she could actually capture the words that they were exchanging but decided that she could fill them in later. A tiny smile graced her lips as the thought flashed through her head. Sylvia sat on a windowsill just inside the doorway, she was shooting distance shots of couples talking. Slowball stood at her side, keeping the rowdies out of her way. His sheer size was enough to keep most of them out of her way, the occasional one needed a poke to keep them moving. This was nothing that Slowball couldn't deal with. Another couple that featured quite extensively in Sylvia's Friday night shots was Billy and Man-Dare. His grey beard flashing all sorts of colours in the disco's lights, and her youth an interesting contrast. Sylvia moved round to the speaker stacks; the DJ smiled at her until Slowball growled at him. Sylvia's camera spent some time focused on other couples, some the beautiful people and others not so much. When Bone and Bandit Queen took to the floor each with a pint in one hand Sylvia focused hard on them, and she thought that the contrast between the two was interesting at the very least. Him a slim yet solid man, her a woman with an immense presence. As they danced, they filled the floor, their eyes displaying their love for each other. Their bodies worshipping each other and their auras creating a space for them to dance in. Lurch moved in alongside, Doris in his arms, smiles on their faces. The flashing lights of the disco made the photography difficult. Sylvia didn't want to use the heavy flash that she had brought, as this would overpower the coloured lights that were giving such interesting contrasts. The brilliant red floodlights made exposures difficult to gauge and made autofocus impossible. Soon the dance floor was packed too tight for her to be able to get any decent shots. Looking around she could find no vantage point to get shots down into the crowded floor, so she retreated to the bar. She watched the interactions of the people. Most were having a good time, though some where already too drunk, or maybe high, despite the hour. She tapped Slowball with an elbow, and he leaned down so she could talk to him.

"Got a beer?" she asked. He pulled a bottle from the inside of his jacket and popped the top with the bottle opener on his key ring. He passed it to her with a smile and getting one in return. With the camera hanging from its strap and her arm tucked through his, she pulled him into the entrance way. Together they walked out into the car park, there was quite a crowd around the roaring fire, so she guided them slowly towards it. Out of the corner of her eye she spotted a dark shape moving around the periphery. She pressed her bottle into Slowball's belly, and he grabbed it. Her hands lifted the camera, the long lens zoomed in to the subject, aperture wide open and iso speed as high as it would go. It took her a second or two to get the focus right, and there filling the viewfinder where Roaddog and Jackie. She turned to him and tipped her head back, he reached down and kissed her softly. Sylvia's shutter clicking continuously, hoping for the one shot that would be perfect. The couple broke the kiss and continued on their way around the grounds, unaware that they had been the centre of such attention. Sylvia let the camera drop back onto its strap and took her beer back from Slowball. She raised it in a toast to the two people who had no clue that she was even there.

"What's that about?" Slowball asked.

"If it wasn't for those two, I'd not be here."

"That's true, any regrets?"

"Only that I didn't do something like this sooner."

"It's been an interesting couple of weeks," he smiled down at her.

"Oh, it's been that." She returned his smile and pulled on his arm. "Let's go over near the fire, all that light might just give me some good pics." As they neared the crowd around the fire. She noticed a centre of excitement; she couldn't hear the raised voices but the facial expressions she read as angry. She pushed her beer off onto Slowball again and raised the camera. It took a few seconds to reset everything, the bright yellow light of the huge pile of burning pallets, made the faces jump out in sharp contrast. As she was focusing in on Bug, Roaddog came up out of the darkness behind him. A heavy hand fell onto Bug's shoulder, the smaller man snapped around and looked up into Roaddog's eyes. A few words were spoken, again the clatter of Sylvia's shutter went un-noticed by those in the pool of light. Bug nodded and turned back to the man he had been arguing with, he reached out a hand the pair shook. Bug walked slowly towards the bar. Roaddog turned away from the fire and walked into the darkness, Jackie under his left arm and a bottle of beer in his right hand. Sylvia's camera snapped onto his back, his jacket and his ass filled the frame. The patches brightly illuminated in the dark, the white dragon and its orange flame with Dragonriders arched across the top, and crossed stilettos glinting in their sheaths on the back of his belt. She worked the shutter speed as he walked away from the fire. The last one down to a third of a second, not really enough to stop his slow footsteps, but it might give a nice effect. She dropped the camera again and reached out for her beer.

"I think that's enough for tonight, tomorrows going to be better with bands to shoot," she smiled up at Slowball. "Let's lock the camera away and get some more beer." The big man just nodded and turned towards the camp. By the time they got to camp Roaddog and Jackie were already there.

"What was going on with Bug?" Slowball asked.

"They were bitching over which Honda is the best. I had a quiet word, it's all fine now."

"We noticed," said Slowball as he opened the lock box on the back of his trike, Sylvia dropped the camera into its case and closed the lid. She took a small camera from the bottom of the box and slipped it into a pocket. Slowball opened the van and filled his jacket pockets with beer bottles, Roaddog did the same.

"No problems?" asked Roaddog.

"Nothing to write home about," grinned Slowball. "You know what these dickheads get like when someone points a camera at them?"

"Yes, they get stupid."

"Stupider."

"Is that a word?"

"It is now," Slowball laughed. "You going back inside?"

"Not yet, I think I'll cruise the perimeter, see what's happening."

"OK, see ya in a bit." Slowball took Sylvia's hand and set off towards the clubhouse.

"Are you worried about something?" asked Jackie after the other two had gone.

"Nothing specific, just being careful."

"Careful of what?"

"That's just it, I don't know, but something is making me uneasy."

"Are you really worried?"

"No, just a sort of dull ache in the back of my head, I don't know, I feel that something is going down, and I'm not seeing it."

"Come on then," Jackie laughed, "let's see if we can catch someone stealing bikes that'll make you feel better."

"Damned right it would." Roaddog took her hand and together they walked towards the gate. When they got there, they found three Centurion guys in yellow jackets manning the gate.

"Anything exciting happening?" Roaddog asked.

"Nothing much," said one of the men, "a couple of scooter riders turned up, they'd seen the fire from the main road and come to see what was happening. They left pretty quick," he laughed.

"No one trying to crash?" asked Roaddog.

"Not with any seriousness, a simple fuck off, normally gets shut of them. Though we did have a car full saying that they were with the band. They wanted in for free."

"Another fuck off then?"

"Pretty much, some of them seem to think we are as stupid as them."

"You guys thirsty?" Roaddog grinned.

"Always." Roaddog reached into his jacket and pulled out three bottles, he handed them over.

"That puts me down to one." He muttered. "I better go and fill up. Have fun guys." Roaddog turned away and set off across the car park back towards the van. Picking his way through the tents, as they approached the van, he noticed two dark shapes crouched at the back of the van. He stopped Jackie and pulled his last beer from inside his jacket. Stepping through the circle of tents he could see that the two men had no patches on their backs, they were working on something at the tail of the van. Roaddog smashed the bottle into the back one head, and then back handed the other as he turned towards him. The first fell to the ground and the second rolled to his feet, not quick enough to avoid Roaddog's right that put his lights out.

"Go get Bone and Alan." He called to Jackie and she set off at a run for the bar.

She returned in a couple of minutes, but not with the two people mentioned. There were considerably more. Both the men had returned to consciousness. Each sitting on the ground on their hands, one bleeding from a head wound.

"What the fuck is going on?" shouted Bone as soon as he was close enough.

"I think they were trying to steal Alan's bike," said Roaddog. "Their bolt cutters were too small for the chain, so they were trying to dismantle the step on the van."

Bone turned to the Centurions president who was standing beside him.

"These yours?"

"None of ours," the president grinned. "Kill the fuckers if you want."

"I've a better idea," laughed Bone. He turned to Alan. "You still got that killer right?" Alan glared at Bone for a moment, then nodded. Bone faced the two on the floor.

"Alan here is a bit miffed that you two assholes tried to steal his bike. So, there's going to be a little contest, one on one fist fights. If you put up a good show, then you'll get to leave once you wake up. If you don't, then you'll be here all weekend, and I am sure the guys will find something to entertain themselves." He pointed at the one with the head injury. "Stand up you're first." The second thief laughed.

"He's old enough to be your granddad, knock him the fuck out." Bone looked around and spotted Sylvia's pocket camera. He caught Slowball's eye and nodded in Sylvia's direction. Slowball engulfed the camera in his huge hand and turned Sylvia away from the action. Bandit Queen saw this and spoke up.

"Right girls, fuck off into the bar." All the girls but Jackie turned away instantly. Jackie checked with Roaddog first, he nodded, so she followed. Bandit Queen of course stayed.

The young man danced around staying out of Alan's reach, so Alan just stood still, he had to come within range at some time. When he finally did, he was paying far too much attention to Alan's right hand. The left caught him completely by surprise, the wide fist connected with a nose and splashed said item across the young man's face. His head snapped backwards, and he dropped to the ground asleep.

"Right, left," laughed Bone. "I always get those confused. Stand up fool your next." He sneered at the second thief.

The second thief stood up slowly, he didn't have any injuries, though he was a little groggy from Roaddog's punch. He looked around and suddenly made a break for it. He failed to get through the encircling bikers and was turned around and pushed back into the centre. He stumbled straight into a right, left, right combination to the guts. Which dropped him on his ass.

"Enough," shouted Bandit Queen. "I heard ribs." The crackle of breaking ribs was unmistakeable.

"Sorry guys," laughed Bone. "Looks like you're staying." He turned to

Roaddog.

"You got gaffer in the van?"

"Should be some." smiled Roaddog.

"Good, tape them up nice and tight, and fasten them to the goalposts. I think they'll make a great toilet for the rest of the weekend." There were peals of laughter all around. The two thieves were hauled to their feet and dragged to the goal post where Roaddog supervised their restraining. Each had their ankles taped and their hands fastened behind their backs, then they were taped sitting with their backs to the uprights. Once the laughing bikers were walking away Roaddog bent down next to thief two.

"If you put too much pressure on those ribs it could be fatal. Do you understand?"

The thief nodded; he couldn't speak because of the gag in his mouth.

"Be patient, make your break for it as it's getting light. Don't think of anything other than getting away alive, if you try anything else, we will hunt you down and kill you, do I make myself clear?" Again, a nod. Roaddog stood slowly, and unzipped his jeans, he pulled his cock out and proceeded to pee on the thief.

"Get used to it, and remember don't piss off the Dragonriders, it's not a healthy way to live." Laughing he turned towards the bar.

25: Saturday Rally Day Two Family Fun Day.

It was about ten o'clock in the morning when Roaddog and Jackie crawled out of his tent.

"I'm not happy with you," said Bone.

"What I do?" asked Roaddog.

"Them thieves got away; you must not have taped them properly."

"I only had one roll, but they were secured."

"Still not happy."

"So how many times did you pee on them last night?"

"Three or four, it gets fuzzy about two o'clock." Bone laughed.

"Well, that's your problem, perhaps they had help?"

"Who'd have helped them?"

"The guys who brought them. They'd not want to let them back into the car though," laughed Roaddog.

"Gotta be fragrant," Bone smiled. Bandit Queen laughed, and said, "They're gonna stink for a while."

"You should have seen them when Man-Dare went to see them." laughed Billy.

"What do you mean?" asked Roaddog.

"Oh, my god," said Billy, "I had a bladder full to get shut of, so I went out to the goal posts, Man-Dare came with me, she watched me as I soaked one of the guys. He'd given up by then. She walked up to the other guy, lifted her skirt, pulled her knickers to the side, and leaned over the top of him. She started to spray him, he opened his mouth and reached towards her. She stepped forwards and pushed her pussy into his face, pumping her piss straight into his mouth. The bastard drank it, mouth full after mouth full until she was empty. It was really surreal."

"He wanted it, he got it," said Man-Dare from behind Billy. He turned and smiled back at her. She reached forwards and kissed him solidly.

"That is just plain sick," Jackie grimaced.

"Some people are like that," Man-Dare laughed.

"At least they've gone now," muttered Jackie.

"We'll have to find some other form of entertainment," said Bone.

"I'm sure we'll find something to keep us amused," said Roaddog.

"What's the plans for today?" asked Bone.

"There's a ride out to Devils Bridge, I'm not sure if Alan is going to go, that old bike isn't really fast enough to tag along with everyone else. I think it's set for departure around twelve o'clock."

"That'd be an idea. Keep the guys out of the bar for a few hours. It's going to be a long day; I don't want them too pissed too early," laughed Bone.

"I'll set up as many of the guys as I can," Roaddog smiled.

"What's for breakfast?" asked Jackie.

"Let's go check the car park, there's usually a burger van at these events." He took her hand and set off towards the clubhouse. As they walked around the corner of the club Roaddog started laughing.

"What's funny?" asked Jackie.

"Recognise the burger van?"

"That's from near the unit, isn't it?"

"Yeah, that's our good friend Andy," they walked up to the end of the queue. In front of them was Lurch.

"Hey Lurch, you up for today's ride out?"

"I think so. Don't want to spend all day here drinking, could get too silly."

"Good, spread the word, Bone would like a good representation from the Dragonriders."

"I'll let people know," said Lurch, he got to the front of the queue.

"Hi Lurch, what you want?" asked Andy from inside the van.

"Burger chips, and a can of pop, cheers." Lurch's head was above the opening of the serving hatch, but Andy had no problem hearing his order. He turned and dropped a basket of chips into the fryer. By the time Andy had filled a burger bun with the relevant onions and relish the chips were ready, a quick shake and a tray full of food was ready. A can from the fridge and Lurch was served, money changed hands and Andy moved on to Roaddog.

"Hi mate," said Roaddog, "how come you're here?"

"The guy they had planned to come here got busted last week and his van is off the road until he gets it up to spec. They came by and offered me a fair price to be here for the weekend. What you want?"

"Two big breakfast buns and a couple of cokes."

"No sweat, will you be around Tuesday, I'm gonna need a restock if this weekend goes well."

"No worries, the shop will be open, just wander round when you've got a moment. You running this on your own?"

"No, I've got a couple of mates coming in later today, they'll have a van of stock and somewhere for one or two of us to crash," Andy laughed as he handed out the buns and took Roaddog's money.

"See ya later," said Roaddog as he turned away, Andy nodded and looked to the next guy in the queue, it was going to be a hell of a weekend for him. Roaddog handed one of the buns to Jackie and they started eating them as they moved around. Roaddog spotted the president of the Centurions and walked over to where he was talking to his second. He stood respectfully by, waiting to be invited into the conversation.

"You OK?" asked the President.

"Ya, just wondering what time today's ride out is scheduled for?"

"On the road about twelve, hopefully, but these things never get out on time, do they?"

"That's for sure, I have another question."

"Go on."

"Is there going to be another food truck coming in? I mean Andy's stuff is good enough, but a little variety would be better."

"Andy stepped in on short notice, but we do have a guy coming in who specialises in some fancy German sausages. There's a guy with a coffee truck coming as well, neither have promised to run twenty-four hours, but Andy has."

"That's great, this ride out, how fast is it likely to be running?"

"You know what these things are like, once we get rolling then the speed just keeps on creeping up, 'we're not racing officer, honest.' But the front runners usually get to be somewhat over the speed limit, less than the speed of sound, but not by much."

"It's going to get more than a little strung out then. But Slowball will be at the back to pick up the fallen." Roaddog laughed loudly.

"How many spare seats does he have?"

"Only two why?"

"Last year we had five bikes hauled off to the shop by the AA."

"What the fuck happened?"

"A dick ran wide on a right hander, hit the kerb and bounced back across the road. The fucker was lucky there was nothing going the other way, he only got run over by bikes."

"I think I'll be just ahead of Slowball," smiled Roaddog.

"What about the vintage bike you've got with you?"

"Alan's dragonfly may just surprise you. The brakes are good, the tyres are modern. Those Earles forks make a massive difference to the handling. If he's been practising, then Slowball is going to struggle to keep up in the corners."

"If they can sort of keep up, they'll get time for a coffee before it's time to come back," laughed the president. Roaddog nodded and turned away. He went to find Alan, with Jackie alongside still munching on her breakfast. They caught up with Alan, he was sitting on the ground at the side of his bike, a spark plug in his hand.

"Everything OK?" asked Roaddog.

"Yeah, I'm fine, just checking the plugs, they look really good. Someone set that damned carb up just about perfect."

"It's what we do, and the plugs are far better than they were in the sixties, the leads too, they only worry I have is the points, but they should be OK. You coming to Devils?"

"Yes, I think so, could be fun."

"You going to be able to keep up?"

"If the rest keep within the speed limits, I'll do all right, but that's not going to happen is it?"

"No, all our guys have been told not to get involved in any road racing, but that's not going to hold them all back. At least you'll have Slowball behind you."

"One or two of the others might be in for a surprise," laughed Alan.

"Try not to get yourself killed," laughed Roaddog.

"I'll do my best."

"If you're going to play with some of the newer bikes then make sure you have the line before you go into the corner. They're not going to be happy if you slip by late and on the inside."

"It may surprise you that this is not my first rodeo," Alan grinned.

"Roll at twelve, be ready." Roaddog walked away and sat in front of his tent Jackie beside him.

"How are you doing?" he asked.

"I'm fine, is it always this exciting at these things?"

"This has been relatively quiet. No fights, no visits from the cops. Looking at that fire last night I was expecting a visit from the fire brigade. No ambulances. It's been good and chilled."

"What about those thieves?"

"That doesn't happen too often, most don't have the balls to show up at an event like this, especially so early in the evening. Three o'clock in the morning is more likely, they were a special sort of stupid."

"What's this ride out going to be like?"

"Most likely it's going to be a sort of controlled road race, with only two rules. Don't get caught, and don't kill anyone."

"You're not going to be taking any risks, are you?"

"Just breathing is a risk, but no, I'm going to be riding relatively sensibly. The others, who can tell?" he laughed.

The convoy left the carpark only a few minutes late, Centurions had the lead and Dragonriders were next. Other lower numbered visitors tagged in wherever they felt like it. Slowball and another trike were at the back with Alan immediately in front of them. Roaddog started off in amongst the Dragonriders, but he knew that wasn't going to last. Once the line of motorcycles had made it through the complex junctions and onto the M61 they sort of settled down for the cruise up to Lancaster. Roaddog dropped back down the line until he fell in alongside Alan, he got a thumbs up from the older man then dropped back to slip in beside Slowball. The weather was surprisingly good, with watery sunlight flooding the motorway. Sylvia was standing up on the seat behind Slowball, a long lens on her camera, Roaddog looked forwards and saw the shot she was after. A column of riders, most with colourful patches on their backs. The sun lighting them up, in some respects it looked like a military procession, almost a cavalcade. Roaddog set off up the line slowly, skipping one place at a time. He passed a few of the visitors and he could tell were going to be a problem once they got to the country roads ahead. There were some serious sports tourers amongst them. He pulled up alongside Bug and Sharpshooter for a moment or two, got a thumbs up from both then moved on. After the switch onto the M6 he caught up with Bone and Lurch, the three cruised together for a while, then Roaddog started to drop back again. As the column started to peel off the motorway at Lancaster Roaddog was all the way at the back, just ahead of Slowball. He looked over his shoulder to check on Slowball and noticed that Sylvia was in the central rear seat and wearing a lap belt. The traffic lights on the exit attempted to cut the convoy up into little pieces, but they were completely ignored, which was no surprise. The twisting country lanes were what the bikers had been waiting for. The commonly posted speed limit signs were treated with no more respect than the traffic lights. None were going completely crazy; the sports bikes were carving their way through the crowd. Alan's little dragonfly was doing quite well, where some of the others were slowing down for the corners Alan was not. He didn't have the acceleration or the top speed of the more modern bikes, but he was holding a good average. Roaddog pushed fairly hard to move up the line, he caught up with Bug and Sharpshooter. Bug looked at Roaddog and nodded his head to get Roaddog to come closer. He moved in until there was only a couple of inches separating their handlebars.

"I'm fucking bored," yelled Bug.

"Tough," shouted Roaddog.

"You seen them pussies on the Hyabusa?"

"And?"

"I want 'em."

"No racing, we've been told."

"They're not even Centurions."

"You cause hassle and Bone will be pissed."

Bug thought for a moment, then looked at Roaddog. He exaggerated a shrug. Then reached down and opened his exhaust pipe. Roaddog backed off as Bug opened the throttle. The little Honda leapt forwards and started to overtake bikes in very rapid succession. He went passed Bone at more than plus forty miles an hour, not bad for a fifty mile an hour limit. Roaddog dropped back until Alan went passed him, and he fell in beside Billy, Man-Dare behind him looking comfortable and relaxed. Billy gave a thumbs up and tucked his beard back into his jacket.

The convoy pulled into the carpark at Devils bridge, it wasn't too busy until they turned up, as the bikes parked up the small area became rapidly full. Only the perseverance of the Dragonriders ensured that there was somewhere for Slowball to park. The day was a little grey, but not raining. The bikers scattered around, some to stand on the bridge and look down into the green water of the river swirling through the narrow arches of stone. Others to join the queue at the burger van. Slowball was in the line at the van, Sylvia was cruising around the crowd with a wide-angle lens on, taking pictures of both bikes and riders. She got some good pictures of the rather heated discussion between Bone and Bug.

"What the fuck was that?" demanded Bone.

"I hate those asses with too much money and no skill." Bug faced Bone and didn't look away.

"I said no racing." Bone snarled.

"That wasn't racing," grinned Bug. "They weren't going fast enough for it to be racing. I went round them both on a long left hander, I didn't even cross the centreline, nor did I put a foot peg or knee down."

"You went round the outside?"

"Of course. I could have dived the inside line, but they'd have shit themselves. As it was one of them got a serious twitch as I went passed."

"How much faster were you going?"

"Not more than plus ten, or maybe fifteen."

"Try not to kill anyone on the way back."

"They'll not even attempt to go past me on the way back?" sneered Bug. "I told Roaddog they was pussies, an' I was right."

"I want no trouble with the Centurions, clear?"

"No problem." Bug turned away to get himself something to eat. Cherie came out of the crowd and walked with him.

It was about two hours later when the convoy formed up for the journey back to Chorley. The departure started out as a procession, but that didn't last long at all, soon it was almost a road race. Even Alan and his vintage Dragonfly were putting up a good show, in what seemed like no time at all they came to the M6 and headed south. Here the number of speed cameras and cops slowed everything down, the strung out line of motorcycles slowly gathered together. Before they passed the junction for Preston north, they had an escort, a motorway patrol car at the back of the group and two motorcycles at the front. The president of the Centurions pulled up hard behind the two police motorcyclists and the rest of the club followed suit. Two by two they made the turn onto the M61, spot on the speed limit, the whole of the inside lane was theirs, at least until there was a truck to overtake. Through the M65 interchange and on to the Chorley junction. The Centurions president slowed the whole group down as they climbed the exit ramp. He was hoping for the traffic light to turn red; this would give the cavalcade a chance to pack up closely. The motorcycle escort almost ran the light as it changed to amber. They both had the front suspension straining under the heavy brakes they needed to stop. Even so they overshot the white line by half a motorcycle length which made the bikers laugh. Once the lights turned green, they all set of at a very civilised pace, they streamed through the roundabout, and on to the next. At the one after that they turned right almost to the place where the rally was being held. They were approaching a set of traffic lights as the president spotted an ambulance coming towards them with its blue lights flashing. He stopped hard, bikes behind him packing up far too close, they took up both lanes, they were all stopped just clear of the entrance to the hospital. The president raised a clenched fist then point to the two lanes of traffic coming up the hill towards them. He was a little late, Roaddog and Bug were already moving up quickly. The pair locked up their back wheels and turned their bikes sideways on the road, blocking both lanes going the other way. By the time that the two police motorcyclist realised what was happening behind them, the ambulance driver was already taking advantage of the empty road in front of him. As the ambulance turned right into the hospital entrance, the sound of revving engines filled the air. Roaddog waved the president of the Centurions off, the president set off with his second, and waved Roaddog and Bug into second place, a position of honour. Only a minute later they turned into the rugby club, the police left as Slowball's trike made it in through the gate.

26: Saturday Rally Day Two Whistle Test.

The afternoon went slowly and almost without incident, a few lively discussions. The German sausage truck was a great favourite amongst the bikers, especially with the German "Senf" mustard. There was a moment when the two guys riding the Hyabusa's were bitching at Bug. Sharpshooter came up to stand beside Bug and Lurch dropped a heavy hand on the shoulders of both the men. At this point the two stopped complaining and went to the bar to get some beer.

"Thanks for that," said Bug, "it's better they walk away."

"Yes," said Sharpshooter, "Bone would be pissed if there was any blood spilled."

"Keep an eye on those two, they could be more trouble once they get pissed." Lurch's gravelly voice made both pay attention. They nodded and went over to the van to get beers of their own. Roaddog and Jackie were sitting on the ground in front of his tent, a bottle of beer next to each. They were eating huge sausages on long buns.

"What the fuck are those hotdogs?" demanded Bug.

"They're not hot dogs," laughed Roaddog, "they're called bratwurst, proper German sausages, they're great."

"Don't let Cherie see them." grinned Sharpshooter.

"To late," laughed Roaddog.

"She didn't?" asked Bug.

"Oh, she did." laughed Roaddog.

"Fuck." said Bug, looking at the inch and a half diameter sausage that Jackie was taking a bite out of.

"God it got messy," said Roaddog.

"What do you mean?" said Sharpshooter.

"Well, the guy in the truck couldn't believe his eyes when she tipped her head back. That damn thing just slid down like a greased piston, straight in it went. Then her face changed, it looked like it got stuck somewhere. Maybe her stomach had just had enough. It came out again, at about Mach one, followed by a fountain of lager. It was glorious." He was rocking backwards and forwards laughing hard, Jackie was shaking her head and grinning.

"Damn, we missed it," snarled Sharpshooter.

"Do you think we can get her to try again?" asked Bug.

"Not likely," said Roaddog, "she was more than a little embarrassed, not to mention queasy. She's been drinking water ever since."

"You're kidding?"

"No, water."

"I'm gonna find her and see how she's doing," Bug walked off quickly.

"She was in the bar about five minutes ago," said Roaddog to his retreating back.

Bug walked into the bar and saw Cherie sitting at the opposite end, leaning both elbows on the hard-polished surface. Bug perched on the stool next to her.

"You OK?" he asked.

"Not really," she shrugged.

"Can I help you?"

"I don't know, my guts are spinning completely out of control. Heart burn that's an absolute killer."

"I got what you need." He smiled and passed her a foil pack with two capsules still in it, the other five already gone.

"What the fuck are these?"

"What you need. Take one now and the heartburn will be gone in twenty minutes or so."

"But what are they?"

"My doc gives them to me, they are absolutely the dogs bollocks for acid reflux, and heartburn."

"Can I drink with them?"

"Yes, but I'd give it an hour or so, and let your belly settle down. You certainly gave it one hell of a shock."

"I know. I've never had that happen before, I mean that damned sausage was all the way down, but it somehow got jammed."

"You're used to frankfurters, they're straight, bratwurst have a definite curve to them."

"Yes, I suppose it could be that." She smiled at Bug and took one of the small capsules from the wrapper and swallowed it without drinking anything.

"How the hell can you do that?" he laughed. He placed a hand on her thigh, and she leaned against him smiling.

"How many should I take?" Cherie whispered to him.

"Just one should do it, take the other tomorrow morning, that should clear everything for you. It stops acid production pretty much instantly. Without the acid burning up whatever damage you've done in there it'll heal real quick."

The two sat at the bar for the rest of the afternoon, drinking slowly and talking.

It was early evening when Roaddog went to Andy's truck to get some food for himself and Jackie, there was a stranger serving.

"Where's Andy at?" asked Roaddog,

"He's having a kip," replied the new guy, "but he's told us about you, don't worry."

"That's good, how's business going?"

"Doing really well, right now. There is some talk about a resupply run for later on, He's got more stock at his house. Looks like we are going to need it before morning."

"That's great news."

"I'm Dave by the way."

"Thanks Dave," said Roaddog as Dave passed him the burgers he had ordered.

Roaddog walked slowly to where Jackie was waiting for her food.

"Shall we grab a seat and a beer?" he asked.

"Why not? I could do with a change from sitting on the grass."

"If we hadn't brought so much beer there'd have been enough space in the van for the seats." He laughed, leading the way into the clubhouse. It was early so there were still a few tables empty, they selected on to the left of the stage, and Roaddog went to the bar to get the beers. As he crossed the dance floor, he saw a man coming towards him carrying what looked like a large speaker, the man had a pink beard.

'Gotta be something to do with the band.' he thought as he strode up to the bar.

While he was waiting to be served a voice shouted.

"Hey Roaddog." Roaddog looked towards the voice and saw someone he didn't recognise.

"What ya want?" Came a voice from the stage, it was the guy with the pink beard.

"How many can we get on the stage?" said the man coming in through the door, he was carrying something that can only have been a drum, a large drum.

"You set up left side, and we can get squirrel and guitar amp on stage, Chris and Gaff will have to be on the floor." Roaddog paid closer attention to the man on stage, he was wearing a t-shirt, a demin cut-off, shorts and sandals. He stepped off the stage and walked towards the door, the back of his cut was as empty of badges as the front. Roaddog took the beers to the table and sat beside Jackie.

"That was weird," said Jackie. "The drummer shouted Roaddog and he was talking to the crazy guy with the pink beard."

"I know. The singer from the saddle told me there was another Roaddog working as crew for a local band, looks like we've just met him." The pair sat and watched the band work, gear came in, it was removed from its cases and set up, then the cases went out of the room. Roaddog could see that they had been working together for a while, in a very short time the gear was in and set up. Bug and Cherie came to sit with Roaddog and Jackie, they brought beer for everyone with them.

"How you feeling now?" asked Roaddog, looking at Cherie.

"Better, and a little less embarrassed," she grinned.

"That's good, I was a little worried that you had really hurt yourself."

"I'm fine-ish now. See drinking beer again." She raised her glass in salute.

"These guys look like they know what they're doing," said Bug.

"They do," said Roaddog, "and the one with the pink beard is called Roaddog."

"You're joking?"

"No, this could get confusing," laughed Roaddog. Looking at the stage he saw the drummer and the keyboard player come down the steps and head off to the bar. The guitarist was tinkering with his amp and pedals. The guy in the shorts was setting up monitors and lights. A shout came from the bar.

"Hey Roaddog, you want a beer?" It was the drummer. The man in shorts stood up and replied.

"Wainrights."

"Same for me," called Roaddog. The pink beard turned towards him and walked slowly up to the table.

"Hi," he said. "they call me Roaddog as well." Looking at the name badge on Roaddog's cut off. "You can call me Mick."

"How come they call you Roaddog?" asked Roaddog.

"I earned that name twenty years ago; I was working for a different band back then and the guitarist christened me Roaddog."

"Why?"

"Roaddog, he's the first guy on the road and the last guy off. He fixes things on the fly and makes sure everything works. When he's not there everything turns to shit. That's what Jay-Kay said."

"I was told about you at Easter weekend by a singer called Paul."

"I know a couple of Pauls."

"It was at the Saddle, Easter Sunday."

"I know who you mean, I almost came to that one, he's a good singer."

"He certainly put on a performance, I left before he finished though."

"I've seen him, but never worked with him," said Mick, reaching out to take the beer that the drummer was offering. "Cheers mate," said Mick.

"Fuck," said the drummer.

"What's up?" asked Mick.

"We don't need two fucking Roaddogs." he laughed loudly, pointing at Roaddog's cut off.

"Well, you got 'em." Snapped Roaddog, grinning. Mick turned to the drummer.

"I'm nearly up, sound check ten minutes, spread the word." He turned to Roaddog. "We'll talk later, I've still got stuff to do."

"No worries," said Roaddog, "I have a question though."

"Make it quick."

"I see no desk."

"Ah," Mick grinned, "state of the art, you'll see it in a little while." He laughed and turned back to the stage, he jumped up onto the stage and picked up a lap top computer. With the computer in his hand, he started some software and then pulled the keyboard off, leaving just a tablet, if a somewhat large one. Roaddog listened carefully and he could hear the monitors on stage being tested. Then the monitors at the front of the stage playing some background music. As Mick walked out from the front of the stage the monitors went quiet, and the background music came from the speakers at the side of the stage. While Mick was tuning the sound from the speakers the musicians started coming onto the stage. They all knew exactly what they had to do, drums first, then bass, then guitar, one by one the instruments came into the mix. Finally, the singer took the mike and joined the rest. He sang only about half the song that was playing before Mick was happy with the sound. He gave them a hand signal, the music stopped, and the singer announced that that was only a sound check we'll be back for the show in a little while. Mick walked over to the DJ and told him that they were done. The music thundered from the DJ's speakers filling the room with some classic Black Sabbath. The musicians came off stage, the guitarist as usual was still tinkering. The drummer walked up to Mick.

"Can I have a little more in my monitors?" he asked.

"There's some head left, what you need?"

"Just a bit more of my vocals and some more of Ste."

"No worries. Consider it fixed."

The drummer nodded and walked off towards the bar. Mick went over to the table where Roaddog was sitting.

"What do you think?"

"Sounds good, and all controlled through that laptop?"

"Yes, digital and wifi controlled. Can you hear everything?"

"Yes, it's fine. How long you been doing this?"

"Twenty-five years."

"What about the musicians?"

"They've been at this sort of stuff for about forty years apiece, so total two hundred years of experience here tonight. I don't think your DJ can match that." Mick laughed.

"How fucking old are you?" asked Bug.

"I'm not sixty, the others are."

"What are you nervous about?" asked Roaddog.

"What do you mean?" replied Mick.

"You never stop looking around, what are you frightened of."

"I've got a lot of expensive kit here, it makes me nervous, I always know what's happening around me." He glanced round again. "And I definitely don't believe that." Mick nodded in the direction of the door, where Billy had just walked through with Man-Dare on his arm. Mick turned towards the stage and shouted.

"Hey Chris." The guitarist looked up from his pedals. A question on his face. Mick looked towards the door. Chris followed his eyes and his jaw fell open.

"Billy," yelled Mick. Billy looked his way, a frown on his brow. The guitarist dropped his guitar into a stand and walked across the floor towards Billy.

"He's going to be depressed," laughed Roaddog.

"Why?" asked Mick.

"That's not Billy Gibbons, he's just Billy, though he does play guitar a little, or so I hear."

"He's a damned good look alike. And he plays guitar?"

"I'm not sure how much," laughed Roaddog, "perhaps we'll find out."

As they watch the guitarist and Billy walk back to the stage. Billy picked up a guitar from a stand and slung the strap over his head, he settled it against his belly. Chris passed him a plectrum and Billy started strumming a pattern, of three cords, just getting the feel for the guitar. Chris kicked a couple of pedals and sound started to come from the amp on the stage. Billy strummed a heavy riff from one of his favourite blues numbers, then he passed the guitar back to Chris. As the two exchanged a few words Man-Dare came from the bar with two beers in her hands, she passed one to Billy, and together they left the stage to join Roaddog, and the others.

"Who's this guy?" asked Man-Dare, pointing at Mick.

"He's the other Roaddog," said Roaddog, a huge grin on his face.

"You OK with that?" she asked.

"Fuck, he's been Roaddog for twenty years or more, call him Mick though."

"Fine, how's it going Mick?"

"OK, sound check was good, just gotta make sure about the monitors." He walked away to the stage area, and for some reason Roaddog couldn't understand started waving the singers microphone around.

"What the fuck is up with that guy? He gay or something?"

"What do you mean?" asked Billy.

"He was staring at my legs, then he fucks off. That doesn't happen."

"He's working," laughed Roaddog. "Try him again when the show is over, until then you'll get nothing from him."

"Wanna bet?" Man-Dare sneered.

"Look at him, he's totally focused on whatever it is he's doing. You'll not be able to drag him away from that. But I'll tell you what, I'll give you a tenner if you can get him so far away from them and while they're playing that he can't hear them." Roaddog laughed.

"You got a bet on that," smiled Man-Dare, turning her eyes towards Mick. He appeared to be making the final changes to the stage, lights were coming on and cables taped down. The DJ sound gradually rose as the number of people in the bar swelled, soon the place was rocking. People were dancing and having fun, some were dancing close and slow, even though the music was fast and heavy. Roaddog looked at Bone and Bandit Queen, they were swaying to their own internal beat, surprisingly soft and gentle. Sharing a lingering kiss, their eyes closed to the world around them. Roaddog watched the others as well, he had only cause to warn Bug once, to slow down, he was drinking too fast.

"What the fuck does it matter?" demanded Bug.

"Those two haven't taken their eyes off you all night." Roaddog nodded in the direction of the riders that Bug had had a minor confrontation with earlier.

"Fuck 'em," snarled Bug.

"Keep an eye on them, they could be trouble later."

"OK." Bug said, just loud enough to be heard above the pounding beat of a Led Zeppelin number.

Soon after Roaddog returned to his seat the DJ cut the music down and introduced the band. The whole room went quiet for a time that seemed to extend itself, the silence almost painful for everyone. People started looking around for the band, wondering when they were going to start, even where they actually were, the stage was still empty. An old tune started to fill the room, pouring from the band's PA. A tune that many remembered it was the introduction to the old TV show, the one the band took its name from. As the drumbeat changed the drummer walked from the bar and took up his place behind the kit. Next the keyboard player walked onto the stage, then guitarist, finally the singer walked up to the microphone. The voice of whispering Bob Harris came from the speakers.

"Tonight we bring you Whistle Test."

The band launched straight into the first number, a classic from Deep Purple. Soon the room was rocking again, as rock song after rock song came from the speakers.

Roaddog leaned close to Jackie and shouted into her ear.

"What do you think?"

"They're good, and damned loud," she laughed as she pulled away.

"Yes, but you can hear everything." Jackie nodded and turned back to the stage to watch the singer as he moved around, sometimes centre stage. Sometimes out on the floor, which slowly started to fill with dancers. Roaddog looked around to see where Mick was, finally through the crowd he saw him, standing at the end of the bar, a beer in one hand and laptop in the other. Man-Dare was standing next to him, but he was paying no attention to her at all. His focus entirely on the laptop, he put the beer on the bar and made some adjustments to the controls. Not anything that Roaddog could actually identify in the sound he was hearing. Mick picked up his beer and walked towards the stage, weaving through the crowd. First to one side of the stage then the other, he put the laptop on the floor behind one of the speakers and put his beer next to it. Slowly he moved to the side and leaned against the fire door. Man-

Dare moved in to stand in front of Mick. Roaddog watched as she moved in close and started to talk to Mick. The singer introduced the next song as a classic by Free. The opening chords had Roaddog smiling, and he watched as Man-Dare recognised it, she actually shivered as the words blasted from the speakers.

"Take off your hat, kick off your shoes." Roaddog leaned in against Jackie and kissed her softly on the cheek. Man-Dare moved in against Mick, pressing her body against him, and she leaned against him trying to talk to him, conversation made very difficult indeed by the nearness of the speaker. Mick placed both hands on her hips, he spoke to her. Then slowly turned her so her back was to the fire door and she was standing beside him. He smiled, she frowned. Roaddog wondered what was happening. The guitarist picked up the solo, the slightly distorted sound cutting through above everything else, all eyes turned to him. Roaddog spotted motion out of the corner of his eye, Mick pushed off from the fire door, and walked towards centre stage where the singer was standing. Roaddog as thinking about that last word of the song, as it arrived the singer passed the mike off to Mick. That last 'Well' rang on in Mick's voice. He strolled through the crowd of dancers, still singing. Round towards the fire door, where Man-Dare was still standing. Mick couldn't cross in front of the speaker, so he raised a hand to Man-Dare and waved her forwards. She came into his arms and writhed against him, her mind filled with memory and her loins with lust. Finally, Mick ran out of air and passed the mike back to the singer. The song ended in a typical rock fashion. Once the applause had subsided, the singer spoke.

"Thanks to Roaddog." Mick raised a hand in salute and moved to the fire door again, this time with Man-Dare close to his side.

27: Saturday Rally Day Two Whistle Test and a Bet.

The first set finished, and the DJ took over with the music again. Roaddog watched as Man-Dare was leaning against Mick, across the room Billy was watching them just as closely. He was wondering if today was the day that Man-Dare moved on. He had enjoyed their relationship so far, he knew it didn't have much of a chance of lasting a long time, but he had hoped for more than a few weeks. Mick left Man-Dare by the door and went up on stage, he was messing with something in the darkness at the back of the stage as Man-Dare caught Billy's eyes. She pushed off from the door and sauntered over to him, she stepped in close and kissed him.

"What's going on with you?" he asked.

"Nothing, Roaddog bet me a tenner that I couldn't get him away from the band while they are playing, I'm gonna do it if I have to drag him away by the dick." A huge grin split her happy face.

"So, you're not taken with him?"

"No, but he is. He's married, I wouldn't mind a quick shag, but it wouldn't be going anywhere." She pressed her belly against his hip and tucked her hand into the back of his jeans. "You'll do for me, old man." He smiled down at her and kissed her as she rubbed her crotch against his thigh.

"You really are a crazy bitch." he laughed. "You know that, don't you?"

"Perhaps, but you want me just the same."

"Of course, I do. We're good for each other."

"That's as may be." She grinned and turned away.

Roaddog and Jackie got up from their table and went to the bar, leaving Bug and Cherie holding hands.

"Shit," said Roaddog. "There's all sorts of romance going on here tonight."

"What do you mean?" asked Jackie.

"Well, those two." He nodded in the direction of the table. "Then Billy and Man-Dare."

"But Man-Dare is hanging with that sound guy."

"Yes, but I've been watching her, she's just cleared her actions with Billy. Could be that there is a spark there as well."

"But he's far too old for her."

"There have been more diverse relationships before."

"There must be thirty years between them." Jackie laughed.

"And?"

"She's gonna kill the old man."

"Maybe, but he'll die with a smile on his face."

"And what about us?"

"I've got used to you being around," he leaned in and kissed her, "you?"

"I've got used to being around as well. It's fun."

"What does your mother think?"

"She's still not happy, but she's getting used to it too."

"Dad?"

"He's cool, but he keeps telling me that he'll kill you if you step out of line," she laughed heartily.

"That is entirely as it should be." Roaddog reached towards her and kissed her again, the kiss slowly became more intense. "Should we go back to the tent for a little while?" He whispered, his lips brushing softly against her ear.

"When the music is finished," she said, "these guys are really good."

"You're not wrong. I'll go get some more beer." Roaddog stood up and went to the bar, it seemed his timing was exactly right. The musicians were returning to the stage as he regained his seat. The second set started with a few fast songs, before the third song Mick had put his laptop down behind the speaker stack and was dancing with Man-Dare, slowly she was manoeuvring him away from the stage. Soon the pair were dancing together in the darkness beyond the reach of the stage lights. Roaddog was smiling, he was certain now that he was going to lose a tenner to the young girl. The singer introduced a new song and the guitarist picked up a different guitar, as he stamped on the pedals a howl of feedback came from the speakers. Roaddog turned to watch Mick, wondering if this was where he was going to lose control of the sound, his laptop was so far away. Mick turned his back on Man-Dare and pulled something from the inside pocket of his cut, his fingers flashed around the screen and the feedback died in a heartbeat, as the screen went dark and the small tablet returned to Mick's jacket he turned to Man-Dare to pick up the dance where it had left off. Roaddog howled with laughter, he knew that his tenner was safe, no matter what Man-Dare did this guy was not going to let go of the sound. Man-Dare leaned in close and spoke right into Mick's ear.

"Bastard."

"What's up?" he asked.

She told him about the bet. He pulled her close and laughed, "You were never going to win that one."

"Bastard," she said again, writhing her crotch against his thigh.

"Much as I'd like to take you up on that offer, you'll have to wait until the band have finished." His hand reached between her legs and cupped her sex, pressing the seam of her jeans against her, causing a minor shudder.

"Bastard," she muttered, far too quietly for him to hear above the sound of the band. Behind him a single note from the guitar rang on and on, all around the crowd were cheering the guitarists skill, sustaining that note was a feature of the song, and the guitarist was doing very well. Man-Dare shook her head and pressed her body against Micks. Their dance continued for a couple more songs, then Mick pulled away and moved towards the stage, taking her with him by the hand. The song playing was Paranoid by Black Sabbath, the dance floor area filled with headbangers. As the guitarist was playing the short solo, Mick dropped Man-Dare's hand and walked into the stage area, taking the microphone from the singer. Once the solo was finished and the band settled down into the main riff, played at a much quieter volume. Mick introduced the band as a whole and the individuals in turn, each played a short solo.

"Last and by no means least," said Mick, "put your hands together for your singer tonight, let's hear it for Gaff the horse in tears." As the applause rolled in Mick passed the microphone back to the singer and stepped out of the lights. When the applause settled down the singer spoke.

"Don't forget the sound guy, the one and the only Roaddog. Let's hear it."

"Ste," shouted Mick. "Special offer tonight only, two for the price of one." He was standing next to Roaddog and pointing.

"Buy one, get one free." Laughed the singer, the crowd roared, many of them knew Roaddog. Mick shook his hand and then turned back to Man-Dare, to see a huge smile on her face. He stepped into her arms and took up the dance as the music played out, to be replaced by another classic as the supposed last song. As normal in these circumstances the band were cajoled into playing two more songs, then the DJ took over again. Mick walked up to Roaddog.

"When does the music stop at these events?" he shouted.

"DJ stops when people go to sleep, usually about four AM."

"Fuck it, I'm not waiting that long, gonna start stripping it down." Mick turned away and started moving gear back from the dance floor, and unplugging things. Roaddog was surprised how quickly the stage cleared of the musician's equipment. It had taken two hours to set up but was stripped and packed in less than forty minutes. Roaddog watched as Mick swept the stage with a handheld search light, finding nothing left behind he walked out to his car, Man-Dare on his heels. Roaddog and Jackie followed at a discreet distance. The two hugged and kissed beside Mick's car, a huge blue people carrier, apparently called Moya. Once Man-Dare had left to go back inside Roaddog stepped forward.

"Hey man," he said, "great show."

"Thanks, it's what we do."

"What you up to tomorrow?"

"Nothing planned, why?"

"We're going up to Rivi tomorrow, just a short ride out, and then back here for another band, you wanna tag along?"

"Who's the band?"

"Fifth element."

"Damned right, I'll catch ya up at Rivi, about lunch time?"

"We'll be there sometime; I wouldn't take this bastard though." Roaddog laughed pointing at the car.

"I'll take the sportster, no worries."

"Great, see ya then, bring a tent."

Mick nodded and shook Roaddog's hand, before getting into his car and driving off.

"He's a nice guy," said Jackie.

"Seems good to me." Roaddog's arm snaked around her waist and walked them both towards the bar. As they stepped inside the first thing they saw was Man-Dare and Billy in an intense embrace, mouths locked together, swaying slowly to the primary beat of a Saxon track. Jackie nudged Roaddog, he leaned in so she could speak to him.

"Don't they look good together?" she asked.

"Yes, despite the difference in ages."

"Definitely, could that be a permanent arrangement?"

"I don't want to predict the future," he said, "but maybe. Who can tell?"

"You think they have a chance?"

"Of course, all sorts of relationships have a chance, there's no less than so many others."

"She's only a child compared to him."

"True, but he has so much to teach her."

"You think she can learn?"

"Certainly, and Bandit Queen has much to teach her as well."

"I'm not sure I understand?" Her question fell on deaf ears, he was looking towards the stage, there was pushing and shoving going on there. Roaddog dropped Jackie's hand and stormed quickly towards the place where things were going badly. He stepped in close and snatched an arm that was rushing to connect with Sharpshooter's cheek. The man behind the strike staggered as his arm suddenly stopped. He looked at the person who had his arm held firmly, then he looked away, dropping the arm and turning to walk away, hoping beyond hope that his arm would be released, and so it was. Sharpshooters' eyes snapped to Roaddog's, and in an instant of understanding they turned to the other three. They looked to the one that was already running for the door. Roaddog caught each man's eye in turn, and everyone backed down. The music was so loud that conversation was impossible, but understanding was achieved and the three followed their compatriot. Roaddog leaned into Sharpshooter.

"You OK?"

"Fine," Sharpshooter replied, "I thought I was going to have to break our agreement with the Centurions for a moment, then you turned up."

"Don't sweat it, who were those guys?"

"They were friends of the Hyabusa guys, that have a problem with Bug."

"And they picked a fight with you instead of him?"

"Yes, he's with Cherie, and some of the others over there." Sharpshooter pointed to the table where Roaddog had been sitting while the band were playing.

"How come you ended up on your own?"

"I was just chilling to the music, ya know how it is."

"I do, watch out for being alone, we are amongst friends, but not everyone here is our friend."

"I understand." Sharpshooter smiled, then walked over to the table where the rest of the Dragonriders where sitting. Roaddog turned and Jackie was immediately behind him, he smiled into her face.

"These things can be crazy."

"I understand." She replied, pressing her body against his. She started to sway to the music that the DJ was playing, his body responded almost automatically. They moved slowly into the thick of the crowded dance floor, swaying to the music, and holding each other close. They danced for a while, then Roaddog led them outside to cool down. Midnight was well passed by the time they made it to the tents, the music still blaring from the clubhouse, much less prominent out here. They sat in front of his tent, slowly drinking beer from the van. Bone and Bandit Queen were sitting back to back on the soft grass, passing a joint backwards and forwards.

"Where is everyone?" asked Roaddog. The response from Bone was a shrug.

"Everything seems to be quiet," said Bandit Queen, "Lurch is watching the bar, the Hyabusa boys have packed up and gone. They made the mistake of picking another fight with an old man this time."

"Who?"

"Geronimo."

"They walk away?"

"When they came to, Lurch and Slowball were standing over them, they opted for discretion over death. Centurions president asked them politely to leave." She laughed and passed the joint back to Bone. Roaddog looked around their camp, Slowballs booted feet were sticking out of his tent. Sylvia's tent was locked up tight, as was Alan's, though there was a chain running from Alan's bike under the flap of his tent, presumably fastened to his wrist, or some other sensitive part of his anatomy. Judging by the noises from Billy's tent he wasn't on his own, it sounded like Man-Dare was taking out her frustrations on him. Though it didn't sound like Billy was putting up much of a fight. 'Another case of discretion before valour.' Thought Roaddog.

"I need a pee before bed." He said, climbing to his feet and setting off for the dark hedge on the perimeter of the camp site. Jackie followed him, walking rapidly to catch up. The lights from the clubhouse faded quickly as the pair walked hand in hand into the darkness.

"Why here?" whispered Jackie.

"It's closer, and I'm lazy." Roaddog chuckled softly.

"It's far easier for you than for me."

"Should have worn a skirt then."

"It's too cold for that."

"That's for sure, could even be frosty in the morning."

"I'm not looking forwards to that," she muttered.

"Don't fret, I'll keep you warm." He said pulling his fly down, while Jackie unfastened her jeans and wriggled them down before she crouched with her back to the hedge. She gasped as the hedge was lit from the other side by a passing car. Roaddog laughed, and helped her to her feet, and waited until she had her pants pulled up before reached for her and kissed her firmly.

"You're crazy," she said pushing him gently away.

"I know," he giggled, taking her hand and walking back towards the camp. As they passed between the circle of tents the sound from the clubhouse dropped away completely, and the lights in the windows began to vanish.

"Looks like the DJ has declared bedtime," said Bandit Queen.

"I'm up for some of that," replied Bone. The two crawled into his tent, Roaddog and Jackie followed suit only a moment later.

28: Sunday Rally Day Three and some business.

It was early when the Dragonriders camp started to wake up, something to with large quantities of beer. Andy and his burger van where more than ready for them, the wind was even in a favourable direction. Wafting the fragrance of bacon butties into camp, making everyone hungry.

Roaddog and Jackie crawled out of their tent and walked into the clubhouse without saying a word to anyone. They went to Andy's van before they returned to camp. Each with a large breakfast on a bun, and a huge coffee.

"How's it going?" asked Bug his voice more than a little rough.

"OK." replied Roaddog. "How's Cherie?"

"Oh my god, has she recovered." Bug grinned. Roaddog laughed, Jackie grinned.

"Hey man," Bug continued, "I could do with a hand this morning, got a lot of deliveries to get moving. Can you give me a hand?"

"How much time do you need?"

"I don't know, we could make the drops in Chorley, it's on the way to Rivi."

"You mean the whole morning?"

"Pretty much, on my own it will take me all day."

"Can't anyone else help?"

"Come on, you trust any of them with this sort of stuff?"

"Fuck no. I wouldn't trust most of them to stand up straight today," he grinned.

"You'll help?"

"I'll have to clear my absence with Bone, but Me and Jackie can help." Bug looked hard at Jackie then back at Roaddog, eyebrows raised high.

"She'll be cool," Roaddog turned to Jackie and smiled.

"I'm cool," she smirked.

"That'll make things easier. I'll talk to Bone as soon as I see him."

"Talk to me about what?" asked a voice from within a tent.

"Got a minute or two?" asked Bug quietly. There was a sigh from the tent and Bone slowly appeared, the heavy shoulders of Bandit Queen behind him.

"What you want?" snarled the leader.

"I need help to get some deliveries out today."

"Does it have to be today?" demanded Bandit Queen.

"Sorry, but yes. Orders came in yesterday, I'm trying to build confidence in our brand, and that is hard enough to do on facebook, the dark web is so much harder."

Bone and Bandit shared a look, then Bone turned to Roaddog, and asked.

"You ok with helping him?"

"Of course, you ok with me not making the run to Rivi? We'll catch up with you there."

"Lurch can take over your responsibilities."

"You sure he won't mind?"

"He'll do as he's fucking told," snapped Bandit Queen. Roaddog glanced at her for a moment then turned to Bone.

"You really ought to feed her before you let her out in public." Silence fell over the group, it lasted for what seemed to be a long time. No one was exactly sure how this was going to go.

"Roaddog," whispered Bandit Queen, the tension rising a few more notches. "You can be a real bastard, one day you will say the wrong thing and die."

"But you love me," his grin split his whole face.

"Damned right I do, so the duty falls to you." She stopped speaking as she walked towards him, he held his ground. Until her considerable chest was pressed against his own. He was struggling not to tense his thighs to block the potential rising knee. He knew she would feel that. Their eyes locked in a long stare, even Bone was beginning to worry when she finally spoke.

"Go get me bacon," she snarled softly. Her right arm raised and pointed in the direction of Andy's van. She smiled then pulled his face down for a gentle kiss. "Bastard," she mumbled, then pushed him away. He passed his breakfast and coffee to Jackie, then walked away to get Bandit her breakfast. Everyone in the small group realised that they had been holding their breath.

"Damn," whispered Jackie. "I'm not sure my heart can stand this sort of excitement."

"You'll do fine, my dear," said Bandit Queen. "There is a strength within all us women, some just don't understand, or believe. Be strong for your man, and everything will come out right in the end."

"Can you be sure of that?"

"It has so far."

"Even Man-Dare?"

"Especially Man-Dare. You watch out for her, she has leader in her, only stand against her if you are certain."

"You still think she's going to try and take over from you?"

"No, but she'll take the opportunity if it comes her way, only stand in her way if you are sure of your backing." Bandit Queen looked at the shape of Roaddog returning with breakfast for both her and Bone.

"I'll follow your advice, but I don't see that opportunity coming for a long time yet, not while there's still life in the Bandit Queen."

Bandit Queen stared hard at Jackie for a long moment before she whispered.

"Thanks for the curse," she turned and walked towards Roaddog, meeting him she took her breakfast and carried on walking towards the clubhouse. Jackie felt very uncomfortable.

"Don't fret," said Bone. "She's had a dream that she will die in the worst sort of pain. Sometimes it gets to her." He took his breakfast from Roaddog and set off after his lady.

"What did I miss?" asked Roaddog.

"Your girl just laid a death curse on Bandit," laughed Bug, shaking his head.

"You're kidding me?" Roaddog asked of Jackie.

"I only told her that she'd be leader while she had life in her," stammered Jackie.

"Good shot, that'll shake her."

"What do you mean?"

"She's a weird chick. She puts a lot of importance in her dreams. She knows that Man-Dare has an important part to play, and that she will die, her dreams tell her, and she believes."

"She strikes me as too much of a realist to do something like that."

"She says there is power within the paradox. She's a realist driven by her dreams."

"Or she's batshit crazy," said Jackie.

"That is another possibility, or a different paradox, I'd not suggest it to her though."

"Do you really think me that stupid?"

"Of course not love, but I want to be sure you'll live until tomorrow at least."

"You'd let her kill me?"

"Of course not love. She's leader, it's her right. I'm master at arms, it's up to me to help her. But I'd not do that."

"I know enough about the dynamics of this group now," she smiled at him. "If she calls for my death and you defy her, then you are pressing the button that tears this whole thing apart. This will all end in conflict and death. Is that what you want?"

"What I want is not relevant," he pulled her by the arm away from the others, once they were out of earshot he continued. "I have talked to Bandit at some length, she believes her dreams. Dragonriders will be torn apart, but not from within. She sees herself dying, and Man-Dare still has things to do, Man-Dare will go on."

"Where are you and I in her dreams? I don't see her dying without you at her side."

"She can't, or won't, say."

"You believe her dreams?"

"There are more things in heaven and earth, Horatio, than are dreamt of in your philosophy," smiled Roaddog.

"Now you're quoting Shakespeare?"

"That and to be or not to be, that's me done," he laughed.

"You dodged that one. Answer."

"Do I believe her dreams? She does, and in some ways that is enough for me. In other ways there has to be more."

"Would you follow her dreams?"

"Bitch, you really ask the hard questions." He paused for a thought or two. "Only if they were going the way I wanted to."

"And what do you want?"

"Bitch is now fishing. You of course."

"Me before Dragonriders?"

"Don't ask that question, this is my family now."

"Fine question withdrawn. Where do we go from here?"

"Today we help Bug make some money for Dragonriders, then we go to Rivi. After that we come back here for another good band and tomorrow can look after itself."

"Sounds like a plan," she smiled up at him, she stepped in close and kissed him.

"You OK with this?" he asked after the kiss ended.

"Not too happy with your prophet, but I'm still having fun, and really enjoying all these crazy people."

"You ready to quit your citizen job and go full time Dragonrider?"

"No. I need the contact with sane people, I need an anchor in the real world."

"What is real?"

"Different bitch asking the hard questions now?" she laughed before going on. "I'm no longer sure what I want to be real."

"Real is the way I feel about you," he said, pulling her tight against his chest. "Know that I will walk into hell for you."

"My hell, your hell, or Bandit Queen's hell?"

"All of these are nothing compared to the hell that rides at my back, my hell rides for you." He pulled her in close and kissed her hard, his tongue probing fast into her mouth. His left leg trapped hers, and he pushed her over onto the ground. Falling on top of her he pressed her into the grass. His need for her obvious in the pressure he placed against her belly, his rampant manhood pushing against her belt, digging the buckle into her soft flesh. Her arms flew around his neck, pulling him in tight. Her legs spread almost by reflex. His weight settled on her, pushing her into the damp grass of the morning. Her heels pressed against the backs of his thighs, pulling him in tighter. Her pelvis rocked against his hardness. Roaddog gasped and backed away, his need still obvious, but rational thought replaced the desperate physical urges.

"Damn girl," he mumbled. "You make me so hot."

"I've never felt this way about anyone before." She whispered, her eyes half closed, and her breath rasping in her throat. His hands pressed into the grass and lifted his body as much as he could against her strong legs.

"Come on girl," he said, "we got lots to do today."

"I got lot's I want to do now," she said softly, pulling harder against his thighs.

"There's going to be plenty of time for that," he smiled down at her.

"Are you sure? I think I can hear the hell hounds coming this way."

"They only come at my call," he laughed, pushing harder, flexing his spine, his thighs pressing hard against the heels of her boots.

"Bastard," she laughed releasing him. "Don't you get too drunk today," she snarled as he lifted from her. Once on his feet he reached a hand down to help her up. Together they walked back into the Dragonriders camp, leaving behind discarded wrappers and coffee cups. More of the bikers were awake now, gathered between the tents chatting in quiet voices. Roaddog caught Bug's eyes with a glance, he looked at the watch on his wrist. Bug held up five fingers. Roaddog nodded.

"We are rolling in five," he whispered to Jackie, she simply nodded and went to their tent, she returned almost immediately with both their jackets. Bug and Cherie both got to their feet, collected jackets. Many faces looked, many eyes asked questions, but no one was willing to press the matter verbally. Some looked to Bone for clarification that was not forthcoming. Two bikes fired up and left the site without fanfare, the slippery grass causing them no serious issues. The run to the Dragonriders home base was without incident. Bug opened the personnel door and cleared the alarm as he walked past. Cherie close on his heels and the other two not far behind. Roaddog closed and locked the door, the heavy bolts crashed home like those of a prison cell. The florescent lights were flashing into brightness as they all walked into the main part of the unit. Bug walked into the back room, more flashing harsh lights, and brightness flooded the place. Dishevelled bunks filled most of the room, except for a space at the back, where three sinks were mounted on the wall, much like those in a barracks room of any military base, anywhere in the world. Bug walked over to the left-hand wall and kicked one of the cracked tiles, one close to the floor. There was a subdued click, and a section of the linoleum covered floor lifted half an inch. Bug lifted the four-foot square section to reveal a ladder leading down into a room below, light flashing into life as he went down. The rest followed him into the hidden room below ground. This space was only twenty feet by eight, but it held all sorts of equipment. It also had quite a strong odour, not unlike urine. That ammoniacal stench that really sticks in the throat.

"What the fuck goes on down here?" asked Jackie.

"Don't fret," chuckled Bug. "Nothing too bad." He went to various pieces of equipment and started them up, LED lights lit up to indicate that things were working properly. A printer in one corner started to spit out sheets of paper, they were documents with details of despatches required. Each showed quantity and address and price paid, via bitcoin of course.

"Right," said Bug. "Weigh the stuff out into bags, as the print outs need. We got twenty-two from the looks of things. Weigh up, no-one gets shorted, they're paying over the odds anyway. Clear?" Bug put a large bag of white powder on a long table along one wall, he started hanging the printouts from a string above the table. Cherie and Jackie started weighing out the powder. A sensitive digital scale made sure they got the quantities right. Bug went to a different machine and started it up, it only took a few seconds for the heat sealer to get to temperature.

"Right," he said looking at Roaddog. "What we do is take the bags, put them in one of these bags." He pointed to a stack. "Then you drop it into the water bath, this squeezes the air out, seal it with the sealer. Just push it closed until the light goes green," he grinned at Roaddog. "Can you do that?"

"Dick," said Roaddog.

"Right, once the bag is sealed, dip it in the ammonia. Lift it out, let it drip for a few seconds, then put it in a new bag, and bag it again. Got it?"

"Got it." snarled Roaddog.

"Right, second gets dipped and dripped, then wiped. Into a jiffy bag and the label from the printout on the outside. Gloves, no fingerprints, got it?" Bug pointed to a box of disposable gloves.

"Yes. No fingerprints, or other possible contaminations," smiled Roaddog.

"That's right, we gotta keep this stuff as clean as possible. There is a chance that the cops can get into this, the ammonia should cause the dogs some problems, and if we can keep prints and DNA out of the stuff, that would be great."

"It fucking stinks though," said Jackie.

"Agreed, but it might just keep us safe. And once you're on the road the stink will blow away real fast," laughed Bug.

In less than two hours the bags were all ready for posting. A final instruction from Bug to make sure there was more than enough postage on each package, and that none of the stamps had been touched with bare hands. The packages were loaded into a carrier bag and gripped between Bug and Cherie as they left the unit, the run to Chorley was calm and without any interruption at all. The two bikes pulled up on the Argos carpark, side by side, a long way away from anyone else.

"Right." said Bug, handing Roaddog a black cylindrical device. "This is a laser torch; the wavelength is set to six hundred and fifty nanometres. Now across the road is a post box, the one we are using today. It has a little problem, there is a CCTV camera covering it. Can you see it?"

"Yes. It's on the top of that pole." Roaddog nodded in the direction of the offending device.

"Right. If you point the torch at it, it'll not be able to see me walk across the road and post the envelopes."

"How do I know I've hit it?"

"It'll light up with the red laser, and the whole lens will flare bright red, you've gotta keep it lit up. We should get a few minutes before the cops come to investigate why their camera has flared out."

"I understand," grinned Roaddog.

"Big problem, if the operator notices the camera going out, he'll try moving it first, keep it targeted. OK?"

"Got it. When?"

"We're still out of shot, you gotta get it hit before I get to the middle of the road."

"Fine. I got the spot on the top of the post already, if you set off now, I'll have it blind before you get to the pavement this side."

Bug got off his bike and taking the carrier bag started to cross the road. Roaddog moved the spot to the lens of the camera and was surprised by the flare he saw from the lens, even in the brightness of full daylight it was clearly visible. Bug walked slowly across the road, taking care not to inconvenience any motorists, he really didn't want to be noticed. He arrived at the post box and started to post the packages, Roaddog noticed that the camera moved a little from side to side. He tracked it with the laser, he was smiling to himself when the camera suddenly switched through a full one hundred and eighty degrees. Now it was pointing completely the other way, slowly it panned back round to where Bug had already finished posting. Bug was back in the carpark before the camera returned to its previous position, Roaddog swept the laser down to his feet and fumbled the switch to turn it off. Roaddog glared at Bug as he walked up to the parked motorcycles.

"You could have warned my, damned camera flipped completely round."

"Sorry, it's a road camera, so it does that sometimes. Did you keep it blinded?"

"Yes, until it switched, but you were back here before it tracked back around, so I didn't bother hitting it again."

"We'll be OK then."

"Why red laser?" asked Roaddog.

"The CCTV cameras are very sensitive to the red end of the spectrum, most of them actually work well down into the infra-red. It's a property of the CCD's used in digital cameras, I noticed it at the unit, I was taking a few snaps of people and the security cameras all come up with a bright circle of LED's around the lens. These are throwing infra-red for the cameras when they are running in the dark, but my camera sees them even when my eyes don't. So, I tried the red laser against them, and it flared them out completely. I talked to a security company that I know and found out the even the most complicated cameras are susceptible to red lasers. That torch is bright enough to kill a camera from over a mile away, just don't point it at people, it's bad for their eyes."

"You really are a mine of useless information, aren't you?" laughed

Roaddog.

"Actually, very useful in this case."

"How long before the camera's get good enough to deal with the laser?"

"Not going to happen, when in night mode they are running in the infra-red band, they need it. There needs to be some serious development to get around that."

"Good, let's go catch up with the guys at Rivi." Roaddog and Jackie mounted up, and with Bug and Cherie behind them left the carpark. Heading along the main road, with all its roundabouts they turned left toward Rivington village.

Only a few minutes later they were looking for places to park their bikes. They struggled because the good weather had brought so many bikers out for a run. They squeezed into a couple of spaces on the edge of the lower carpark. Together the four walked across the circle heading for the bar.

"That fucking ammonia gives me a serious thirst," said Roaddog.

"Yes, it does that." laughed Bug.

"My hands still stink of it," said Roaddog.

"It'll go away, don't worry," Bug smiled.

"But I smell like I've pissed myself."

"This is new?" grinned Bug.

"Fuck you," snarled Roaddog, which only made Bug's smile even wider.

"It's no different for me."

"I wondered if some local tomcat had been making his way into the clubhouse, but it seems that pong was you in the cellar," Roaddog looked hard at Bug.

"It's not really a cellar though is it?" asked Jackie.

"No," Roaddog laughed. "It's on no plans, it is a short container sneaked in over an Easter weekend a few years ago. It goes under the back carpark area, that took some damned digging out. But it's paid for itself since, it gives us some storage space that no one knows about. Hell, the cops have torn the place apart at least three times and not found it."

"I saw air vents and I heard fans, surely the power and air can be traced?"

"Only if you go looking for them, the air vents look like just another boiler vent pipe in the roof, to find the junction box for the power you'd have to take four bricks out of one of the walls in the garage bay. The drains go to a small sump, and then a pump lifts the water up into the soil pipe for the toilets. No toilets in the underground, did you notice?"

"Not specifically. But I don't think I'd like to be down there with the door closed."

"It's not that bad, so long as the power doesn't go out." They walked into the darkness of the barn, as they approached the bar a voice called out.

"Roaddog."

He turned towards Bandit Queen; she had a pint in her hand. The four walked over the where the Dragonriders were sitting, beers were handed to them.

"How did you know we were here?" asked Bug.

"You were seen as soon as you came into the circle," Bandit Queen smiled.

"Everything go OK?" asked Bone.

"Yes," replied Bug, "no problems, five K already in the bank and all the goods despatched. Should all be delivered Thursday, parcel farce not up to much as usual. All the customers have been advised that the packages are on the way. More happy customers, I was getting thank you messages before I had finished sending out the confirmations."

"How much is that for the week?" asked Bone.

"Ten."

"We going to need some more stuff?"

"Not this week, maybe next week. Most of these guys are buying enough for a month."

"What the fuck are we going to spend this on?" demanded Bone.

"We don't need to," said Bug. "It doesn't actually exist, keeping it as bitcoin it's untraceable."

"And un-usable," Bone snapped.

"What do you want? You can buy a nice new Harley using bitcoin now."

"You're kidding?"

"No, just sell the bitcoin and put the cash in your account. Watch out for transaction limits though, don't want to attract the attention of HMRC." Bug laughed.

"But if we get too flash too quick, then the plods are going to come looking."

"True. We just gotta go a little slow."

"I don't want to go slow though," Bone sneered, "slow is for citizens."

"Help me out here," said Bug looking to Bandit Queen, she grinned and turned to Bone.

"Go easy for a few weeks, and we'll have an awesome summer, we could go to some of those big rallies, I fancy a solstice rally at Stonehenge." She took his hand and smiled at him.

"Fine," snapped Bone, he turned back to Bug. "Stack us some cash and we'll have a blow out in June, and we'll go to Americana in July."

29: Sunday Rally Day Three, Rivi and back to camp.

Bug turned to Roaddog and raised his eyebrows; the question was clear in Roaddog's mind. 'Has Bone lost the plot?" Roaddog shrugged and lifted his chin only a millimetre, Bug's returned nod was of a similar inclination. They both knew that they would talk later. Talk circulated around the tables, discussions of the rest of the day and the night to come. Suddenly Bandit Queen spoke softly.

"Fuck."

"What's up?" asked Bone.

"Fucking Hopkins and Lewis." Bandit Queen nodded in the direction of the entranceway. The two plain clothed officers paused for a while as their eyes became accustomed to the darkness on the inside. Once their vision cleared, they walked straight to the table where the Dragonriders were sitting.

"Good afternoon," said Hopkins, a smile on his face.

"Hi," said Bandit Queen. "What do you want now?" she sneered.

"Nothing, my dear," smiled Hopkins, "I have some information for you."

"Well?" her monosyllabic question long and slow.

"The unicorn is dead."

"What do you mean?"

"Someone killed him in his cell. There are so many candidates we aren't sure we will ever be able to decide who actually did it."

"What do you mean?"

"There are a dozen, at least, who are ready to plead guilty to his murder."

"Actually, fourteen," laughed Lewis.

"You came here to tell me or arrest me?" demanded Bandit Queen.

"Actually," Hopkins smiled and looked at Lewis, "I can't link you to any of the volunteers, not a single one. Not that we can actually decide which, if any of them actually strung him up from the bars of his window."

"I am not sure I understand," said Bandit Queen.

"With so many saying they did it, and no physical evidence to point to any of them, the most inept of barristers could muddy the waters so no jury could ever convict, and they are all going to get legal aid, no damned barristers for them, QC all the way. CPS has decided not to prosecute any of them."

"There's something else you are not telling us," Bandit Queen laughed.

"You're right of course. There is physical evidence, found at the scene."

"And?"

"It points to someone known to be dead for at least ten years."

"That's one hell of a pickle for you," she smiled.

"Fucking aye," grinned Hopkins.

"Sadly, I can't help you with your problem, I couldn't even find out which jail you had him in."

"That's one of the things I made sure of, he wasn't even registered under his own name."

"I only knew him as Simon," smiled Bandit Queen.

"Fuck off," Hopkins chuckled, "you had his phone, I know you did. I think you had his surname as well. You have a surname at least."

"But is it a real one?"

"No less real than Cross," Hopkin's grin split his face.

"Fuck you," Bandit Queen snarled, her quiet tone had her people reaching for pockets and boots, she started to come to her feet.

"Relax," snapped Hopkins, stepping backwards. "I've done my research, I know where you come from, I meant no offense."

"Fuck," whispered Lewis, seeing that Roaddog was already on his feet, a twelve-inch black stiletto in each hand.

"Stand down Dog," whispered Bandit Queen. "How far back did you have to go?" Her voice louder and calmer. Two knives collapsed and returned to a belt, but Roaddog didn't return to his seat.

"Shit," muttered Hopkins, "a damned long way, have you any idea how many favours I had to use to get that name?"

"Ancient history, and not who I am now."

"Isn't that true of us all?" He held his hands wide, open and palms up. "How is your past so well protected?" This question brought more tension from Roaddog, though the knives stayed in the belt. "Can you make your Dog relax? His posture is attracting a lot of attention?" A look around the room showed that Centurions were moving forwards, and Satans Sons already had the door, people were leaving quickly and quietly, but no one was coming in.

"What else do you know?" asked Bandit Queen gently.

"Fuck all," snapped Hopkins, "and that really pisses me off. Who are you?"

"Bandit Queen," she smiled, "that is all you need to know."

"Damn it. Did you actually get to the unicorn?"

"You've already said that you can't prove it," she laughed.

"Proof isn't always everything."

"No, I didn't get to him, could be there are bigger players on the field that you can't see."

"Now that really scares me. Getting information on you was hard enough, to think that there may be others involved, please don't do that to me."

"Who can tell? Not me, that's for sure. My history has been buried and cancelled. Digging it up would not be good for you. Do you understand?"

"I think I am beginning to see." Hopkins looked around the room, only patch wearing people remained. "Now I have a boon to ask."

"What do you need?"

"I could do with an escort for myself and my comrade from this place."

"You have my word that you and yours will not be harmed at this time," her smile did nothing to calm him.

"The future?"

"No comment." She looked round. "Roaddog, escort them out, and open the doors again." Roaddog nodded and stepped forwards, a hand signal made Jackie stay where she was. With the two detectives he walked slowly towards the main door. He nodded to the Sons that were guarding the door, grim faced bikers surrounded the cops and guided them to their car.

The president of the Centurions walked up to Bandit Queen.

"Do we need to leave?" he asked softly.

"No, it'll take them hours to get a force together big enough to take us on. Hopkins won't want that, he doesn't know what is going on, and that makes him frightened. So long as he gets out, he'll drop it."

"You sure?"

"Death and taxes."

"Bitch, you make everyone nervous, don't you?"

"I try my best." People were returning to the barn, it was filling slowly, there was some trepidation amongst the newcomers. "Have a beer and relax," she smiled.

It only took a few minutes for normality to return to the barn, though the Dragonriders took longer to relax. The tension was slow to ebb from their nerves, even after Roaddog returned with the president of the Sons.

"They've gone," said Roaddog simply.

"What the fuck was their problem?" demanded the chief of the Sons.

"Some guy I wanted dead, sort of died whilst in their custody. That always pisses them off, especially when they can't pin it to me."

"Who was he?"

"A rather prolific paedophile, one they'd been after for a long time."

"Did you arrange his demise?"

"No, I couldn't even find him. I'd have made sure he didn't simply strangle."

"I've heard that about you."

"And so have the damned cops," she laughed loudly.

"You are crazy," said the Son turning away and walking back to the door, in a flare of invading sunlight he vanished.

"It's never boring," laughed Jackie.

"That's for sure," agreed Sylvia, she turned to Slowball. "Go stand in that doorway, I want the sun light and your shadow." She hefted her stills camera, mid-size lens already loaded. Slowball walked over to the door and opened both of the doors, highlighted by the sun pouring in. The air of the barn flaring as the dust was illuminated by the sun. He waited a few moments then returned. Sylvia got to her feet and hugged him.

"Awesome," she whispered into his ear.

"Me or the photo?" he asked.

"Both obviously," she chuckled, reaching up to kiss him firmly on the lips. The inside of the barn returned to a more normal atmosphere as more and more people came in. The bar and the café were doing a roaring trade, but the citizens were giving the bikers plenty of room.

"When do you think we should leave?" Bandit Queen asked Bone, his reply was a shrug. She turned to Roaddog; eyebrows raised to ask the question again.

"I don't want to leave until that other Roaddog gets here," he laughed.

"Any idea when that will be?"

"Not a clue, we didn't specify a time, just lunchtime-ish." Bandit Queen nodded slowly then relaxed back into her seat, one hand reaching out and snagging one of Bone's. He looked at her and smiled.

"I'm going to cruise the outside," said Roaddog, "see what's happening." He stood and held out a hand for Jackie to take, she took it and went with him. Hand signals from Bone sent Slowball and Bug with him, along with these went Sylvia and Cherie.

"Does he think I need a bodyguard?" asked Roaddog, turning to

Slowball as they walked into the sunlight, and the crowds in the circle. Slowball just shrugged. Sylvia's left hand found his, her camera in the right. The circle was busy, packed tight with bikes, and people. It was quite difficult to walk without bumping into people or tripping over dogs. There seemed to be far more dogs than normal, but then the weather was good, and lots of people came to walk in the local countryside, so dogs came with them.

"What are all these people doing here?" asked Jackie. "They don't seem to be very interested in the bikes." She turned to glance at Sylvia whose shutter was chattering as she fired off a sequence of photographs.

"There's lots of pretty walks here," laughed Roaddog, "or so I hear."

"You've never left the carparks, have you?"

"No." he smiled back. Something lit up his peripheral vision, his head snapped to the right and he froze. Slowball was already looking in the same direction, Bug soon turned the same way. Two police motorcycles were rolling backwards into parking spaces. The two new arrivals dismounted and lifted the bikes onto the centre stands. Roaddog continued to watch as they removed their helmets, sure enough he had seen this pair before, and in the very same location. The sergeant's eyes swept the carpark and locked onto Roaddog; the cop smiled. He started walking around the circle, his compatriot a step behind.

"Fuck." whispered Roaddog. He remained still waiting for the cops to reach him.

"Hi Roaddog." said the sergeant nodding to the others.

"What's up?" asked Roaddog.

"You lot have been burning up the airwaves today."

"What do you mean?"

"Some dicks are more than a little pissed at you lot."

"You'll have to be a little clearer, that's a long list for today, and it's barely lunchtime."

"A couple of detectives from Wigan way, seems they had to ask for safe passage out of here."

"Their own fault, they pissed off Bandit Queen, shouldn't go rooting into her past."

"They're still breathing, I reckon that puts them up on the deal."

"Anything else interesting on the radio?"

"Like I'd tell you," laughed the sergeant.

"You two the scouting party, or have you really pissed someone off?"

"We heard you were here and decided to stop by for a burger. The only guy we've pissed off is a pussy of a camera operator."

"How did you piss him off?"

"I called him a pussy and told him to grow a pair." The sergeant laughed loudly; his colleague grinned.

"Seems fair to me," laughed Roaddog.

"Less than an hour later he had a call from HR." laughed the constable.

"Damned pussies," smiled Roaddog.

"Hey Phil." said a voice from behind Roaddog. As the bikers turned to the new presence the sergeant spoke slowly.

"This is going to be fun, two Roaddogs in one place. I wonder which has the biggest bite. Hi Mick."

"Too late Phil, we met last night, he's an OK guy," said the newcomer.

"Mick is that damned bike of yours road legal?" asked Phil.

"You expect me to tell you if it's not?" Mick grinned.

"Probably not. Where'd you two meet?"

"Whistle Test were playing the rally they're all at. We met there."

"Good gig?"

"Yes, great. Went down a storm, you missed a cracker."

"I'll have to catch you lot again some time."

"Fleetwood next weekend," Mick's smile was contagious, soon taken up by Roaddog.

"You two know each other then?" asked the biker.

"Yes," replied the cop, "I've seen his band a few times, they're almost always good, even on the bad days they are better than most."

"We try," laughed Mick.

"What pissed off Bandit Queen?" asked Phil looking at Roaddog.

"It seems Hopkins had spent some favours trying to find out about her past, and he came up with the name Cross."

"I don't believe it." Phil laughed out loud, holding on to his sides as he did so. "All he had to do was ask me, I've known her for a long time, we went to the same school."

"What was she like back then?" asked Roaddog.

"She was a nutter even then," laughed Phil.

"Some things don't change," Roaddog grinned.

"That's for sure, anyway we gotta circulate. Spread a little oil on the choppy waters hereabouts."

"More like, give the bikers someone they all hate, that way they won't start trouble between the clubs. We're here with a load of Chorley

Centurions, and there's more than a few Satan's Sons here as well."

"There is some of that in it as well, you be careful." Phil turned and tapped his constable on the shoulder as they walked away together, towards the queue for the burger van.

"Well Mick, who is this lovely lady with you?" asked Roaddog.

"Roaddog, meet my wife, Jackie."

"You're kidding." Roaddog shrugged his shoulders and turned Mick's wife. "Jackie, meet my girl Jackie." He pointed to Jackie. "And these are Slowball and Sylvia, Bug and Cherie. I'm very pleased to meet you. But we are going to have to do something about these names, it's going to become very confusing as more and more drink is consumed."

"I have a solution," said Mick, "before I was Roaddog, I was known as Hawkrider and she was Jet."

"And where on earth to those names come from?" Roaddog frowned.

"Early eighties, citizens band radio."

"Oh my god, you are old."

"Thanks for that," said Mick.

"You're not Roaddog," said Jackie/Jet quietly, looking Roaddog hard in the eye.

"I may not have been Roaddog as long as your husband, but it is a name I earned in battle, as he earned his for his abilities in other fields." His eyes swept her, taking in everything about her, from the long blonde hair, down passed her large breasts and wide hips, to her sturdy legs. She was not as powerful as Bandit Queen but there was far more to her than his own Jackie. "I would appreciate it if you would accept me as a Roaddog, if not yours." She stared into his eyes for a while before she nodded, actually it was more a tiny twitch of the head.

"Ok." said Bug. "What the fuck have you done with the real Roaddog? Someone's left a damned politician in his place and we hadn't even noticed."

"Who you calling politician?" demanded Roaddog.

"You," grinned Bug, "far too polite."

"New friends can't scare them off yet," laughed Roaddog. He looked back at Jet and smiled. She returned the smile and shook her head.

"Let's go back inside and meet some of the others," suggested Roaddog. He took Jackie by the arm and turned towards the barn. Hawkrider and Jet followed, with the others behind. There was still a heavy presence around the doors, but they were only watching. A couple of the guys shook hands with Roaddog and nodded to the other Dragonriders. Hawkrider and Jet were ignored as they wore no patches.

Mick smiled to himself as he walked through into the darkness. Roaddog lead them to the bar, and back to the tables once hands were filled with glasses.

They were about three strides from the tables when Man-Dare stood up, she stepped quickly up to Mick and threw her arms around his neck. She kissed him firmly, he could do little with a beer in one hand and his wife in the other.

"What the fuck?" demanded Jackie quietly.

"You his wife?" asked Man-Dare breaking the kiss and looking to Jackie.

"Yes, and if someone doesn't explain real quick, then he's going to be without bollocks."

"Your man can be a real bastard, you know?"

"Go on."

"Last night I did everything I could to distract him, and got nowhere, I thought I had him when the sound went off and we were by the bar, but he turned his back on me and pulled a phone from his pocket, he fixed the sound in a heartbeat."

"He does that," smiled Jet.

"I had some hope for the end of the night, but he kissed me, then got in his car and drove away. I was so horny I raped Billy," she nodded in the direction of the older man, "damn near killed the old fool."

"Hey Mick," called Billy laughingly, "if you're going to wind her up like that again, please do it when I'm somewhere else." Mick nodded, Man-Dare released him and looked to Jet again.

"He's one of the good guys, don't lose him." She stepped in front of Jet and enclosed her in a tight hug, Man-Dare pressed her cheek against Jet's and held her for a couple of breaths, the whispered. "You smell fucking gorgeous, what's that perfume?"

"Dune," Jet's whispered reply.

"I gotta get me some of that," said Man-Dare releasing Jet and returning to her seat next to Billy.

"Some of what?" asked Billy, a cheeky grin on his face.

"Her perfume, you dirty bastard."

"Watch out for that stuff," Mick laughed, "it's damned expensive."

Conversation continued around the tables, light and fun. Until the leader of the Centurions came up to Bone.

"I think we should get out of here before the guys get too pissed."

"Agreed, thirty minutes to roll?"

"Why so long?"

"There's a lot of people to get together, and I've just bought another beer." The pair laughed loudly and agreed to thirty minutes.

Once the president had left Bone spoke to Roaddog.

"Put the word out, roll in thirty." Roaddog nodded and got to his feet to arrange the departure of the Dragonriders.

Thirty minutes later a long convoy of motorcycles left Rivington Barn, bound for Chorley. The return journey was without major incident though the cavalcade did cause a few issues at some of the junctions along the way. It seems that red lights and give way signs don't actually apply to motorcyclists when they are moving in such a large group, certain motorists were irritated enough to sound their horns, but no one was actually going to challenge them directly. Mick and Jackie were in the group right at the back, only followed by Slowball. He had Sylvia mounted in the centre rear seat, from her elevated position her camera got more than a few good shots of the procession. One such was as they were crossing the reservoir, a long straight road, climbing up from the level of the water far ahead of her. A solid stream of motorcycles the leaders only just visible in the distance. They arrived at the rugby club mid-afternoon, there were a few bikers there, some that hadn't joined in the ride out, and some new arrivals. Mick followed the other Dragonriders and pulled up just outside the main circle of their tents. It only took him a few minutes to have his own tent up and filled with the gear from his rack, and the rucksack that Jackie was carrying. Hand in hand they went into the bar, to find the others getting stuck into the drinking. No one was planning to be driving anywhere. Roaddog looked towards the door as it opened, two guys came in pulling a heavy flight case on wheels between them. He turned to Mick.

"Hey Mick, why don't you get wheels on your gear, makes moving it easier."

"Yes it would, but then it wouldn't fit in the car and I'd have to get a van like theirs. I prefer the car." Mick replied, the men pushing the heavy box looked up. They smiled at Roaddog and Mick, they carried on with their work. Roaddog watched them roll the case to the stage then lift it up and roll it into the right corner. Covers front, back and top were removed and the mixing desk in the top lifted up to its operational angle. The two came off the stage carrying the covers. They walked up to Mick.

"You gonna lend a hand?"

"Not until you get shut of all that heavy gear and go air."

"You can't beat the sound of the EV gear." said Neil, who is the guitarist.

"I agree, but the punters can't tell the difference, they don't have our ears. Switch to powered cabs, lose the amps, and get an air desk of some variety. I've seen a Midas 18 that's awesome, or the cheaper Behringer that's almost identical. You could cut the weight down by fifty percent and the overall size of the rig by thirty percent. Imagine not having that amp-rack and desk."

"I could do without that bastard," replied Peter the bass player.

"If you get up to date, I'll help you out until you get used to it," Mick laughed.

"We got too much money in the PA," said Neil.

"And everyone is switching to the new gear, yours has very little resale value."

"It's a real bitch, we bought it from a band that was going powered and air."

"And it seemed like a real bargain."

"It was a price I couldn't turn down," Neil looked down.

"Now you're stuck with it, at least for a while."

"Well," said Neil, "At least you can look out for the sound for us tonight, you are staying aren't you?"

"Of course I will, I'll be here for sound check and keep an eye on me for the first few songs, we'll get it right."

"Cheers Mick," Neil and Peter left to get the next items of heavy gear from the van.

"I didn't understand most of that," said Roaddog.

"They've got some cracking gear, but it's heavy and bulky by the current state of the art."

"Neither of them are lightweights, so they can manage." Roaddog smiled.

"That's true, and they've been doing this a while now," Mick turned to Jackie. "I'm hungry, how you doing?"

"I could go a snack," she laughed.

"Let me introduce you to our favourite chef," said Roaddog. He led them outside and over to Andy's van. There was no queue, so they walked straight up to the serving hatch.

"Hey Andy," said Roaddog. The thin face of Andy looked down on him from the inside of the van, the fluorescent lights glaring behind his head.

"What you want Roaddog?"

"These are friends of ours."

"If they're friends of yours then they're friends of mine. What you need people?"

"Burgers and chips," said Mick.

"Cheese?" asked Andy.

"That'd be nice," grinned Mick.

"Heavy and real cheese," said Roaddog.

"Of course," Andy smiled. Roaddog dropped a tenner on the stainless steel of the opening. Then he turned to go back to the bar. Waving to the pair.

"These people are strange," muttered Jackie.

"They're crazy bikers, but they're fun people as well." said Mick, then he turned to Andy. "How long you been a friend of these guys?"

"A few of years now, they're generally good guys, but don't cross them. You know what I mean?"

"I do. Where are they based?"

"They have a garage unit on Walton Summit, easy to find, if you really want to."

"Not sure I do, but it's nice to know they are local."

"They do cars as well as bikes."

"Yes, and they seem to be quite busy, so they can't be bad at their jobs."

"Perhaps I should try taking the car to them?" Mick looked at Jackie.

"But you like Uncle Jim," she replied gently.

"That's true, Jim's great. I'll take the bike to them though."

"I'm OK with that," Jackie leaned against him and kissed him softly.

"Here's your burgers," Andy said, "you want Roaddog's change, or should I give it to him later?"

"You deal with it." Mick smirked, leading Jackie away from the van towards their tent. The campsite was quiet, it appeared that most were in the bar, or in their tents resting.

Roaddog and Jackie watched from their place by the bar as the two guys carried the heavy gear on to the stage, he was surprised just how much more there was that the previous night. As he watched the drummer start to bring his gear in, he pulled Bug to one side of the stage for a quite conversation.

"How are we doing for stock?" he asked.

"We're OK, we should have enough for another couple of weeks, at the current rate, if demand goes up, we could be struggling in a week or so."

"I'll talk to the Manchester guys, see about some more stuff. Just how much money are we making at the moment?"

"Enough, if demand goes up too much more, we're not going to be able to spend the stuff fast enough, no matter how many rallies we attend."

"Any suggestions?"

"Yes, leave it in bitcoin, but then it's just sitting there, and if bitcoin crashes were going to lose a lot of money."

"If we can pay for the stuff in bitcoin, then that'll help."

"Of course, but we're making so much money at this it's going to be difficult to hide."

"You've set up a bitcoin wallet for the club, set up another for yourself, split the proceeds, then we can still keep some of it, even if the cops get wise to one of the accounts."

"I'll do that, you want me to syphon some off into your account as well?"

"Seems prudent, if we're going to be making so much, damn I never thought I'd have the problem of too much money."

"It's not too much, it's just hiding it from the authorities that's the issue." Bug chuckled, thinking that he was in much the same position as Roaddog.

"I'll advise Bone what we are planning, wouldn't want him to find out by accident." Roaddog's grin was wide.

"I'll tell Bandit Queen, so she's in the picture as well." Bug glared at a musician who was suddenly standing way too close to them. He had a speaker in his hands and was trying to lift it onto a pole. Roaddog stepped in and took one side of it, to help him position it correctly. The musician crossed the stage to the other side and picked up another speaker. Roaddog nodded to Bug then went to help the musician. Once the speaker was settled neatly on the pole, Neil spoke.

"Cheer's mate, these tops are heavy."

"No problem, I'm looking forward to the show."

"You seen us before?"

"A couple of times and always good."

"That's what we want too."

"You got any more rallies set up for this year?"

"I think we've got a 'Rock the Lakes' for the middle of the year sometime, but don't ask me for details, I don't look that far ahead." Neil laughed and walked away to carry on with the set up.

By the time Roaddog walked back to the bar Bug was already talking to Bandit Queen, so he went to find Bone. After a brief conversation it was clear that Bone really didn't care, so long as there was going to be enough money for them to party, he was happy. Roaddog turned and caught Jackie with his eyes, and she followed him outside into the open air. They walked towards their camp, him with an arm around her waist.

Together they walked up to the back of the van, and opened the doors, Roaddog was looking for more beer. Off to the right he saw Mick and Jackie talking to some people, so he picked up a half full case and went to talk to them. With the case in one hand he passed a bottle then his keys to Jackie, she opened the bottle using the keychain he had given her, then passed the beer to Mick.

"Hi Mick," said Roaddog, "friends of yours?" Passing a second bottle to Jackie.

"You're the other Roaddog we've heard about." said one of Mick's friends, a tall thin guy, with a bandana on his head. The other friends smiled.

"Yes," Roaddog spoke slowly, "I understand that Mick here has been Roaddog longer than I have, and that he earned his name in a different fire than I did. I have come to accept him as a friend, I hope that you can perform the same curtesy for me." Roaddog held his hand out.

"I'm the one that gave him that name." said the thin man. "They call me Jay-Kay." He reached out and shook Roaddog's hand. Roaddog looked at the other two, then back at Jay-Kay.

"These are John and Dianne, long-time friends, and fans of Fifth Element." The two nodded in turn as they were introduced.

"It's so nice to meet you all, any friend of Micks is a friend of ours." Roaddog dropped Jay-Kay's hand and spoke again. "Beers?"

"Not for me." said Jay-Kay pulling a bottle of water from an inside pocket.

"I'll have one," said John, a shorter and somewhat wider man than Jay-Kay, and older as well.

"Me too," said Diane, from her body language so obviously married to John, and he to her. Two beers came from the case and were opened by Jackie for the newcomers.

"So," Roaddog said, "How long have you lot known my new friend Mick?"

"We've known him for," John paused, thinking back through time, "Shit it's more than twenty years."

"It's that at least." Laughed Jay-Kay.

"How long have you known him?" asked John.

"Oh my," Roaddog grinned, glancing at his watch. "it must be just over twenty," he paused, "yes, definitely just over twenty hours." He laughed. "I met him yesterday."

"And what do you think?" asked Jay-Kay.

"He's damned good at what he does, he's a nice guy as well."

"He learned that in the fire that was Rubian," said Jay-Kay.

"What happened to this Rubian?"

"As with most bands, they fall apart eventually," laughed Jay-Kay.

"So, tell me about this Rubian."

"No," interrupted Mick, "those tales are better saved until everyone is too drunk to remember tomorrow."

"You want to be the sole possessor of the truth? Don't you?" asked Jay-Kay.

"Damned right," laughed Mick, holding up his bottle for Jay-Kay to touch by way of a toast. Jay-Kay did exactly that.

"What truth?" Roaddog asked.

"There are many truths in the path through life," Mick grinned.

"You've gotta give me something?" demanded Roaddog. Mick paused for a while before continuing.

"Fine, gig was in Barrow. The run back from Barrow is a long one, real long. I'm tearing along the A590 as fast as that big van will go. A musician says 'I need a pee.' No surprise there. 'Me too.' Says another. So, I pull over into the next layby. Three musicians get out of the side door. They are happily peeing against the side of the van and I see a cop car coming towards us, blue lights flashing merrily. I drop the van into drive and roll forwards ten feet. Three musicians are waving their dicks at a passing cop car. He's busy so he can't stop. This is the sort of thing that happened way back in the Rubian days."

"Fucking awesome," said John, "don't forget the Americana gigs."

"They were completely crazy," said Jay-Kay.

"Tell me more." said Roaddog.

"No, later," laughed Mick.

30: Sunday Rally Day Three, Fifth Element.

Long before the show was due to start Roaddog went into the bar with Jackie on his arm, the table he was hoping to get, the one they had been at the night before was already taken by Mick and his friends. Roaddog smiled as he joined them.

"How's it going?" he asked.

"Fine," Mick replied, "sound check should be very soon, then the show can start on time."

"How long have you known this band?"

"I don't know, a few years."

"I've seen them a time or two, and always been impressed."

"They're good," said Jay-Kay. While they were talking the musicians started to assemble on the stage. The singer came over to the table.

"Hi John," she said, smiling at Jay-Kay.

"Hi Ann, how's it going?"

"Fine, keep an ear on it for us."

"No problems, and we got a Roaddog as well."

"Sorry Mick, didn't see ya there."

"I know," laughed Mick, "You saw John and forgot everyone else."

"It's not like that," laughed Ann, turning away going to the stage. As with the band from the previous night, she was on the floor, as the small stage only had enough room for the drummer and the bass player, Neil the guitarist, who would be running the sound from on stage was going to be up and down. Sound check was a fairly simple affair, the band had been doing it for so long that there was little to change. Once the individual instruments were set up it was only a matter of balancing them one against the others. Again, experience showed, and it all came together in the first few bars of a single song. The only issue came from mixing in the vocals, and the monitors. Again, this didn't take too long, well before the song was finished everyone appeared to happy with what they were playing and what they were hearing. Once they had stopped playing Ann thanked the audience for their patience and told them that the show would start shortly.

"Neil," called Mick as the guitarist walked past.

"What's up?"

"Knock the eight hundred down touch in the monitors, that's where the feedback is starting."

"What feedback?"

"I said starting." Mick shook his head. Neil thought for a moment, then briefly went back on stage.

"I've put eight hundred down 2dB and six-thirty and one K down one."

"That should do, it should give some more headroom on the monitors as well."

Neil smiled and walk towards the bar.

"Does that actually mean anything?" asked Roaddog.

"It means a lot to the sound guys," Jay-Kay grinned. "For the rest of us it just feels like magic."

"How long you been a guitarist?" Roaddog asked.

"Forever," responded Jay-Kay, "I started when I as very young. I teach as well, if you know anyone interested in learning?"

"I don't know anyone, but I do know that one of our group plays a little. You've seen Billy?"

"Yes, he looks a lot like the real Billy Gibbons."

"I've no idea what his name actually is, but as soon as I saw him, I called him Billy."

"Perhaps we'll find out how good he is later," said Jay-Kay.

"That sound like fun," said Mick, "How many guitars you got?"

"I've brought mine, and John's got his. That should be enough," Jay-Kay smiled.

"Party time," laughed Mick loudly.

"What the fuck are you two on about?" snapped Roaddog. Mick chuckled.

"It could be a long night, we got two acoustic guitars, if only we had a bass as well, but I'm sure we can find enough singers to fill in the bottom end. Once the gig is over there'll be a party somewhere on this site, with music and singing."

"Mick uses the term singing in its loosest possible form," Jay-Kay laughed.

"I know how he sings," replied Roaddog, "we heard him last night."

"And you survived," Jay-Kay slapped Mick on the arm, "Well done."

Bug and Cherie walked up to the table, each put a tray of glasses down.

"Wainwrights," said Bug pointing at one tray, "lager." The other. People with empty, or nearly so, glasses started to reach out for the beverage of their choice. Bug tapped Roaddog on the shoulder. A glance was exchanged, and Roaddog stood up.

"Be back in a bit," he said as the two walked away from the table. Out into the open air, he followed Bug until they were sure they couldn't be overheard.

"Go on?" said Roaddog.

"I've been online again, we're going to need more product and real soon, sales are going through the roof."

"Put the price up. I'll talk to the Manchester guys."

"Price isn't that important, it's delivery that counts."

"Do it anyway. When do we need delivery?"

"Tuesday would be good."

"You're kidding?"

"No, I have orders for almost all of our current stock already. By Tuesday I'll have tons more."

"Right." Roaddog thought for a few moments. "Go dark for a couple of days, flag the site as moving location back in a couple of days. That way the customers won't go looking too seriously for another supplier."

"Consider it done." Bug took out his phone and went online to the website. Roaddog took out his own phone and called a number from his encrypted contacts list.

"Hi Wolf," he said, once the call was answered.

"Hi Roaddog. What's up?" Wolf's voice returned quietly.

"We are having a bit of a run on our stock, can we buy some from you?"

"How much do you need?"

"Call it six kilo's cut, or one uncut, and we can cut it ourselves."

"Where you selling all this?"

"All over the country, we still haven't sorted a way to get it out of the country yet, but we are working on that."

"So not in our territory?"

"Nothing into Manchester, it seems we can't compete with you guys on price."

"How much are you charging?"

"Buckets full, and still selling loads."

"What the fuck? Hold on." Wolf went quiet for a while then came back.

"When you need this?"

"Tuesday would be good."

"Hold." Again, Wolf was speaking to someone else. "We'll be there with the goods around one PM. OK?"

"Great, see ya then." The line went dead. Roaddog turned to Bug. "Delivery one PM Tuesday."

"Did they specify cut or not?"

"No, but that's not too important, we can be ready to cut it once they get here."

"This is getting entirely out of hand," muttered Bug.

"Agreed, we need to slow things down, or someone is going to notice."

"Right, what sort of price hike do you think?"

"I'd say, reopen for deliveries on Wednesday, twenty-five percent higher."

"Right. That might just slow things down a bit, but our reviews are going crazy."

"What do you mean?"

"Recommendations galore, and so many people pissing themselves that postman Pat is delivering for us."

"We need to find some way of getting another delivery service involved."

"I'll think on it," Bug nodded and turned back towards the club. As Roaddog followed him he thought about the other delivery services. There were none that had the flexibility of the post box, they all required personal contact at the point the package goes into the system. That would make the sender identifiable. He shook his head as he walked back into the bar, a quick glance at the table showed him that the trays of beer were now empty. Turning to the now crowded bar he joined the waiting throng. Jackie walked up behind him and slid one hand around his waist.

"Need a hand?" she said.

"Would be good, can you bring the trays?" She held up the other hand to show that she was ahead of him. He smiled and lean in for a kiss, the man left between him and the bar turned with his hands full of glasses. Roaddog eased to his left to allow the man to move away from the bar, while blocking the man on his left from getting into the empty space. As the brass rail pressed against his hip Jackie caught the eyes of the barmaid, without even breaking the kiss. Roaddog turned to the barmaid.

"Eight Wainwrights, and eight lager, please my lovely." She laughed and went to the currently vacant Wainwrights pump and started pulling beers. She leaned back as she pulled the handle down, her small bicep straining against the weight of the beer in the pipework, her back arched and her thigh tensed.

"Damn, she's going to put some muscle on tonight," he said to Jackie.

"She looks far to light for this sort of job, even too young," was the soft reply.

"She's definitely short and light, but I think she's older than she looks."

"She surely a pretty little thing," smiled Jackie, watching the half-filled glasses pilling up on the bar.

"Love that black strappy vest."

"She's cute."

"You want to share her? We could invite her back after she finishes."

"I'm greedy, I don't want to share you. We could invite her anyway; she could be fun."

"I like the way her tits jiggle when the handle hits the stop," he laughed.

"There's no bra under that shirt, she'll have someone's eyes out with those." giggled Jackie. The barmaid came toward them with three full pints in a group, she dropped them carefully on the tray, and went to get some more. Once the hard work of pulling Wainwrights was over, she switched to lager, this was much easier, but not as much fun to watch. One by one the lager glasses filled, without the pump ever being turned off, full replaced with empty in a fraction of a second, a simple motion that spoke of plenty of practice. When the second tray was full Roaddog waved his card, the barmaid rang in the purchases and returned with the payment machine.

"You want to join the party when you finish?" asked Roaddog inserting his card into the slot.

"Can do," she smiled.

"What time you finish?"

"I made it very clear that when the band finish their first set, I'm off the clock." Her grin told him that she was glad of the invite, the smile shared equally between Roaddog and Jackie.

"Oh," said Jackie, as the barmaid reached under the bar top for the receipt, "she's sure to be fun." While the barmaid passed the paper to Roaddog Jackie stared hard into her eyes, then leaned forwards over the bar, her hips pressing hard against the edge, reaching she offered her lips. The girl reached up and kissed her, only for a couple of seconds then she stepped back and moved on to the next customer. The two turned from the bar, each carrying a tray. When they had forced their way through the crowd Roaddog stopped.

"What was that kiss about?"

"What's that song? I kissed a girl and I liked it." She started towards the table again, now there were no empty seat, but once the trays were on the table one appeared, and then another. Cherie gathered a load of empty glasses and carried them off to the bar, before she returned the musicians were taking to the stage. The DJ turned his music down and introduced the band, to applause from the crowd, lead mainly by Mick and Jay-Kay. The singer smiled their way.

"She looks great," said Roaddog. Taking in her long dark brown hair, her t-shirt, short black leather skirt, and knee length high heeled boots.

"Wait 'til you hear her," said Jay-Kay.

The band crashed into their first number, 'Tie your mother down' a classic from Queen. People were up and dancing immediately, Ann's voice clear as crystal filling the room with Brian May's lyrics. They watched enthralled as she strutted around the stage area, catching the eyes of one of the audience, then moving on to another one. The song crashed into its ending, and the audience applauded loudly. Ann turned to Neil and pointed to the monitors, and then pointed up. He stepped back to the sound desk and twiddled something, then looked at Mick. A quick hand signal told Neil to turn the bass up a tiny bit. Neil moved a slider and then stepped down to the lower stage again.

"I'd like to thank Chorley Centurions for the invitation to share this party with you all," said Ann, smiling at the crowd as the Centurions members went wild.

"And all the others," she continued, "there are a couple of other clubs here tonight, always so good to see you guys. Next is a classic from Free." Roaddog looked at Jackie then they both looked at Man-Dare, waiting with bated breath for the song to start. They all breathed easier when the first few notes were struck, and the song was not wishing well. They shared a smile and returned to listening to the music. As the set progressed, they danced to some songs and sat out for others, more beer arrived at the table, Lurch brought these, Doris almost fastened to his hip. Slowball and Sylvia were moving around the room, her camera shooting almost continuously. The lights that Fifth Element brought were more than good enough to light most of her shots, she focused mainly on the singer. In the middle of one song the singer moved out into the audience to dance with those gathered in front of the stage, Neil was banging out an excellent solo and Ann was dancing with the crowd,

Sylvia followed her into the crowd to get close ups with the audience. Ann's motion through the crowd suddenly stopped and she looked back at the stage. Her microphone lead was jammed under one of the monitors, but before she could get back to the stage to free it Mick was there, with a flick of the wrist the line was cleared and Ann was dancing with the crowd again. Knowing that the guitar solo was going to end soon Ann set off back to the stage, following her microphone lead as if it were a trail of breadcrumbs. When the lyrics came back in, she was facing the drummer and rocking her hips from side to side as the beat swirled in everyone's brains. The set moved on at a rapid pace, flowing from one song into the next, until Ann finally announced the last song of the first set, a fast rocking number from ZZ Top. When the song ended, the bands lights went down and the DJ came back with something a little heavier, Metallica shaking the floor as the bass bins bounced. The band left the stage and went straight out into the open, presumably to cool down, Mick and Jay-Kay followed. Roaddog watched them go and thought that they would be discussing the sound and whatever it is musicians talk about. He laughed to himself and grabbed Jackie by the waist pulling her in tight for a kiss. Jackie felt a tap on her shoulder, so she turned away from Roaddog, only to have her lips captured by those of the barmaid. This kiss far longer and much hotter than the one snatched over the bar. Eventually the barmaid moved away breathing hard.

"Hi, I'm Jane."

"Hi Jane, I'm Jackie," was the equally breathless reply. Jane's wide brown eyes bored into Jackie's.

"Are you gay?" Jane's question as quiet as she could make it given the noise that the DJ was making, which meant that everyone around the table could hear it.

"I didn't think so, but suddenly I'm not so sure," laughed Jackie. Jane grinned as she stepped across Jackie's legs and sat on Roaddog's lap. She turned to him and kissed him just as energetically as she had Jackie.

"There's no doubt about her inclinations," said Bug loudly.

"Damn girl," said Roaddog as she broke away, "what are you after here?"

"Just some fun, but the boss as put me on a short leash, I'm allowed to stay out front, but I've gotta collect glasses, there seems to be a shortage behind the bar just now."

"Well, you're not collecting too many sat there are you?" he asked.

"You want me to get up?" she wriggled her ass against his crotch.

"That doesn't bother me, it's not as if these people haven't seen it all before."

"Now you are definitely starting to sound like my sort of people," She stood and glanced down at the swelling in his jeans. "Not bad."

"Little girl, you stay away from Lurch, he'll split you in two."

"That sounds like a challenge," she looked around and found Lurch not too far away. "Damn, he's a big guy."

"He's that all right." Jane looked back to Jackie.

"You want to help me collect empty glasses?" This fell into the gap between two songs played by the DJ, so everyone heard it. Bandit Queen smiled.

"Come on girls," she shouted above the sound Deep Purple's Smoke on the water. "Let's help Roaddog's new plaything collect some glasses." Somehow her smile seemed more than a little evil. She stood and eased out from her position against the wall.

"I'll start with you Roaddog, give me your glass."

"It's not empty."

"It's close enough, empty it or I will." Roaddog shook his head and emptied the glass, passed it to Bandit Queen and lifted another one from the table.

"That's how you do it girls." she shouted. "Anything less than half full is ours." The Dragonrider girls and Jane swept through the bar, collecting empties and suggesting that glasses were close enough to be emptied. Then they followed Jane outside, here they discovered where all the glasses had been accumulating, the outside picnic tables were covered in empties, and there were more scattered around. walking slowly through the pitched tents Bandit Queen found more and more, these were all collected, despite the complaints that they were needed for the party after the bar was closed. For those that put up too much resistance the approach of Bandit Queen was usually enough to have the glasses handed over with no further comment. Only once did a biker get a slap from the heavy right hand, his glass taken from his unconscious grip. Only Cherie's grip on her shoulder prevented the man from getting the kicking Bandit Queen felt he deserved. The elder woman glared at Cherie for an instant, then turned and stamped off towards the bar.

"What's up with her?" asked Jackie.

"No idea." was the simple reply. Jackie passed her stack to Cherie and set off at a run to catch up with Bandit Queen, she caught up just before the woman reached the door.

"Hey," she called softly, "what's wrong? You were ready to kick that guy to death."

"What's it to you?" the snarled response.

"I see pain in you, and I want to help."

"What do you know of pain?"

"Probably not as much as you, so tell me."

"Why should I?"

"Pain shared?" Bandit Queen saw the others getting closer, she was in no mood to share with them, not even certain she wanted to talk to the newcomer. She grabbed Jackie by the arm and pulled her away from the entrance, taking her towards the carpark. Her glare at Cherie told the younger girl everything she needed to know, she stopped Jane from following the two as the disappeared into the darkness.

"They want some alone time," said Cherie. Jane nodded and went inside with her stack of empties. Once the girls had deposited their cargo on the bar they returned to their seats, Jane to Roaddog's lap. He glanced round, Cherie stepped in close and whispered.

"Jackie's talking to Bandit Queen."

"What's wrong?"

"No idea, we'll find out in a little while."

"Should I tell Bone?"

"Nah, he'll find out. Maybe he already knows, he's been a little quiet." She returned to Bug's side, sliding her hand onto his thigh and leaning against him.

Bandit Queen led Jackie into the darkest corner of the parking area. Jackie looked around and smiled to herself, not that long ago she'd have been frightened to be so far from the lights, the darkness only alleviated by the streetlights that were so far away, the eerie yellow of sodium made Bandit Queens face look jaundiced.

"What's going on with you?" asked Jackie.

"I don't know." Bandit Queen stared at the ground.

"What do you mean?"

"I feel strange, like something is coming, and I have no idea what it is. Normally I have some sort of feeling about things. Only I can't sleep."

"Not sleeping can have all sorts of effects."

"No, it's not just the not sleeping, it's the dreams."

"You're not making much sense."

"The dreams usually give me the hints, I can feel when something is coming, and the dreams tell me about it, now all I get is a jumbled mess. There is darkness, featureless, empty, and huge."

"What have you to be afraid of?"

"That's the problem, I have no clue." Bandit Queen shook her head slowly.

"You can't be afraid that Roaddog is going to take over, I'm sure we have convinced you of that."

"But that's not the impression that the dreams give, I see him riding to war, death rides at his back."

"So why does this mean he's taken control away from you and Bone?"

"Because he should be riding at my back, he rides alone."

"Where am I in these dreams?"

"Nowhere."

"You're not there, I'm not there, he's riding to our rescue."

"That's not the way it feels, he's different, the fire in his eyes tells of pain. He's planning on burning someone's world down."

"I don't think we have anything to worry about, he'll be there for us when we need him, I'm sure you can see that?"

"I don't see that at all. I feel that I have abandoned him, but I can't see that ever happening. He's family to me."

"I know that, and so does he."

"So why would I leave him, when he needs me so?"

"I don't know, dreams can be more than a little strange."

"Not mine, they generally tell me the truth."

"Sometimes I wish that mine would do that?"

"No, you don't. Ignorance is bliss."

"It seems that a little knowledge is no fun either."

"You're not wrong. I hate it when things are this muddled. Why would I abandon him?"

"I'm sure things will sort themselves out, it could be anything."

"I wish I had your confidence."

"I've never seen anyone with more confidence than you," Jackie laughed.

"It's an illusion, especially just now."

"Well, hold on to that illusion, until things get straightened out. You can't go just killing some dick because he pissed you off."

"I wouldn't have killed him."

"Yes, you would, if Cherie hadn't stopped you."

"You know me that well all ready?"

"Maybe I don't but the look in Cherie's eyes told me that she was worried."

"Fuck, she knows."

"She's worried about you, and now so am I."

"She could use this against me."

"Not a chance, she's real family."

"She might try, it wouldn't be too hard."

"No, she loves you. She'd never turn against you, but you have to get control of yourself."

"Why do you suddenly care so much?" Bandit Queens voice dropped to a whisper.

"Maybe I've come to love you crazy bunch of bastards as well."

Bandit Queen looked into Jackie's eyes; Jackie watched the heat drain slowly from the older woman. The cold calculation that was normal there returned.

"Right," she snapped. "Call it PMS, no one will question, only Bone will be sure it's a lie."

"Fine," replied Jackie. "You better smile, when you tell them."

"Fuck that, you can tell them."

"Great, that makes me look as much of a bitch as you."

"That's the idea." Bandit Queen linked her arm through Jackie's and started back towards the entrance. The two were walking around a corner into a slightly better lit area, Bandit Queen was practicing her false smile, a voice shouted.

"Oi, cunt." A fist came flashing towards Bandit Queen's head, she faded away from it and pushed Jackie towards a wall, fast though she was the knuckles still caught a glancing blow to her head. Before the fist was recovered, she was stepping in, two fast strikes to the lower body, left and right, had the man staggering backwards. She got her first look at the man; he was the one from earlier. He was a good five inches taller than her and a fair bit heavier. He punched for her head again, this time unhindered by a friend on one arm, she side-stepped, the blow missed and again she stepped inside. Left, right and left, starting low and rising, driving all the air from the man's lungs. He started to reel away as the next right hand took him square on the cheek, he spun round and toppled to the ground. Jackie was happy to see that he had no patches on his back, that was a complication they really didn't need. Bandit Queen was panting with effort and adrenaline. She shook her right hand while checking the knuckles for damage.

"Fuck that feels better." She prodded the fallen man with a foot and watched briefly to be sure he was still breathing; she saw a trickle of blood come bubbling from his lips. "Now I need a drink." She took Jackie by the hand and walked to the front entrance, it was only as they stepped into the light that Jackie noticed the blood running down Bandit Queen's face, there was a small cut on her right temple. She almost swaggered up to the table where the others were sitting. Jackie was a little upset to see Jane sitting on Roaddog's lap again.

"Who's got Jacks?" Demanded Bandit Queen loudly. Three flasks appeared from inside pockets, she grabbed the nearest, and emptied half of it in a few seconds. She dropped the flask back into Roaddog's hand and smiled her thanks.

"What the fuck happened to you?" Yelled Bone.

"Some dick tried it on, he's sleeping in the carpark," she smiled, the one she had been practicing.

"You ok?" said Bone, much quieter this time.

"Fine, beer me," her grin even bigger.

31: Sunday Rally Day Three, onto party time.

"Ladies and gentlemen put your hands together for Fifth Element," called the DJ. Further conversation was made difficult by the rock music pouring from the speakers at either side of the stage. Ann was moving to the beat and singing another classic. Bone got up from his seat and took Bandit Queen in his arms, together they took to the centre of the dance floor. He wiped the blood from her cheek and held her close, everyone could see that they were talking, but no-one could hear them.

"You really OK?" he asked.

"I'm fine, just some dick who fancied himself."

"He still breathing?"

"Yes, well he was when I left him."

"Badly damaged?"

"No just bleeding from the mouth, I certainly can't have caused any brain damage."

"He should have had more brain."

"Perhaps he left it at home," she laughed and kissed him hard.

Their bodies moulded one against the other, her arms around his neck, his around her waist. They moved together as if they were one, as far as anyone on the outside could tell the music they were dancing to was not the same as everyone was hearing. They occupied an entirely different time and space from the rest of the room. Jackie smiled to herself watching them dance together. She turned the smile to Roaddog, who still had Jane sitting in his lap. She shook her head slowly and sat down next to him. Taking a beer from the table she really didn't care who it belonged to. Roaddog leaned towards her and shouted above the music.

"You ok?"

"Not sure," her short reply followed by a glance to Jane and back to him. The response was not what she was expecting in any way. Jane stood briefly, turned about and sat down in Jackie's lap. Jane threw an arm around Jackie's neck and leaned against her. Her lips almost against Jackie's ear.

"I really liked our kiss earlier," her voice loud enough for Jackie to hear but not Roaddog.

"So did I," her reply straight into the younger woman's ear, "and that is not me."

"Kiss me," said Jane.

Jackie looked at her for a moment, then reached forwards to make contact, their lips met. Their lips blended together, tongues touched, and then reached. Breathing raced between the two. Suddenly Jackie pulled away. Two pairs of eyes stared into each other.

"I kissed a girl," said Jackie.

"And I liked it," said Jane. The two hugged and laughed together. Then they both turned to Roaddog and looked hard at him. He leaned forwards and kissed first Jackie then Jane.

"Is there room for me in this arrangement?" he asked a huge smile on his face.

The two girls nodded, and reached towards him again, pulling him in for a three-way kiss. The pounding of rock music filled their minds and they climbed to their feet to join the dancers, even Billy and Man-Dare were on the floor, swaying in each other's arms, his thigh firmly between her legs, and her sliding forcibly up and down it.

Drinks flowed freely as they always do at these events, and more and more couples and groups took to the floor, to dance in time to the music of Fifth Element. Ann often amongst the dancers, and singers. Though none were up to her standard.

All good things must come to an end, and after a final song, and then three encores, the show finally ended. Ann and the guys more than happy with the responses from the audience. There were group photographs and band drinks, many of which were refused. Very soon the bands gear started to be stripped down. Mick and Jackie, along with Jay-Kay and his two friends sat to one side of the stage. simply watching the work going on and smiling.

"You could lend a hand," shouted Neil, with a heavy speaker in one hand.

"No thanks," said Mick.

"Not me," said Jay-Kay as he stood and left. He paused by the door, but only to hold it open for Neil to go through. A couple of minutes later, when Neil was back on the stage dismantling something else Jay-Kay returned, this time with an acoustic guitar, not that anyone was going to be able to hear it over the pounding of heavy bass from the DJ's speakers. Roaddog came back from the bar, with Jackie and Jane, each carrying a tray of beer. They all sat down drinking slowly and listening to the music from the DJ's playlists. Suddenly all the lights in the bar flashed and the DJ announced last orders at the bar. Mick and Jay-Kay stood up and removed the last few pints from the trays before going to the bar. When they reappeared, the table had been cleared of empties and Jackie along with Jane were moving around the room collecting even more. Very soon the grills came down to the bar top, and the DJ apologised for the fact that current licencing rules mean that the music has to stop at one AM, one last dance for any that can still stand. Roaddog was struggling to dance with both Jackie and Jane, until they pushed him away, and he returned to his seat leaving the two in each other's arms. Looking across the table he saw that Mick and Jackie were holding hands and smiling into each other's eyes, Jay-Kay was strumming softly on the battered Guild guitar. When the last song finished the dancers returned to their tables to find that the bar staff had been removing more empties, and they were patrolling and cajoling people to drink up. They were having nowhere near the success that Bandit Queen had achieved earlier. Roaddog looked to the dance floor and even though the music had stopped Jackie and Jane were dancing together, Jane somehow looked even younger pressed up against Jackie's prominent chest. Bandit Queen crossed the dancefloor finishing her pint on the way to the ladies. Jay-Kay started to play a song that Roaddog recognised, that classic from the Eagles. Jay-Kay and Mick started singing together, "On a dark desert highway, cool wind in my hair." Roaddog smiled and joined in quietly, keeping his voice low so as not to disturb the much better voices already joined in the delicate tones of the song. He glanced at the dancefloor, Jackie and Jane were coming towards him, smiling and holding hands. Behind them he saw Bandit Queen coming towards them, she put her half full pint down on a table as she passed. He caught her eyes. She smiled. He shook his head and grinned, losing track of the lyrics as he did. She sat beside Bone and he slapped her hard on the thigh, she blew him a small kiss and laughed gently. Jay-Kay was playing out the guitar solo at the end of the song when two strangers came into the room. Looking even more out of place than they would in normal circumstances, cheap suits not exactly de-rigueur for bike rallies.

"Fuck," snapped Bandit Queen. "No good deed goes un-punished." After a quick scan of the room the newcomers walked straight over to the table where the Dragonriders were sitting.

"What the fuck do you want now?" demanded Bandit Queen.

"We've actually come to give you some good news." said Hopkins, Lewis looking a little nervous at his side.

"Good news, bad news, I suppose," said Bone.

"Maybe," smiled Hopkins, "we have so much evidence that we really can't charge anyone over the death of the unicorn. I thought you'd like to know." He stared hard into Bandit Queens eyes.

"You could charge them all," she growled.

"We could, but if we lose, then we lose them all at the same time. There has been talk of making them draw straws to decide which is guilty. That didn't go down too well as you can imagine."

"You came here at this time of night to give us this non-news?" asked Roaddog, making the policemen turn to face him.

"We have other news as well."

"Please say on," interrupted Bone, "before everyone gets bored."

"Fine," the smile on Hopkins' face lessened in no way at all. "Remember that quote meth lab un-quote, that burned down in Leyland a few weeks ago?"

"We remember," mumbled Bone.

"Well, it wasn't a meth lab, it was a drug processing plant, but with almost no drugs on the premises. What we found was top quality coke, but in tiny quantities. The current theory is that persons unknown raided it, cleaned it out and then set fire to it on their way out. Would you know these persons?"

"I believe we were all up at Rivi when that place was burned, and we have some excellent witnesses to that effect."

"We are aware of your witnesses. A thought has occurred to me though, what if someone else did it, and split the take with you?"

"Who would do that? And what would we do with a load of coke?"

"What about your current hosts?"

"That is simply laughable," said Bandit Queen, "Centurions are a simple bike club, you should try a different club."

"Anyway," said Roaddog, "if you had any real suspicions, you'd have searched our clubhouse already, in which case you've found nothing and are here fishing."

"We haven't been able to search the place, not enough evidence pointing your way as yet, but I did walk a couple of sniffer dogs passed, they were not happy, but could give no real indications."

"That's sneaky," laughed Roaddog, "we use all sorts of chemicals, thinners, paint, and we have nitrous oxide on the premises, it could be these that are upsetting your dogs."

"That was pointed out to me by the handlers, and it's only down the road from the dog food factory, so the poor animals could be getting confused."

"So, you're still fishing?" asked Bandit Queen.

"Perhaps," smiled Hopkins. "We did get more motorcycles from south Manchester passing through the area on that particular Sunday, so maybe they had a beef with the bikers from Manchester?"

"So, you're sure it has nothing to do with us?" said Bone.

"Unless you met with some from Manchester on that fateful Sunday?"

"We'd obviously tell you if we had," said Bandit Queen, "fishing."

"I just thought we'd swing by and let you know."

"Some swing, quite a way off your patch?" she asked.

"Special knowledge, you know what I mean?"

"I do. Anything else?"

"I don't think so, we have done everything we could hope to here." The detective smiled and turned away, Bandit Queen got up to follow him, Roaddog went with them. As the foursome walked towards the policeman's car a voice shouted from the darkness.

"Bitch you called the fucking cops." A dark figure came rushing out of the blackness, something silver flashing in his hand, straight for Hopkins, low and rising. Roaddog was quicker, he stepped across and twisted the wrist holding the long knife. Then spun the man around, wrist flexed up his back until the blade fell with a clatter to the ground. Roaddog's left hand snatched a knife from his belt, in an instant that blade was against the man's throat, he froze.

"Your call Bandit," said Roaddog.

"Dog." shouted Hopkins. The biker looked to the cop. "I believe you may have just saved my life, as such I'd prefer it if you didn't cut this man's throat, I wouldn't like to be forced to testify in court." Roaddog looked to Bandit Queen, she nodded, and the knife disappeared from the man's neck.

"What you going to charge him with?" asked Roaddog.

"That's another issue," said Hopkins, he thought for a few moments as Roaddog released the man's arm, there wasn't actually much they could charge him with, at least not without involving Roaddog and Bandit Queen. With a sudden flash he punched the man in the face, he toppled slowly to the ground. Hopkins turned to Lewis.

"Lewis, you are too young, but there was a time when such an action would have been perfectly acceptable, sadly those days are gone."

"I don't know what you are worrying about," said Bandit Queen, "he's the one that should be worried." She nodded towards the man lying on the tarmac of the carpark. "He's been knocked out three times tonight, twice by a girl and once by a cop. He really ought to find some gentler friends."

"I'd suggest a sewing circle for him," said Lewis, he paused before continuing. "I think we need to be somewhere else, after all we haven't been here, have we?"

"Good man," said Hopkins. "Sometimes I really miss the old days, things were simpler. Come on." They walked around the groaning man and got into their car. In a moment they were gone.

"Stay down," snarled Roaddog, the man stopped making any attempt to stand.

"What the fuck happened?"

"You attacked a cop, I stopped you, he prevented me from killing you. Then the DI punched your lights out, the DC thinks you should join a sewing circle. What happens next is entirely up to you. Think before you respond."

"Seems that I'm not having a good day." The man paused for a short time. "I'd like the opportunity to apologise to the lady, perhaps even get to know her better. She appears to have some serious muscle, and people to back her up."

"You are correct about the lady, from what she has said about you, it is clear that you should have died three times tonight. One third of your lives are gone pussycat."

"I don't understand," the fallen man whispered.

"The first occasion, Cherie stopped her from giving you a good kicking. The second my girl was with her and that restrained her. This is something we will discuss later. On the third occasion a cop begged for your life."

"Fuck, I've definitely had a bad day, and missed most of it."

"True," Roaddog grinned.

"Lady," the man spoke slowly, turning to look up into the hard eyes of Bandit Queen. "I am deeply sorry for the way I have behaved tonight; I should have given you the respect you deserve right from our very first meeting. I have nothing of import to say in my defence, I am alone here, and at your mercy. Tell me how I may serve you to make things right between us."

Bandit Queen smiled for a moment.

"Groveller you understand that such service must be given freely and completely?"

"I understand and."

"Stop right there." Roaddog interrupted. "I know her, and your servitude could easily include a quiet nap on the railway tracks waiting for the arrival of the Glasgow express."

"Bastard," muttered Bandit Queen. "Nice idea though."

"Roaddog, I understand. My life is a mess, right now I would be surprised if anyone at all even noticed my death. So, I offer my service to the lady and ask only a place in the world where I can be accepted once I have earned my place in her good graces."

"Shit man," said Roaddog. "She can be a real bitch."

"Whatever it takes."

"Fine Groveller, I accept your service, know this it is going to be distasteful in the extreme for you, it may even break you permanently, do I make myself clear?"

"Yes lady, I am your slave until such time as you release me."

"Perhaps you will learn something, it may even make you a better man. Your first test is going to be a hard one, are you ready?"

"Yes lady." Groveller's voice more than a little shaky.

"We are going back inside, you will follow on your knees, you will go where you are told and do what you are told, do you understand?"

"Yes lady."

Roaddog shook his head as he and Bandit Queen walked slowly towards the entrance, with Groveller behind them. Roaddog held the doors open for Bandit Queen and her new puppy. He followed the odd couple as they approached a table where the Dragonriders were not sitting.

"Kneel Groveller." She said pointing at the floor next to the table.

Once he was in position she spoke again. "That drink there is yours, drink it all." She pointed to a glass that was half full.

"Lady it might belong to one of these people," said Groveller picking it up.

"No, it is one that I put there earlier, it's a booby trap to catch a minesweeper. Drink it." One of the men at the table started to shake his head slowly, as if he couldn't believe what he was seeing. Groveller put the glass to his lips and looked into Bandit Queens eyes, hoping for a reprieve, but none was forthcoming. He drank half of it in one draught, he stopped and choked as he swallowed.

"What does it taste like?" she asked.

"Lady, to be honest it tastes like piss."

"That is no real surprise to me. All of it, or this is over," she whispered. With tears in his eyes Groveller drank the rest of the glass. He choked even more as he tried to swallow the pungent liquid. Finally he succeeded and turned a shaky smile to Bandit Queen.

"Bandit Queen, you can be a real bitch," said one of the men seated at the table. "That one almost got me earlier, but I noticed that it was warm, before I got it even close to my mouth. Was there really someone pilfering drinks tonight?"

"There was, and I was hoping for him to make himself known. It seemed a pity to let it go to waste."

"This guy must have really pissed you off."

"Some, but he has offered to be slave until I see fit to release him," her smile made the man shiver.

"He's doing ok, well, he's not puked yet." The man laughed.

"Groveller stand up." She smiled at the people around the table and turned away. She went to regain her seat next to Bone. Groveller took an empty seat as close to her as he could.

"You picking up strays again?" asked Bone.

"Only a little bit," smiled Bandit Queen leaning in to kiss her man.

"Who's the new guy?" asked Bug.

"His name is Groveller until I say different," said Bandit Queen.

"Hey Groveller, what's your story man?" Bug questioned.

"Well," Groveller replied, "I'm having a bad day and looking for a way out that doesn't include death."

"Ok Groveller," laughed Bug, "you're still breathing, so that's a positive. It might even make you a rarity."

"That's as may be, but I'm not sure where I go from here."

"Just go with the flow. What's your history?"

"I was married until recently, my friends were supposed to be here with me this weekend, but they all seemed to have bailed. I am alone."

"And you managed to piss off Bandit Queen?"

"Oh, my god, did I fuck up there. She's certainly a powerful woman."

"We know that already, it sometimes takes a while for others to learn the truth."

"I now have experience," Groveller smiled.

"Groveller," said Bug, "if you run now, she's unlikely to chase you, and if you stay out of sight, you'll be free."

"This is going to sound strange, and I'm not even sure that I believe it myself." Groveller replied. "I feel freer now than I ever have in my life, I give my servitude to Bandit Queen and nothing else matters, I have no decisions to make, no life to live, only as she decides. There is no greater freedom."

"You understand how this could end?" asked Bug.

"Roaddog has already pointed that out to me. The ex will get the life insurance and my children will be far better provided for than I could ever manage while I was alive."

"You regard yourself as dead already?" asked Cherie, goaded by Bandit Queen's smile.

"Yes, and no." replied Groveller. "Perhaps the old life is over, and a new life begins, in the servitude of Bandit Queen."

"Likely to be a hard life," said Cherie.

"That's as may be," said Groveller, "but I've a feeling it's going to be living in the largest of ways."

"That's to be decided," snapped Bandit Queen, as the steward walked towards them.

"Ok people," the steward said, "time to leave. The bar needs to be closed, but the toilets, and the showers will remain open. Ladies use the visitor's showers, I am sorry, but they are more set up for males than females. If the ladies wish to share with their menfolk, please use the home team showers, but I have not said this."

"Agreed," said Bandit Queen. "Everybody out," she shouted, standing up. "Party time is now outdoors. We have musicians, and beer, what the fuck more do we need?" The only answer was people standing up and leaving the bar. The whole group moved out to the campsite, the morning was cool, but not cold, and the grass was beginning to show a little of the dew that would cover it by morning. Bandit Queen breathed deep of the cool night air and looked up. The cloud cover was high and widely spaced, many stars were clearly visible to the naked eye. She looked around and then pointed up into the sky.

"Orion, won't you give me a star sign," she said softly.

"A great song," said Mick, "Jethro Tull, one of my favourites."

"Hey man," said Jay-Kay, "I'm not playing second fiddle to some ass that stands on one leg and plays a fucking flute." Not too quietly at all, strumming a heavy minor chord.

"Still a good song," said Bandit Queen, as she walked into the circle of their tents, Jay-Kay's friends were approaching from the direction of their camper, one with a bottle of JD and the other with a case of beer. Roaddog opened the back of the van and lit the floodlights, the whole site was covered in a hot white LED brilliance.

"Back them the fuck down," snarled Bone. Roaddog reached inside and turned a control the lights faded until there was just enough to reach the outer circle of tents, but not enough to light the road through the hedge.

"Do you think you've brought enough beer?" asked Jay-Kay, looking at the cases stacked up in the van.

"Should be enough," said Roaddog, "we didn't drink so much last night, so there's quite a bit left."

"What do you mean? There's nowhere to put any more."

"Oh, there were two more rows in front of that lot," smiled Roaddog.

"Damn you guys can drink," said Jay-Kay, grinning.

"You remember those days?" asked Mick.

"Not so much, but you do you bastard."

"Someone had to be sober enough to drive."

"Crazy days," Jay-Kay, dropped to the grass and settled the guitar in his lap, strumming a chord pattern that everyone knew, around the circle voices other than Jay-Kay's started to pick up what lyrics they knew of "Hey Joe". Gradually the people got more and more drunk, as the beer flowed, and the songs went on. Only twice where Lurch and Roaddog called upon to quiet things down, Roaddog suggested that someone was drunk and should go to sleep. Lurch was less subtle, he returned from a trip to the toilet to find a man pressuring Doris to go to his tent, she told him no. As the man tried to pull her to her feet Lurch arrived. He said nothing but the punch came all the way from his boots, it struck the man just above the belt. The man folded over the ramrod arm as it continued upwards slowed surprisingly little by the suddenly acquired mass. The man's heels lifted from the grass as the fist's unrelenting upwards progress carried on. Finally the fist withdrew, and the man fell to the grass on his back, a fountain of beer and burger spewing from his mouth.

Drenching him in the noisome mess.

"Someone turn him over before he drowns," said the leader of the Centurions from the darkness of the edge of the camp. With a casual poke of one boot Lurch did just that. The Centurion walked fully into the light and took the beer that Roaddog offered automatically. He turned to Lurch.

"I'm sorry about that, sometimes the lightweights just don't know when to quit."

"He was told no," said Lurch, looking down at Doris, her smile told him everything he needed to know.

"He'll be sore as hell in the morning, he'll apologise, you can be sure of that." Lurch nodded his thanks and sat down again beside Doris, who crawled up into his lap and kissed him with real passion.

Jay-Kay and Billy were both playing guitars, a rolling twelve bar blues thing that switched from one to the other in an unpredictable manner, at least for those that weren't guitarists. Mick was smiling and nodding to the beat, Jackie nestling in his arms almost asleep. Things calmed down as the drunks wandered off to their tents, Billy and Man-Dare retired after handing back the guitar, leaving only Jay-Kay to play for the much diminished audience, he strummed quietly, fragments of tunes here and there, some that they knew and some that they didn't. Out of the darkness came a gaunt figure, thin almost to the point of starvation. His hollow cheeks and sunken eyes gave him an almost cadaverous appearance in the lights.

"Hey guys," he said, his voice surprisingly lively. "I'm gonna be shutting the van down for a few hours to get some kip, if you want something to eat speak now."

"Thanks Andy," said Roaddog, a small order was assembled, and Andy retired to the darkness again. A few minutes later he returned with a box full of food, he sat in the shrunken circle, and accepted a beer from Roaddog, joining in the conversation and taking his share of the passing joints, a mellowness spread all about. It soon became very clear that this party was heading for bed. Then a voice came out of the darkness.

"That's the bastards that tied us to the goal posts." Roaddog Lurch and Bone rolled to their feet and turned towards the speaker.

"You guys better make a run for it," said Andy. Roaddog looked at Bone.

"You want to sit this one out, there's only eight of them."

"Nah, I feel like a little exercise before bed."

"I was thinking of your age, you're getting on you know." Roaddog was looking straight at Bone, almost as if he was ignoring the men coming towards them.

"Who you calling old?" demanded Bone.

"You're not as young as you used to be." Roaddog only needed one more step, he didn't have to wait any longer for it, the first of the invaders stepped just too close, Roaddog spun towards him and took both legs out with a sweeping leg and took the man's consciousness away with a blow to the head as he fell. Lurch lunged into the fray, every flash of his large fists took a combatant out of the game, Bone took one with a kick to the knee and another with a right to the head, Roaddog was caught briefly between two of them, another spinning leg sweep and a fast kick to the head, the last fell to the ground. Roaddog passed amongst the fallen, gathering the weapons that they had dropped, a baseball bat, a short pool cue, a pocket knife or two, a rather brutal looking machete, 'sadly in need of a sharp' he thought as he ran his thumb along the edge.

"What the fuck are we going to do with them this time?" asked Lurch, one tried to get to his feet, only to feel Lurches heavy boot on the back of his head, only for an instant then the surge of pain put him back to sleep.

Roaddog pulled the leader to his feet and punched him in the guts, just to be sure that he understood that things were not going his way. He presented his captive to Bone. Bone looked into the man's eyes for a short time, then turned to Roaddog.

"What's that line from the movie? Oh, I remember. I want your finger." He held up his middle finger just to be sure the man knew what he meant. "Lurch," he continued, not releasing the frightened man's eyes, "the bolt cutters are in the van."

"Anyone runs," Bone continued, "I'll be collecting cocks."

"Damn it, you could have saved me a couple," came a new voice, Roaddog looked across to see Alan staggering to his feet, wearing only his boxers.

"Any that run you can have," laughed Roaddog.

"They don't look like they've got a run left between them." Alan reached into the van and took a bottle from an open case, twisted the top off, and took a swig. Lurch dropped from the back of the van and presented Bone with the bolt cutters.

"I believe these are the ones we confiscated Friday night, sort of poetic don't you think?" Roaddog twisted the man's arm and presented the right hand.

"Why the middle finger?" asked Bone. "The French declared that they were going to take the middle fingers of any British archers captured at the battle of Agincourt, since then the raised middle digit has been a symbol of defiance. For you it's something a little different, you'll not be able to ride a bike until it's fully healed, and even then, it's going to be difficult. I do have one question." He closed the hardened steel jaws of the croppers on the man's soft flesh. "Why have you got such a hardon for this bike?" The wrists twitched and the man flinched.

"I've got documents that prove that Sean Connery owned and used a Dragonfly during the filming of From Russia with Love in Scotland in 1962. It's an easy fix to make this Dragonfly match the papers I have."

"Then it could be worth millions."

"That's the plan, though it'll only go as high as a hundred thousand, and only in the right auction."

"Trade." snapped Bone.

"Trade what?"

"Your finger for the documents," again Bone twitched the cutters.

"Deal," said the man.

"Right," said Bone, "you bring the papers here tomorrow before noon, you come alone, at noon I'm going to start chopping chunks off," he paused and glanced around the men on the ground. "That one there." Lurch grabbed the younger man by the back of the neck and lifted him to his feet.

"Fuck, he's my baby brother."

"I thought so, just a little more incentive. You understand? Anything not clear for you?"

"I understand. Here before noon or you start to cut bits off my brother."

"I think we have a deal." Bone smiled and released the man's finger. "Run." he whispered. That was all it took, the seven ran, back towards the hedge they had come through.

"Can you do it?" asked Bone looking at Roaddog.

"Easy, change the chassis plate, and the engine number, present it as a barn find, re-register it under the new identity, discover the documents and hey presto a hundred K motorcycle."

"You OK with that Alan?"

"I don't want to sell it, even for that much."

"Fine, you keep it until you want to sell it, but make sure you keep it insured, and make sure your family know how much it is worth."

"You don't want a share?" asked Alan.

"No, it's your bike, it just gonna get an upgrade," Bone smiled and turned to Lurch. "Chain that fucker up in the van, no way he's getting away before big bro shows up."

32: Monday Rally Day Four. Breakfast and Phone sex

Roaddog woke slowly, the light coming through the roof of the tent showed him that it was sometime after sunrise, but not much. He still felt very tired, it had been a long and busy night for him, in his arms was Jackie, soft and warm and pink. Even in her sleep she must have sensed his wakefulness, she pressed her naked ass against him sighing when she felt his hardness between them. She didn't wake. In her arms was an equally naked Jane. 'Fuck, what a night.' Thought Roaddog, suddenly there was an issue with beer that really needed to get out. He flicked the edge of the sleeping bag off himself and onto Jackie, releasing her he rolled slowly away. She writhed as the cool air moved against her skin, he covered her with the still warm bag. She settled again. He made his way on hands and knees to the flap of the tent, then slowly out into the light of dawn. Stretching his body high onto the very tips of his toes, he breathed in until he felt like his lungs were going to burst, then slowly he breathed out, settling back onto his feet and relaxing every muscle in his body.

"Damn you're beautiful, like a big scary cat," whispered Man-Dare, she was walking towards Billy's tent. He smiled and nodded. "If you're going to the toilets, then you ought to put some clothes on." She continued. Roaddog nodded, reached back into the tent and pulled out his cut, settling the leather waistcoat on his shoulders he looked at her. She smiled, shook her head and crawled into Billy's tent. Strolling slowly through the tents towards the club house where the dressing rooms were open for showers and toilets, he passed a few early risers. There were a few smiles and some giggles, but no one made any serious notice of his nudity. It was as he walked into the building that he realised that he was a long way from his four stilettos, he was more nervous of this than his lack of clothes. Having completed his current mission he returned to the outdoors. A swirl of wind brought a sudden fragrance to him, that unmistakable odour of cooking bacon. Following his nose he soon arrived at Andy's van.

"Hey Andy," he said softly.

"Hi Roaddog, hey man, have you heard of these things called clothes they seem to be fashionable in these parts?"

"Yeah, but had some beer to get shut of. Three bacon please."

"And let me guess, your wallet is in your other pants." Laughed Andy, fishing rashers of bacon from the pile and dropping them onto barm cakes.

"These jeans don't have any pockets," smiled Roaddog.

"Here ya go, later ok?"

"No worries. Catch ya in a bit." Roaddog retreated to the Dragonriders campsite carrying his as yet free bacon rolls. As he passed Bone's tent Groveller started to rouse from his place by the flap, curled up like a faithful hound at his master's door. Roaddog smiled to himself. 'More like mistresses' door.' He corrected himself. He crawled carefully through the opening into his tent, and woke the girls, passing each a bacon roll. These were devoured with gusto.

"How are you two feeling today?" he asked.

"I'm fine," said Jackie.

"Me too," said Jane, "I stink like a polecat though."

"Damned fine polecat, I must say," laughed Roaddog, reaching out with one finger to collect a drip of bacon fat that had fallen between her small breasts.

"I could go a shower," said Jackie.

"I haven't brought any clothes, or towel, or well anything, I was expecting to go home last night," said Jane.

"You can share mine," smiled Jackie.

"I thought we already did that," Jane looked at Roaddog, and grinned.

"That too," said Jackie.

"Did you enjoy last night?" asked Jane quietly.

"It was different, and fun, and hot, and sexy."

"First time for you with a woman?"

"Yes. I kissed a girl and I liked it," Jackie giggled.

"It was fun for me too," said Roaddog.

"Let's go get clean," whispered Jane, reaching for Jackie's hand.

"Yes," said Jackie, turning to get her towel and other things, as Jane started to collect her clothes. Roaddog was dressed and standing outside by the time the two girls emerged.

Together they walked hand in hand in hand towards the clubhouse, Jackie in the middle with both hands filled. Roaddog headed towards the home team's dressing room. As they walked in through the outer door Jackie dropped his hand and took Jane into the visitors changing rooms, before they vanished from his view, they both turned and blew him a kiss. While they were undressing Jackie laughed and spoke.

"Did you see that sad puppy look on his face?"

"Oh, my god, it was just too precious," smiled Jane, as she walked towards the bank of open showers, turning one head on, and standing under the falling water, turning slowly.

"He honestly expected to take us into the guy's showers and show us off." Jackie took the shower next to Jane, letting the hot water wet her hair and run down her back.

When they walked out into the open again Roaddog was there waiting.

"What took you so long?" he asked.

"We had to share a towel and everything else," laughed Jane.

"We had to make ourselves beautiful for you," said Jackie standing to his left and putting her right arm around his waist. Jane mirrored her position and smiled up at him. His arms fell across their shoulders and he grinned.

"Let's get some coffee," he said guiding them towards Andy's van.

"Hi Roaddog. What would you like?" asked Andy.

"Three coffee's and make them big 'uns. And don't forget the bacon butties I owe ya for."

"I'll not forget," Andy's characteristic cackle of a laugh filled the van and made the girls giggle. Three large paper cups landed on the serving hatch, money changed hands and the three walked away, leaving Andy to his continued amusement.

"What you got planned for today?" asked Jane.

"Whatever," said Roaddog. "Last day is usually quiet, stripping down the camp and going home, we'll start wrapping up about twelve, and then wend our merry way home in the early afternoon, most have to be ready for work in the morning."

"Well," said Jane, "I don't have work until Thursday."

"Me too," said Jackie. "Well Wednesday for me, but hey, that's far enough away."

"I've got the shop to open, I've got a couple of jobs booked in," said Roaddog, he was actually thinking about the delivery he was going to get from the guys in Manchester. The trio walked through the campsite, greeting the people they knew, and nodding to the ones that they didn't.

Roaddog was quite enjoying the feeling of the two girls pressed against him, their arms around his waist and thumbs locked into his broad belt. His arms rested on their shoulders, walking at a slow and yet complicated pace, guided by subtle movements, mere suggestions in the pressure of a hip, or the lean of a shoulder. As they approached the Dragonriders camp he was struck by the arrival of three faces that didn't belong. A sudden breath filled his lungs and he realised that the girls were too close and blocking his access to his blades. The three moved as one, he raised his arms and shrugged his shoulders, both girls released their grip on his belt and stepped away and behind him, his arms slashed rapidly down and two long stilettoes snapped from the pockets in his jeans, unfolding as they came forwards, the click of the blades locking into position seemed so loud as to be deafening.

"You were supposed to come alone," he snarled at the newcomers.

"You think I'd come here alone; I've come for my brother," said the man in the centre, his arms wide and empty. His friends a full pace wide and half a stride behind, looking nervously at the slowly twitching black blades.

"Bone," called Roaddog, "asshole has come for his brother, and he's not alone."

"You deal with it, I'm busy." Came a muffled voice from inside Bone's tent.

"Hell of a time to be getting head." mumbled Roaddog, as he watched Lurch, Slowball and Bug moving closer. "Show me the papers," he growled.

The man reached behind himself and pulled a sheaf of papers from his belt. He moved slowly, holding them towards Roaddog. Roaddog signalled for Jackie to take the bundle, he didn't want to release either of his knives. He smiled when Sharpshooter stepped up to take them.

"You can see there is a log-book, that shows Connery's name and signature, and the address he was living at in London at the time, all these can be verified."

"If these are forgeries," said Sharpshooter, "They're damned good."

"How would you know? You young pup," snapped Alan's voice from behind. Sharpshooter passed the log-book to Alan. In a few seconds Alan confirmed that this did look very good, maybe even real.

"Fine," said Roaddog, "you can have your brother back in one piece. You have one other task to perform. It's nothing terribly difficult, do you accept?"

"What do you want now?"

"Simple, Alan's bike is now your responsibility, if anything happens to it, then we will come looking for you, you make sure nothing happens to that bike. Is that understood?"

"Agreed," The man mumbled looking at the grass beneath his feet. Roaddog nodded to Lurch, who jumped up into the van and returned in a moment with the younger brother.

"You OK?" asked the elder.

"I'm fine, they tied me up and went to bed. I was expecting you back as soon as it went quiet." He spoke softly held in the arms of his brother.

"It took me until now to get these two to come back, the rest were too chicken, I'm sorry."

"Good," said Roaddog, "You four can leave, remember what happened here, and the promises you made, we will not forget them, we will hold you to them.

"We'll not forget, Alan." He looked to the old man. "I'm going to need your phone number so that we can arrange security details for your bike."

"No worries." Alan called out his number as the man punched it into his own phone. Still holding his younger brother by the waist the man turned to Roaddog.

"How come you guys are so together? I thought our group was real good."

"We're not just a group of friends, it goes much deeper," said Roaddog.

"How do you do that?"

"It's not easy to get to be a member, it takes work and time, you've got to prove yourself to be accepted. We're not just some guys who meet in the boozer on a Friday night."

"I need some new friends."

"Pick them carefully."

The man nodded and turned away, never letting go of his brother, the other two walked with them towards the hedge again.

"Well, that was nearly exciting," said Roaddog as the two girls returned to his side, muffled voices and grunts from Bone's tent indicated the completion of the activity within.

"Oh god," mumbled Bone.

"Yeah," said Bandit Queen.

"I hope you didn't find the action out here distracting," called Roaddog.

"Just enough," laughed Bandit Queen loudly.

"Fuck you," grumbled Bone.

"Yes you did," she laughed even louder, joined by many on the outside.

"You're all a bunch of bastards," muttered Bone, though many could actually hear him.

Gradually the camp returned to a more relaxed state, Mick and Jackie surfaced and wandered over to the camper where Jay-Kay was with his friends. Andy's van was doing a roaring trade in coffee and breakfast, the competition had already left.

Bug and Cherie walked away from Andy's van breakfast barm cakes in hand.

"I'd have preferred one of those German sausages." said Cherie.

"You sure?"

"Yes, I didn't really taste the last one." She leaned against him and laughed. "When you planning on leaving?" she asked.

"Soon, I got lots of shit to do. These online sales are going potty."

"You need some help with that stuff?"

"If you feel up to it, it can be a smelly job."

"No worries, can't be any smellier than some of the jobs I have done in the past."

"What's the worst you've ever done?"

"Chicken factory. Trucks full of birds come in, and millions of chicken portions leave. It's a real messy process, and seeing as the waste skips only get emptied when they are full, the whole place gets real stinky especially in the summer."

"Is that place in the middle of Preston?"

"Yes."

"I think I've followed one of their waste skips. Surely the worst thing I have ever smelled. Really foul."

"Fowl. Jesus, the old jokes are the old jokes." She laughed despite the poor joke.

Mick and Jackie walked slowly into the centre of the Dragonriders camp, having finished their breakfast with their other friends.

"Hey Roaddog," said Mick.

"Hey Roaddog," laughed Roaddog, "how's it going?"

"Fine, good brekkie and feeling sober about now."

"Beer? We can fix that sober thing."

"No thanks mate, gotta get home, work tomorrow, ya know?"

"Yeah, I know. Me too."

"It's been great to meet you and your club, perhaps we can do this again some time."

"You'll always be welcome were ever we are. Let us know when your guys are playing in the area next and we'll turn up and make a racket."

"That would be wonderful, the guys will really appreciate that."

"No problem," Roaddog reached out a hand to Mick. They shook and hugged, then Roaddog turned to Jackie, and gathered her up in his arms, he kissed her on both cheeks. "You are always invited whenever you want, you don't even have to bring him with you." Roaddog smiled returning her to her feet.

"You know that will not happen." She grinned up at him, then turned away. After a couple of steps, she turned back. "Didn't you get enough with two girls in your bed last night? You really want to take the chance of pissing them off?"

"You have a great point there, however, the invitation stands."

Mick slapped Roaddog on the shoulder as he walked past. In less than ten minutes Mick's tent was down and strapped to the back of his bike, the Harley barked into life and the two mounted up, with a final wave they rolled slowly across the grass and off into the morning sun.

"He's a nice guy," said Jackie.

"That he is," agreed Roaddog, taking her hand in his. Jane took his other hand and looked up into his eyes.

"I need to be going soon, my mum will be wondering where I am."

"Didn't you text her to tell them you were staying over?"

"No, my phone is in my car, and I couldn't be bothered getting it, we were sort of busy."

"I suppose," he dropped her hand. "Go and tell her, but don't do what

Jackie did."

"Go on, what did she do?"

"I was silly," said Jackie. "I met him on a dark country path, after midnight. He told me to take his picture and send it to someone. So, I sent it to my mother."

"She must have had kittens," laughed Jane.

"She was less than impressed when I turned up with this lunk and covered in blood."

"Not yours I hope?"

"No, the blood was mostly his, it was the start of a beautiful friendship."

"You certainly seem to be good together," Jane paused, "I'll go get my phone, don't run off." She turned and walked quickly away.

"I like her," said Jackie.

"She's cute," replied Roaddog.

"And sexy as fuck."

"Did you ever think you'd say that?"

"Not about a girl."

"How would momma deal with that?"

"She'd throw a fit."

"Who would she prefer me or Jane?" his grin split is face.

"I honestly have no idea." Jackie looked across the campsite to where Jane was returning, her phone pressed against her ear and her small breasts bouncing with every hurried stride. Jane smiled at Jackie.

"I'm fine mum, there's nothing to worry about, I've made friends with this guy called Roaddog." Her pace slowed as she listened. "No mum, his girlfriend is here as well, she's really nice." Again, she listened. "I'll be home about lunch time, don't fret." She faced Jackie, leaned forwards to kiss her, still holding the phone to her ear.

"Mum, I'm perfectly safe here, you should see the size of Roaddog, he's huge."

Jackie reached her hand in under Jane's skirt and slid it slowly upwards.

"Mum, I'm going to have to go, Jackie is stroking me." She spread her legs a little to give Jackie better access.

"Yes mum, it does feel good." Jackie stopped moving. Jane started to rock backwards and forwards pressing more firmly on the hand, feeling a finger slowly raise.

"God mum, it feels so good." Jackie smiled and kissed her, as Roaddog moved in behind Jane, and pressed against her back.

"Mum, I'm going to have to go, Roaddog has pressed up against my back, he's so tall that his cock is pressing against my kidneys." He stroked her neck and kissed it softly.

"No mum, he's still got his pants on, but I can feel it, and he's kissing my neck." Jackie raised her hand so that Jane could taste herself on her fingers.

"No Mum." Jackie pulled gently on Jane heading towards the tent.

"No mum, let me go." Jackie's arm was now at full stretch, Jane had to move or let go.

"Fine." snapped Jane, flipping the phone down and punching a button.

"Roaddog," said the phone, "are you and your girlfriend going to fuck my daughter?"

"That seems like the plan," said Roaddog.

"You're not forcing her, are you?"

"In no way, if she want's to walk away she can do that at any time, but she's not going to, she's going into the tent now."

"I am jealous as hell, it's been fifteen years since I had a good fuck, since her no good daddy fucked off with that tart."

"Hang on," said Roaddog. Then he raised his voice. "I got a MILF in serious need of a good fucking, anyone available?"

"Did you just do that?" asked the phone.

"Yes and I got three raised arms, sorry two, one just got kneed in the nuts by his girlfriend."

"You can't mean that?"

"I can, give me your address and someone will be on the road in less than three minutes."

"You're crazy."

"And you're thinking about it."

"Not with any seriousness, no I'll not give you my address."

"Should I get it from Jane?"

"No, please don't do that."

"Fine." he raised his voice again. "Sorry guys she chickened." looking back at the phone. "I really need to get inside that tent before I miss out on something."

"OK," said the phone, "just do me a favour, don't hang up, and put her phone somewhere near. Does that sound bad?"

"I suppose it would to your average straight, but not to us. You want me to keep you informed as to what is happening?"

"This sounds so bad, but yes, just don't let Jane know."

"She'll not know until it's way too late." Roaddog, went into the tent and got undressed, placing Jane's phone on top of his discarded jeans.

Some twenty minutes later, as Jane was coming down from an earth-shattering orgasm, she noticed the sounds coming from her phone.

"What the fuck is going on?" she moaned weakly.

"I'd say that was your mum getting off," laughed Roaddog.

"Bastard," mumbled Jane.

"Don't be mean," said the phone, "you bring those nice people to meet mama."

"Not a chance mum, these are my friends." said Jane, scooping up her phone and breaking the call.

33: Monday Rally Day Four.
Post coital discussions and Homeward Bound.

"I can't believe that you did that," said Jane after she recovered from the breathlessness.

"Hey," said Roaddog, "she seemed like a desperately lonely person. As she said, since your father left."

"You mean she has been alone since the asshole left us?"

"That's the impression I get," said Roaddog, "she's still a woman after all."

"She's mum."

"And everything else as well?"

"Not as I'd thought of it, until now."

"Well, she's a woman, and a real woman at that. She has needs, and I have to believe that she has repressed her feelings in favour of you."

"I don't understand," mumbled Jane.

"She's done everything she can for you as a mother and denied her own needs in the process."

"I'm not sure I understand."

"Come on girl," said Jackie, "your mama hasn't had a fuck in fifteen years, could you do that for someone else?"

"I offered to send a guy for her," said Roaddog, "and she turned them down, on the proviso that I let her listen in to you having fun."

"What do you mean, offered to send her a guy?"

"I called out for any guy available and got two takers, she turned them down."

"You think she did that for me?"

"Could you have dealt with a new father?"

"No, not really, and she would have known that." Both Jackie and Roaddog looked at her and smiled. Jane looked at them and grinned. "You're right, it seems I've been selfish. I'll have to talk to her about this when I get home."

"You could call her," said Roaddog, "I'm sure the guys haven't left yet."

"No way, I'm going to get some random guy to follow me home to fuck my mother."

"Fine, but talk to her, find out how she really feels. You could even bring her to the clubhouse to meet some of the guys. She might take a shine to one, or maybe two." he laughed.

"OK, we'll talk about things. Will I get to see you two again sometime?"

"It's possible," said Jackie, "it's been fun. Far more fun than I'd have expected."

Jane flung her arms around Jackie's neck and hugged her, then she did the same to Roaddog. "I really gotta go," she whispered. Phone numbers were exchanged while the trio got dressed and readied themselves for the outside world.

"I'll call you," said Jane as she walked quickly away towards her car, she glanced back at them a time or two before she was gone from sight.

"She's a nice girl," said Roaddog taking Jackie's hand in his own.

"She's that," agreed Jackie.

"Hey Roaddog," called Bug from some distance away.

"What's up?" asked Roaddog.

"Is the van ready to take on camping gear? I have shit I need to do today."

"Yes, just drop it near the back, I'll sort it before we leave. It'll be in the van at work tomorrow."

"Cheers man." Bug carried his already collapsed tent over to the van then returned to where Cherie was waiting by his motorcycle. In a couple of minutes, they were gone as well.

"It's a bit depressing," said Roaddog to Jackie, "watching all these people starting to leave, it's like the weekend is over."

"Yes, back to the real world." She leaned against him and put her arm around his waist.

Alan added his tent to the pile and shook Roaddog's hand before kicking the dragonfly to life and rolling slowly for home. The pile of tents was getting quite large by the time Roaddog started to think about lunch.

"You want something to eat?" he asked Jackie.

"Why not?" she smiled in return. Then he looked over at Andy's van to see the serving hatch fall into place and Andy lock it up.

"Damn," he whispered. "Looks like we are too late." Jackie shrugged and together they started to load the gear into the van. Very soon Groveller turned up to lend a hand, bringing with him Bone's tent. Leaving the two guys to the heavy work Jackie started to pack the gear from their tent and she added this to the pile for loading. Bone and Bandit Queen were sitting on the grass watching the work going on as Andy came strolling up, a cardboard box in his hands.

"Hey guys," he said, "I got some leftovers for ya'll."

"Cheers mate," said Roaddog jumping down from the van. "Good weekend?"

"Damned right, ya can get your own food tomorrow, I'm going to be sleeping."

"No sweat," grinned Roaddog. Grabbing a burger from the box, before passing the box on to Jackie, who snaffled a bacon butty for herself. The box progressed slowly around those still present. Roaddog passed out bottles of beer, not forgetting Andy. Shortly, all the gear was loaded, and everyone was ready to leave, Man-Dare decided to drive the van from where it was, there had been no rain, so the field was very dry. She did get Roaddog to roll it out of the depressions its wheels had created, but from there on there was no problem for her. The Dragonriders convoy left the rugby club, leaving many more behind, they were waved off by the leader of the Centurions. As they drove back to the clubhouse gradually riders peeled off for home, there were only six bikes, the van, and Slowball's trike when they got back to the club. The gates were already open, and the doors were unlocked. Cherie and Bug were huddled up close on one of the sofas. Man-Dare parked the van and climbed straight onto the pillion of Billy's bike, she tossed the keys to Roaddog and with a wave they were gone. Sharpshooter got beers from behind the bar and distributed them. Bone and Bandit Queen occupied one of the comfy chairs, Lurch and Doris the other, Slowball and Sylvia squeezed in with Bug and Cherie. Roaddog and Jackie took stools at the bar, with Sharpshooter and Groveller leaning nearby.

"That was a good rally," observed Bandit Queen.

"That's for sure," agreed Cherie. As Roaddog selected a rock radio station and let the music spill gently from the speakers.

"I definitely had fun," said Sylvia.

"You get some good piccies?" asked Bone.

"I'm sure I got some, won't be able to tell until I get them home and sort through, but I think I've got some real gold in there."

"How about a slideshow for the website?" asked Sharpshooter looking at Roaddog.

"I don't see why not. The web guys can deal with that sort of thing. Sylvia, can you pick the best, say fifty shots?" He replied.

"I'll try, but it might be difficult to decide on the best fifty."

"I've just thought of something," said Slowball.

"Now that is rare," chuckled Bandit Queen.

"Bitch," snapped Slowball, smiling. "Someone is not in the pics." He looked at his trike standing as it was in the bright sunlight. He nudged Sylvia. "Go get a camera and set it up for an idiot to take pictures." She shrugged and climbed out of his lap, she retrieved a camera from the box on the back of the trike, flicked the switch to 'auto'.

"Ready," she said. Slowball took the camera and waved towards his trike.

"Take a seat." he grinned. Sylvia frowned and climbed up onto the trike, taking her usual seat on the back.

"No, front seat, one hand on the handlebar, and the other on the gear lever." She hitched forwards into the front seat, her right hand on the throttle, her left below her left hip on the gear lever. She smiled at Slowball, he shook his head slowly.

"Give her your shades," he said to Sharpshooter. Sharpshooter raised his eyebrows but took his large mirrored aviators over to Sylvia. She settled the glasses on her nose and looked back at Slowball. He paused.

"Nearly." he muttered. Taking the handlebar he heaved the wheel over to full left lock, he took her right hand and draped it over the throttle, so that the hand hung down between the brake lever and the twistgrip. He looked long at Sylvia and shook his head again. Reaching into his jacket he took a pair of black leather fingerless gloves and passed then to her. She put them on and placed her hands exactly as he had set them. He nodded and moved back. He crouched down, then moved right, then left. Finally, he was happy with the angle.

"Right." he said. "Look over my right shoulder." She did. "A bit further." She did. "Now tip your head up just a little." She did. "A bit more." She did.

"Just take the photo will ya," snarled Sharpshooter.

"Down just a tiny bit," said Slowball. Sylvia moved as he requested.

He held his breath for a moment, then the camera clicked.

"OK," said Slowball.

"Don't you want a second just for luck?" asked Sylvia, trying not to move.

"Don't need it," said Slowball passing her the camera. She turned the camera around and looked at the picture he had taken. She nodded.

"Great shot."

"Now you can be in the slide show as well." He said softly, pulling her to her feet and kissing her. He put his gloves back in his pocket and handed Sharpshooter his sunglasses.

"What was all that fannying about for?" asked Sharpshooter.

"I wanted to get the light right, just a bit of sun flare off the glasses."

"He did a damned good job too," said Sylvia, she turned the camera so Sharpshooter could see. "It'll look a lot better on a big screen, or in print." She went on. They all returned to their seats and the conversations settled down into the usual relaxed atmosphere of a quiet Sunday afternoon.

As evening rolled in the clubhouse slowly emptied, Sylvia had Slowball take her home, she had post processing to do, or so she said. Roaddog smiled as the VW rolled out of the yard, he knew that Slowball would not be coming back.

"Fancy a beer?" he asked Jackie.

"We've been drinking all day," she whispered.

"I know but I fancy a change of scenery."

"Where?"

"Railway?"

"Fine." She stood up and Roaddog waved to Bone. Then he called to Bug.

"I'll see ya in the morning, don't forget we got a delivery due in." Bug nodded without taking his eyes off Cherie. As the pair walked slowly to Roaddog's bike she glanced at Bug and whispered.

"I think they're going to be an item."

"Most likely, it might even last a while." His grin told her that he knew more than she did, but the noise of his motor was such that further conversation was impossible.

Jackie rested against his back as they flew along the now familiar roads to the Railway. They walked into the pub to find it quite busy, families eating together, children running around, Nigel waved to them as soon as he saw them, so they took up a place at one end of the bar and waited patiently for Nigel to serve them.

"What can I get for you?" he asked.

"Wainwrights and lager," said Roaddog.

"How's things today?" asked Jackie.

"Busy, but we're doing OK," smiled Nigel. He went on to bitch about a couple of the waitresses, seems there was some friction between them. Roaddog's phone bleeped softly, he replied to the text message while Nigel and Jackie were talking.

"I'll just be a little while," said Jackie to Roaddog, before she walked into the kitchen.

"What's happening?" asked Roaddog.

"She's going to sort out those two. Tears before bedtime," laughed Nigel, taking Roaddog's money.

"You need an escort tomorrow?" asked Roaddog.

"Thanks, but no, it's been a sort of steady but busy weekend, and I have had a visit from the cops this afternoon. You remember the ones that followed us back from the bank?"

"I remember them."

"They say they're going to be here about ten in the morning, quick ride to the bank, and back for coffee."

"So, they do have some use," smiled Roaddog.

"Seems so, I think it hurt their feelings that you helped me out when they should have."

"I've no problem with that," laughed Roaddog. Nigel watched as the door to the bar opened and a young girl came in, a quick glance round and she ran straight up to Roaddog, threw her arms around his neck and kissed him firmly. Nigel glanced at the kitchen door in time to see Jackie walk through it. She paused for a moment then came striding over.

"If there's going to be trouble here, I'd prefer that you take it outside," said Nigel. Jackie took the girl by the shoulder and spun her around, then grabbed her by the neck and kissed her equally firmly.

"What the fuck?" whispered Nigel.

"Don't ask," said Roaddog. Jackie broke the kiss and looked at Nigel.

"I kissed a girl," she said.

"And I liked it," laughed Jane.

"You people are crazy," mumbled Nigel. Then he nodded in the direction of the kitchen. "You get them sorted out?"

"I told them that if their stupid squabble made me work this evening, then I would feed them both to my boyfriend."

"Perhaps you should have threatened them with your girlfriend instead."

"I didn't know she was here. Why are you here?"

"Well," Jane glanced down at the floor, then squared her shoulders, "I had a long talk with mother, and we've come to a sort of understanding. She's going to take her love life off hold, and I'm going to be more than happy for her."

"How did she deal with our situation?"

"There's still a lot of work to do there, but I think she'll come round. Though she did make some extreme threats if either of you hurt me."

"No problem," said Roaddog, "Beer?"

"No," replied Jane, "coke, full fat, I need the energy." Jane laughed, as Jackie took her by the arm and guided her to an empty table in the window, leaving Roaddog to collect the drinks.

"What is going on with you?" asked Nigel.

"I'm not sure, but it's definitely exciting."

"Keep them both happy if you can, if you can't then run like a bastard." Nigel laughed and turned away.

The girls were sitting and laughing when he caught up.

"So, what happened?" asked Jackie.

"We had a long talk; she was surprised when this lunk left the phone line open for her to listen." Jane nodded in Roaddog's direction and snatched her coke as soon as it hit the table.

"She certainly enjoyed herself," laughed Roaddog.

"That's for sure," smiled Jane. "We had a long talk about that. She was more than a little surprised that I usually favour girls, not guys. Last night was a first for me. I think I want more, if you two can put up with me?"

"I have no issue," laughed Jackie loudly.

"So long as there's space for me in this craziness, then I have no problem," smiled Roaddog.

"Well," Jane looked slowly into his eyes, "that really goes without saying."

"Thanks," mumbled Roaddog.

"I'm sorry," said Jane. Getting confused looks from the other two.

"I was more than a little greedy last night. I loved the way that you two made me the centre of attention, it really made me feel so special. I'm sorry if I appeared to be too pushy."

"No sweat," said Jackie.

"Oh, there was plenty of that. I smelled like a polecat again by the time I got home. Mother mentioned it." Jane took a long gulp of her coke and followed that with a loud belch. "Do you think there is some mileage in this crazy three-way?" she looked down, as if dreading the answer.

"I think we can have some fun for a while at least," said Jackie.

"I hope so," said Jane looking up again.

"The only issue I have," said Roaddog, "is that I only have one pillion seat."

"You could get a trike." said Jane.

"That's not happening." said Jackie.

"Why?"

"You wait until you feel that motor shaking underneath your ass," laughed Jackie.

"Doesn't a trike shake the same?" asked Jane.

"No way," grinned Jackie, "I've tried both, the bike is better, way better."

"Don't I get a say in this?" asked Roaddog.

"No," said both together.

"Just thought I'd get that straight." He grinned knowing that they'd sort this out between them. "Better get another spare lid," he mumbled.

"Do it," laughed Jackie, taking one of his hands.

"I get the feeling I'm being railroaded here," he muttered.

"I suppose you are," replied Jane, "but you'll enjoy it for a while at least."

"Maybe I should kick you both to the kerb," he said gently.

"Like that's going to happen," laughed Jackie.

"Don't worry Dog," smiled Jane, "we'll make sure you get fed." She wriggled in his lap.

"How will your mum take all this?" he asked, looking straight at Jackie.

"To be brutally honest," whispered Jackie, "she's been such a bitch that I really don't care."

"I'm not sure that is the right attitude," he muttered, reaching out to take her hand.

"I know, but that's the way I feel. She can accept it, or she can fuck off."

"Your dad?"

"He's a sweety, he'll not care just so long as I am happy."

"And are you?" asked Jane. Jackie's' head snapped round to face the younger girl.

"I would never have thought that you would ask that."

"Ask I do." Janes eyes turned down, as if she really didn't want the answer.

"I think we can be happy as a trio," Jackie released Roaddog's hand and reached out to Jane's chin, she lifted the girls face and smiled into her eyes. Jane leaned forwards and flung her arms around Jackie's neck. The two hugged long and hard. When they finally separated, there was a much younger girl standing next to the table.

"You want something?" asked Jane.

"Yes," the girl paused before going on, "you lot kept my dad out all weekend, and he came back with some very strange tales this morning. What is going on with you lot?"

"You're Alan's daughter?" asked Jackie.

"Yes, I don't like him out all weekend."

"He's a grown man, he can do what he wants with his spare time," Jackie smiled.

"He's too old to be sleeping in a tent with a load of hairy bikers."

"That's his decision to make, not yours."

"I don't want him taking up with some biker chick."

"I see," said Jane, "you just don't want to share him with someone new."

"Have you met Man-Dare?" asked Jackie, Roaddog spluttered into his beer.

"Who's he?" asked the girl.

"She, not he, she. Your dad turned down the chance to jump her."

"I don't understand."

"He said he couldn't do it, because she reminded him too much of you, seeing as she was draped over garden furniture at the time."

"Ouch." whispered Roaddog, Jane frowned at him.

"How do you know?" mumbled the girl.

"He told me, I did put him under some pressure, I refused to believe that any man could turn down a good looking girl like Man-Dare, so he explained it to me."

"So, you know?"

"Oh yes, he explained in detail, and I understand why he turned down Man-Dare, she does look more than a little like you."

"He told you?"

"He did, and he said that he didn't want you to take up with the hairy biker lifestyle."

"He thinks I'd hang around with bikers kipping in some sweaty tents, no way."

"I'll tell him," said Roaddog, "you do know that you are talking to bikers who kipped in sweaty tents last night, don't you?"

"Damn was that a sweaty tent," laughed Jane.

"Your mother enjoyed it," said Jackie, Jane smiled broadly.

"You people are disgusting," said the girl turning on her heel and stamping off into the pool room, to be with her younger friends.

"Well, I think we've managed to convince her that she shouldn't take up with bikers," laughed Roaddog.

"I'm not so sure that Alan is going to be terribly happy about it though," said Jackie.

"He'll get some stick from her, but he'll at least be sure she's not going to turn up at the club looking for him."

"Or us," laughed Jackie.

"Well," said Roaddog, "I don't know about you two, but I've had a long weekend and have work in the morning, so I'm going home to bed."

"Sounds like a plan to me," said Jackie.

"I'm up," smiled Jane. She got to her feet, with Jackie only a moment behind.

"Come on then," said Jackie. Roaddog shook his head slowly and followed the two out of the pub.

34: Tuesday Off to work and a delivery.

Roaddog woke slowly the light from the curtains showed him that sunrise was not far away. His bed seemed more than a little crowded. Pushing back against his belly where the small soft buttocks of Jane, his ass was almost hanging off the edge. He slid his hand forwards and stroked the warm hip of Jackie. He patted it gently.

"Come on girls, it's time to get up, I have work and I'm sure that you two have something to do today" His voice quiet in the soft light. Jane pressed back some more against him.

"Don't wanna," she whispered.

"Me either," mumbled Jackie.

"Tough shit," he spoke a little louder, and pushed back against Jane. Then he rolled away and stood up.

"I'm going to make coffee, get your sexy asses out of bed, and get moving." He turned and went downstairs. In the kitchen he set the kettle to boil and went to check on his miners. It only took him a few moments to get through the security checks and he smiled when he saw his figures, three good hits overnight, and more bitcoin to go into his bank. His batteries were almost empty, but the sun was coming up very soon.

Back in the kitchen he made coffee for them all and called up the stairs.

"Come and get it, coffee for all."

He carried three steaming mugs into the living room, and fired up the radio, he took a seat on the sofa, looking out of the front window, the sky was lightening rapidly, but there were more than enough clouds to hide the sun. He heard the giggles as the girls came down the stairs, Jackie came into the room and sat down next to him, leaving the chair for Jane. Jane was a little concerned about the fact that the curtains were open, but she dropped into the chair and hid herself from the view of passing strangers, Jackie laughed.

"See," she said, "it's easy."

"But it feels so wrong," answered Jane.

"Don't worry about it," smiled Roaddog. "What you two got planned for the day?"

"I'm working this evening," said Jackie.

"I've got nothing on," said Jane.

"That's sort of obvious," laughed Jackie.

"Well, I've got to be at work in less than an hour, so drink your coffee's and skedaddle," he said.

"Can you take me home first?" asked Jackie.

"I can take you home," interrupted Jane.

"Fine, that should blow mothers mind," Jackie laughed, then she saw a figure turn into the garden path. "Looks like Sylvia's here." She stood and went to open the door.

"She's going to answer the front door naked?" asked Jane.

"It's only Sylvia," observed Roaddog.

Sylvia had most of her clothes off by the time she walked into the front room, her jeans and boots were gone before she sat down.

"Tea?" asked Roaddog.

"That'd be nice," smiled Sylvia. Roaddog went into the kitchen to make another cup.

"What happened to Slowball?" asked Jackie.

"He had to go and get some clothes for work, and I was busy with the weekends photos, so he went home about ten last night."

"You two ok?"

"We're fine, I'm sort of hoping this will last, but it's early days yet."

"You think you might get bored of him?" asked Jane.

"Not for a while, he's an interesting guy."

"Good sex too?" Jane grinned.

"Better than I've had in a long while. What about you three?"

"Damned fine," laughed Jane.

"Fine what?" asked Roaddog passing a mug to Sylvia.

"Fine sex," laughed Jane.

"Slowball's a great linguist," said Sylvia.

"So's Jackie," replied Jane. Jackie blushed brilliant red from her cheekbones to her shoulders.

"I'm no slouch," said Roaddog.

"That's true," said Jackie, "but you ain't got that girl touch." She reached out and patted his hand. She glanced down and the conversation was having a pronounced effect on Roaddog, she slowly reached across and stroked him.

"Now that is indecent exposure," he muttered.

"You're not stopping me," she replied.

Suddenly he stood up, breaking her hold on him.

"I'm going for a shower, you lot sort out what you're doing with the rest of today." As he left the room Sylvia spoke out.

"Need a hand with anything?" The three laughed loudly as his heavy steps climbed the stairs.

"That was cruel," whispered Jane.

"Only a little," replied Jackie.

By the time he returned to the living room he was fully dressed.

"I got to go to work. Can you lot lock up on your way out?"

"I'll do it," said Jackie, she stood and threw her arm around his neck, kissing him and pressing her body against his. No sooner had she returned to her seat then Jane had taken her place, wriggling her soft belly against him.

"Looks like your shower didn't do much for your little problem," she said as she sat down.

"Not so little from this angle," said Sylvia.

"You bitches will be the death of me," he laughed as he turned and left. The roar of his harley soon filled the air as he set off to work.

He was unlocking the door to the workshop when he heard the rumble of Slowball's VW, he turned and waved to his friend, as the trike rolled slowly backwards into its normal parking place. Slowball walked through the roller door as soon as it was high enough for him to step through without ducking.

"What we got for today?" he asked.

"There's a VW Sharan due in, guy said he'd drop it off in about half an hour."

"What does it need?" asked Slowball.

"You could check the book you know," laughed Roaddog.

"Can't be arsed, whatever it is we can do it."

"It's got a dodgy clutch."

"Shit, that's clutch and flywheel."

"Yes, but the cash is good."

"It's going to be most of the day though."

"We can't have easy days all the time. The parts are going to be here midmorning."

"We should have it stripped out in a couple of hours," grinned Slowball. "Coffee?"

Roaddog simply nodded as Slowball retired to the back room to make the coffee. By the time he came out with two mugs in his hands there was a dark blue VW attempting to climb the slope into the garage.

"Hey man," shouted Roaddog, moving his hand across his throat to tell the driver to kill the engine. The big diesel rattled into silence and the man wound a window down.

"We'll pull it up on the winch," said Roaddog loudly. The man got out and handed Roaddog the keys.

"Damned thing's a bitch to drive when it's slipping that bad," he spoke slowly, Roaddog couldn't quite place the accent, thinking it might be Irish.

"Don't sweat it. We've got your details; we'll call you when it's ready."

"This morning?" a hopeful question.

"Not likely, it's an old car, and we got a lot of work to do."

"Should have at the price you're charging."

"Take it to the dealer, they'll tell you that it's a discontinued part, and sell you a nice new car. Oh, and a loan to go with it."

"Yes," the man chuckled, "been there, done that, told the assholes to fuck off."

"We'll start it immediately, the parts are due in this morning, we should be just about ready for them when they arrive. With the best will in the world you're looking at one PM at the earliest. If the drive shaft's a bitch to split, then two o'clock is likely."

"I understand, just soon as you can please."

"We'll do what we can. Call you later." The man nodded and turned away, walking out into the street to get into the van that was waiting for him, it was a white bodied flatbed with caged sides. Roaddog watched them drive away and caught the plate as they turned round in the street. He went straight to the office and ran the number through the systems.

"What's up?" ask Slowball.

"That flatbed is registered to a PO box in Birmingham."

"Strange."

"We need to be careful with this one, I think we are dealing with gypsies."

"You run the VW?"

"Yes, registered in south Manchester and the MOT is well out of date."

"Well at least it'll be cash in the hand."

"If they decide not to collect it today, then we put security in for the night."

"Fuck, you know that's going to be you and me."

"It is what it is. I'll set up the winch, you see if you can drive the damned thing any better than him."

Roaddog tossed the keys to Slowball and went to the other end of the four-post lift, to free the winch. While he was working the mechanism, he heard the VW start, then stall.

"Hey Dog," shouted Slowball, "this thing's got no handbrake, but the electric won't release."

"Handbrake is on the other side of the driver's seat dick."

Slowball looked down and sure enough there was a very traditional looking hand brake lever.

"Why do they do that?" Shouted Slowball.

"Don't know, but it does give you twelve feet of flat space from the tail to the centre console."

"Not very wide."

"You can stand a door up in it, or a worktop. How many cars can do that?"

"Not many, you ready?"

"Just get the damned thing a little closer."

Slowball reversed slowly, then pulled forwards to line the heavy car up with the ramp. Every time he revved the engine the clutch just spun. He dropped back from the ramp again, and then using only idling revs let the clutch up, before he arrived at the ramp the clutch was fully engaged and the shear mass of the people carrier got the front wheels up on the ramp, the rears were never going to make it, so he stamped on the brake and pulled the handbrake. This took two attempts because he reached between the seats on the first one.

"Good shot," called Roaddog running the cable up to the front of the car and hooking it around the anti-roll bar. Slowball watched the cable tighten then he dropped the handbrake and the big car rolled sedately up onto the ramp, Roaddog stopped the winch when the nose was level with the end of the ramp. Slowball pulled the handbrake, and the car was now ready for work to start.

The two men set to work with a will, they'd been working together for long enough to know exactly what to do. In just over two hours the car was ready for the replacement parts.

"Coffee?" asked Slowball.

"Yes, you get that, and I'll contact the parts guy, see where he's up to." By the time that Slowball returned Roaddog was just hanging up the phone.

"He's about ten minutes out, and I got a text from Bug, he's running late."

"Ten minutes is good, Bug, well fuck him," said Slowball, "how'd it go last night?"

"It was good, but this morning Sylvia turned up, and I had all three of them in the front room, so I just cut and ran, left them to it."

"What the fuck where they doing?"

"They were talking, that Jane is crazy, and Sylvia's turning into a naturist."

"So, just so I can get this straight in my head, there were three naked women in your living room, and you came to work?"

"Yes. Unlike you I knew what was coming in today, and I wasn't going to leave you with this bitch to do all on your own." Roaddog nodded in the direction of the VW on the lift.

"I'd have called in one of the others."

"Anyway, Sylvia's with you, isn't she?"

"So far, not sure how long that's going to last though, it's early days yet."

"Well, I'm not getting in the way of that," Roaddog smiled.

"Thanks, I think," said Slowball.

Further conversation was prevented by the arrival of Bone and Bandit Queen. As the pair walked towards the open doorway Slowball called out.

"Brew, or beer?"

"Beer," snarled Bone. Slowball went to the corner bar to get beers for the new arrivals. Bone dropped hard into the seat Slowball had just left.

"What's up with you?" asked Roaddog.

"Fucking cops, that's what," snapped Bandit Queen. She twitched her head in the direction of the street outside, a car rolled to a stop. It had two occupants, and far too many aerials. "They've been on our ass all morning, they were parked outside the house when we woke up, and they've been with us ever since."

"What do they want?" asked Roaddog.

"No idea," grunted Bone taking a bottle from Slowball. "they could be onto our dealing, or they're looking for a way to pin the death of that paedophile on us." He glared at Bandit Queen.

"Hey, I had nothing to do with his death, if I could have found a way then I'd have done it, but I didn't. They can track down everyone I've talked to and find out that I couldn't find the bastard. I tried, but I found nothing."

"Well, they're still on our asses."

"I'd give them something to do," said Roaddog.

"What the hell do you mean?" demanded Bone.

"Whatever you got to get them away from here before we get our delivery from the guys in Manchester. So, give them something to do. You got nothing on for the day, have you?"

"Nothing major planned, why?"

"Go to devils bridge. Meet a guy, Bug can be there in less than an hour. Then take them to the other bridge. Meet a guy, say Sharpshooter, then bring both guys back here."

"That's one hell of a ride," said Bone, smiling broadly.

"The current record for the bridge run is about two and a half hours, but think of all the different areas those bastards will have to check in with as they go, hell they're even crossing into a new country."

"They think we're up to something and they'll not want the local plod getting in on the act, so they'll keep them off us." Bone grinned.

"If you think I'm riding that pillion to fucking Wales and back, you can kiss my sweaty ass," laughed Bandit Queen.

"Even better," said Roaddog, "they'll not know which one they should be following, if another car turns up here, then we'll know they are really serious."

"I'm liking this even more," said Bone, "set it up."

Roaddog pulled his phone from his jeans pocket, but stopped before he made any calls, a small white van had pulled into the yard, he went out to meet the driver, and collected the heavy box of parts from him. He passed the box to Slowball and then made his calls. Five minutes later he said to Bone.

"All set up, Bug's going to be on the road in about ten minutes, just make sure he gets to the bridge before you do. Shooters going to set off for the other bridge about twelve, so that should give you lots of time to get there after him. You can all be back here by about five o'clock, I'll get Chinese and beers ready for y'all, and we can laugh at the coppers."

"What if they drop another car out there to watch me?" asked Bandit Queen.

"Slowball can take you out for a beer or two. Wolf's not going to be here until about one."

"I'm up for that," laughed Bandit Queen.

"Good, everything is set up," said Roaddog, "and I've got a damned dual mass clutch to fix." He went over to the ramp and set about fixing the car with Slowball. Things went surprisingly well, considering the age of the vehicle, there wasn't one stuck bolt or dodgy ball joint. Twenty minutes later Bone made a big thing of running to his bike and setting off like the devil himself was on his trail. The cop car peeled rubber as it turned in the street to follow him. In less than fifteen minutes another car took up station in the street.

"Looks like they're serious," said Bandit Queen.

"It's early yet," replied Roaddog, "let us get a bit more done on this car, then Slowball will take you out for a beer."

He'd only been back under the car a few minutes when a red escort pulled into the yard. Jackie and Jane got out and walked into the garage.

"You ok, lover?" said Jackie, as Roaddog slid out from under the car.

"I'm fine, but busy," he said softly as she kissed him. As soon as she stepped back, Jane came in for a kiss.

"You smell funny," she whispered as she broke away.

"It's called work."

"My work stinks of beer not sweat and oil," she smiled up at him. "Do you know there's a cop car parked outside?"

"Yes, Slowball's going to take Bandit Queen for a beer, they'll follow them for a while."

"I've a better idea," grinned Jane.

"I'm all ears."

"How about me and Jackie take Bandit Queen shopping, we can get those cops out of their car and walking around for an hour or two."

"Hey Bandit Queen, you wanna take some cops for a walk?"

"Where?"

"Jane suggests you go shopping with her, and make the bastards walk for a bit."

"What sort of shopping?"

"I was thinking we could go to Debenhams in Preston, we could go dress shopping."

"Do I look like a woman that wears dresses?" snarled Bandit Queen.

"Every woman wears a dress for a wedding or a funeral," laughed Jane.

"That sounds like real fun," said Jackie.

"Dog, I could hate you," said Bandit Queen, "conditions are, I'm buying nothing, other than beer and food. OK?"

"Great," said Jackie, "we can stop by one of those fancy pubs for lunch on the way back. I know just the one, it's far too snobby for its own britches." She smiled as she took Bandit Queen by the hand and walked her towards Jane's car. Bandit Queen looked back at Roaddog, her face a mixture of hatred and resignation.

Roaddog chuckled quietly to himself as he returned to the job on the VW, it was about midday when his phone bleeped in his pocket. He pulled it out and punched in his access code, Slowball watched as his friend's eyebrows raised slowly.

"What's up?" asked Slowball.

"Wolf is going to be a little late, but he's still coming."

"Shouldn't be a problem, especially if we can get shut of this thing before he gets here." Slowball slapped the side of the VW, none too gently.

"Might be a possible," replied Roaddog, "get your finger out and get that housing back on."

"Bitch," laughed Slowball, lining up the housing and catching the first bolt. The other bolts located and tightened in only a few moments, a single raised finger as a hand signal for his friend.

At one o'clock the office phone rang, Roaddog snatched it from its cradle, just before the answer machine took it.

"Yeah," he growled.

"Hi, is the Sharan ready yet?"

"Not yet, but it's only a few minutes away, quick final test, and it should be completed in about fifteen minutes."

"That's great, we'll be there in about half an hour. A seven fifty right?"

"No, as agreed a thousand, the damned parts are six hundred."

"We'll be there in half an hour."

The phone went dead.

"I got a bad feeling about these guys." said Roaddog.

"Think they may be trouble?" said Slowball. "Should we call in some guys?"

"Nah, we'll handle them." Roaddog grinned and put on his leather and cut, checking the placement of his stilettos. In short minutes the

Sharan was finished, Roaddog rolled it off the ramp then put another car on the ramp. This car he raised to the limit of the four-post lift. Then he drove the Sharan back under the ramp.

"You get on the buttons as soon as that pickup shows," smiled Roaddog, turning the key that overrode the safety interlocks.

They didn't have long to wait until the white bodied pickup pulled into the yard. this time the front seat was full. Three large men got out, two of them carrying baseball bats.

"If you think I'm paying a grand for a fucking clutch you're crazy." Snarled the one in the centre. "Give us the fucking keys now."

"No," snapped Roaddog, he fingers clicked and the lift dropped a couple of inches, Slowball smiled.

"You'll pay for the work that we have done on your damned car, or we will crush it right here right now." Another snap of the fingers and another drop of the ramp.

"No fucking way," said the man, "I'm gonna break every bone in your body." The visitors had missed the latest arrival. A motorcycle had rolled into the yard with a dead engine, the rider walked up behind the man in the middle. The man froze when he heard the click of the hammer locking back, and felt the muzzle of the gun against his neck.

"Hey Roaddog," called Wolf, "you got a problem here?"

"Not so much I think," he turned to the batsmen, "put those bats down and sit on the floor with your hands under your asses, or Wolf here will spread your friend's brains, such as they are, all over everywhere." The two looked to the leader, and then did as they were told.

"Now you owe us a thousand pounds, if you've come even a quid short, then were gonna take both fucking cars and you bastards can walk home. Do you understand?"

The man nodded slowly, then moved one hand towards his jacket.

"Be very careful what you take out of that jacket, Wolf here can be quite jumpy."

Slowly the hand came back into view, this time carrying an envelope.

"The money is all there."

Roaddog took the envelope and made a point of counting the cash slowly. It was indeed all there. He poked one of the seated men with a boot.

"You," he snarled. "get in your pickup and drive it up onto the street outside." Roaddog pulled a knife from his jeans and flipped the blade into place. "If you make one unfriendly move with that truck, Wolf is going to kill your boss, and I'm gonna take your friends head, are these terms acceptable."

"Do what he says," groaned the boss. The man rolled slowly to his feet fired up the van and drove it out of the yard.

"Now you," said Roaddog, to the other seated man. "Take your fucking VW and get out onto the road, the keys are in. Same conditions, one wrong move and your boss loses his head." This time the thug didn't even glance at the boss, just did exactly as he was told.

Once the MPV was parked out on the street Roaddog turned to the boss.

"You've paid the agreed price for the work we have done on your car. No one has been hurt. If we see you or yours again the outcome will not be so polite. Do you understand?"

"I do," whispered the man.

"That's good," said Roaddog, "now that we have an understanding you walk slowly to whichever of the vehicles you want to go home in and do just that. Rest assured taking your cars to the main dealers will be cheaper for you in future."

"I understand." snarled the man, walking towards the road.

"Hey Wolf," said Roaddog as the man walked to the passenger door of the pickup. "Where'd you get a revolver?"

"It's a fake, or an imitation, or a model, depending on who you're talking to," laughed Wolf.

"You're fucking shitting me," shouted Slowball.

"What's up?" asked Wolf.

"I thought you had a gun to the bastards head, and it was a toy."

"Not a toy," laughed Wolf, "an imitation."

"Fuck," muttered Slowball going to the bar and snatching up a bottle of JD. He took a large swig straight from the bottle and then passed it to Wolf, who did the same.

"Now that we've sorted out your local issues," said Wolf, "how's about some international trading?"

"Fucking Manchester is another country now?" asked Roaddog.

"No, but the damned product is."

"Agreed, cash we don't have but bank transfer we can do, though bitcoin would be better."

"What the fuck is bitcoin?" asked Wolf.

"Cryptocurrency doesn't exist physically, but is currently worth about eighteen hundred pounds each. We're dealing a lot on the dark web, and we have bitcoin to spare, we can change it to sterling, or transfer as bitcoin, which would sir prefer?"

"I'd prefer folding."

"Folding is traceable, folding has serial numbers. Bitcoin is not."

"I've got ten thousand's worth in my saddle bags, and you want to pay for it in some micky mouse money?"

"It ain't micky mouse, I promise."

"I'll have to check with the boss."

"Go ahead," Roaddog smiled.

Wolf glared at Roaddog, then walked out into the yard pressing his phone to his ear. Wolf returned a few minutes later.

"Bank transfer will do, but the boss ain't happy. This is usually a cash business."

"How many times have you seen in the news stories of a network busted and suitcases full of cash recovered, cash doing fuck all but sitting in a tin box under the mattress? Our cash is working for us, I'm actually making more money with the bitcoin than with anything else at the moment." Roaddog laughed.

"I see what you mean," said Wolf, thinking about the stash that was currently hiding in his garage, in the pit, covered by a two inch thick steel plate.

"I'll make the transfers as two fives," said Roaddog.

"Why?" asked Wolf.

"Banks start to pay attention at the ten K mark, they have to report it to the tax assholes."

"We don't want that now do we," smiled Wolf, passing the bank details over to Roaddog, who got busy with his phone making transfers from bitcoin to sterling and on to the required bank account. In only a few minutes everything was completed.

"OK for you?" asked Roaddog.

"Fine," replied Wolf getting a package from his saddlebags. Roaddog passed it to Slowball who took it into the back room, where he washed it and bagged it. When he returned to the seating area the other two were already sitting and drinking beers.

"Hey Slowball, we got any spooks left?"

"Yes I think we've got a couple why?"

"Register one to us for the ten we just spent and sell it on for fifteen, puts fifteen from the bitcoin accounts into the general funds."

"I'll do that." Slowball went into the office to make the necessary changes.

"Ok, I'll bite," said Wolf. "What the fuck is a spook?"

"Well, bitcoin is a currency that doesn't exist."

"I get that."

"Spooks are expensive motorcycles that only exist in the computer, you've just sold us one for ten and we'll sell it on for fifteen tomorrow, tax man is none the wiser and we've got fifteen K in our bank that is completely legit."

"Don't the DVLA have something to say about this?"

"They're all too busy trusting what their computers tell them that they actually have no idea what is going on in the real world."

"We need to get in on that action, how do we do that?"

"You need access to their rinky-dinky systems."

"You have that?"

"We do, but we use it sparingly, don't get greedy and attract attention, someone somewhere in Wales may actually be awake."

"Nah, they're too busy chasing sheep," laughed Wolf. "Can we buy into this?"

"I'd rather not increase the traffic through this thing, I can put your guys in touch with our network wizards, see if they can help you, is that OK?"

"That'll have to do I suppose, does it really work?"

"Yes, we've been using spooks to cover cash exchanges for a couple of years, but no more than a couple a month, and nothing really major."

"I call fifteen thousand major," said Wolf.

The three men were still sitting and drinking beer two hours later when the three women returned in Jane's car. The plain clothes police car parked just outside the gate, Bandit Queen waved to them as the three went to the bar to get themselves beers.

"Did you have fun?" asked Roaddog.

"We had a great time," laughed Bandit Queen, "we dragged them all over the shopping centre, and then onto the pub for a burger, they must have been starving sitting outside."

"And thirsty," smiled Jane, sipping her beer.

"Bone should be on his way back from Wales by now." grinned Roaddog.

"I wonder how his followers are doing?" asked Bandit Queen.

"I dare say we'll find out later." Roaddog's smile turned to a frown as another car rolled into the yard. Bandit Queen turned, and muttered "Fuck."

35: Tuesday more meetings with the cops.

Hopkins got out of his car and walked towards the group in the workshop, his side kick wasn't the normal one, this one was a spaniel.

"If it isn't DI Hopkins," growled Bandit Queen, "what can we help you with today?"

"Nothing much," smiled the cop, "I see you've been having a little fun today."

"I went shopping," said Bandit Queen.

"And your man?"

"He's off on some trek somewhere, I didn't feel like that many hours in that damned seat, makes my ass numb."

"I don't believe that the idea was entirely yours," said Hopkins turning to Roaddog.

"Are your people having fun?" asked Roaddog.

"Unlike some of my colleagues I knew as soon as Bone turned onto the M56 where he was going. And that it was all a wild goose chase. Then Bandit Queen going dress shopping," he turned to her, "anyone who actually knows you would never fall for that, I am sorry, but it's true."

"It only goes to show just how bright the local plod are," laughed Bandit Queen.

"Was that your idea?" asked Hopkins, as he casually dropped the lead on the dog. "Be good Sparky," he said, the dog wandered over to meet the people, each got a quick greeting.

"No that was Jane's," said Bandit Queen, "I would have just gone for a beer and a burger, but she thought it would be fun to take them for a walk."

"They got a walk all right, and then they got to sit outside a damned gastro-pub while you had a meal."

"We had burgers and chips and got a window seat so they could see us from the carpark," smiled Bandit Queen. Sparky sat in front of Roaddog and barked.

"Is this damned dog house trained?" demanded Roaddog.

"That dog is trained like you won't believe, but he doesn't normally make that much noise." Hopkins glanced at the police car by the gate, realising just how far away they were.

"Looks like he's caught on to one of my worst habits," said Roaddog, his voice low and menacing. Roaddog's left hand fell casually on Wolf's right arm as he hitched forwards in his seat, his right hand went to his pocket and slowly came back into view, this time with a biscuit in it. He broke the biscuit in half and passed one half to the Sparky and bit into the other half himself.

"Boneo's," he said, "I've been trying to cut down but they're so full of marrowbone jelly." The crunching of the dog's teeth on the biscuit only lasted a few seconds, then it yapped again. So Roaddog tossed it a complete biscuit.

"Fuck." whispered Hopkins.

"You brought a drug sniffer dog here?" asked Roaddog,

"Not officially," laughed Hopkins.

"That took balls," said Bandit Queen.

"I knew that he'd find nothing, but I wanted to be sure. Who's the new guy?"

"This is Wolf, he's just passing through, he's from Manchester way." Roaddog knew that Wolf's plate would be run through the system in a heartbeat, so there was no point in hiding his identity.

"Long way from home Wolf?" asked Hopkins.

"Yes, trading a bike with our friends here."

"How are you getting home then?"

"I didn't sell my bike, it's one we've got still in Manchester."

"Seems that you trust each other quite a lot?"

"I did," snapped Wolf.

"Did?" asked Hopkins.

"Yes," snarled Wolf, "I sold it to him for ten grand and now I find out he's already sold it on for fifteen, bastard."

"Hey," said Roaddog, "you were happy with the ten, I made very sure of that before we made the transfers."

"I didn't know how much you were making on the deal then."

"I can't help it if I found a sucker to buy the damned thing," smiled Roaddog.

"And one to sell it," said Wolf.

"The used motor trade is a cut-throat business; we all know that."

"I didn't expect a brother to cut my throat."

"You were happy with the ten," smiled Roaddog.

"So, you guys trade bikes as well?" interrupted Hopkins.

"And what of it?" asked Roaddog.

"Would there be any dodgy vehicles around here?"

"Always the fucking cop?" asked Roaddog, "Run every plate you can see they are all legit," he snarled. "Except possibly for the two just arriving." He looked pointedly at two pick-up trucks that had pulled into the yard, each carrying more people than they had seats for. Eight men unloaded from the pick-ups, all armed to some degree, bats and chains in evidence, one with what looked like a shotgun.

"Ladies in the back," snapped Roaddog.

"Fuck that," said Bandit Queen, as the other girls retreated through the small door, "Blade me." One of Roaddog's stilettos flashed through the air towards her, the other appeared in his right hand. Slowball grabbed a bat from behind the sofa.

"You better call back up while you still got the chance, and get in the back with the girls," said Roaddog to Hopkins.

"They're rolling, less than a minute out," Hopkins smiled.

"Bastard," muttered Roaddog as the men approached.

"Give me my money back you bastards or we're going to fucking kill ya all," yelled the boss man from earlier, pointing his shotgun straight at Roaddog's head.

"Why all the bats?" shouted Roaddog, "Shotgun not enough?"

The boss pointed the shotgun to the sky and operated the slide, then pointed it back at Roaddog.

"You've been watching too many movies, you dickhead, gun's a phoney." Yelled Roaddog as the place was filled the shattering of blue lights and the howls of tortured tyres. Three brightly decorated cars pulled to a halt and uniformed cops, some with guns unloaded in a hurry.

When the boss saw the AR80 pointed as his head he dropped the shotgun like it had bitten him and held his hands up in the air, the others around him followed suit in only moments.

One of the armed police called out to Hopkins. "Their plates are bogus."

"Round 'em all up, attempted armed robbery at the very least, and whatever else you can get on them," shouted Hopkins.

"What about that lot?" asked an armed officer, indicating the bikers by pointing his gun, "I see knives and bats."

"Self defence, they were under attack. Get the rest of these assholes out of here."

"You sure boss?" asked the uniformed policeman.

"Yes I am." As the men were being cuffed Sparky came up to the leader and sat as his feet.

"Search that one." shouted Hopkins, "he's carrying drugs of some variety." He turned to Roaddog. "Get your people to stand down, we have things to talk about, once I've sorted these assholes out."

"Fucking right we do," said Roaddog, he gathered the rest into the bar area, and started popping the tops of bottles of beer.

Hopkins showed Sparky to the pick-up trucks and got indications from both. Three vans turned up with cages in the back, before the men were loaded in, they were presented to Sparky, he identified three more that smelled suspicious to the dog.

"What about that lot?" asked one of the armed police of Hopkins.

"I'll get statements and bring them in, you get that bunch on ice, I'll be along presently."

"They should be brought in for questioning."

"I'll call in my assistant, won't be an issue."

"They should be questioned at the station."

"Listen constable there are things going on that you don't know about."

"That's sergeant, sir."

Hopkins raised his eyebrows, the officer nodded and walked away. Hopkins had a short phone call with Lewis, then walked into the Dragonrider's workshop.

"What the fuck is it with you Hopkins?" said Roaddog angrily.

"Someone with a lot of clout has suggested that you are major players in the local drug dealing scene."

"So, you bring a sniffer dog here, again, and find my freaking boneo's."

"Yes, that's about it, I am fairly sure that any drugs don't come through here, Sparky would have found them." Sparky looked up at the mention of his name and went to Roaddog and yapped for another biscuit, that was of course instantly forthcoming.

"That's a bastard's trick," snarled Roaddog, "why shouldn't we just kill your lying ass and throw you in the river?"

"Because you love me, and Lewis is on way here. All those uni's know I'm here, and you're not that fucking stupid," Hopkins laughed.

"I could really get to hate you," growled Bandit Queen.

"Perhaps," Hopkins smiled, "but for now we will get along fine. Now to questions of the moment, what the fuck happened with those pikeys?"

"For god's sake, you're not even allowed to think that nowadays, let alone say it," said Roaddog.

"Well, I'm sure no one here is going to be upset by my language in this case."

"You're not wrong, after all they did just try to rob us with a gun."

"A question springs to mind," said Hopkins, looking at Roaddog. "How did you know that pump was a fake?"

"If you're serious about using a shotgun," Roaddog smiled, "you load the tube until it is full, then jack one into the chamber, and refill the tube. Dropping the hammer slowly is a scary moment. If a guy points a shotgun at you and threatens you with it, then sometime later actually loads it, it's most likely a fake. If he points the gun and pulls the hammer back, most likely he's serious."

"It really bugs me when I see that in a movie," agreed Hopkins, "until that cartridge is loaded into the chamber it's not a gun, it's a metal club," he paused for a moment before going on. "So, what happened?"

"We did some work on a car and they didn't want to pay for it, they were convinced that they should pay the agreed price, and they left, with the newly fixed car and no injuries, only I suppose the boss man's pride a little pained."

"So, you were lucky that I was here, and backup so close?"

"No, they were."

"They had a gun, and you were outnumbered."

"The gun is a fake and there were only eight of them"

"That's two to one against."

"Yes, but we had a Bandit Queen, and she's worth at least three of them."

"And you've got a Roaddog." smiled Hopkins.

"That also is true."

"Here's a thought," said Hopkins slowly, "how many corpses if the boys in blue hadn't turned up?"

"Now you're asking me to predict a future that didn't happen," laughed Roaddog.

"I feel that the tenses got more than a little scrambled in that statement."

"I don't think I'll worry about it," said Roaddog.

"Probably best not to dwell on it," said Hopkins, as everyone looked to a new car pulling into the yard. As the engine stilled Lewis climbed out, Sparky went over to meet him, after a moment the dog sat on the ground, looking at Lewis.

"Hey Lewis," called Roaddog, "you got dog biscuits in your pockets?"

"Why the hell would I have dog biscuits in my pocket?" He looked for a while at the smiling faces, and then at the dog sitting before him. He turned his gaze to Hopkins.

"You are having a laugh," he shouted. "have you any idea how many regulations you have broken to bring the damned dog here?"

"I don't think Hopkins has anything to worry about," laughed Roaddog, "the real question is, why does that dog believe that you are carrying drugs?"

"Been busting some asshole in Leigh, there was cocaine all over his flat, as a dealer he was very messy. That is of course irrelevant, what am I doing here? What's the damned emergency?"

"Simple," laughed Hopkins, "these poor people have just suffered a terrifying attack by some gypsies. We need to collect their statements, and maybe share a beer or two."

"You do know that the beer these people serve is going to be cheap bottled lager, not the stuff you usually drink."

"I'd dispute cheap," said Roaddog.

"You sure?" asked Slowball, "we are still drinking Alan's free beer."

"I suppose that is true." Roaddog turned to Lewis, "What does he usually drink?"

"You know, cask ales, hand pumped, whatever he can find really. There is a whole inspector Morse thing going on with him," laughed Lewis.

"He's even got the right sidekick," said Bandit Queen.

"Please don't remind me of that," replied Lewis, "I've watched some of those old TV shows, and as Lewis there are times I would have slapped Morse." He turned to Hopkins, "Still might."

"All this isn't getting the job done," said Hopkins, "go get the gear and we'll get these statements sorted out in no time." In less than half an hour they had all the paperwork sorted out, though there wasn't much in the way of paper. Statements written and uploaded to the main data base. As Roaddog passed out some more bottles of cheap beer, Wolf's phone started to play that classic from Black Sabbath, the opening riff from Paranoid is unmistakable. Wolf walked into the open air to answer it.

"I'm still stuck in Preston."

"Making statements for the cops."

"Nothing to worry about, just an attempted armed robbery."

"I said nothing to worry about, I'll explain it all later." He returned to the group.

"They worry about me," he said.

"Well, mister Wolf," said Hopkins, "thanks for your help, but I don't think we need to detain you any longer."

"We just call him big bad," laughed Roaddog. "See ya later bro, give our best to the guys in Manchester."

"I will," said Wolf, "but I'm gonna warn them not to deal in bikes with you lot again."

"If you feel that way, then I cannot argue, but if you've got something to sell give us a nod and we'll help you shift it."

"How come you're so flush with buyers round here?" asked Wolf.

"Local aerospace industries are doing well, and there's quite a bit of disposable income waiting for the latest toys."

"I'll keep that in mind, we might just set up a railroad for bikes, especially if you're going to get so much better prices than we can." Wolf reached out a hand to shake with Roaddog, then waved to the others and left to the beat of a heavy Harley motor.

"Hey Lewis," said Hopkins, "I think we need new jobs; these guys appear to be doing fine, but they've only worked on one car today."

"It does seem a little quiet round here," said Lewis.

"I have no idea what you gentlemen are insinuating," said Roaddog, "but we took five hundred from the gypsies, and five thousand from that bike deal with Wolf, I think we deserve a rest after all that hard graft."

"It does look more than a little like graft," smiled Hopkins.

"You know," replied Roaddog, "sometimes we can go for days without getting a single job in, so we gotta make gravy while the sun shines."

"The saying is hay," grinned Hopkins.

"You make what the hell you want in the sun, we want gravy," laughed Roaddog,

"Fine," said Hopkins, finishing his bottle of beer. "I think we better get back to the station and see what else we can pin on those diddycoys."

"Hopkins," snarled Lewis, loudly.

"Fine, we shall go and interview the, as yet innocent gentlemen of no fixed abode and see if they can be accused of any other criminal actives. That will make the local magistrate really happy as his park land is currently inundated with their houses on wheels. Happy now?" he raised his eyebrows at Lewis.

"Not really, the words fit the currently accepted norms, but we all know the thoughts behind them."

"As yet my thoughts can be policed by no one but me," smiled Hopkins.

"Don't bank on that lasting too much longer," laughed Roaddog.

Hopkins waved as he loaded Sparky into the back seat of his car, then the two policemen left.

"Well, that was interesting," said Bandit Queen softly.

"It was indeed," replied Roaddog, "that bastard copper is just too bright for his own good."

"He's definitely got balls that clank," her smile was extremely broad.

"Yes, I could almost get to like him."

"Me too." The two shared a look then returned to the workshop.

"How the fuck did that damned dog not find the drugs that Wolf brought?" asked Slowball.

"I told him how to wrap them, we'll find out when Bug gets here to start work on it later."

"We'll need security for a few nights," said Bandit Queen.

"I know, just until the gypsies have moved on."

"Should we move the stuff elsewhere?" asked Slowball.

"Nah," replied Roaddog, "there's nowhere as tight as the underground. We'll need to get it repackaged and moved out as soon as we can though."

"Where to?" asked Bandit Queen.

"I've got a floor safe with some space in it," said Roaddog.

"I've got a heavy lockbox in my garage," suggested Slowball.

"That should do, as soon as Bug gets back from Wales he can start splitting the stuff down into saleable quantities, and we'll ferret them away, it will take all night as least."

"You and Slowball can be security for the night," said Bandit Queen, "Bone can bring in Lurch and Sharpshooter for tomorrow's work, maybe some of the others."

"Did all the cops leave?" asked Slowball.

"That is a damned fine question," muttered Bandit Queen, she twitched her head at Roaddog, and he walked slowly across the yard, up to the gate, in less than a minute he returned to the others.

"I can't see any cops loitering out there, but they could easily put a long lens on us from a few places," he said.

"I think we need to get this place looking busy for tonight at least," said Bandit Queen. "I'll ring a few and see if we can get some down for a bit of a post rally party."

"Good idea, I'll call a few guys I know and get them to come round."

"Get Billy to come down and bring his guitar, he was really quite good Sunday night."

"Looks like we're having a party." Laughed Roaddog, taking his phone from his jeans pocket and starting to make some calls.

It was just after four o'clock when Bone, Bug, and Sharpshooter rolled into the yard and parked up.

"What the fuck has been going on here?" demanded Bone as he walked towards the workshop.

"We've had a right old time," laughed Bandit Queen, hugging him firmly. She went on to tell him everything that had happened. After some laughter he spoke loudly.

"That bastard Hopkins is a little too sharp for my likings."

"He's that all right," said Roaddog.

"It also explains something."

"What?"

"We stopped for a break and a piss on the A fifty-five just outside Chester, the car that had been following us pulled up alongside and the passenger wound his window down, he called us smart arsed bastards."

"I'm betting Hopkins told them what was going on," laughed Roaddog.

"Do you think they may have a camera on us?"

"It's possible."

"Give 'em something to film then," laughed Bone. He walked into the middle of the yard, unzipped his fly and peed into the drain, once this display was finished, he returned to the workshop for a beer.

Gradually the yard filled up with bikes and the occasional car, the music got louder, and the party got into full swing, Roaddog was dancing slowly with both Jane and Jackie when Bug and Cherie appeared from the back room, they had been gone for a long time but hopefully anyone watching wouldn't have noticed that. Cherie pulled Roaddog away from the girls and took his place, pushing him towards Bug.

"Anything happening out here?" asked Bug.

"Not anymore, now that your chick has stolen both of mine," laughed Roaddog.

"You know what I mean."

"Nothing of any import, little traffic, no police. You?"

"It's all cut, packed and ready to be moved. There's eleven packages ready to be posted. I'll do those on my way home, OK?"

"Fine, just be careful, I'll make a run out with Slowball, stash the rest and get some pizza's on the way back here. I'll let Bone know, you get some rest, it's been a long day."

"No worries, I could do with a beer or two." Bug walked over to the bar where Man-Dare passed him an open bottle of beer. She nodded in the direction of the coffee jug on the back of the bar. Bug shook his head; he really didn't need any more stimulants just now.

After a short conversation with Bone and a longer phone call Roaddog climbed up onto Slowball's trike and left the yard. It was about half an hour later when the two returned with a stack of large pizzas, a bag of heavy donner kebabs and a Sylvia. The revellers fell on the food like they hadn't eaten in days.

The food had all been eaten, more beer had been drunk, the sun was almost disappearing below the buildings to the west, when a car pulled into the yard. Bandit Queen motioned for the others to stay where they were, she walked slow towards the car as it stopped, its engine remained running quietly, the soft haze of diesel smoke drifting from underneath. The driver looked uncertain as to what he should do, he looked around as if he was expecting something other than an approaching woman.

"Any of you guys know Jethro Tull songs?" she asked, looking in through the drivers open window. Puzzled looks were all she got.

"Car full of young boys looking for a fight, it's a line from Rocks on the Road," she continued, "seemed sort of appropriate. Is it a fight you're after?"

"Your guys turned my dad into the cops."

"Actually, your dad pointed a dummy shotgun at a certain Detective Inspector Hopkins, he was a little pissed. Then ARU turned up and carted everyone away, the vans have been impounded and at least three of the guys were carrying drugs, according to Hopkins little dog. We had nothing to do with their current problems. The big question is, do you want to make today even worse for your families?"

"What do you mean?" asked the driver.

"They were eight and armed, you are five and outnumbered. The mathematics of the situation are not too difficult."

"We could have guns," replied the driver, reaching into his jacket.

"If you had guns then your dad would not have come here with an imitation," she looked at each of the teenage boys in the car, "the choice is yours, bad day or worse day?" The young man looked around for a few moments then turned back to Bandit Queen.

"Did Pa really give up without a fight?"

"He had an AR-80 pointed at his head; he dropped that plastic pump action like it was a venomous snake." The driver looked at his friends, a quiet voice came from the back of the car.

"What sort of man gives up without a fight?"

"Shut up," snarled the driver then he turned back to Bandit Queen. "What the fuck where the cops doing here anyway?"

"That was something entirely different, and the bastard brought a sniffer dog."

"They were looking for drugs?"

"It appears so, but the only drugs the damned dog found were in your vans and on your people." Suddenly the young man's eyes opened wide, and he looked around scanning the rooftops, peering into the setting sun.

"Yes," said Bandit Queen, "the bastards could still be watching." She paused for a breath or two.

"Looks like, you're not going to fight this night, I suggest you prepare your vans, and as soon as your guys make bail, change your plates and head for Yorkshire."

"We'll head south," said the driver, he selected reverse and waited for Bandit Queen to step back before releasing his handbrake and slowly manoeuvring out of the yard. Bandit Queen watched them as they drove out into the road and were gone, there were some raised voices within the car, but she couldn't tell what they were saying. She walked slowly back towards the garage, smiling.

"For fucks sake," whispered Bone. Bandit Queen frowned at him then heard the tires on the tarmac behind her.

"Hopkins?" she asked softly. Bone nodded. She shrugged and heard two car doors slam. She released the buckle on her belt, unbuttoned her jeans and lowered the zipper. She pushed her jeans down off her hips.

"There you go bastard," she shouted, "you fancy my ass so much ya can kiss the damned thing then fuck off and leave us the hell alone." Hopkins walked up and stood alongside Bandit Queen; he threw his arm around her shoulders.

"Tempting as you offer is my dear, I think I'll pass, I'm an old man, and the shock may be too much for my heart, it will have to remain a dream that can never come true. I'd like to introduce my governor; this is DCI Hunt." Bandit Queen looked over her shoulder at a new face. The man was obviously in his late forties, greying hair, wide jaw, and cold grey eyes that bored into her own.

"I've heard of you," she said.

"I'm not surprised, Hunt is a difficult name for a policeman to live with, I'm known as Hunt the cunt amongst the criminals hereabouts," he paused for an instant, "and within the ranks of my own force." He smiled at Bandit Queen. "You can put that away, it may be Hopkins unfulfilled dream, but it is not mine." Bandit Queen pulled up her jeans and refastened her belt.

"So why the fuck are you here?" she demanded.

"I was hoping for kebab and beer," said Hopkins.

"Shut up," snapped Hunt. Bug brought two opened bottles from the bar, handed one to Hopkins, and the other to Hunt. "Sorry the foods all gone." Hunt watched as Hopkins took a sip from his bottle of beer, he shook his head.

"You are impossible," he whispered, taking the bottle from Bug and nodding his thanks. "If you weren't so fucking good, I'd have cashiered your ass years ago." he snarled at Hopkins. He turned to Bandit Queen.

"I'm here, because someone has been misappropriating police equipment, and misusing said equipment, even though he captured some major dealers, and some assets, the misuse was targeted against yourselves. I'm here to ask if you wish to press charges against this man?"

Bandit Queen turned to Hopkins.

"Equipment?" she asked. Hopkins nodded and replied.

"Sparky."

"Sparky," laughed Bandit Queen. All the others joined in with the laughter.

"Yes," grumbled Hunt, "a damned sniffer dog, which he brought here without permission, I'm not going to mention the ARU's on standby, nor the damned goose chase into Wales."

"Twice," said Roaddog.

"What do you mean twice?" asked Hunt.

"He said he'd brought a dog by here when we were closed, just for a look see."

"Fuck," muttered Hunt glaring at Hopkins. He turned back to Bandit Queen.

"And it seems that the apprehension of the unicorn was more your work than his, but I'm not supposed to ask about it."

"We heard it on the grapevine," said Bandit Queen. Hopkins smiled.

"He says that you would have killed said unicorn?" asked Hunt.

"I'd have hung him up by his bollocks," snarled Bandit Queen, "and he'd have begged to die."

"But you couldn't even find out which jail he was in."

"Correct," snapped Bandit Queen.

"So," said Hunt, "do you want to press charges of harassment against DI Hopkins?"

"No," said Bone loudly. "we won't."

"Why the fuck not?" demanded Hunt.

"Bastard has been straight with us."

"That makes no sense to me."

"We're straight-talking people," said Bone, "we don't like cops, but we do see them as a necessary evil in this batshit crazy world."

"I thought I had a real chance of getting rid of him with you lot. I've no idea what sort of criminal activity you are involved with, but I'm fairly sure there's something."

"If there is," interrupted Hopkins, "you'll never find it, but I might."

"See Bone, he's going to keep on digging. Press charges of harassment and I'll have him working in records, in the bowels of headquarters until he retires."

"No, he'll catch more random murderers and perverts than anyone else in your whole damned force, he makes you look bad that's why you want him out."

"No, it's just that he's a right royal pain in the ass."

"He's that alright, but he's good at his job."

"Bone," said Bug, "you can't do this, you have to shoot the fucker down."

"No. He knew about the devils bridge run when it was still morning, none of the other bastards had clue one. Without bright cops like him more murderers and rapists and perverts will get away with it, we can't help those cunts."

"You forgot the drug dealers," said Hunt.

"Actually, we didn't," laughed Bone, "where did today's drugs come from?"

"That information is not being made public as yet," said Hunt.

"Hyde," said Roaddog, "most likely it's coming out of Hyde."

"How the hell did they know that?" demanded Hunt staring at Hopkins, "Did you tell them?"

"No," sighed Hopkins, "but you just did. How the hell did you get to be DCI?"

"We know how you didn't get to be DCI," laughed Roaddog.

"I know," shrugged Hopkins, "too much desk time and not enough out on the mean streets of Chorley," he laughed.

"What about Lewis?" asked Roaddog.

"He'll make DCI easy, he'd have made that mistake last year, but not now. He might even make Chief Constable. He's got what it takes."

"So long as his association with you doesn't kill his career."

"Don't worry I'll not let that happen."

"There you go Hunt," said Bone, "that's why we need bastards like him."

"I don't get it," said Hunt, "I just don't get it."

"You never will," said Roaddog.

"Is there anything else we can help you with?" asked Bandit Queen.

DCI Hunt looked at Hopkins with raised eyebrows. Hopkins shook his head.

"No," said Hunt. "Come on Hopkins, looks like I don't get to fire you today."

"I think I'll stay," said Hopkins, "if that's alright with you Roaddog?"

"Fine by me," said Roaddog.

"For god's sake why?" asked Hunt.

"Because it's likely to be a long night, and these people may need a fair witness come sunrise," said Hopkins.

"Just because they've saved your career, doesn't mean they get any favours." Snapped Hunt.

"Dog," sighed Hopkins, "you tell him."

"Detective Chief Inspector Hunt, we already understand that there will be no favours from Hopkins, to get favours we need to go to a more political animal entirely, someone like yourself will trade favours for that Deputy Chief Constable, or maybe the soul of your firstborn for Chief Constable. Hopkins is more of a Dixon of Dock Green sort of guy."

"I don't understand, I'd not do any sort of favour for a promotion." Hunt turned to Hopkins. "What about your car?"

"Leave it in the compound at Hutton, leave the keys on the front seat,

I'll pick it up in the morning."

"I can't do that, what if it gets stolen?"

"It's in a secure compound at police headquarters, who's going to steal it?"

"Anyone could."

"Your confidence in your fellow officers is astounding."

"Don't even think about booking this as overtime," snarled Hunt.

"I clocked out an hour ago, what about you?"

"Beside the point," replied Hunt, "I'll see you tomorrow, we still have to find out where these damned drugs are coming from."

"Tomorrow bright and early," said Hopkins tossing his keys to Hunt. Everyone watched as Hunt drove out of the gate.

"God, I hate that cunt," said Hopkins.

36: Still Tuesday, evening and party time.

Hopkins sat chatting with the bikers for a while, then more started to arrive, first was a car with Billy and Man-Dare, the two strolled hand in hand to the club house.

"What's wrong with the bike?" demanded Roaddog.

"Nothing, just a little short on luggage space," replied Billy, lifting the hard cased guitar in his left hand. He took a stool by the bar and tuned his guitar, the martin sounded fat and smooth, with rich overtones and a deep resonance that could only come from a quality instrument. Billy smiled at Man-Dare and started to strum a simple blues pattern, she grinned briefly then joined in, to sing almost diffidently a song from a movie. Her voice was nowhere near as full and forceful as Aretha Franklin, but "Think" came across quite clearly for those that knew it. Before the song was finished Alan arrived on his Dragonfly. Gradually more and more members of the club turned up to fill the ranks. Hopkins looked concerned and dragged Roaddog off to one side.

"What is going on?" he asked.

"What do you mean?"

"It's Tuesday after a rally, everyone should be broke and recovering, this place should be like a morgue."

"It's been an exciting day, perhaps people want to be involved the stimulating happenings."

"Balls. You're up to something."

"Fine, called the guys in for a show, the more traffic we have, the less likely the pikies are to respond to their people being captured by the damned cops." Roaddog smiled broadly.

"And the less likely our long lenses are to spot your nefarious activities."

"You still think we are up to something?"

"Some do."

"Your dog found nothing; you have nothing but still you doubt us?"

"Yes and no."

"What do you mean?"

"There has to be something going on here, but I have no idea what."

"We offer specialist garage services, and these are expensive."

"You find people to pay your prices?"

"Today we had pikies paying, so yes."

"But they had no intention of actually paying, did they?"

"Probably not, but they paid up in the end, then lost more to your colleagues."

"I think they'll be back tonight."

"There will be some people here if that happens."

"And I'll be one of them."

"Much depends on when they get out of your cells."

"According to my latest reports they've got some high-powered lawyers, they'll be out before it gets dark."

"That's not far off now," said Roaddog checking the sky.

"Could be very soon," agreed Hopkins.

"If they do turn up, I want you in the back room with the girls."

"I'll hide with the girls so long as Bandit Queen is there."

"You know that's not happening."

Hopkins's phone chirped in his pocket, he took it out and glanced quickly at the message.

"They're out on police bail, conditions are they don't come here, and they don't leave the area."

"I'm certain they'll abide by those conditions," sneered Roaddog. "Bone." he shouted, "Pikies are out and could be on their way here."

"Time for a couple more beers then," called Bone. The men started to move to the outside picnic tables and the women closer to the narrow door to the back room. Roaddog turned an earnest gaze to Hopkins.

"You and Billy hold that door to the back room, if it gets really bad call back up, otherwise you stay the fuck out of it, do you understand?"

"I got it Dog." Hopkins smiled.

"Fuck I hate having cops this close, you be cool man OK?"

"Coolest. They could of course simply fuck off."

"Not likely, and you know it."

"True, let's have another beer." Hopkins led the way inside and took up station near the door.

Tensions climbed rapidly over the next fifteen minutes, Roaddog checked his stilettos every few seconds, even taking a diamond hone to the edges, just to ensure their sharpness. By the time another fifteen minutes had passed the bikers were beginning to think that nothing was going to happen. It was only when Hopkins attracted Roaddog that they knew something was going to happen.

"What's up?" asked Roaddog.

"My guys have lost them," said Hopkins, "they scattered, we can't watch them all."

"What about their camp?"

"Vans are prepared and ready to roll, some even hooked up to towing vehicles, but other than that we've no idea what is happening."

"Bone," shouted Roaddog across the compound, "cops have lost them, they could be on their way here now."

"Everyone get hot," called Bone, even as he said it three white transit vans rolled slowly to a stop across the entrance. One of them showed dark outlines and brilliant white paint, as if decals had recently been removed to show the pristine surface beneath.

One door opened and a single person climbed down, he stepped away from the van, slowly pulled his shirt from his pants, showing his bare midriff he turned slowly, so that everyone could see that he had no weapons concealed in his waistband. With arms spread wide he walked slowly down into the front yard. As he got closer Roaddog recognised him as the boss they had dealt with earlier in the day.

"I wanna talk," the man called as he stopped still some distance from the assembled bikers.

Bone snapped his fingers and Roaddog glanced at him, as nod was all it took, the two walked slowly towards the gypsy leader, hands open and empty.

"Speak," said Bone.

"I'm Jonas," said the leader.

"Speak Jonas," said Bone.

"This is hard for me," Jonas spoke slowly, "I underestimated you people, and that doesn't happen often."

"I can agree with that," replied Bone.

"Your back up was damned impressive."

"Nothing to do with us, damned cops," smiled Bone.

"And you still got one here?"

"Yes, they're more difficult than dog shit to get off the boots."

"Agreed," laughed Jonas, "I'd like to consider the business between us concluded, is that acceptable to yourselves."

"We can agree that everything is finished."

"I only have one outstanding issue," said Jonas.

"Explain," snapped Bone.

"My son and his friends came here this afternoon, they came looking for a fight, and were convinced to leave without getting out of the car, my son feels that he has lost face before his friends, this makes him unhappy."

"He was a little distressed that you surrendered without a fight as well."

"He's young I'm hoping he will learn."

"What do you want from us?" asked Bone.

"My son would like you to name your champion who he will face in single unarmed combat. Thereby he can regain some respect amongst his friends."

"He's going to lose," said Bone.

"Even in losing he can gain face, if he puts up a good show."

"I'm sure we can do this for a young man," said Bone. "Any champion?"

"Anyone at all," said Jonas looking directly at Lurch.

"Fine," said Bone, "bring out your fighter."

Jonas waved an arm in the air and the rear doors of all three vans opened, from the centre one came the young man in question, already stripped to the waist, and ready for battle. Roaddog watched as people unloaded from the vans, lots of people.

"It's all right if the family and friends watch his humiliating defeat?" asked Jonas.

"Not too close, you understand," replied Bone. Jonas nodded and indicated a line halfway down the entrance ramp. The spectators stopped exactly where he indicated.

"We have to decide who our champion is going to be," said Bone.

"We'll wait here." said Jonas.

"We'll be as quick as we can," said Bone turning away. Roaddog smiled and followed Bone. They walked towards the clubhouse.

"What do you think about Lurch?" asked Bone.

"That'll be over in a heartbeat."

"You want him?"

"No worries, he's got some muscle, but he's too light to bother me too much."

"We're looking for a champion to take on the kid, anyone interested?" asked Bone of the whole group.

"Too easy for me," growled Lurch.

"Too short for me," laughed Slowball.

"I'll take him," grinned Sharpshooter.

"I've a better idea," smiled Bandit Queen.

"No," said Bone.

"Yes," said Bandit Queen, "he's mine," she snarled and challenged everyone with a look. None of the men even thought to contradict her. So, it was decided.

The three walked slowly out to where Jonas and his son were waiting.

"So, who's your champion to be?" asked Jonas.

"She's here," said Bone as Bandit Queen peeled off her leather jacket, her short gloves, and her necklace, she kissed the large turquoise stone before she passed it to Roaddog.

"He can't fight a woman," said Jonas.

"She convinced him to stay in the car simply to save his life, now she wants the chance to prove herself against him, how can this be a problem?" said Bone.

"But she's a girl," muttered Jonas.

"This is the twenty-first century," said Bandit Queen, "if I lose, he'll have a great victory under his belt."

"Or he'll be branded as a beater of women," said Jonas.

"This will be a fair fight," said Bandit Queen, "but I'm not taking my shirt off, he'll be too easy a target while he's watching the girls bounce." She held her breasts in her hands briefly to emphasise the point.

"I don't fight girls," said the young man.

"I ain't a girl," laughed Bandit Queen, "I'm the sort of bitch that'll cut off your balls as soon as laugh at you."

"Son," said Jonas leaning in close, so that no one else could here, "She's not a girl, she's a guy with an amazing set of pecs. Take her breath, put her down, and everyone walks away alive. Got it?" The son looked into the father's eyes and nodded. By this time it was obvious to the gypsy crowd that the youngster was going to be fighting a woman, they were unhappy about this and making their feelings known. Jonas thought for a moment, before speaking to his followers.

"It is unusual, but by no means unheard of for our women to fight alongside their menfolk, they fight with the spirit of a lioness defending her cubs, it is their choice so to do, and we have no right to gainsay that choice. I suddenly find myself in need of a little exercise, anyone willing to step up?"

"Damn," said Bandit Queen, "I like your style." she turned to the young man. "Come on kid, let's get this done." With one last look to his father the young man stepped away into some clear space. Bone looked to Lurch, then to Hopkins, Lurch understood immediately, and walked up to the policeman, grabbed his wrists and picked him up in one hand, a quick search of his pockets liberated a phone and a two-way radio. Lurch released Hopkins and smiled. Before walking back towards the front of the biker crowd. The electronic devices in his pockets.

"Can we clarify the rules for this confrontation?" asked Bone loudly.

"It's a bare-knuckle fist fight, what rules?" asked Jonas, while the son was looking to his father Bandit Queen struck, a front kick straight to the balls, the son turned a thigh inside just in time to take the weight out of the hit.

"Damn it John," shouted Jonas, "get with it before she kills ya."

"Hey John." said Bandit Queen, raising her hands in front of her face, "nice to have a name for the gravestone."

"Loser pays for the gravestone bitch," replied John, just before a right from Bandit Queen blew the air completely from his lungs and had him retreating. She followed him casting blows randomly at body and head, none with any intention to actually strike with any force, until a left hit him in the belly and blew his air out again. John countered with a left, right, left combination to Bandit Queens not inconsiderable belly, however, inches of fat over a large barrier of muscle meant that this had little effect, her open handed slap to his face almost felled him, and left him staggering a little to his right. He jabbed with the left and then drove in hard with a low right, this one making enough penetration to push the woman backwards and stop her attacks for a moment. She breathed briefly then bounced forwards again, this time she walked straight into a hard right to the breast, again she was pushed backwards.

"Fuck," said Bone, he so wanted to step in, but knew that he couldn't.

Bandit Queen shook her head and went back into the attack, a fast series of body blows were exchanged which culminated in a right cross that took Bandit Queen in the jaw, her lip split and she spat blood across John's chest, she stepped back and looked him in the eye.

"Oh god," whispered Bone, "she's gonna fucking kill him for that."

"You hit like a girl," snarled Bandit Queen loudly. John was enraged by this and attacked hard with low left and right, then followed in with the right cross, Bandit Queen turned inside this and pulled the arm through, yanking John off his feet, she fell on top of him, only the part that hit him was her fist, her whole falling weight behind it. More than a hundred pounds per square inch landed on the lower three ribs on his left side, the unmistakable sound of breaking twigs was heard by everyone. Bandit Queen knelt beside him and readied the final blow.

"Yield." she whispered. John heard nothing, only the roaring of the pain filled his mind. Jonas knew.

"Lady," he shouted, "please don't kill my son."

"Call me lady and he dies," she yelled.

"Bandit Queen you bitch let my son live," cried Jonas. She paused.

"Bandit Queen," shouted Jonas, "Kill me, send your giant against me," he pointed at Lurch, "Send your cold eyed leader against me," Bone this time, "Or your psycho," Roaddog gets the moving finger, "or all three, but let my son live."

"I've never had a son," growled Bandit Queen.

"Please don't take mine." begged Jonas, he could feel his relatives getting more and more restless, as could Bone.

"Bandit Queen my love," he said, "let the boy live." She looked down into the boy's eyes.

"Is your need for respect satisfied?" John nodded slowly. Her fist relaxed, the arm un-cocked, and she stood slowly. She waved Jonas in, and walked to Bone. He hugged her and kissed her, despite the blood all over her face. Behind her Jonas supervised the careful movement of his son into the back of one of the vans. As the rest of the visitors returned to the vans Jonas walk slowly up to Bone and Bandit Queen.

"You are indeed a fierce fighter," he said, interrupting their embrace.

"And your point is?" asked Bone.

"Had I known that this morning I would not have made the mistake that I did. I apologise for the way I underestimated you all, I thought you were trying to rip us off because you knew who we were."

"I quoted a fair price on the phone, without even meeting you," said Roaddog.

"But you knew who we were when we dropped the car off."

"Only because of your dodgy plates, did I jack up the price?"

"No, you did not."

"How did our price compare to others?"

"You were half the price of a main dealer, and about the same as the other independents I asked."

"So why come to us?"

"Now I have a confession to make, this will not sound good. I had planned to rip you off, much kudos to be gained from robbing a gang of hells angels."

"That particular stupidity almost cost your son's life," said Bone.

"I am fully aware of that," said Jonas looking down.

"Only your willingness to die for him kept him alive," said Bandit Queen.

"I am grateful dear lady," smiled Jonas.

"Call me lady again and it's not too late to kill someone today," she snarled.

"Perhaps," said Jonas, "but the moment is passed and the emotions are not running so high right now."

"I don't know about that," said Roaddog, "I'm not at all happy about psycho."

"Spur of the moment thing," said Jonas, "but that is how you portray yourself. You were to one betting every one of your friends lives on your belief that my shotgun was an imitation."

"True, I suppose," replied Roaddog.

"It is time I left," said Jonas, "the family are getting restless. Before I go," he reached into his pocket and slowly pulled out a phone, he passed it to Roaddog, "There is one number on that phone, if you find yourself in need please call. We will help you in any way that we can, you have proved to be far more honourable than I would ever have believed." He held his hand out to Bone, and then Roaddog, finally he turned to Bandit Queen, he opened his arms and stepped up close, he hugged her and kissed both bloody cheeks.

"You are now as a sister to our clan, and I thank you for sparing your brother's life." He turned on his heel and strode confidently towards the waiting vans.

As Jonas walked away Hopkins walked up behind Roaddog.

"I don't suppose I can get a look at that phone?" asked Hopkins.

"Not a fucking chance man," laughed Roaddog, stuffing the phone into his jeans pocket.

"Well that was something different than what I expected," said Hopkins.

"Yeah," said Bone, then he turned to Bandit Queen, "You OK love?" he asked.

"Getting a bit pissed at this lip getting busted, but I'll live." She smiled and turned to go into the back room to clean up.

"Am I mistaken," said Hopkins, "or are the Dragonriders now honorary gypsies?"

"God, I hope not," said Bone.

"I don't believe that your hopes are even a factor, they think that you are, and that's all that matters to them," laughed Hopkins.

37: Wednesday Hopkins is a pain.

Slowball rolled into the yard, only Roaddog was there ahead of him, he strolled into the garage and called out.

"Hey Dog." He elicited a muffled response from the back office. The large monitor on the wall flashed into life and a map of the northwest flared into being, many blue trails lead across it.

"What's that?" he asked as Roaddog came out of the back.

"That's where that green civic has been in the last week, it's been all over locally, and three runs to Hyde, always the same place in Hyde, it's a truck depot of some variety."

"Maybe a processing plant?"

"Could be, seeing as their local one had a fire, they'll have to process it there and ship this way."

"Unless they have another site nearer."

"I don't think so, our delivery boy has been busier than pizza guy during the world cup. He's dropping to dealers."

"Could we hit the dealers, either as new supplier, or just steal their stuff?"

"We'd have to put a tail on him, and he's quite a nervous driver."

"What do you mean?"

"In the last week he's made at least three high speed runs, then returned in a few minutes once he was sure he was no longer being followed." Roaddog manipulated some controls and the display changed. "Reds are way over speed limit." There were three red stripes on the map, each lasted a short time, and then once the speed was back down to more legal levels he returned to the same area.

"He's paying close attention to the cars around him."

"Could we put a bike on him? After all Bug did OK."

"I'd not want to push that, even Bug can make mistakes, if he tried to keep up on one of those high speed runs, then delivery boy would know for sure that someone was following him."

"So what do you want to do with this information? Leak it to Hopkins?"

"I don't think so, file for now, we know where we need to go if we are in need of some supplies in a hurry."

"Not going to be an easy target to hit."

"We could get the Manchester guys to help out."

"Not really our style though is it? Way too serious, if you know what I mean."

"I agree," Roaddog laughed. "We're doing OK, we're shifting enough, and making enough money, I don't really want to join the big time."

"Let's stick to being small time crooks," grinned Slowball.

"Yeah, you've seen the newspaper reports, drug dealing cartel smashed by the drugs squad, hundred and fifty thousand pounds found in mattress. If ya can't spend it why bother?"

"So is bitcoin our modern-day mattress?" Slowball said, starting the coffee machine up.

"Perhaps," laughed Roaddog. "but the damned cops can't get at it as easily."

"Can they get at it at all?"

"I'm not sure, they could try to force the passwords out of us, now there's a thought."

"Go on."

"The usual tactic is to put up a fight and tell them nothing, then give in, and tell them something, victory for the pigs and they stop looking."

"It has been known to work, I'd not attempt it with that bastard Hopkins."

"Agreed, but a second layer of bitcoin accounts, with almost no transactions, just a few thousand of cash deals that HMRC never knew about. Then the cops stop looking for the big money from the other stuff."

"It might work, but we gotta get Hopkins out of the picture."

"That bastard is way too sharp, you thinking of dog food?" asked Roaddog, a large grin on his face.

"Someone would miss him, that Lewis is no slouch either."

"Could we set him up for a brothel raid?"

"DI Hopkins found hanging in a dungeon, dressed in latex with a dildo up his arse," laughed Slowball. Roaddog reached out and killed the large monitor, as a car pulled into the yard.

"What we got due?" asked Slowball.

"Not these bastards that's for sure."

"We can get a blue light and put you a nice desk in a corner if that's what you want," shouted Slowball without even looking round.

"I am sorry to bother you so early in the morning," said Hopkins as he walked towards the two.

"Yeah right," laughed Roaddog, "You want coffee?"

"Coffee would be nice," said Lewis, Slowball got up to make two more.

"We have cots in the back room," said Roaddog, "save you a lot of travelling."

"Can you believe that those damned pykies have scattered and we don't have a clue where they are?" growled Hopkins.

"I have heard that your lot can't find their asses with both hands and a map." replied Roaddog.

"True, but you have a contact number for them."

"I have a landline number that is most likely just some answering service, you'll get nowhere from that."

"Where's it at?"

"Area code is 0161, so Manchester, you really want to waste your time tracking that one down?"

"No, they'll just give us the fucking run around."

"What about three transit vans? I'm sure you got their plates."

"All stolen yesterday and recovered at the Ibis hotel Preston north."

"That's a hundred yards from the M55 M6 interchange," laughed Roaddog.

"Your local knowledge is impressive," grumbled Hopkins.

"He's taking this quite hard you know," said Lewis.

"It wasn't you the bastards pointed a shotgun at," snapped Hopkins.

"It wasn't real," said Roaddog.

"I didn't know that, and neither did you."

"I guessed it was a fake."

"Until the ARU turned up that was a pump action twelve bore pointed in my direction."

"It can't be the first time someone has pointed an imitation gun at you?" asked Roaddog.

"Seventeen years in the force and no one has ever pointed a gun at me before."

"Well, ain't you the lucky one," laughed Lewis. "Seventeen weeks and some asshole in Lewisham shot at me and my partner."

"Well, that's London for you, it's not like that around here."

"That very much depends on where you go," said Lewis. "Hyde is no holiday camp."

"What's wrong with Hyde?" asked Roaddog.

"Other than everything?" asked Lewis.

"That bad?"

"In places yeah, drug dealers and bikers fighting for territory, the place is a mess."

"I've not heard of anything from our groups," said Roaddog.

"Outlaws," said Lewis.

"They're all outlaws," said Hopkins.

"He's not actually that stupid, is he?" asked Roaddog.

"He does a good impression," laughed Lewis.

"Fine," snapped Hopkins, "Outlaws in Hyde and Hells angel's affiliates in central Manchester, but they're not currently squabbling with anyone, it's sort of peaceful."

"And absolutely nothing to do with us," said Roaddog.

"That's not what Hunt tells us."

"So, it's Hunt that thinks we're involved in the drug trade, is that correct?"

"I can't confirm that," said Hopkins slowly.

"Well, I fucking can," snapped Lewis.

"Why's he so against us?" asked Roaddog.

"It seems his brother got involved with a bike gang and ended up dead." said Lewis.

"We're not a gang, we're a club," smiled Roaddog.

"The gypsies didn't think you are a club."

"We will defend ourselves when someone threatens us," smiled Roaddog.

"You could just call the cops you know," said Hopkins, "That's what we are here for."

"Yes, your lot would be just too late, as normal. Turn up when the action is over and arrest the guys for bleeding without a licence."

"Hey, we weren't late when that guy pointing a shotgun at you."

"No, but you were here for something else at the time, again a tip off from Hunt."

"Actually Hunt was real pissed at me for that particular episode, as he made very clear at the time."

"I know, but if he is so sure about us, why was he so anti?"

"He wants the bust that takes you lot down to stick hard, he wants it by the book. We both know that by the book is not going to get you lot off the streets."

"You think we are guilty as well?" demanded Roaddog.

"If you are I've no idea how you are managing it, and that worries me," muttered Hopkins.

"Worried that you might just be barking up the wrong tree? Could your time be better spent chasing the real drug dealers?" laughed Roaddog.

"When Wolf was spotted coming this way, Hunt was sure he was making a delivery, so I got in real quick, and nothing. All it got me was a bollocking."

"So why not go after Wolf and the Manchester guys?"

"Tried that but Greater Manchester Constabulary told us to fuck off and mind our own business. They even threatened to bust me if I stepped inside the M60."

"Sounds like something is going on with them," observed Roaddog.

"You may be right there," said Lewis, "but we can't do fuck all, big city police forces can be a law unto themselves."

"You think they're involved?" asked Roaddog.

"Wouldn't surprise me," mumbled Lewis.

"What do you mean?" asked Hopkins.

"We've been warned off too many times. And warned hard."

"True, the deputy chief constable did suggest that I could wake up and find myself in the Strangeways hotel."

"They're definitely involved somewhere," snarled Lewis.

"Prove it without ending up dead," smiled Hopkins.

"All it takes is one straight copper," said Lewis.

"They got one, Chief Constable is straight as a die, but surrounded by assholes."

"How can they get away with it?" asked Roaddog.

"Simple," replied Lewis, "even if the CC finds real evidence, he can't do anything without tearing the whole force apart, everyone they've put away in the last ten years may have grounds for appeal. The guy is a sharp cookie, he's taken a couple of the big players out already, but he's got to isolate them first, can't risk the whole shooting match falling down around his ears, that sort of shit is bound to stick."

"I get the urge to burn the whole thing to the ground," snapped Hopkins.

"Me too," replied Lewis, "bigger picture and all that."

"Where does Hunt the cunt fit in all this?" asked Roaddog.

"Strangest of all, bastard is as straight as they come," laughed Lewis.

"So, what's his problem, just burn the bastards down," said Roaddog.

"I think he's after the CC job, but he wants it to be worth something when he takes it."

"How are these CC jobs awarded?" asked Roaddog.

"It's complicated," laughed Lewis, "there's a whole load of factors to be taken into consideration, many of which Hunt is good with, but he doesn't want the job until the bad apples have been cleared out."

"So why doesn't our friend Hopkins take it?" asked Roaddog.

"He's pissed off too many members of the local lodges," laughed Lewis.

"Funny handshake brigade?" asked Roaddog.

"Yes, they don't like him because he won't do favours for members."

"If they're criminals they need to be stopped," snarled Hopkins.

"Sometimes he's so black and white," laughed Lewis.

"Criminals need to be stopped."

"There are criminals and criminals," said Lewis, "some are worth chasing, some not so much."

"The ones that get me are those that believe they are above the law because they are a member of a club," snapped Hopkins.

"That almost never happens."

"Almost and never are mutually exclusive terms," snapped Hopkins, "how do you think that GMP got into the mess it is now, slow step by step, protecting the members, trashing statements, convincing people not to press charges as they'd most likely lose, 'Your word against a pillar of the community,' this shit is where it starts and systemic corruption is what we end up with. I'll never back that shit."

"Chill man," said Roaddog, "you're preaching to the choir here."

"It's just typical of the world we live in. I have a story for ya'll. My friend was driving to an appointment to help and old friend, a dark rainy night, some asshole side swiped her at a set of traffic lights, when the pair pulled over, he spotted the hair dryers and scissors in her footwell. 'You drove into me.' He said, 'Some damned tax dodging mobile hairdresser.' He said. 'I'm a pillar of the community.' He said. 'I'm a teacher.' He said. 'Who'll believe you.' He said. She finally got her head together, deciding that her old Vauxhall Astra has seen its last journey. That old Astra limped to its appointment. She talked to her old friend, this was a woman who was very important to her, this was a woman who had helped her when she needed it the most, this was a woman who had paid for her law degree exams when she couldn't afford them. The next day when the hairdresser turned up at her day job, the leader of the legal practise said to her. 'That asshole is going to jail if he thinks he's better than one of my lawyers.' The hairdresser thought for a moment, 'My new Hyundai coupe is being delivered today, I think I'll take on this bastard myself if that's alright with you.' She said. 'We're all behind you.' Said the boss. This is what happens when the 'Pillars of the community' believe themselves to be above the law." Hopkins sighed.

"So what happened?" asked Roaddog.

"So called 'Pillar of the community' was out with a woman not his wife, a hundred miles from the meeting he was supposed to be at, he lost his job and his marriage, and his lover. This is what happens when pillars of the community believe themselves to be above the law."

"Seems about right to me," said Roaddog, "anyway you want something else other than the contact number and to bum some coffee of us?"

"No," said Hopkins, "that's about it really, I was hoping to get here at breakfast time though."

"If you want feeding go talk to Andy, he'll see to you, and while you're buying." Slowball let the sentence drop and chuckled softly to himself.

"Nice plan," replied Hopkins, "but I gotta watch my figure, too much time spent sitting down these days."

"Yes," said Lewis, "he doesn't even do much of the driving."

"I was hoping for a mobile I could track." said Hopkins.

"So, without them giving me a phone number, those upstanding members of society just walk away from firearms offences?" asked Roaddog, a large grin on his face.

"Pillars of the community and drug trafficking offences," said Lewis.

"Bastards," sighed Hopkins.

"Sorry we can't help you," said Roaddog.

"Come on," said Lewis, "we do have other work to do."

"He's right, you know," smiled Hopkins, "we've got actual drug dealers with drugs in their pockets, and nasty reputations." He looked round. "Thanks for the coffee guys, we'll see ya around, no doubt."

"It's always nice to meet the local cops," said Roaddog, as the two stood up.

"Don't tell lies," said Hopkins, "I can tell when you are lying, well, most of the time."

Once the cops had left Roaddog turned to Slowball.

"I think we need to throttle back for a while, once we've got shut of that load we have scattered about, that bastard's not going to stop sniffing."

"You'll have to bring that up with Bone," said Slowball. "We're making plenty of money."

"Speaking of sniffing," said Roaddog, "is it just me? Or does it smell like we have tom cats around here?"

"That'll be the ammonia, looks like it works to confuse the dog, but I think we're going to need more ventilation."

"Eventually Hopkins is going to notice," said Roaddog. "I'll talk to

Bug, he'll know some way of getting rid of the stink."

"Let's hope so." Slowball smiled as a car rolled into the yard.

38: Friday night Bandit Queen's advice

Roaddog was sitting in the corner of the club house, drinking slowly, it was one of those rare nights when both Jackie and Jane were working. Bandit Queen dropped onto the stool next to him, the music was subdued, there were some members present, but not many. For some reason the mood was sombre.

"What's up?" he asked.

"I don't fucking know, something's just off right now. It's like some fucker has died."

"I know what you mean."

"You're just lonely and wondering what your bitches are up to."

"Yes and no, and no and yes," he laughed softly.

"You struggling to keep up?"

"Not at all, but not sure where it's going to end up."

"How do you want it to end?"

"That's the thing, I don't, but do they?"

"Well, I'm fairly sure I couldn't share like you three are."

"It's all very exciting, but it's new yet."

"And you're already worrying about the end?"

"I suppose."

"Stop it, it'll end when it ends. If you get that sudden pain in the back, then you know that you've missed the signs."

"But what the fuck are the signs?"

"It's your story, you're writing it, you decide," her soft smile did little to cheer him up.

"Why you so down? Your relationship is solid."

"Is it? Is it really?"

"Of course it is, Man-Dare is settled with Billy, you've got nothing to worry about."

"For now, what about the next young thing that comes along?"

"What about the last one?"

"Man-Dare? I don't understand."

"Bone may be naive but he ain't stupid."

"I'm stupid, explain."

"Fine, it'd been a while since there was any challenge, the girls were changing, it was time for the great BQ to flex her not inconsiderable muscles again."

"You saying he led her on?"

"Not consciously, but she was getting pushy, maybe he prodded her a little in the right direction. She came on too strong, you slapped her down."

"I could have killed her. I was certainly mad enough."

"No you weren't. I've seen the killing rage in you, that wasn't even close."

"You know me too well you bastard."

"We're much alike. She was begging for help, you couldn't kill a child begging like she was. The other side of the coin is also true."

"What do you mean?"

"If she'd attacked and hurt you, you'd have backed off."

"Fuck that," Bandit Queen snapped.

"If she'd been strong enough to take you, then you'd have walked away. Bone needs a strong woman beside him, as far as you are concerned, you'll do until someone better comes along."

"You believe there is someone better?"

"Not a fucking chance. You my dear are state of the art. Though the gypsy kid did have Bone scared."

"Scared?" How?"

"When the kid split your lip, Bone was certain you were going to kill him."

"I did consider it. That damned lip has been busted too often recently."

"I wasn't worried that you would kill him, he was still a kid in your eyes."

"You're not wrong, you do know me too well."

"I have something else I'd like to ask you to help me with if you would?" said Roaddog, looking around to see if anyone was within earshot.

"Ask away," whispered Bandit Queen.

"The cops believe we are major dealers, we need to slow it down for a bit, until they start looking somewhere else."

"And?"

"Talk to Bone, we need to shut down for a while."

"I've tried, but he just sees cash coming in."

"It's cash we can't spend without giving the game away."

"I know, but he likes the feel of all that cash."

"It ain't even cash, it's bitcoin."

"And it's value just keeps on climbing."

"That can't last forever, it's gotta crash at some point."

"I agree, for fucks sake, it doesn't even exist, it's far worse than any real currency, when people turn away from it, and they will, it'll vanish without a trace."

"No but it'll settle for a much lower value than it is now."

"How much?"

"I can't even guess; it might get as low as five percent before people get interested in it again. That'll really hurt us, because we got in when it was already high."

"That'd be real bad."

"It's not like it's supported by a country, I mean, sterling is important to the United Kingdom, it's value has a real importance to the whole country, bitcoin, no one gives a damn. And they'll all be laughing up their sleeves at anyone who gets burned when it crashes. We really need not to be in that crash."

"So, what do we need to do?"

"We need to convert to currency, sterling would be good, euro, not so much, US dollars forget it. I might suggest converting it to oil, but that market is even more crazy. Last year the price of oil screwed up big time, it actually cost money to get it out of the ground."

"What? That makes no sense at all."

"Indeed, the price crashed from fifty dollars a barrel to minus fifteen dollars a barrel. Which mean the oil producing companies were paying for processors to take the oil away from the well head. Nut's I know, but that's the way the markets work."

"You're kidding?"

"No, minus fifteen dollars a barrel. It was for real, and I have no idea how it happened, but it did."

"You're saying this insubstantial currency could be worse than actual crude oil in the ground?" asked Bandit Queen.

"So much of the world's economies are affected by the price of oil and yes it went to minus fifteen."

"I'll talk to him; we need to find some way to turn that bitcoin shit into real money that we can spend."

"I'm not going to argue with that statement. It's not urgent right now, but we may not have much in the way of warning before it crashes."

"Fine, but this doesn't solve your other problem."

"Yes, well, I think I'll just have to let this one slide until something happens, then learn to live with the results."

"Good philosophy, just hope that you survive."

"You're the Tull fan, never too old to rock and roll."

"If you're too young to die," she laughed so loudly that Bone turned to look. She smiled at him to reassure him that everything was fine between them.

"He's worried that he may lose me to you," she whispered.

"You're jesting?"

"No, he's quite insecure, he thinks he's getting old."

"Is he?"

"No, he's more than enough man for me."

"Does he know that?"

"I keep telling him, but whether he hears me is something else."

"He's a good man, you'll have to look after him."

"I try, but this doesn't get anywhere near your problem."

"I think I'll just ride that dragon to the end," Roaddog laughed.

"Just don't let go, or the bastard will bite ya."

"Don't I know that."

Lurch strolled up. "You guys doing ok?" asked that gravelly voice.

"We're just putting the world to right," smiled Bandit Queen.

"Is there still a place in it for me?"

"Always, my friend," said Roaddog, "always."

"Good," said Lurch, "pass me a beer." Roaddog reached under the counter and lifted a bottle of beer for the giant standing behind him.

"How's things with you and Doris?" asked Roaddog.

"We're fine, she seems to be happier when she's with me, in fact she's told me that I have to collect her before I come here."

"Not unusual," said Bandit Queen, "she's serious about you."

"I know that."

"But she shows it by not coming here alone."

"So why am I alone now?" he growled.

"She's giving you space, to see if you're going to chase some other chick," smiled Bandit Queen.

"That doesn't make any sense," snapped Lurch.

"You expect women to make sense?" laughed Roaddog.

"You're crazy," said Bandit Queen, smiling at Lurch. "You can't understand us, hell, I don't even understand us."

"So, what the hell am I supposed to do?" sighed Lurch.

"You keep an eye on her, talk to her occasionally, and behave as if everything is normal," said Bandit Queen.

"What the hell is normal?" demanded Lurch.

The other two simply shrugged, Lurch shook his head and wandered off, in the direction of Doris, who was sitting in a corner with two other girls giggling about something or other.

"He's got it bad," observed Bandit Queen.

"I'm hoping they'll stay as a couple," said Roaddog, "he needs someone stable in his life."

"He's fairly stable, at least compared to some of the others."

"Everyone is stable compared to Sharpshooter, Lurch is a nice guy, but he's so strong he breaks people by hugging them."

"I have the advantage," said Bandit Queen.

"What do you mean?"

"I've seen him lose it."

"What happened?"

"There were only a few of us and we were attacked by a group of young thugs."

"And?"

"One of the fools stuck a short knife in his belly, he lost it completely, it was scary, he just started flinging them all around, anyone that got inside his reach was hit so hard they bounced off walls, cars, hell, one of them landed on top of a bus shelter. It was pure chance that he didn't actually kill any of them."

"So, what happened?"

"We got the fuck out and left them to it."

"Any fall out?"

"None worth talking of. A certain DI turned up some days later, he told us that the youngsters had been convinced not to press charges, after all, eight of them armed, and beaten to a pulp by one man. It was not going to look good, and he'd make very sure of it. He also let us know that he would be watching."

"It wasn't Hopkins?"

"Worse."

"You gotta tell me."

"Hunt the cunt."

"How long ago was this?"

"Before you turned up on the scene."

"He's been watching us ever since?"

"I don't believe for one moment that he has had any interest in us at all, he's much more focused on his career. He's got a five-year plan."

"What do you mean?"

"He's planning to make Chief Constable, it may not be five years, but he's running to some schedule, and no-one better get in his way."

"Are we in his way?"

"I don't think so, we're at best a very minor irritation to him. Watch out if he wants to be your friend, I'm fairly sure that is something none of us can afford."

"Was he being our friend this week?"

"No, he was trying to get Hopkins in the shit."

"Why?"

"Perhaps he sees Hopkins as a challenge to his plan."

"That can't be right, Hopkins has already burned those bridges, he's not enough of a politician to make it to the top."

"We only have Lewis's word for that, he could have a lot of support from people he has helped out in the past."

"Do you really see Hopkins in behind the CC desk?"

"To be honest, no. It's not part of who he is. Hunt, is a bird of a different colour."

"This shit is starting to make my head hurt."

"That's why you are master at arms," laughed Bandit Queen.

"Good," nodded Roaddog, "tell me who needs hitting."

"No one today, no one today, I certainly point them out to you when the time comes."

"Thanks," he paused, then carried on, "Jane is picking up Jackie, and they are supposed to be coming to mine after work."

"Your point is?"

"I am struggling with the tension, I'm hoping they will turn up, and dreading that they won't."

"I know what you need," she smiled and took his hand.

"Go on."

"You need to burn."

"Right." Roaddog put his half full bottle of beer on the bar, leaned over and kissed her on the cheek. He turned away and walked out of the clubhouse without talking to anyone. He snatched his helmet from where it was hanging on his handlebar and jammed it forcefully on his head. As his engine fired into life. Bone called across the garage.

"What's with him?"

"Women troubles," replied Bandit Queen, "he's just gotta burn." Her voice was almost drowned by the howl of Roaddog's V-twin, and the scream of rubber as he threw the clutch out, up the ramp and out onto the street, without slowing and without looking. In a moment he was gone. Bone shrugged as Bandit Queen walked towards him, she dropped into his lap and kissed him, saying quietly.

"I love you."

Chapter 39: Friday night Roaddog on the road.

Out of the yard on onto the road, he throttled back. No clear idea where he was to go, the first thing he needed was fuel, the bike was about half full, but he had no thought as to how far, or how hot this burn would be. Across the M6 roundabout and on to Sainsbury's, this is an automatic action as it's the nearest cheap fuel to the clubhouse. It's generally where the club fuel up before a run, with thoughtless ease he rolls to a stop at a vacant pump. He puts his card into the machine and opens the filler cap in front of him. Pin number punched and the card approved, 'You can spend one hundred pounds.' the machine told him, and he laughed quietly, the pump kicked off at only twenty quid. He returned the hose to its holder, snapped the filler cap down and jabbed the 'no receipt' button. Slowly cruising out of the petrol station heading towards the roads, a question flashed through his mind, over and over, awaiting an answer. 'A or M'. 'A or M'. Approaching the traffic light he made the choice and shouted "M". Left at the lights and heading for the M6 motorway, the next choice is 'North or South?' this was only asked the once, turning onto the northbound carriageway at the roundabout he wound the throttle up and clicked through the gears. Very soon he was in the right-hand lane making one hundred miles an hour, the big V-Twin merely plodding along at two thousand revs per minute. The riding part of his brain took over the handling of the bike, leaving the rest for his other thoughts. Even when the volvo changed lanes and pulled across in front of him, automatically the throttle shut, and the brakes dabbed. As soon as the volvo was settled in the outside lane, the throttle snaps open and he squeezes over to the left-hand section of the right-hand lane, his bike flowed past the volvo and back into the centre of the lane, returning to the two thousand RPM necessary for a hundred miles an hour. Knowing that the riding was taken care of his mind turned to the other issues that he felt were a problem. Leaving the autopilot to run the motorcycle he thought about his life ahead with Jackie and Jane. An ancient adage came to mind. It goes along the lines of 'Image your life without a person in it.' If all you see it darkness, then your life has no purpose without this person. Considering both Jackie and Jane, individually and together, he saw only darkness for himself. There was no longer any doubt in his mind that he loved both equally, the outside world impinged briefly on his inner turmoil, the sign read, Lancaster south half a mile. His conscious mind took over the piloting again and he started to make his way towards the exit, three lanes to cross and thirty miles an hour to dump, and only twenty seconds to do it in, in a blaring of horns Roaddog made the exit, braking hard up the ramp he flipped onto the roundabout and off in a moment. Heading towards the main north-south road he had a decision to make, a small signpost lit up in his mind, Glasson. Pushing well beyond the speed limits and driving hard through the corners it only took him another ten minutes to arrive at the lock gate, where the burger van normally is on the Sunday run out. He dropped the bike over onto its side stand, and killed the motor, the silence was quite a shock for him, he shook his head as the ringing subsided. He was alone on the dockside; the only sounds were the plaintive calls of the gulls and the slap of the rigging on the boats in the harbour. Then came the ticking of his own cooling exhausts. He walked to the rail and leaned over it, looking down into the murky depths of the dock, then up into the lowering sun. He smiled gently, 'the darkness of despair and the brilliant light of joy.' He thought, how this covered everything that he was feeling. Looking down into the darkness and thinking about Jackie and Jane he heard that unmistakeable beat of a classic Harley, it slowed and made the turn into the carpark, it pulled up alongside his own and stopped. Roaddog finally looked round at the biker as he dismounted.

"Damn you're old," he whispered. The elderly biker dropped his helmet on the handlebars and walked over to where Roaddog was standing.

"Hey man," he said.

"Hi," replied Roaddog.

"It's great, this place. Nothing better after a shit storm day at work, listen to the gulls, and watch the sun go down," he smiled.

"All I need is a beer," laughed Roaddog.

"Not so much of that for me these days, damn near killed my liver a few years back, so real easy now," he paused, "Dragonriders, see you lot on the weekends mainly, to what do we owe the pleasure today?" The old man turned so that Roaddog could see the back of is cut-off. Though the front was covered in all the sorts of badges and patches that a bike club member's cut should have the back was without emblem or rockers.

"You a member of a club hereabouts?" asked Roaddog, looking for a name tag on the front of the jacket, all he could find was 'gentle'.

"Not for a while, sorted drifted away."

"You Gentle?"

"Ay, that is how I was known, you Roaddog and master at arms?"

"That's me, why Gentle?"

"Anyone old enough to have be taken fishing by their grandfather, and having read the books Mr Crabtree goes fishing, will know what Gentle refers to."

"Sorry I don't fit into that category."

"Fine," smiled the old man, "the term Gentles is used for the maggots that Mr Crabtree uses as bait. Sometimes bike clubs can be quite cruel when they assign people names."

"I suppose you had to fight quite hard to live up to it?"

"Oh yes, but what of your problems?" asked Gentle.

"Women, isn't it always?"

"You got women fighting over ya?" laughed Gentle.

"Actually no, they seem more than happy to share."

"You're not happy being shared?"

"I'm fine with it."

"You can't keep up?"

"Not a problem as yet, anyway they get on so well together, they don't actually need me around, if you know what I mean."

"You're feeling left out?"

"Well no, everything is going along fine, I'm just worried about how this will all end."

"You're planning on ending it then?"

"No, but I don't want either of them to be hurt, you know, when this all falls apart."

Gentle laughed heartily and leaned over the rail alongside Roaddog. "I know what your problem is young man, it's quite simple. You need to grow a pair." His laugh rolled and then changed to a short echo, and it was gone. Roaddog looked down into the water and noticed that Gentle's reflection was not visible. He shivered, and turned slowly to his left, there was no one there, turning further round there was only one motorcycle parked, he was alone on the dockside.

"Fuck," he muttered, thinking slowly, 'Where did the old geezer go? How did he go? And finally was he here at all?' In two strides he was mounted on his bike, he left the carpark, the rear wheel spitting gravel into the dock, no more settled than when he arrived. Running back towards home he asked himself the same question over and over again. 'Who was he going to tell? Was he going to tell? What was he going to tell?' By the time he got back to the club house he had no more answers than when he left, other than the one from a guy who wasn't there. The clubhouse was empty and dark, the gates locked so he turned around and went home.

He was sitting in his living room, listening to music and drinking Jacks when Jane's car pulled up on the front and the girls got out laughing and joking. The two walked up to the door arm in arm, they walked in and he heard the door lock behind them. They came into the front room, Jane dropped into his lap and Jackie kissed him.

"What's up lover boy?" asked Jane, seeing the look on his face.

"You're not going to believe me," he said having decided to tell them and see how they felt.

"You've turned gay, and no longer like girls?" asked Jackie with a grin.

"You're planning on taking holy orders," smiled Jane.

"You girls are crazy," he shook his head and went on the recount the meeting with Gentle.

"Spooky," said Jane.

"Definitely weird," said Jackie.

"Crazy dead biker aside," said Jane. "The real problem is this nutso relationship of ours."

"We're having fun," said Jackie perching on the arm of the chair, holding Jane's hand and stroking Roaddog's face at the same time. She leaned down and kissed him softly. Then leaned down further and kissed

Jane. When the kiss broke Jane reached up and stroked the other side of Roaddog's face.

"This is a beginning," she said, "it's far too early to be worrying about an ending. It'll end when it ends and everyone will hurt, it could be tomorrow or twenty years. It'll last as long as we all want it to last."

"I don't want it to end," said Jackie looking at Jane. "You?"

"I don't want it to end," said Jane turning to Roaddog. "You?"

"Of course I don't want it to end, but I know that at some point it must, and I don't want you two to be hurt," he whispered.

"Why should it end?" asked Jane softly.

"I'm pushing forty, and you're not."

"You're a crazy biker with a limited life expectancy," laughed Jane, "so what?"

"We all know it's very unlikely that you will die of old age," said Jackie, "when it happens, we'll have each other."

"We might look around for a replacement guy, or not." said Jane.

"Don't worry about it," smiled Jackie, "long way off."

"Fine," said Roaddog shaking his head slowly. "I want you two to make me a promise, will you do that?"

"Depends what it is," said Jane, Jackie simply nodded.

"OK. If anything in this crazy situation starts to really get on your nerves, tell us, talk about it, fix it before someone gets really hurt, can we agree to that?" he said.

"Of course we can," laughed Jackie.

"Yes," said Jane. "I've got something that starting to get on my nerves."

"What?" asked Roaddog.

"We've been here fifteen minutes and you haven't offered us a drink yet, what's that all about?" she continued.

"You know where the glasses are, go get them brat," he laughed loudly.

"I'm comfy," she said wriggling in his lap. She looked at Jackie.

"Fine," said Jackie standing up from her place on the arm of the chair, "I'll get them." By the time she returned from the kitchen with two glasses Roaddog and Jane were kissing.

"I thought you were thirsty?" she laughed.

"I got distracted." replied Jane breaking away and taking a glass from Jackie, three glasses were filled and Roaddog held his up in the air.

"To us, and a crazy future," he said, two glasses clinked against his and large sips were drunk.

"We have a future?" whispered Jane.

"For now," said Jackie leaning forward to kiss Roaddog. As their tongues fenced in each other's mouths she felt a hand slide slowly up under her shirt and grasp her breast through the brassiere, the hand was too small to have been a man's. She pushed forwards against both the hand and the man, pressing her body against them both. Roaddog groaned softly into her mouth and the wondered what Jane was up to with the other hand, she pulled back to find out. Sure enough, Jane had his jeans opened and his hardened member out. Jane sank to the floor releasing Jackie's breast and engulfing Roaddog in her hot mouth. He groaned again and pushed towards her, his left hand fell to Jane's head and pulled her even closer, forcing himself deeper into her throat, his right hand went to Jackie's crotch and pressed hard in the moistness there. Jackie grunted and lunged in to kiss him again. Jane broke free of his hold and pulled back, a glance at the front window showed the outside to be so dark that only reflections of the room could be seen. She smiled as she watched Jackie writhing against his heavy right hand.

"Enough," Jane said loudly. "Upstairs, and you lover boy need to get a bigger bed." She pulled him to his feet by his left hand and nodded to Jackie to lead the way. Jackie smiled and walked backwards so as not to break contact with the hand between her thighs. Once they arrived at the stairs Jackie knew that contact could not be maintained, so she turned and ran up the stairs. By the time Roaddog and Jane walked into the bedroom Jackie already had her shirt and bra off and she was struggling with her tight pants. Jane pushed her over onto the bed and started to pull her pants off, Roaddog reached down and removed Jackie's shoes. The dark pants flew into the corner of the room, with the pale blue panties inside them. Jane held Jackie's legs apart, she knelt at the edge of the bed and dived face first into her crotch. Jackie moaned loudly as she looked into Roaddog's eyes. He smiled down at her, watching her writhe on Jane's tongue, while slowly removing his own clothes. Once he was naked, he started work on Jane's clothing. The jeans and pants were gone in a heartbeat, but to remove her shirt he'd have to break the contact between the two women, this he was loathed to do. He slid his right hand gradually down Janes exposed buttock and then between her thighs, his middle finger went straight to her clitoris and she moaned softly into her friend's crotch. Jackie stared hard at Roaddog.

"Fuck her," she whispered. Roaddog smiled and moved in behind Jane. Slowly he slid into her tight body, she moaned some more, and Jackie grabbed her hair, holding her tight to her own body. Every thrust that Roaddog drove into the young woman pushed her hard against her friend's vulva. Each shock made Jackie's breasts bounce.

"God, I love this," said Jackie.

"Me too," said Roaddog.

There was a muffled agreement from Jane, but it was choked off by another plunge from Roaddog.

"Faster," called Jackie. Causing Roaddog to increase both the pace and the ferocity of his thrusts. Jackie lifted her legs and pressed her thighs against the sides of Janes face, she groaned loudly closing her eyes. Roaddog grunted as Janes whole body clenched, her sudden tightness was enough to bring him to a shattering orgasm. All three slumped to the surface below them, each breathing hard and trembling with the aftermath of orgiastic delight.

"Fuck that was good," whispered Jane, looking up from the edge of the bed, first at Jackie, then round at Roaddog.

"Damned right," mumbled the man.

"Yeah," said Jackie, as she slowly turned around to kiss Jane. Roaddog moved in to make the kiss a three way, tongues fencing and breath whistling between the happy three.

"You really worried about this ending?" asked Jackie, breaking away.

"It's just so scary," replied Roaddog, "it's so intense that if it blows apart, then it's going to blow big time."

"We have to make sure it doesn't," smiled Jane, "now fuck my girlfriend while she returns the favour I just did her."

"You're a dirty girl," laughed Roaddog as Jane moved up onto the bed, she straddled Jackie's head forcing her onto her back and lowered herself until Jackie had no choice but the lick the pussy presented, this sight was enough to get Roaddog ready again, he moved onto the bed and on his knees moved into Jackie. Her moan was seriously muffled but was still audible to all. Things moved much more slowly this time, the urgency was gone, but the enjoyment was no less.

40: Saturday Clubhouse and new information.

He opened his eyes to the dim light of early morning and looked straight into the eyes of Jane.

"Do you know you bark like a dog when you're asleep?" she asked quietly.

"It's more like a muffled growl really," said Jackie.

"I was not aware," smiled Roaddog, "no one else has ever mentioned anything."

"Well it's true," laughed Jane. "You know something else?"

"No, what?" he dreaded her answer.

"You need a bigger bed and a bigger shower." Jane rolled quickly from the bed and moved towards the bathroom.

"You need a shower big enough for three," said Jackie following Jane.

"No room for you," called Jane from the bathroom as the shower curtain rattled on its rail. He laughed softly to himself and rolled out of bed, a quick glance in the bathroom showed him that they were indeed right. there was no space for him. He went downstairs and put the kettle on, coffee would be order of the day soon enough.

Going into his back room he opened up his mining computer, soon he learned that not only had he had a good hit during the night, but that the club account was thriving, bit coin coming in faster than he could deal with it.

"Damn Bug is shifting a lot of stuff," he muttered. He bounced most of it through some Russian accounts and on to the Cayman Islands. A quick check with the broker sites showed him that the value of his bitcoin was still going up, and quite quickly at that. He shunted some more of that into his Sterling accounts and reset the miners to full operation, the batteries were full, and they were running on free electricity. If the sun shone, they could run all day at full power without costing a single penny. He returned to the kitchen and made three coffees know that the girls would be down soon, though listening to the noises they were making he was no longer sure of that. He opened the back door and stood in the doorway, letting the cool air of morning blow over him. He heard peals of laughter from the bathroom above and wondered what the girls found so amusing. Then the drain at his feet lost its fragrance of apples and turned to something more acrid.

"At least they're saving water," he mumbled, to no one in particular. In only moments the flow into the drain lessened and stopped. Soon the sound of footsteps on the stair told him that they were coming down.

The girls walked into the kitchen and each picked up a coffee cup, they nodded their thanks to Roaddog, then kissed him in turn.

"Should you be standing naked in a doorway?" asked Jane.

"It's far too early in the morning for anyone to be up, and if they are this might just make their day."

"You may have something there," said Jane stepping up next to him and dropping her towel on the table beside the door.

"Did you bitches leave me a dry towel?" he asked.

"There are none left in your cupboard," giggled Jackie.

"And your neighbours may like the smell of a hot sweaty working man," replied Jane.

"Smells fine to me," said a voice. The three looked around but could see no one. "He certainly looks fine," this time the voice was accompanied by a hand waving from a frosted window across the alley, "I wish my husband looked that fine. I think I'll give him a surprise when he gets in from his night shift, only in my mind it won't be him I'm riding, loverly boy." Her laughter rang out filling the alley with happy sounds.

"Hey bitch," called Jane, "four's a crowd."

"If I had hold of that I'd share it with no one," the hand waved and the window closed.

"I wonder who she is?" asked Jackie.

"Why? You want to meet her?" said Jane.

"Maybe, I'd like to know who's dreaming about my man, while she's shagging her husband."

"Whose man?" asked Jane.

"Our man, OK?"

"Of course, just because you saw him first," chuckled Jane.

"None of this helps me with my shower, I don't have a towel," grumbled Roaddog.

Both girls threw their damp towels at him.

"Now ya got two," laughed Jane.

"Fine," he said, "what you got planned for the day?"

"I'm working lunch time shift," said Jackie.

"I'm on this evening at the club, till late," said Jane.

"One of the problems with this crazy thing of ours is the simple logistics of getting people where they need to be," said Roaddog, "and getting together again."

"No worries," said Jane, "I'll take Jackie home so she can get changed, then I'll drop her at work, you pick her up, and I'll text to find out where you are after my shift. Simples." The last word spoken as a meercat from a TV advert.

"You are making me feel like a package that needs to be carted around," said Jackie gruffly.

"Sorry love," whispered Jane, reaching out for her hand, "it's just logical."

"And think how impressed your mother is going to be when you come home in a car," laughed Roaddog.

"And think how shocked she's going to be when I kiss you goodbye." All three laughed at this, Roaddog finally went inside to get a shower and set up for the day. When he came downstairs again the girls were dressed, he was not.

"You planning on going to work like that?" asked Jane.

"No, but there's plenty of time."

"Time for what?" asked Jackie.

"I was thinking of some toast and another coffee," his reply slow and even.

"After last night," replied Jane, "I feel like something more substantial, I'm thinking breakfast barm cakes from some greasy roadside caravan."

"Fine I'll go and get dressed, Andy should be open by the time we get to the clubhouse." he turned and ran up the stairs.

"Look at that butt scuttling up the stairs, I just want to eat it all over again," said Jane. Jackie laughed loudly.

"It wasn't that funny," said Jane.

"No, but it reminded me of something my dad used to say all the time."

"What was that?"

"After every day at school he used to ask 'What's the scuttlebutt?'"

"And what the hell does that mean?"

"You've never heard of it before? It means gossip, rumours, that sort of thing, I think it comes from the navy or something."

"Was he in the navy?"

"No but he watches a lot of those old navy movies, you know, black and white and real crappy effects."

"Yes, my grand-dad likes those as well, but I don't watch them."

"Are you sure you're OK with taking me home? There's bound to be lots of questions."

"Fine, it'll be nice to chat to your mum, I'm sure she's going to be more than happy to find out what you've been up to," laughed Jane.

"Oh my god," muttered Jackie, "you're loving this just too much."

"Don't fret love," said Jane softly leaning in to kiss Jackie, their arms encircled each, their bodies pressed together, until they heard the heavy tread on the stairs.

"Damn girl," said Jackie glancing at the mirror over the fireplace, "you've smudged my lipstick, we'll have to start wearing the same colour."

"Bugger that," laughed Jane, "I'm gonna wear black and then everyone will know when I've been kissing you."

"You're crazy." Jackie leaned in for another peck on the lips.

"Breakfast girls?" asked Roaddog, "Or are you already eating it?"

"Jealous much," grinned Jane.

"Definitely, either of you want to ride pillion?" he asked the question almost sure of the answer before the words had made it from his mouth. His suspicions were confirmed by the holding of hands.

"Fine," he was a little depressed that he would be riding alone, but then he thought of the solo and the freedom it brought, his smile returned in no time at all.

"OK, you set off and I'll catch you up." He stamped his feet into his boots and was zipping them up as the girls turned to leave.

"You'll never catch us," said Jane. Roaddog laughed loudly.

"Go on, I've still got to get the bike out," he said pulling his jacket on, and starting the zipper upwards. He walked towards the front door, waving the girls before him. Jane pecked him on the cheek and ran out of the door. Jackie kissed him more firmly on the lips then followed the younger girl. Roaddog locked the door on his way out, he walked to his garage and heard Jane's car set off along the road, tyres scrabbling for traction as the motor howled. Taking the usual care to secure the garage doors he straddled the Harley, the motor almost warmed up while he was checking the alarms. He smiled to himself as he kicked the lever to engage first gear. He wound the throttle to half-way and then threw the clutch out, the rear wheel spinning as the engine's torque far exceeded the available grip, the uneven surface of the alley offered little in the way of acceleration, but he was using all that it would give, left on to the road, and then right at the main road. He was making twice the speed limit before he got out of second gear, he failed to catch Jane before the first roundabout, but she was in sight by the time he came off the roundabout. They were side by side at the next roundabout, the traffic lights were against them. This pattern repeated until they hit the roundabout that crossed the M6, no traffic lights here, Jane's little car couldn't match the power to weight ratio of the big Harley, by the time he got to the gate to the clubhouse Jane was two hundred yards behind. He unlocked the heavy gates and latched them back into the opened position, then rolled his bike down the hill into his parking place. By the time Jane rolled past him into the yard his helmet was off, and he was grinning hugely at them. He dropped his helmet onto the handlebar and walked to where Jane had parked.

"Shall we go get some breakfast?"

"How fast were you going?" asked Jane as they climbed out of the car.

"Fast enough," laughed Roaddog.

"Give me some numbers," she snarled.

"I only got as high as sixty, I didn't need anymore," he grinned, understating by only twenty.

"Nuts, you were going a lot faster than that, I was making sixty."

"Yes," he answered, "but my sixty comes up in three seconds, not eleven."

"Bugger," snapped Jane.

"Breakfast?" he asked again.

"You're paying," snarled Jane, she was just not used to people driving faster than she did, her little car was not in any way standard. He smiled and reached out to take her hand, in the other hand he captured Jackie's. They walked out onto the road, and towards Andy's van as they came around the bend and the van came into view it was obvious that something was wrong. There was a van parked next to Andy's car, one man inside, three clustered around the caravan, one with a baseball bat, trying to hit some target on the inside. Roaddog dropped the girl's hands, in a flash each was handed a stiletto from his belt, then he ran towards the caravan, pulling a stiletto from each pocket, he closed on the three rapidly, a rising knee put one on the floor and a flashing elbow smashed the nose of another, leaving only the batsman. Roaddog held a blade to his throat and whispered harshly into his ear.

"If my friend is hurt, then I'm going to cut your dick off." The bat fell to the ground with the characteristic clatter well-formed wood. Jackie moved to the driver's door; knife held where the driver could see it. The driver opened the door quickly, but he didn't hit Jackie as hard as he had intended because she was already moving away when the door lock snapped open. His right leg was on the floor when the door slammed shut, all of Jackie's weight behind it, it didn't quite make it to closed, there were a couple of shattered bones in its way. The driver screamed.

"Shut the fuck up, or my knife maidens will give you something to really scream about," shouted Roaddog, as the drivers voice choked down into silence.

"Andy, you OK?" called Roaddog.

"Hey mate, am I glad to hear your voice," said Andy rising up from behind the counter.

"What the fuck is going on here?" demanded Roaddog.

"Assholes want insurance money," snarled Andy.

"Hey asshole," said Roaddog, "don't you know that this estate is ours?" He pressed the blade against the batsman's throat, just enough to draw a thin line of blood.

The man didn't dare to speak or move, he could feel nothing other than the cold steel against his skin.

"You've come here to collect money," said Roaddog, "let's see how successful you've been. Wallets girls." Jackie opened the van door and tapped the driver on the knee, he stifled a scream and wriggled his wallet from his hip pocket, trying his level best not the move the damaged leg. Jane waved her knife at the two on the ground, the man with blood streaming down his face handed over his wallet without a moment's thought. The thunder of a heavy motorcycle filled the air, followed by the howl of rubber as it slid to a stop, the pillion passenger stepped down to the pavement and walked over to the man who was without obvious injuries, though clearly in some pain.

"I believe we are collecting charitable donations today," said the pillion.

"Fuck you," said the fallen man.

A flashing boot ended his lack of visible injuries, his face ripped by the studs in the side of the sole of the boot. He rolled face down on the ground, consciousness shattered by the heavy boot. The pillion pulled the man's wallet from his jeans and walked towards Roaddog.

"Just you left," whispered Roaddog. The batsman found his voice.

"You can't do this, they'll kill us."

"And we won't?" snarled Roaddog, holding the knife hard against the man's neck he passed the other to the pillion passenger. In less than a second the man felt the point of the blade penetrate his trousers and come to a stop in the skin to the side of the root of his penis.

"I don't know what is going on here exactly, but I am fairly sure that I can give you a real close view of your cock, and then I'm going to get Andy to fry it for ya, you might be lucky enough to see it cooked before you bleed out. Wallet or it's frying time."

"Whatever you say bitch," said the man.

"Damn it Man-Dare, you got some balls," said Jackie.

"So's this guy, for now," called Man-Dare, not taking her eyes from the man before her.

"Hey Billy," shouted Roaddog, "you not been feeding her enough?"

"Hey man," replied Billy, "she's been cranky all morning, fuck knows what's going on in her head."

"Wallet, asshole," said Man-Dare. Moving slowly the man pulled his wallet from his back pocket, it was fat, but not too much. Man-Dare looked into his eyes, seeing fear there she whispered.

"There's more."

The man shook his head. The knife in her hand twitched cutting just a little deeper. The man nodded. Slowly he moved his right hand into his jacket.

"If the wrong thing comes out of that jacket, you head and your cock will be lying in the road," snarled Roaddog. A long narrow packet came out into view, it was quite thick. Man-Dare took the packet and opened it.

"Someone has been busy, must be a couple of grand here."

"Who do you work for?" demanded Roaddog.

"I'm not going to tell you that," he said. Man-dare smiled and jabbed the knife just a little more.

"OK, OK, just keep this bitch off me, I work for a group from Hyde, we're planning to move into this area, we have a lot of product to shift, and we hear that you guys are selling a lot as well. We thought for some venture capital from some simple insurance policies."

"Well, you are going to have to pay taxes for coming into our area, this time the price will be simple, everything you have. If we ever see you again, we will take everything that you are, and no one will ever find the bodies. Do I make myself clear?"

"I understand everything you say, you will not see us again."

"That's sensible, you look like the only one fit to drive. I suggest you get in your van and get your friends out of Lancashire as soon as you can."

"I agree to your terms, though my superiors may not be happy about this turn of events."

"They can vanish as well. We have quite a capacity in our processing systems. Give your superiors a piece of information and some advice. Will you?"

"I will report everything."

"That is good. Information, we are selling across the country, not just locally. Advice, before they move against us, consider the iceberg." Roaddog snapped the knife away from his throat and moved it so that the batsman felt it prick his back just where his right kidney was. Man-Dare stepped back, the hand with the package moved behind her back, and stuffed the envelope in under her belt, leaving both hands free.

The batsman loaded his friends into the van, the driver was moved to the back, the others took front seats and finally the batsman climbed into the driver's seat. Before he could get the engine started Billy fired up his bike and moved it into the yard, it was too tempting a target, so he thought. The batsman looked one last time at Roaddog, for a long moment he stared then he let the clutch up and the van pulled slowly away.

"It's not fucking over," whispered Man-Dare.

"I got that as well," smiled Roaddog.

"What the fuck is iceberg?" she asked.

"If they have anyone that can actually think in their operation, they'll understand that I am telling them that they see is an iceberg, only ten percent is visible above the water, ninety percent is hidden. Hopefully they'll reconsider before they take this further."

"Is there any chance of that?"

"Who can tell, some of the guys have real brains, but not so many, most are just thugs that have grown big on the drug trade."

"If they are thugs?"

"I'll have to explain to them about icebergs."

"Can I come along?" she was obviously excited by this possibility.

"Of course my dear, you can come and watch the education of the idiots. Andy how you doing?"

"I'm OK Dog, fuck I thought I was dead."

"Luckily my ladies were hungry for something other than toast for breakfast today."

"I for one am happy for the appetites of your lady friends."

"You and me both mate," laughed Roaddog, "you need anything"?

"I'm fine, no damage, just fucking scared."

"That's good, once you've got your shit together, I'll have three large breakfast barm cakes." Roaddog turned to Man-Dare, the look question enough. She nodded.

"Billy?" he whispered. She nodded again, with a big smile and she rubbed her belly smiling.

"Make that five please," said Roaddog.

"No worries mate, be a few minutes OK?"

"No sweat, we'll be here."

"You go to the club house and I'll bring them," said Andy.

"You sure?" asked Roaddog.

"No worries."

Roaddog turned to the girls, collecting his knives and starting walking back to the clubhouse.

"That was one hell of a hit," he said to Jackie.

"I just knew what he was going to do, I rode the door out and then sent it back to him."

"Good hit girl."

"Not as good as this bitch," said Jackie pointing at Man-Dare.

"She's had more practice," laughed Roaddog, grabbing Man-Dare around the waist and hugging her close, "someone it setting her up for a good job in the future."

"What the fuck are you on about?" demanded Man-Dare.

"Bandit Queen is training you to be boss lady, hadn't you noticed?"

"No, I thought she was being a bitch as normal."

"She's getting old and she knows it, she needs someone strong to take over, you'll either get strong or break."

"She could have said something," grumbled Man-Dare.

"She couldn't and nor should I, so you've not heard this from me, bitch will have my balls on a wire round her neck."

"Hey," said Jane, "I need your balls, she can fuck off."

"Just you?" asked Jackie.

"Sorry lover, we need his balls."

"That's better," smiled Jackie, "we gotta share him proper."

"Fine," laughed Jane, "you can have one ball and I'll have the other."

Roaddog turned to Man-Dare, "I begin to worry about my future."

"You have no future without us," said Jackie, sliding her right arm around Jane's waist.

"Damned right," agreed Jane.

"They're not wrong." said Roaddog quietly to Man-Dare.

"You don't fancy taking over from Bone?" asked Man-Dare watching the other two girls walk arm in arm ahead of them towards the club.

"Hell no. I'm in this for the fun, that sort of power and responsibility I don't need."

"You think I do?"

"Not specifically, but you'll get to enjoy it."

"We'll just have to see how that develops," said Man-Dare. As they came down the road into the yard Roaddog realised that the door wasn't open, he wondered where Slowball had got to. He opened the doors and started setting the shop up for business. His last task was to set up the coffee machine, once this was done he looked round, Jackie and Jane were on one sofa, and Billy and Man-Dare were on the other.

"Everybody comfy?" he asked, not really expecting an answer, the replies he got were all hand gestures. Andy walked in through one of the shutter doors with a box in his hands.

"Thanks guys, I was actually frightened for my life," he said.

"No sweat," said Man-Dare, "I don't think they'll be back."

"I hope not," said Andy slowly, his voice quieter than the gently bubbling coffee maker. He passed the box to Roaddog, and just stood there. Roaddog reached into his jeans for his wallet.

"No man," said Andy, "Your money's no-good today."

"Something else on your mind?" asked Roaddog.

"Yes," Andy looked down at the ground for a moment before he made eye contact with Roaddog again. "I've had enough of this shit, I'm gonna get out of this business as soon as I can sell that fucking van, you know anyone that wants it?"

"Hey man," said Roaddog, "I'm sorry that you feel that way, but I fully understand. I'll ask around, you do know that we'll miss you. Just don't rush into something."

"It's been a good craic and the money's always been good, and mainly cash, so the damned tax man can go whistle. The hours are long, but I've never been bothered by that. Today has just been too much."

"OK, I'll ask around and let you know, how much do you want for it?"

"I don't know, I've never even thought about it before."

"I'll see what I can get for ya, hey man, it's been great knowing ya."

"Cheers Dog, I think I'm going to fuck off and think about things, maybe I'll be back tomorrow."

"Tomorrow's Sunday."

"See, I don't even know what fucking day it is." He turned slowly away, "See ya later," he said, his shoulders slumped.

"Poor guy, this has really hit him hard," said Man-Dare.

"He has a family to support," said Jackie, "he's worried about them more than himself."

"At least he's still alive," said Man-Dare.

"We're going to have to do something about those assholes from Hyde," snarled Roaddog.

"Do you really want to get involved in that sort of thing?" asked Billy, egg yolk running from his breakfast to fall in yellow strings into his beard.

"Not really, but they're coming this way, I don't want to move from here, we've got a good thing going, I'm going to fight for it."

"It could get very dangerous."

"Well, they've already found out how dangerous it can get for them." Roaddog laughed. He grabbed the remote for the big screen and activated it, flashing through the menu's so fast that no one else could read them, suddenly a huge map appeared, a line drawn all across the map, Roaddog focused on the eastern end of this line, several times the line went through a small industrial estate on the edge of Manchester. Roaddog focused down and tighter until the blue lines covered the screen. He shook his head slowly. Finally he chose an item from the menu at the top of the screen. A payment screen popped up, he clicked through accepting the charges. The popup vanished and the small map slowly morphed, the wide blue bars became gradually thinner, until they were simple threads that crossed the yard in front of a warehouse unit, several times this line ran in through the door of the unit, and then out again.

"What the fuck is that?" asked Billy.

"That's where a car has been, I tagged it. This is an industrial estate in Hyde. This particular car is super-hot, it's a civic running monster nitrous tanks. What are the chances of a different group from Hyde moving into our area, when the civic driver comes from around here?"

"Unlikely." Billy paused. "I saw the payment screen, what did you just pay for?"

"The free service is good enough most of the time, but if you want real precision ya gotta pay more."

"How precise?"

"They say that their trackers are true to about five feet."

"You're kidding?"

"Why?"

"Satnav is good to about one hundred feet, with some clever coding and sampling that can be improved to fifty feet, if they are getting five feet, that's military grade, how much did that cost you?"

"It's fucking expensive, a hundred quid gets ya a month at high def."

"They're hacking military accuracy there. The damned yanks will get pissed if they find out."

"Get it from the dark side of the web, they'll be well hidden," laughed Roaddog.

"So now you know where they are?"

"I think so, but I'll have to talk to the driver to be sure."

"You think he'll tell you?"

"I can be very convincing," the smile said far more than Billy wanted to know. The un-mistakeable sound of Slowball's VW preceded his arrival.

"You'll never guess what I've just seen," said Slowball as he walked towards the gathering.

"Andy's van leaving," said Roaddog.

"Fuck, how did you know?" Roaddog told him about the mornings action.

"Poor fucker," muttered Slowball. "Perhaps I should buy his van."

"You'd eat all the profits, and besides that you'd not fit inside, it's tiny in there," laughed Roaddog.

"So what are we going to do about these assholes?" asked Billy.

"Not my decision," said Roaddog, "I'll call Bone and set up a war council, maybe later today, it's still a bit early for some."

"I'll call Bandit Queen," said Man-Dare, "she'll get shit moving." Her phone call was indeed very short.

"What the fuck did you just do?" demanded Roaddog.

"I lit a fire under her ass," smiled Man-Dare.

"We got anything booked in for today?" asked Slowball.

"Nothing, we're here for the casuals." said Roaddog, turning to the road as a motorcycle came screaming into the yard, and slid to a halt in front of the doors.

"Bug," yelled Roaddog, "cover that fucking pipe you noisy bastard."

"What's bitten your ass?" demanded Bug moving the plate that closed off the pipe.

"Bastards from Hyde came collecting protection money."

"They dog food?"

"Not this time, but we can drink for a few weeks on the cash they had already collected," smiled Roaddog.

"And Andy is selling his burger van, they were giving him a hard time when Roaddog stepped in," snapped Slowball, "Hey, what am I going to do for my breakfast?"

"There's always the guy on the other side of the estate," said

Roaddog.

"Salmonella Sam, fuck that I'll go to Sainsburys."

"Come on," said Bug, "Sam hasn't poisoned anyone in weeks."

"You mean none that we have heard about," sneered Slowball.

"That is a possibility," smiled Bug, "we only hear about the survivors."

"Hey Roaddog," called Slowball, looking across the workshop to where Roaddog was staring at his phone, "what are we going to do about the bastards that pissed off Andy? I feel the need to hurt someone."

"Council of war will be convened, today or tomorrow."

"Let's go burn the bastards out, we know where they are."

"We think we know where they are, need confirmation from that driver."

"Let's go pick the little bastard up."

"Not until Bone has made the decision." Roaddog was trying to calm his friend down, Slowball was building up to a serious explosion, not something that was needed just now. Slowball took control of the big screen and tracked the civic to its current location.

"What the fuck is he doing in Fleetwood?" he asked.

"Who can tell," replied Roaddog, "probably making deliveries."

"That's a long way to go. Isn't it?"

"Maybe he's visiting family, we have no idea what is actually going on, but there is no way I am going to Fleetwood on the off chance of some information. We wait until we have a solid plan."

"Fine," Slowball was quieter but by no means happy about things, he wandered off into the back room.

"He really that upset about Andy quitting?" asked Jackie.

"Sometimes he really struggles with change."

"Why?"

"Just the way he is, maybe borderline OCD."

"He just seemed so angry."

"He'll calm down, it'll take a while, but once he's got it sorted in his head, he'll be fine."

"What if he'd been there when it was just you and us?"

"If he'd closed that door there would have been leg on the floor. He packs one hell of a hit."

"I wish he had been there and not me," interrupted Jane.

"You OK?" asked Jackie, taking hold of both of Jane's hands.

"I've seen a few fights, but never been so closely involved before.

That Man-Dare is scary."

"No she's not, Bandit Queen, that's scary."

"No shit," smiled Jackie as the air was filled with the sound of heavy motorcycles. Bone, Lurch, Sharpshooter, Renegade, Red-Devil, and Groveller. By the time they had parked up and killed the engines. More bikes could be heard in the distance, and that distance was decreasing quickly. Bandit Queen came over to Roaddog and asked.

"What the fuck went on?" He told her and the gathering crowd.

"How much had they already collected?" she demanded.

"Looks like about two grand," said Roaddog, fishing the envelope out of his jacket and passing it to Slowball. He handed the four wallets to Bandit Queen. She pulled the cash and handed it to Slowball, then held the wallets up in the air.

"Bug, where are ya?" The small man shouldered his way through the crowd. "There you are," she went on, giving him the wallets, "find these bastards, I want to know everything about them, including what they had for breakfast." Bug nodded and took the ID's from the wallets, tossing the wallets on the ground.

Bandit queen forced her way through the crowd out into the open air, Bone and Roaddog followed. Groveller was only a few feet behind, a glare from Bone sent him back into the clubhouse.

"What's with him?" asked Roaddog.

"He's fixated on her," replied Bone, "he crashed on our sofa last night, it's starting to get a little weird."

"He just likes to be near a strong woman," said Bandit Queen.

"He makes a pass and I'll kill him," murmured Bone.

"He hasn't got that much balls," laughed bandit Queen.

"He's getting creepy," said Bone.

"The only way he'd make any sort of pass is if I fucking told him to, he needs to be told. And I think he's only just found that out."

"He's not that important right now," snapped Roaddog.

"True," snarled Bandit Queen, "I want those bastards dead. They can't come into our backyard and frighten our people. They can stay in fucking Manchester."

"We have to be sure who we are dealing with," said Roaddog.

"We know who they are, don't we?" she said.

"We have evidence that there is a link from Hyde to the burned out place in Leyland, but the only connection we have is the damned driver, and that shit box civic."

"You think it's a good connection?" asked Bone.

"I'd say it's exceptionally likely that he is a member of the group that were here today," said Roaddog, "I'm more than ninety percent sure."

"Well I can't make the decision without the backing of the council, so how about, you take a crew and collect that bastard and his car, bring them back here before lunch, we can present his evidence to the council, sound like a plan?"

"Sounds good to me," said Roaddog.

"Great," said Bone, "if we get to voting before you get back, how would you vote?"

"War, you know me."

"Damned right," snapped Bandit Queen.

"Make it happen," said Bone turning towards the clubhouse. Bandit Queen and Roaddog followed him. Roaddog looked straight into the eyes of Jackie, he could see that she was worried, and Jane standing next to her was no less frightened.

"What's happening?" asked Jackie.

"I got a run to make, intel gathering sort of, the council will decide and something might just get done tomorrow."

"Are you in any danger?" asked Jane.

"Not much, I'll be back here this afternoon, you two should carry on with your plans for the day, I'll text you both as soon as something is decided, OK?"

"I'm not sure," said Jackie, "suddenly I'm feeling frightened."

"Me too," said Jane.

"I'll be fine, and you two will be safe away from here," he slid an arm around each waist and pulled them in tight.

"You think there could be danger here?" asked Jackie.

"If anyone comes here with bad intentions, they better bring an army, it looks like Bandit Queen has called everyone in," he glanced over his shoulder as more bikes arrived. Jane reached across Roaddog's chest and grabbed Jackie's arm, the two stared into each other's eyes for a long breath, and together they came to the same decision, each nodded.

"What's just happened?" asked Roaddog.

"We're staying here, work can go to hell," said Jackie.

"What can go wrong?" asked Jane, "look at all these men, I feel much safer now that they are all here."

"Well, if you're going to stay, take your lead from Bandit Queen, there's not so many girls here, keep the beer flowing but slowly."

"You think it'll turn into a party?" asked Jane.

"If the beer goes slow, then it'll turn into a party, if it goes too fast these mad fuckers will go off half cocked, they'll ride to war with no plan. Keep them safe."

"Fine," said Jackie, "who you taking with you?"

"A few, and we're leaving very soon."

"Remember that we love you," whispered Jane reaching up for a kiss. Her kiss replaced by Jackie's.

"Damn, you bitches are hard to walk away from." They both smiled up at him. He turned away, shaking his head slowly. He walked into the noise of the club house, Jackie and Jane behind him, they went to Bandit Queen to see how they could help. He walked up to Slowball.

"You're with me," he said, the only response was a nod. "Sharpshooter," he called, "You're with me." Sharpshooter walked towards the two preparing to leave.

"Where's Bug?" demanded Roaddog, just as the small man came out of the office, a sheaf of papers in his hand, these he passed to Bandit Queen.

"Bug," he yelled, "with us, we got a ride out." Bug smiled and walked out into the open space of the carpark. Slowball was surprised when Roaddog climbed up into the back seat of the trike, frowned a question.

"Someone's gotta drive that shit box civic back here. Driver may not be fit to drive."

"Where's the fucker at?" asked Slowball.

"Still in Fleetwood, so M6 north, M55 to Kirkham and then north, we'll track the bastard down." The small convoy left the compound and headed out, north, west then north again. Slowball pushing the trike as fast as he dared, except for the roadworks sections, damned average speed cameras. Off the M55 and into the open fields, the Saturday morning traffic was quite light, so they made good time. They came to the Norcross island and Roaddog tapped Slowball, indicating a turn, the target was moving south. They came off the island heading towards the promenade. Well that's what Cleveley's calls it. Following Roaddog's directions they turned into beach road, the speed bumps were difficult for Slowball, but up ahead they saw the civic, it was parked outside a pub, the Travellers Rest. They parked up behind the pub.

"Slowball, you go in the front door and we'll pick him up as he comes out the back door."

Slowball sauntered along the pub and in through the front door, moments later the driver came out the back, he walked straight into Roaddog's arms.

"You my friend are in the shit up to your neck, you're coming with us, and if you are lucky you may just live."

"You can't be serious," the driver said.

"Serious like you will not believe. We will take your car." Roaddog took him by the elbow and guided him towards the civic.

"Keys," he said, "I'm driving." By the time they got into the car. Slowball and the two bikes were waiting for Roaddog to pull out. The crackle of the civic exhaust brought a couple of young men out of the pub, Slowball stood up on the trike, looking down on them and they scampered off inside.

"You just sit nice and still," said Roaddog, "think about the things you have done recently, and how you may be able to help us, failing to help us is not an option for you, do you understand."

"Yes, I know all about you lot, you have a history."

"You have things that I need to know, and you will tell me, but before that we are going to meet with a group of men, they have a decision to make. You are connected with a group out in Manchester, aren't you?"

"Yes, I run their stuff back and forth, I've been delivering this morning."

"Still carrying?"

"No made the last drop to a guy in that pub."

"That's great, I don't want to be at risk of carrying drugs around."

"But your more than happy to kidnap me?"

"I'm more than happy to gut you like a fish if you don't co-operate."

"I'll tell you anything, everything."

"That's good."

"You need to know that I was called earlier, they asked me if I knew anything about the Dragonriders, I told them where you are, which they knew, and I told them of your maximum strength."

"How many?"

"I said thirty, no more."

"You're wrong by at least fifty percent."

"What there's only fifteen of you?"

"Wrong way dick."

"You mean forty-five?"

"Yes, and more coming in every moment."

"Well they didn't seem too impressed."

"What do you mean?"

"They said they were going to sort you out."

"When was this going to be?"

"I have no idea, but it could be soon." Roaddog was silent for a mile or so, then made the decision. He wound the window down reached a hand up into the air, he made a gesture like a motorcyclist pulling the throttle open. In a moment Bug and Sharpshooter came flying passed Slowball, Roaddog stamped on the accelerator, the civic leapt forwards, even Bug was struggling to keep up, Sharpshooter's harley maxed out at about a hundred and fifteen, the civic was starting to fly, the bikes were falling behind. Slowball was a memory in the mirrors, Roaddog suddenly got a feeling of intense dread that flooded his brain. He turned to the driver.

"Nitrous." he shouted over the screaming of the exhaust. The driver reached across the centre console, turned a tap, and pointed to a button now lit in red. Roaddog reached down and pressed the button, the whole engine note changed, then a monstrous surge of power made the front of the car lift, the rev counter set off for the red and the speedo leapt up and up, one eighty, one ninety, in four seconds the car reached one ninety-five. After ten seconds Roaddog released the button, the engine note dropped so much it was almost as if it had become silent. Roaddog watch the M55 fly backwards, the roadworks came up and he kept the pedal to the metal, the oil temperature gauge started to rise, and the pressure started to drop. The M6 interchange came up and the lightness of the civic helped him to negotiate the right turn at more than a hundred miles an hour, he snapped straight into lane four and thumbed the nitrous again, the compression at the bottom of the hill was intense, it felt like a fighter making a vertical loop. Up the hill and past the M61 cut-off, he released the noise button again and the car started to slow, but the junction was coming up, heaving the brakes on he snapped into the left-hand lane and up onto the surface roads. The howling of hot rubber filled the air as he made the roundabouts and finally the turn into the yard. He stopped with the nose of the car pointing towards the clubhouse. Without looking at the car's driver he spoke slowly.

"You are dead."

41: Saturday Clubhouse and what he found there.

Roaddog opened the car door and climbed out of the low seat.

"What's your name kid?" he asked quietly.

"I'm called Tom, I had nothing to do with what has happened here," he muttered.

"Tom, get out of the car, if you run, I will take your legs and you will bleed out slowly."

Tom got out of the car, and followed Roaddog as he walked towards the building, the only sound was the distorted crackle from a destroyed speaker hanging from a wall. Once they got closer the crunch of brass under their boots, the ground was covered with spent 0.45 inch cartridge cases.

"Tom, you check for living, I'm looking for two girls. Try the back room." Roaddog set about checking his friends in the vain hope that he could save some, he turned over Bone, to find his belly torn to pieces, at least twenty shots had turned it into mush, red steaming and stinking, as the contents of his abdomen slowly seeped out onto the ground. He looked up as Tom came out of the back room, Tom leaned against a wall and heaved, the contents of his stomach splattered over the wall and floor, he was trying not to puke on the dead.

"Any girls in there?" demanded Roaddog,

"No, only guys, all dead." said Tom and he leant against the wall, it seemed he wasn't quite empty. Roaddog walked over to the bar, he picked up a fallen bottle of Jacks, took a large swig from the broken neck, and smashed the bottle against the far wall. He heard a groan from behind the bar, he ran around to find Groveller face down, from the number of holes in his back there was no way he was alive. He grabbed Groveller's arm and flipped him over, Bandit Queen looked up at him, her chest was covered in wounds, her breath sounded wet and strained.

"They took the girls," she whispered.

"How did they do this?"

"Machine guns, small with big silencers. Groveller saved me."

"No he didn't," said Roaddog.

"I know, but I'm talking to you because he took a whole clip in the back."

"Agreed."

"Light a fire for me and Bone," her voice fading.

"I'm going to light a fire, the like of which god himself has never seen."

"Send them all to hell."

"They'll go there screaming," whispered Roaddog moving closer.

"I've always loved you, my favoured child," her last breath dribbled blood from the corner of her mouth.

Roaddog rose slowly with tears in his eyes. He turned to Tom.

"I had nothing to do with this," whispered Tom.

"You sent them here."

They both looked to the outside as Bug's Honda came screaming into the yard. Bug staggered from the bike and ran over to front door. There he stumbled to a stop.

"What the fuck?" he asked quietly of no one in particular.

"Bandit said small gun big silencer and looking at this shit some serious rate of fire."

"Fucking Mac-10," replied Bug, picking up an empty case, and nodding as he read the impression in the end. "Bastards."

"I'm going to kill them all," said Roaddog.

"Starting with this cunt," snarled Bug, looking at Tom.

"No. He has things to tell us and things to do before he dies."

"Fine," replied Bug, begrudgingly giving in to Roaddog's authority.

"I need something from the office." said Roaddog, "You keep the kid alive, and get the bodies downstairs, he can help, he can't puke much more."

"Why downstairs?"

"Bandit Queen wants a fire and she's damned well going to get one."

"We got stock down there."

"Had."

"What do you mean?" demanded Bug.

"This is over. The bastards took the girls, we're going to get them back, and then this is over."

"I'm in," said Bug, taking Tom by the arm and guiding him into the back room, there they opened the hidden trapdoor and went down into the container that was the basement. Bug and Tom started moving things around to make space for all the bodies that had to be moved. By the time he went back upstairs Sharpshooter and Slowball had arrived.

"You want the barrels out?" asked Bug.

"No, they are the fuel for the fire."

"You set fire to that lot and you'll be lucky not to blow the place to pieces."

"I know what I am doing," mumbled Roaddog, he went into the small office and tipped the desk up so that it rested against a wall, he ripped up the carpet tiles and opened the floor safe.

"How long has that been there?" asked Bug.

"For ever," was the terse reply. Roaddog got a heavy case out of the safe then dropped the lid closed, he didn't bother to lock it. He went into the back room and looked around at his friends, all of them dead, many with far more holes in them than was needed to actually kill them. From the look of Lurch he had been standing in the doorway, he was stitched from head to crotch and from shoulder to hip, the forty-five calibre slugs had made a real mess on the exit. Roaddog sat on an empty cot and opened the case.

"Fuck," said Tom, "that's a tommy gun."

"It was," replied Roaddog, he lifted a round drum out of the case and opened it. He oiled the mechanism and checked the clockwork drive, oiled it and checked it again. Finally happy with the function of the drum he started to load it with cartridges from a box, a large box.

"Those aren't bullets," said Tom.

"Right, these are four ten shotgun shells, modified by me, heavy load of powder and shot that is very special."

"Why?" asked Tom.

"Because it's not lead, it's a bit softer, it won't penetrate as far as hard lead shot would, but it gives far better energy transfer. It hits a fuckload harder. Another advantage it won't ricochet, we got friendlies where we are going, I want no strays hurting my people."

"What about my people?" asked Tom, already knowing the answer.

"They are all dead."

"So why should I help you to kill them?"

"There are many ways to die."

"You wouldn't do that."

"The woman that spoke to me, she fed guys to an industrial meat grinder, and she did that while they were screaming, and I helped. You can die with a single knife thrust to the heart, or you can go in the container with the corpses, in the dark and wait for the fire to start. Incendiaries are on a timer, could be ten minutes or it could be ten hours, even ten minutes can feel like ten hours. It's the waiting."

"How have you modified that gun?"

"I've changed the bolt, the block, and the exit port, the barrel is now smooth, it's not designed for long range work, it's for chopping people into pieces at close range."

"How many rounds in that drum?"

"A hundred-ish, driven by clockwork, it won't jam, not ever. The exit port is another matter, it could jam because the cartridges aren't hard brass. But simple yank on the bolt will clear almost any jam, and off you go again."

"How long have you had this thing?"

"I modified it about five years ago, never thought I'd actually get to use it."

"So why make it?"

"I was in a very bad place back then, and now I found myself in the dark again."

"They've got three uzi's at least," said Tom.

"Mac-10's according to Bug, it could be that this is a one way, but it's got to be done, I can't leave the girls in the hands of your friends."

"I wouldn't say friends, those guys are nuts."

"They don't actually have a clue what nuts is, I'm going to show them."

"Good luck with that, you're going to need it."

"What I need is a diagram of their place, numbers, doors, windows everything, you've been there, draw it for me."

"How?"

Roaddog turned on the TV in the back room, it was still connected to the computer he pulled up the satellite image of the truck depot, and gave Tom a stylus, "Draw on the building what is inside, don't make any mistakes."

Tom nodded and set to work, it was not something he was used to, but he got the idea quite quickly.

Roaddog went to help with the moving of the bodies.

"Lurch Bone and Bandit Queen go last." he said to Slowball, who had already come to the same conclusion.

"I've not seen Billy," said Roaddog.

"He's not here," said Sharpshooter.

"I wonder if he took Man-Dare with him when he left?" muttered Roaddog. It took all four of them to carry the remains of Lurch down into the container, as they were climbing back up the narrow stairway he laughed.

"What the fuck is funny?" demanded Slowball.

"All we need now is for Hopkins to show up," said Roaddog.

"You've mentioned the bastards name now, you're the one that let the demon out of the bottle," smiled Slowball.

"I thought it was a genie in the bottle," said Sharpshooter.

"Demon, Djinn, same thing," said Bug.

"Bone next," said Roaddog. They each picked up a limb and lifted the heavy man. Halfway to the office what was left of Bone's spine finally gave up. The four staggered as the body came apart.

"Damn," said Roaddog.

"He never could keep it together," said Sharpshooter. The four smiled and carried the separated parts down into the container, they paid no attention to the parts that fell from the body cavity.

"The Queen last," said Sharpshooter.

"The Queen last," replied Roaddog. He glanced into the back room; Tom was hard at work on the drawing he was creating.

"Tom," he called, "come help with the Bandit Queen." Tom looked for a moment then did as he was asked. Roaddog dragged her out from behind the bar, into a place where they could all get a grip.

The four bikers took a limb each.

"You hold her head," said Roaddog to Tom.

"Damn she a big girl," said Sharpshooter.

"Always has been and always will be," said Roaddog.

"Jesus christ." Muttered Bug as they manoeuvred into the back room.

"What's up Bug?" asked Slowball.

"How the fuck did she walk around all day with all this weight?"

"Practise," said Roaddog, "stop bitching."

When they made it into the container they laid her on the top of the pile.

"Fuck," muttered Tom.

"What's up?" asked Roaddog.

"There's so many, it didn't look like so many when they were all spread out."

"Yeah, and these are all personal friends of us four. Show me what you've got for me." He followed Tom into the back room, the picture of the garage was covered with additional information.

"Right," said Tom, "The big roller door is wide enough for two artics to park inside, but normally there are a few cars to one side of the bay, the rest is empty. At the back left hand side is a double door that leads into the office section, well it's the processing rooms. If you come in through the shutter door the wall to your left is breeze block to about five feet high, and plasterboard for the rest. To the left of the shutter is a normal door, entry to reception area, it goes back about fifteen feet, single door into another room, another fifteen feet and a double door into the back room. The back room has double door into the loading bay, and a single fire door to the side of the building. The windows on the side are frosted and wired, for security, and they've put bars on the inside. I've never seen more than five guys there, but after today's raid, they could have called in some extras."

"Good, this is exactly the sort of information I need," said Roaddog. "Now I have an important question for you."

"Ask," said Tom quietly.

"Why did you take up with these drug dealers?"

"How else is a guy like me going to get to drive a car like that?" He nodded in the direction of the green civic. "And you guys aren't doing too bad out of drug trade, or so I hear."

"Perhaps not the best time to mention that," interrupted Bug.

"Maybe," replied Tom, "but I'm not wrong, and they knew where you were when your gang attacked them this morning."

"Gang?" laughed Roaddog.

"Yes, you beat up four of their guys."

"Actually, your four enforcers that were extracting insurance monies were beaten and robbed by myself and three girls, not a gang as such."

"Not the tale they are telling, mob handed and brutal, is the word."

"Well, brutal I can agree with, Man-Dare turned up late and kicked the shit out of one of the mouthy bastards."

"What about the one with the smashed-up leg?" demanded Tom.

"He made the mistake of hitting one of my girls with a car door, then getting out of the car when she shut the door on him. Schoolboy error," laughed Roaddog.

"They're saying they took on ten guys and were lucky to get out with their lives."

"I took their cash and let them go, with a warning not to come back," said Roaddog.

"Well, the guy with the busted leg is the leaders brother. As far as they are concerned his word is the truth."

"He told lies and they came here with machine guns?"

"Looks like it,"

"What do you think would have happened if he'd told the truth?" asked Roaddog.

"He'd have been the laughingstock for weeks. He wasn't really up to the sort of work his brother expected of him."

"What about you?"

"Shit," replied Tom, "I don't even carry a knife, I'm taxi driver, that is all. I certainly couldn't shoot anyone. I don't really need to; everyone I deal with knows that I work for the guys with the machine guns."

"Fuck kid, I'm beginning to hate you."

"I thought you already did."

"No, I wanted to kill you for bringing death to my friends. Now I hate you because I can see that you are simply a petrol head that fell in with the wrong people.

"And that means what to me?"

"You live. I'm not going to be popular with the guys that are left, but I cannot in all honesty kill you in cold blood. Is the information you have given me accurate?"

"Absolutely, though I'm in no way sure if your machine gun will punch through the stud wall in one hit, it might take a few."

"Maybe I'll find out, maybe I'll die. Give me your phone."

"You notice that I have made no attempt to use it since we got here?"

"Yes, I had noticed, and I had been watching."

Tom handed the phone to Roaddog, without another word.

"You understand that the phone is forfeit, as is the car, but your life I return to you, is this acceptable?"

"Of course." Tom almost smiled.

"Bug," yelled Roaddog, he waited until Bug appeared at the doorway. "Lock the kid in the container, leave him the lights."

"You're going to burn the fucker alive?"

"No, he's going to survive."

"Fuck off."

"No, he lives, but those stairs can be fucking dangerous."

Bug grinned and dragged Tom into the office. He returned a couple of minutes later.

"You were right about those stairs, poor kid fell down them twice," laughed Bug.

"Damaged?"

"Bruised and hurt not broken, but I still don't see why?"

"You left him the lights?"

"I did as I was told."

"Thanks for that. It's not really his fault, the dickheads Man-Dare and Jackie damaged claimed they were attacked by ten of us."

"They couldn't tell that they had been beaten by a couple of girls," laughed Bug.

"Right," said Roaddog, "I have a battle plan, let's get this shit on the road. We have no idea how long they've been gone." The two walked into the main section where Slowball and Sharpshooter were passing a bottle of vodka backwards and forwards.

"We need to be moving," said Roaddog, "But I have a call to make first." He held his phone to his ear and talked briefly to the person that answered.

"That's set up," he said, "Billy's coming over, if we're not back in three hours he's going to let the kid out and start the fire, but let's see if we can bring our girls back alive."

"You mean your girls," said Sharpshooter.

"They got Cherie and Man-Dare, if they only had them, we'd still be going," snapped Roaddog, "I had a hard enough time making Billy stay here, you wanna stay here and I'll take Billy instead?"

"Fuck no," said Sharpshooter, "he's an old man, sorry I spoke without thinking, it's one of the things that I do. It was a joke really, I know you and I know the others, we go."

"Right, I got Vera, you guys got anything useful?" picking up the heavily modified Thompson,

"I got a sawn off," said Bug, hefting a double barrel twelve bore, "Only two cartridges though.

"Short gun for a short guy," laughed Sharpshooter, he held up a pump action twelve gauge, "full load, one in the pipe, and five in the tube."

"I ain't got a gun," mumbled Slowball.

"You're driving, and you're far too big a target, you stay with the van, if the place gets too hot you split with whatever we've managed to get on board. Plan is I'm going to send that civic in through the big door, that should seal it nicely and give us only two doors to deal with, one on the front and one at the back on the side, we'll have a quick recon before we go in." He placed a small box on the bar. "Questions?"

"What's the box with the red button?" asked Slowball.

"It starts the fire, it activates the pumps on the fuel barrels, spraying fuel into the air, it activates the fans, blowing air through the container. I reckon it should make six hundred degrees for about an hour before the pumps fail, damned fire bobbies aren't going to able to stop it."

"That's why everything goes on down there," laughed Bug, "Shut the doors, fire the incinerators and there's no evidence left."

"Fire bobbies aren't going to open those doors, too much chance of a back blast. Awesome man, just awesome," said Sharpshooter.

"Hang on," said Bug, "I've been working in a crematorium for months?"

"There's almost no chance of the fire starting while you are down there," laughed Roaddog, "I only armed the pumps five minutes ago, checks show that they are working. The air blowers work all the time, they're what make the place breathable, when they come on later they're going to be running flat out, not just ticking over."

"And where the fuck does this fire vent?" asked Slowball.

Roaddog looked around the room and laughed.

"We're standing in the exhaust from a crematorium?" asked Slowball.

"Yep," smiled Roaddog, "and the firemen won't understand why it won't go out."

"Fuck," whispered Sharpshooter.

"We need to be on the road," said Roaddog, "leave the door unlocked, Slowball you and Sharpshooter in the van, you go south then east on the M60, me and Bug in the civic got east then south, we meet up behind the building, everyone understand what is happening today?"

Slowball nodded and snatched the keys for the van from the board beside the bar.

"Fucking ay," said Sharpshooter grabbing a bottle of Jacks from the bar ad following Slowball out to the van.

"You're mad," said Bug, "but so am I. Lock and load, let's hit the road."

"Contact by zap only," yelled Roaddog. Slowball nodded.

"Why zap?" asked Bug, "sorry stupid question, encrypted both ends. Please ignore any stupid comments I may make, it's a bit of a crazy day." He smiled and walked outside to the Honda.

42: Angels run.

The trip on the motorways was fairly uneventful, though Roaddog did have considerably more miles to go, but the Honda was more then up to the pace he was setting, he got a message from the van that they were only minutes away from the target when he was still showing ten miles left, one quick stamp on the go pedal and those miles passed in only a very few minutes. Conversation had been sparse; the two men knew that they were going into a very dangerous situation but go they must. Roaddog pulled up behind the red van and got out to talk to Slowball and Sharpshooter.

"We need to know that there are people there before we go breaking the doors in."

"I'll get close and see if I can hear anything," volunteered Bug, he immediately climbed through the hedge and up to the back of the building. He returned in only a minute, with a huge grin on his face.

"What the fuck?" demanded Roaddog.

"They're there, and some bitch is giving them a real hard time about, well, about everything, from their parentage to the size of their tiny dicks, she's giving it to them real hard."

"Would that be Man-Dare's dulcet tones you are hearing?"

"I think so, do you know another chick that swears like a docker?"

"Actually I know a few," replied Roaddog. "Plan is unchanged we go now, before they get pissed enough to just kill that bitch." He thought for only a moment, "Can you get to that back door?"

"No," replied Bug, "big steel fence in the way, we're going to have to come it from the front."

"Great," snapped Roaddog, "you're with me. Let's get this thing done." He got back in the Honda with Bug and Sharpshooter only seconds behind him, it was only seconds to the front of the building Bug and Roaddog got out of the civic, he had stopped it so that it was pointing straight at the main roller door, at a distance of fifty yards. He reached into the car with a couple of sticks he had collected before they left the Dragonriders clubhouse. The first stick he used to jam the clutch pedal down, the second jammed the accelerator pedal to the floor, the motor howled up into the rev limiter for the seconds it took him to close the door and cock the Thompson, the report of the gun was hidden by the scream of the engine. The stick holding the clutch pedal was destroyed by the shot and the clutch engaged in an instant, with a tortured scrabbling of rubber the fluorescent green car set off towards the industrial door. Smoke was pouring from the front wheel arches as the car ploughed into the steel shutter. The pedestrian door opened as the car approached, then shut instantly. The car buried itself into the door, pushing a good five feet through, there it stopped, wheels still spinning, pouring dense smoke into the air around the doors. With a sickening crunch the engine finally expired, and silence fell.

A hand came round the front door and waved the Mac-10 around spitting twelve hundred rounds a minute, three seconds and the clip was empty. The hand disappeared, only to return a few seconds later, as it came into view the Thompson fired three times, the hand disintegrated under the barrage of shot and Bug started running in towards the door, another hand appeared and this time it was Bug's sawn off that returned fire, both barrels ripped a massive hole in the door and in the person standing behind it. Bug dived to the ground and came up with a Mac-10 in each hand. Sharpshooter started running down the side of the building pump ready, the fire door flew open, and a man stepped into view, as he crouched behind a snub nosed thirty-eight he opened fire catching Sharpshooter in the chest, the heavy boom of the shotgun knocked both men to the ground. Sharpshooter staggered to his feet and wobbled over to where the other man was beginning to move, the man's shirt was destroyed by the shotgun blast but underneath was the kevlar of a ballistic vest. The man still on the ground raised his pistol and fired twice up into Sharpshooters body, the heavy shotgun fired again this time turning the man's head to a bloody stump that gushed blood into the bushes behind the building. Sharpshooter tried to operate the slide on the pump, but found he no longer had the strength to do so, nor the legs to hold himself up, he slumped to the ground and spat his last breath against the man's chest.

Bug ducked into the doorway and sprayed a short burst into a man hiding behind a desk, in the panic of the moment he hadn't realised that his knees and feet were visible beneath the desk, especially when viewed from Bugs low angle. Roaddog approached the shutter door where the car was buried, smoke from the wrecked engine was drifting from under the car, through a gap between the door and the front wing of the car he saw a large black suppressor pointing his way, firing from the hip he sent about a dozen loads of shot through the gap and the machine gun silencer fell from view. Roaddog walked up to the door and gave it a hefty kick, one of the strips finally gave up its grip to the next one and the bottom three feet of the door fell to the ground, Roaddog rolled under the door and came to his knees with the Thompson ready, in front of him was a fallen man, his chest torn to ribbons by the small shot, Roaddog kicked the machine pistol from his hand and moved into the room, three men came out from behind a parked van, one was armed and pointing a gun towards Roaddog, again the Thompson chattered spinning the gunman round, he slowly pirouetted to the ground, the other two men held their hands up and fell to their knees. Roaddog gestured that these two should open the doors to the back room, the Thompson would brook no disobedience, they opened the doors, and a voice rang out.

"Dog, get your ass in here, what the fuck took you so long."

"Coming darling," shouted Roaddog pushing the two men ahead of him, once inside he shouted. "Bug, Shooter, rooms clear." Bug came in and checked the other door.

"Sharpshooter is dead," he said.

"Quit gawking and get me off this fucking table," screamed Man-Dare. Bug set about cutting the ropes that held Man-Dare onto the table, her clothes were in tatters, she was bleeding from several minor wounds, bruises were starting to show over much of her body, there was very little of it hidden from view. Bug finally cleared the last of her bonds and helped her to sit up.

"Are we safe?" she whispered.

"Yes," answered Roaddog, "Slowball is bringing the van now, we'll be going home in a few minutes."

"Thanks Dog." she mumbled and slumped in Bug's arms and passed out.

"She breathing?" asked Roaddog, Bug checked her breathing and her pulse.

"She'll be fine, just fainted, sort of," said Bug. Roaddog started to release the other girls, from where they had been tied to chairs around the table. As nearest he started with Jackie, it only took seconds for his knife to cut the gaffer tape holding her to the chair.

"Are you hurt?" he asked.

"Not to any real extent, not as much as Man-Dare. They only made us suck their dicks after they'd fucked her, and still she didn't shut up taunting the bastards." Roaddog moved on to Jane, and released her, her arms flew around his neck and she buried her face in his neck, sobbing loudly. A small hand slid down his arm and gently tried to pull the Thompson from his grip, he looked up into Jackie's eyes, and gave her a small smile, and released the gun. He moved on to release Cherie as Slowball came into the room.

"Sharpshooters outside that door," he said, a nod indicating the door in question, "get him in the van, he goes in the fire with the rest." Slowball nodded and went outside.

"They said that they were going to get us hooked on drugs and sell us into Pakistan, seems white girls get more money in the whorehouses there," said Jackie.

"Well that's not happening is it?" said Roaddog.

"Not to us," said Jackie, she raised the Thompson and pulled the trigger, five rounds tore into the plasterboard, raining dust and paper fragments down into the room. Before the echoes had died the gun was trained on the two survivors again. She glanced at Roaddog and turned to the survivors again.

"Hicks was right, it does kick some," she smiled before going on, "but they could still do it to someone else."

"I'm sure you could get promises from them not to do such a thing."

"But could I ever believe them?"

"I'm not in anyway sure of that," laughed Roaddog as Cherie stood shakily from her chair. Cherie pointed at one of the men.

"That one made me suck is cock after he fucked Man-Dare in the ass."

"This is going to sound like a really bad question," said Roaddog, "was he the first one to fuck her ass?"

"Yes," replied Cherie.

"That particular privilege was returned to Man-Dare by Bandit Queen," said Roaddog, "no asshole should have taken that from her." Jackie pointed the Thompson somewhat carelessly and pulled the trigger. The pellets tore the man's knee to shreds, he screamed and rolled onto his back, moving his hands to the damaged part, but not actually daring to touch it, his friend decided to make a run for it, Jackie tracked him as he ran through the doors, the third round took him in the calf, taking the lower leg away completely. Jackie walked up to him slowly and pointed the machine gun at his crotch, she pulled the trigger. Not even a click. She turned and glared at Roaddog.

"The knob of the top, that's the bolt, it's jammed halfway, pull it back hard," he called.

She pulled it and released.

"Again," he called.

This time the bolt pulled clean and dropped firmly into place.

"It's cleared the jam, ready to go," Roaddog laughed.

This time when she pointed it at his crotch and pulled the trigger the gun fired straight and true, three rounds turned the crotch of the guy's jeans to pink mush. In a few seconds he even stopped screaming. Jackie returned to the first guy, the pain from his tattered knee was such that he hadn't even moved. Again the Thompson trained on his crotch. Three rounds, and he didn't even scream, the man was simply waiting to die. The rate of blood loss was more than enough to tell him that he didn't have long left to worry about the pain. Jackie didn't give blood loss chance to kill him, three more rounds turned his head into minced burger meat. The process she then repeated on the last of the men.

"I think it's well time we left," said Roaddog, he turned to the girls, "you lot can walk?" Jackie nodded and put her arm around Jane's waist. Cherie simply gave him a thumbs up. Roaddog took Man-Dare from Bug and lifted her from the table, he carried her towards the door. Slowball preceded him out of the front door, stepping carefully of the two dead bodies the van was there, Roaddog stepped up into the van and laid Man-Dare on the floor, near to but not touching the tarpaulin covered shape that was already there. Jackie followed and helped first Jane, and then Cherie up before taking her place in the back of the van. Roaddog looked at Bug.

"Blow the fuel tank," he said.

Bug turned one of the Mac-10's loose and sprayed the car just in front of the rear wheels, once petrol started to pour from the underside, he targeted the tarmac, the sparks from the ricocheting bullets started the fire.

"Hey," said Bug, "is there NOS on board?"

"Yeah," replied Roaddog, "two huge cans of it."

"I suggest," said Bug, "that we skedaddle with extreme alacrity."

"I'll agree with that," replied Roaddog, he pointed Bug towards the front of the van, and climbed in the back before shutting the doors and shouting. "Go."

As the van headed for the motorways Roaddog sat amongst the rescued girls.

"Is Man-Dare going to be alright?" asked Jane.

"She's had a heavy day, I'm sure she'll be back with us very soon," smiled Roaddog, in no way certain as to the truth of his words.

"Fuck you asshole," mumbled Man-Dare.

"Where do you hurt?" asked Roaddog.

"Everywhere," she muttered, "nothing major, no broken bones, them pussies hit like girls, and fuck like five-year-olds."

"Jesus girl," said Jackie, "how the hell did you do that?"

"I had to," said Man-Dare, a little stronger this time. "I knew that Dog would be coming, but I didn't expect you to take that long."

"Hey," replied Roaddog, "we set off as soon as we had a workable plan. I wasn't even sure where you were until Bug had a listen at the back windows. You were definitely giving them a hard time."

"I had to, the others couldn't deal with that sort of shit," snarled Man-Dare.

"I couldn't deal with watching it," whispered Jane, Jackie hugged her hard, and whispered in her ear, something the rest couldn't hear.

"Did Bandit Queen survive?" muttered Man-Dare.

"Long enough to tell me that you'd been taken," replied Roaddog.

"Good," snapped Man-Dare, "anyone else survive?"

"No one that was there," said Roaddog, "Dragonriders is now only three guys and you four girls."

"So Dragonriders is over," mumbled Man-Dare.

"Sadly yes," replied Roaddog, "I'm going to tell Billy to affiliate with Chorley Centurions, and take you and Cherie with him, you will be able to find a home there. I'm going to have to run, I'm going to move away from our base, I have a plan, sort of, but what the hell, I'm going to take Jackie and Jane with me, if they want to come. I'll call Bug and Slowball in once I'm set up. It's not going to be easy for a while."

"You not going to take me with you?" asked Man-Dare.

"No, I think you'd be better here. Stay with Billy, until you find something better."

"With you gone, where am I going to find someone better?"

"You'll have Billy, once you get your claws into the leaders of whatever club, I'm sure you'll find something to satisfy your lust for power."

"You know, with Bandit Queen gone, there is just no challenge anymore."

"Then be happy with what you got, I was, and this shit happened."

"I'll come with you," said Jackie. "My parents will be royally pissed, but I'll come with you."

"Thanks for that," said Roaddog, "that makes me feel so much better." he turned to Jane, leaving the question unasked.

"No," she whispered, "no," louder, "no," almost a scream. "last night was wonderful, this morning fun, this afternoon hell. I went from smiling happy people to drugged prostitute in Pakistan in the space of five hours."

"But some of that didn't actually happen," said Jackie, taking Jane's hand in her own.

"In my head it happened, when that asshole held my nose until I was forced to open my mouth to breathe, and then he shoved his stinky cock in it, I may as well have been in Pakistan."

"But you weren't," said Man-Dare.

"In my mind I was, it was as real as if it had happened."

"Rest assured," said Roaddog, "even in Pakistan, I am coming, I am loaded for bear, I am the angel of death, and I ride for you."

"Even that feels like it's not enough," said Jane.

"Can you believe that I would ever abandon you?" asked Roaddog.

"No," whispered Jane, "but there are challenges you cannot overcome."

"Do you believe that I would ever give up on you?" asked Roaddog.

"No," answered Jane, "but you would die trying and unlike today, rescue would not happen, no matter how much I prayed for it."

"You know that I will never give up on you, but you won't give me the same?"

"I can't, if you die, I end up as a prostitute in Pakistan, or maybe somewhere worse."

"Or you end up in a loving relationship with two wonderful people, both of whom would die for you," said Jackie.

"If you both die, then I have nothing to live for."

"So," said Roaddog, "will you go back to your old life, and forget all about the rest of us?"

"I can go back," said Jane, "but I can never forget."

"If that is what you want," replied Roaddog, "I can do nothing other than abide by your wishes."

"I can only do the same," said Jackie, "rest assured you will be missed, I have thoroughly enjoyed our times together, but I am not prepared to give up on this man who was prepared to die for us today."

"I am too frightened," said Jane, "this has been so scary for me, I just can't deal with it."

"Fine," said Roaddog, "if that's how you feel, then I, or we, cannot press you any further. I have things I need to do today, and then I will be leaving. The damned cops are going to be on my back over the things I have done today, I have to leave and hopefully become someone else. Jackie will be coming with me," he looked at Jackie and got a nod, "when we are sorted and stable, I will contact you, you can come over to join us, if you still want that. I hope that you do because both of us will miss you."

"We will," said Jackie.

"Please," said Roaddog, "give us the chance, think about it, and say yes when I've got things safe for you again."

"I might do that," said Jane, "or not, it depends on what happens in the meantime."

"Give me the chance to make things right," said Roaddog, "please give me a few months, say six to sort things out?"

"Six months is a long time."

"Fine," said Roaddog, "If something, or someone better comes along, then tell me to fuck off when I contact you, if not, give me the chance to bring you back into the fold. That is all that I can ask, I can't believe that I will ever be happy to lose you, but your wishes have to be paramount."

"I don't want to lose you either, but I can't lose this man either," said Jackie.

"I can't live with the things that have happened today," said Jane, "Jackie, you actually shot and killed two guys, I could never do something like that."

"You will never need to," smiled Jackie, "leave any rapists to me, I could have been far harsher, but we really needed to get out of there."

"So, what did you do to them?" asked Man-Dare.

"She shot them in the crotch and then in the head," muttered Jane, shivering as she did so.

"Go girl," said Man-Dare, "if you had more time what would you have done?"

"I don't know," said Jackie, thinking for a while, "perhaps I'd have had them suck each other, while I blow bits off them, maybe the pain would cause them to bite each other's cocks off," she laughed loudly.

"That's just sick," mumbled Jane.

"Rapists deserve nothing better," said Man-Dare.

"How are you feeling?" asked Jackie, taking Man-Dare's hands in her own.

"Fuck," snapped Man-Dare, "my ass, pussy and throat are sore, but

I'll survive. Billy's going to have to make do with hand jobs for a few days."

"You better think about something else," said Jackie, "there's no saying that some of those guys weren't diseased in some way."

"Oh my god," mumbled Jane as she leaned over and her stomach started to heave, there was nothing inside her, the earlier abuse had seen to that, but it tried to find something to throw up for a couple of minutes.

"Aye," said Man-Dare, "doctors' visits for all of us, those guys were definitely sick, and it was terminal."

"I'm planning on moving across the country," Roaddog spoke directly to Man-Dare, "Do you want to come with us, once we're all set up of course?"

"Ask me nearer the time, I might just be happy with the way my life is going by then," Man-Dare smiled.

"God, I hope so," said Jackie.

"You don't want me to come over?" asked Man-Dare.

"Not that, I just want you to be happy, that's all I want for all of us," said Jackie.

"I'm not sure that I will ever be happy," mumbled Jane.

"Of course you will love," replied Jackie, "someday all this will be a distant memory, you may even enjoy telling the tale of how the hero's came to rescue you with crashing cars and guns blazing, it'll make your grand-children laugh, they'll not believe that granny had such an exciting life."

"Horrifying more like," said Jane.

"Excitement, horror, simply a matter of degree," smiled Jackie.

"Give it a few weeks," said Man-Dare, "you'll start to feel better about it, it's never going to be a happy memory, but at least you survived."

"Without becoming a drug addled whore in a foreign land," said Jackie.

"I was so scared when he said that I could see it happening."

"You think that would have stopped this Roaddog?" asked Man-Dare. Jane looked into Roaddog's smiling face.

"I suppose not," she said.

"You're being very quiet," said Roaddog looking at Cherie.

"I'm thinking," she replied softly.

"Thinking like Jane?"

"No, thinking about that bastard Bug, I'm going to make him marry me."

"I thought you enjoyed the freedom of not being tied down?"

"I'm not planning on being tied down, but he's going to be."

"That should be a match made in hell. Can I warn him?" asked Roaddog.

"No, I think I want it to be a surprise."

"Oh, I can't wait for that penny to drop," laughed Roaddog.

"I'm sure he'll get the message eventually," said Cherie.

"I don't think he'll be too upset," said Jackie.

"You don't?" asked Cherie.

"No, he's ready to settle down, and you two get along so well. Made in heaven." laughed Jackie.

The van swayed as it made the turn onto the roundabout.

"Looks like we're nearly home," said Roaddog, he caught Jackie's eyes with his own and sighed. She reached out and took his hand in hers. He reached out to Jane with his other hand, slowly she took it and smiled wanly at him. There was still love in her eyes. Jackie took her other hand and the circle was complete. The van made a few more turns and pulled to a stop. Roaddog opened the back doors and slowly climbed out, the stress of sitting on the floor in the van had caused him some pain in the knees, but he knew this would pass quickly once he started moving again. He walked into the clubhouse through the pedestrian door, and found Billy sitting on a sofa, a beer in his hand.

"Shit man," said Billy, "you have about twenty minutes before I have to do something, have you any idea just how scared I am right now?"

"Hey, Billy. Sorry to drop this shit on ya, but I got no one left."

"You mean that?"

"Yes."

"What the fuck happened?" demanded Billy.

"You didn't look? The kid is still in there?"

"I didn't look, because I didn't want to know."

They both turned to look as Slowball and Bug came in through the door carrying a tarpaulin covered shape.

"Who's that?" asked Billy.

"Sharpshooter, he died a hero, he goes on the fire with the rest."

"Fuck," muttered Billy, as he opened the door to the back room and then followed the others in. The narrow stairway was difficult for Slowball and Bug, but they managed, the door to the container was a different matter, Slowball couldn't open it with one hand, nor did he really want to put his burden down on the ground. There was no way the others could get past to open the door, so Sharpshooter was placed gently on the ground, then lifted into a sort of seated position so the door would open without fouling on his head. The door came open and Tom rushed out, he saw the people in the confined space and retreated into the container.

"I thought I was going to die in here," he said.

"I said that I would be back, or someone would let you out," said Roaddog.

"That was fucking hours ago," snapped Tom.

"Yes," said Roaddog, "two and a half hours ago."

"Seems like about five to me," said Tom.

"Modern generation, no watch," laughed Roaddog.

"You took my phone."

"Yes, you have no phone, you have no car, you only have the life that I give you, do you understand?"

"I think so," said Tom.

"Our mission was successful," Roaddog flipped the tarpaulin off Sharpshooter's face. "This man gave his life to save his friends, your friends are all dead. Do you have any friends that you would give your life for? Don't answer that, more important do you have any friends that would give their lives to save you? Again don't answer. I think you need a whole new batch of friends."

"They were business acquaintances at best," replied Tom, "I assume that they are all dead."

"There were seven men at the Hyde location, they are all dead."

"I've never known of more than eight there. So you missed one."

"I saw no one with a broken leg so that one must have been still in the hospital."

"I don't believe he's going to be a problem, he's not what you'd call up to it, if you know what I mean," laughed Tom.

"So, the leader's brother was just a poseur?"

"Oh yeah, without big bro he's a real wimp."

"Fine," said Roaddog, "I think we can consider the matter closed, you need to find a proper job, get walking man." The others made way so that Tom could climb the stairway, up into the office and then on to the fresh air. The others followed a little more slowly. Roaddog threw his phone into the container before he locked it, he followed them with the trigger in his hand.

"Right," he said, "as I see things, Dragonriders is over. The survivors need to keep a low profile, damned cops are going to be sniffing around, me and Jackie are leaving, we'll be setting up somewhere else. Man-Dare you should go with Billy, join Centurions, Bug and Slowball the same with respective ladies, I'm hoping that the fire will wipe out all the evidence, if the hardware hangs together it should burn for a good few hours. Anyone any questions?"

"What are you going to do?" asked Billy.

"I have a plan, if you don't know it, so much the better, in a few day's you'll each received phones, I will be in contact. If any of you want to come over to the new location you will be more than welcome, but we will be starting again from scratch."

"Call me and I'm there," said Bug. Roaddog smiled, before going on.

"I know that things can change in a few months, but any who chose to come will be welcome, always." He looked round at the faces of his friends, knowing that he wouldn't see them for a long time.

"We need to get out of here, it's going to get real warm," he said pressing the button and tossing the small box into the back room. He hugged each of them and said his goodbyes. When he got to Jane, he held her for a long time and wiped the tears from her eyes.

"Can you give us a ride back to my house?"

"What about your bike?" asked Billy.

"If it's here the cops will think I am, at least for a while."

"Sure," said Jane. There was a deep thump from somewhere below ground, smoke started to rise in the corner of the workshop, the back room and behind the bar.

"We need to move," said Roaddog, ushering everyone out he closed and locked the doors. With a final look they all left to go their separate ways. As they left the yard Roaddog turned to Jackie.

"Call your parents. Let them know, tell them not to believe the cops or the papers."

After a five-minute phone call with the father, she handed her phone to him, he broke it over his knee and threw the parts out of the car window. Jane's car rolled to a stop outside Roaddog's house. Jane stayed in the driving seat with tears rolling down her face.

"Remember," whispered Roaddog, "we still love you and always will, I'll send you a phone and we can talk about this in a few days." He kissed her and stepped back so Jackie could say her goodbyes. The two went inside, Roaddog went straight to the back room, he woke the computer up and checked the systems over, he transferred all the money into his travelling accounts then activated the final shut down.

Big red letters on the screen asked him three times if he was sure. Each time he hit the OK button.

"What's that all about?" asked Jackie.

"Military grade wiper program, once that progress bar hits one hundred percent there is no more data on the PC." Together they watch the bar climb slowly to one hundred, it flashed briefly, then the screen went dark. Roaddog stood up, removed the hard drive caddy from the front dropped it on the floor, and stamped it into fragments.

"What's that all about?" asked Jackie.

"Biker grade wiper, fix it first motherfuckers." He smiled and opened the floor safe, retrieved his other phone and turned to Jackie.

"Let's go," he said.

"What about that damned machine gun, you just going to leave it here."

"I can't do that." He picked it up and in less than forty seconds it was reduced to its component parts. "There," he said, "It'll drop in the bottom of the panniers now."

"So," snapped Jackie, "we're leaving town, most likely forever, and you're taking your machine gun, while I've got the knickers I am wearing. You do know this is madness?"

"How can it be madness when we are together?"

"You sentimental fool," she laughed as she followed him outside, he walked down the side of the house to the garage.

"You left your bike at the clubhouse," she said.

"That was the harley," he said opening the door. He walked into the darkness at the back of the garage, pulled a sheet off something, then rolled a black motorcycle forwards into the light. He dropped the gun parts into the left-hand pannier. Threw a leg over the saddle, thumbed the starter, the soft rumble of a heavy v-twin filled the air, he nodded to Jackie, she took her seat behind him. He pulled slowly from the garage and onto the road, heading for the future, whatever it held for them.

Authors Note

More of me in the earlier works, the epic fantasy The Doom of Namdaron. This one has been two years in the making, it's been a long road. Every journey starts with a single step, and this journey is not over, there is more to come for the survivors of the Dragonriders, could be another two years. It should be worth the wait.

Michael Porter

Printed in Great Britain
by Amazon